Also by Elizabeth

*The Greatest K*

*The Scarlet Lion*

*For the King's Favor*

*To Defy a King*

*A Place Beyond Courage*

*Shadows and Strongholds*

*The Outlaw Knight*

*The Summer Queen*

# THE
# WINTER
# CROWN

### A NOVEL OF ELEANOR OF AQUITAINE

## ELIZABETH
## CHADWICK

Published by Sourcebooks Landmark, an imprint of Sourcebooks, Inc.
P.O. Box 4410, Naperville, Illinois 60567–4410
(630) 961–3900
Fax: (630) 961–2168
www.sourcebooks.com

Originally published in 2014 in the United Kingdom by Sphere, an imprint of Little, Brown Book Group.

Library of Congress Cataloging-in-Publication Data

Chadwick, Elizabeth.
  The winter crown : a novel of Eleanor of Aquitaine / Elizabeth Chadwick.
    pages cm
  Includes bibliographical references and index.
  (pbk. : alk. paper) 1.  Eleanor, of Aquitaine, Queen, consort of Henry II, King of England, 1122?-1204--Fiction. 2.  Henry II, King of England, 1133-1189--Fiction. 3.  Great Britain--History--Henry II, 1154-1189--Fiction. I. Title.
  PR6053.H245W555 2015
  823'.914--dc23
                            2015011727

Printed and bound in the United States of America.
                VP 10 9 8 7 6 5 4 3 2 1

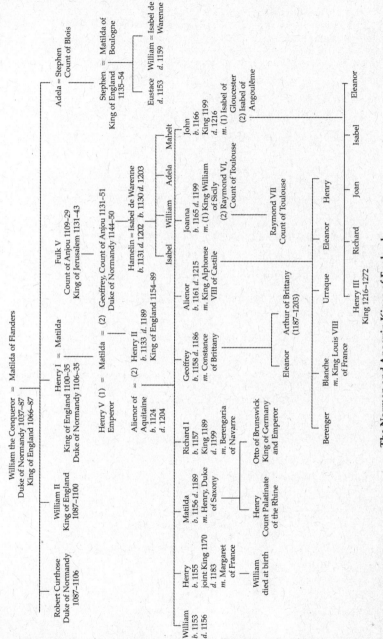

**The Norman and Angevin Kings of England**

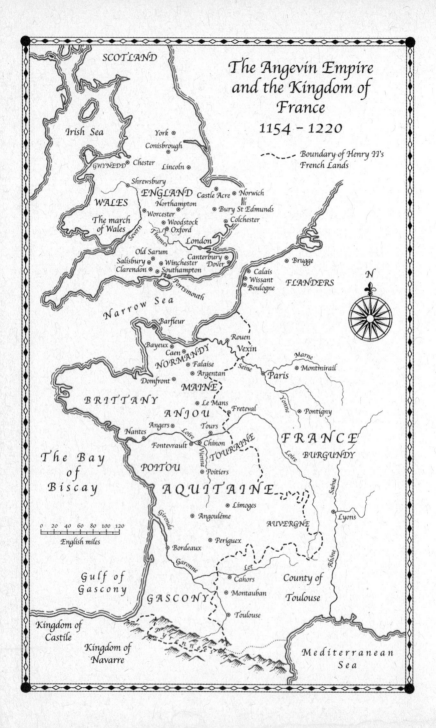

## NOTE FOR READERS

I have called Eleanor "Alienor" in the body of the novel, rather than Eleanor, because Alienor is what she would have called herself, and it is how her name appears in her charters and in the Anglo-Norman texts where she is mentioned. I felt it was fitting to give her that recognition.

# 1

At the precise moment Theobald, Archbishop of Canterbury, placed the golden weight of a crown on Alienor's brow, the child in her womb gave a vigorous kick that resonated throughout her body. Clear winter light rayed from the abbey's Romanesque windows to illuminate the Confessor's tomb in the sacrarium and cast pale radiance upon the dais where Alienor sat beside her husband, the newly anointed King Henry II of England.

Henry gripped the jeweled orb and the sword of sovereignty with confident possession. His mouth was a firm, straight line and his gray gaze purposeful. In the mingling of gloom and light, his beard glinted copper-red, and he exuded all the glow and vigor of his twenty-one years. He was already duke of Normandy, count of Anjou, and consort duke of Aquitaine and had been a force to be reckoned with ever since leading his first battle campaign at the age of fourteen.

The archbishop stepped to one side, and Alienor felt the full focus of the congregation strike her with the intensity of a fixed beam of light. Every bishop, magnate, and English baron was gathered to bear witness, to pay homage, and to usher in an era of peace and prosperity during which the wounds suffered by decades of civil war might be healed by the young king and his fertile queen. An air of anxious optimism filled the air. Everyone was eager to seek favor and advantage from their new sovereign. In the months to come, she and Henry would have to pluck the jewels from the piles of common stones and discard the dross.

This was the second time Alienor had worn a crown. For almost fifteen years she had been queen of France until her marriage to Louis had been annulled on grounds of consanguinity. The latter had been a convenient box in which to conceal the true reasons for parting, not least that she had only borne Louis two daughters of their union and not the all-important sons. That she was more closely related to Henry than to Louis gave Alienor cause for sardonic amusement. Money, influence, and human imperatives always spoke more loudly than conscience and God. In two years of marriage with Henry, she had produced one healthy son and expected another child before winter's end.

Henry rose from King Edward's carved throne, and all knelt to him and bowed their heads. He extended his hand to Alienor, who sank in a curtsy, her silk skirts a flood of gold around her feet. Henry raised her up by their clasped fingers, and they exchanged glances bright with exultation and a mutual awareness of how significant this moment was.

Cloaked in ermine, hand in hand, they paced down the abbey's great nave, following the archbishop's jeweled processional cross. Frankincense-perfumed smoke and the vapor of icy breath swirled heavenward. Alienor held her head high and walked with a stately tread and straight spine in order to balance the weight of the jeweled crown and the swollen curve of her womb. Her gown shone and flared with each step, and the choir sang triumphant praise, their voices soaring to twine with the smoke and carry all to God. Within her the child tumbled joyously, flexing and testing his limbs. It would be another boy; all the signs were auspicious. Their firstborn son, sixteen months old, was being cared for at the Tower with his nurse, but one day, God willing, he too would be anointed king in this cathedral.

Outside the abbey, crowds had gathered in the sharp December cold to watch the spectacle and to fete England's new king and queen. Ushers and marshals held the throng at a distance, but the mood was cheerful, the more so when servants of the royal household showered the gathering with fistfuls of silver pennies and small loaves of bread. Alienor watched the scramble, heard the cries of blessing and approbation, and although she barely understood a word of English, the sentiments were clear and made her smile.

"We have made an auspicious beginning," she said to Henry.

"Given what has gone before, it would be impossible not to do so." His own smile was wide, but Alienor saw his glance flick across from the abbey to the palace of Westminster and harden for an instant. Once a grand residence, it had become ruinous during the later years of King Stephen's reign and needed urgent repairs to make it habitable. For now he had set up his administration at the Tower and his domestic quarters across the river at the manor of Bermondsey.

"But you are right," he said. "We have made a favorable start. Long may it flourish." He placed his hand on her rounded womb, deliberately displayed to their subjects through the parting in her cloak. Being fruitful was a vital part of queenship and never more than now at the start of their reign. He gave a delighted chuckle to feel the baby's firm kick against his palm. "This is our time. We should make the most of every moment." Taking a handful of coins from an attendant, he flipped them into the crowd. A young woman standing near the front with a small child caught one in midair and sent him a dazzling smile.

❖ ❖ ❖

Alienor was tired but still bright with excitement as the barge bumped against the jetty on the river entrance to the Tower. A crewman cast a rope around a mooring stake and hauled the vessel closer in to the steps. Attendants hastened with lanterns to illuminate the winter night and escort the royal party from landing stage to apartment. Splintered gold reflections spilled across the dark waters of the Thames, heavy with the salt scent of the estuary. Alienor's teeth chattered despite her fur-lined cloak. She had to step carefully on the frost-rimed paths, wary of slipping in her thin kidskin shoes.

Talking animatedly to a group of courtiers, including his half brother, Hamelin, Vicomte de Touraine, Henry strode ahead, his voice ringing out in the clear night. He had risen long before dawn, and Alienor knew he would not retire until the small hours. Their domestic use of candles and lamps was a major item of expenditure in winter; no one could keep up with him.

Entering the Tower keep, she slowly climbed more stairs to their chambers, pausing for a moment to rest her hand on her womb. A swift peek into a partitioned alcove reassured her that the heir to the new throne was sound asleep in his crib tucked under soft fleeces and blankets, his hair a burnished gold flicker in the light of a single lamp. The nurse smiled at her with an expression that said all was well, and Alienor turned to the main chamber where she and Henry would spend the night before crossing the river to Bermondsey the next day.

The shutters were secured against the bitter winter's night, and a fine red fire blazed in the hearth. Alienor went to stand within the arc of heat and let the comforting warmth envelop her and banish the chill left by the icy gusts from the river. The reflection of the flames danced hypnotically on the surface of her gown, inscribing stories in the silk.

Her senior maid, Marchisa, came to disrobe her, but Alienor shook her head. "No," she said, smiling. "I want to savor the day for a little longer; there will never be another like it."

Henry's half sister Emma handed Alienor a cup of wine, her hazel eyes shining. "I shall remember this all my life."

Until Alienor's marriage to Henry, Emma had dwelled at the abbey of Fontevraud in the hall for laywomen. She and her brother Hamelin were Henry's illegitimate half siblings, and both had places in the household.

"We all shall," Alienor said and kissed her. She was fond of Emma, valuing both her gentle company and her embroidery skills.

Henry arrived, his energy still bubbling like a cauldron over a hot fire. He had exchanged his coronation robes for a tunic of everyday wool and donned a favorite pair of boots that were worn to the shape of his feet.

"You look as if you are ready to spit on your hands and begin work." Giving him a knowing look, Alienor eased herself carefully into a chair before the hearth and arranged her gown in a full sweep around her feet.

"I am." Henry went to fiddle with an ivory chess set arranged ready for play on a small bench near the window. "Unfortunately, I am constrained by the sleeping habits of others. If I don't let them rest, they become as dull as blunt knives." He shifted the pieces about to create a scenario of checkmate.

"Perhaps you should take the opportunity to sleep for a few hours too."

"What use is there in being dead to the world?" Abandoning the board, he sat on the bench facing her and purloined her goblet for a swallow of wine. "The archbishop of Canterbury will attend me at first light. He has a candidate to put forward for the position of chancellor."

Alienor raised her brows. The business of bargaining for favor and position was hard apace. She had already deduced from their brief exchanges before the coronation that Theobald of Canterbury was a wily one. His benign, myopic expression concealed the fact that the man himself was as strong as sword steel. He had defied King Stephen and prevented Stephen's eldest son Eustace from being acknowledged heir to England, for which he had been exiled for a time. His stand had kept Henry's cause afloat, and favors were owed. Theobald's reputation for gathering around him men of rare and keen intellect was renowned.

"Thomas Becket, his archdeacon and protégé," Henry said. "London born but educated in Paris and eager to demonstrate his skills as a fiscal genius."

"How old is he?"

"Thirties, so not in his dotage like half of them. I have spoken to him in passing but have not garnered any particular impression yet."

"Theobald must have a reason for putting him forward." She retrieved her wine from him.

"Naturally he does. He wants one of his own in my household because he thinks to influence the way I govern and promote the interests of the Church. And the man will have a keen brain, I am certain." He gave a taut smile. "But if I choose this Thomas Becket, he will have to change allegiance. I do not mind men in my service seeking advancement, but never at my expense."

Hearing the edge in his voice, she gave him a searching look.

He stood up, restless as a dog in a strange place. "Loyalty is a virtue rarer than hens' teeth. My mother told me to trust no one, and she is right."

"Ah, but you trust her, do you not?"

He sent her an evaluating glance. "I trust her with my life, and I trust that she always has my best interests at heart, but I do not always trust her judgment."

There was a small, difficult silence. Alienor did not ask if he trusted his wife's judgment, because she suspected his reply would disappoint her.

The child kicked again, and she stroked her womb. "Quiet, little one," she murmured and gave Henry a rueful smile. "He is like you—barely sleeps and is always restless, especially in church. I think he was running a race during the coronation!"

Henry chuckled. "Doubtless he was excited at the notion of being born the son of a king. What children we shall make between us." He came to crouch at her side and took her smooth hands in his calloused ones, bridging the gap that had briefly opened between them. He strengthened the repair by sitting on the floor at her feet like a squire, while he shared her wine and asked her opinion upon matters pertaining to the appointment of other court officials. It was mostly him talking while she listened, because these were English affairs and concerned men she barely knew, but she was pleased to be asked and ventured opinions here and there. They agreed that Nigel, Bishop of Ely, a former royal treasurer, should be persuaded out of retirement and his expertise used to set the exchequer to rights and start revenues flowing again. Richard de Lucy, a former official of King Stephen, would take up a senior administrative role together with Robert Beaumont, Earl of Leicester.

"It does not matter to me where men have sided in the past," Henry said. "It is their abilities I seek and their good service now. I said I trust no one, but I am willing to give men of backbone and intelligence a chance to prove their loyalty. Both de Lucy and Beaumont know where their best interests lie."

Alienor gently ruffled his hair with her fingertips, loving the way firelight played over the red-gold waves. She must cultivate these men too. When Henry was absent from England, she would have to deal with them, and better as allies than enemies.

"Stephen's son I shall keep where I can see him," Henry continued. "Even though he has rescinded his claim to the crown, he may still prove a rallying point for dissent."

Alienor cast her mind over the courtiers she had met in recent weeks. King Stephen's surviving son, William de Boulogne, was a pleasant, unremarkable young man a couple of years younger than Henry. He walked with a limp from a broken leg and was hardly the stuff of which great leaders were made. The only threat, as Henry said, was from those who might use him as a spear on which to nail their banners. "That seems prudent," she agreed, her words ending on a stifled yawn. The long day was catching up with her; the fire was warm, and the wine had gone pleasantly to her head.

Henry rose to his feet. "Time to bid you good night, my love."

"Are you not coming to bed for a while?" she asked with a note of entreaty. She wanted to end this glorious day wrapped in his arms.

"Later. I still have business to attend to." He kissed her tenderly on the mouth and briefly laid his palm over her womb. "You are everything a queen should be. I have never seen a woman look as beautiful and regal as you did today."

His words softened her disappointment and filled her with a warm glow. She watched him go to the door, his tread still as buoyant as it had been that morning. On the threshold he turned and gave her a melting smile, and then he was gone in a draft of cold air.

After a moment Alienor summoned her ladies and prepared to retire for the night, regretful to be alone, but still with a deep contentment in her heart.

❖❖❖

Henry's squire tapped softly on the door of the rented house in Eastcheap, a short walk from the Tower. The bolt slid back, and a maidservant quietly admitted the young man and his royal master before closing the door and kneeling.

Henry ignored her and fixed his gaze on the young woman who had dropped in a curtsy as he entered the room. Her head was bowed, and all he could see was the heavy ripple of her ash-brown hair against the pale linen of her chemise. He went to her and lifted her chin on his forefinger so that he could look into her face.

"My king," she said, and her full lips parted in a smile that stole his heart. "Henry."

He raised her to her feet, crushed her against him, and kissed her passionately. She circled her arms about his neck and made a soft kitten sound. Feeling all the warm points of her body against his, he buried his face in her abundant hair, inhaling scents of new grass and sage. "Ah, Aelburgh." His voice caught. "You're sweet as a meadow."

She nuzzled his throat. "I did not think you would come to me tonight. I thought you would be too busy."

"Hah, I am busy, but I have time for this."

"Are you hungry? I have bread and wine."

He shook his head and cupped her breast. "I have eaten a surfeit today. There is only one appetite I need to sate just now."

Aelburgh gave a soft laugh and eased from his embrace. Taking a lamp from a trestle, she led Henry up the steep stairs to the sleeping loft.

❖❖❖

The lamp was guttering by the time Henry reached for his clothes and prepared to leave.

"You could stay." Aelburgh stroked his naked back with languid fingers.

He gave a regretful sigh. "I have too much business to attend to, my love. The archbishop of Canterbury is visiting me in a few hours' time, and it would not be fitting to greet him still warm from the bed of my mistress, no matter how enticing that bed may be." He raised her hand to his lips. "I will come again soon, I promise."

"The queen looked very beautiful today," she said quietly.

"She did indeed—but she is not you."

Aelburgh sat up a little straighter and preened.

"My love, you are a different part of my life." He tucked a tress of her hair behind her ear. "There are duties…and then there are pleasures, and you are surely of the second sort." Especially while Alienor was great with child and he could not bed her.

From a small curtained-off section beyond the bed came the soft wail of a child waking from slumber. Aelburgh donned her shift and disappeared behind the hanging, returning a moment later with a red-haired infant boy cuddled in her arms. "Hush, little man, hush now," she crooned. "See, your papa is here."

The child stared at Henry, and his chin wobbled, but when Henry made a face at him, he giggled and hid his face against his mother's soft white neck before turning to peep at Henry again out of round blue eyes. Henry was amused and delighted. There was nothing worse than a screaming child that kept on screaming.

"I will provide for him," he said. "He is the son of a king, and he will have everything he needs to make his way in the world."

Fear flashed in Aelburgh's eyes. "You will not take him from me? I could not bear that."

"Don't be a foolish wench." Henry ducked around their son to kiss her again. "A child belongs with its mother in the early years." Of course, once intellect, reason, and physical strength had progressed sufficiently for his son to be educated, then the maternal ties would be severed, but he was not going to say that now. "I must go." He tugged a strand of her hair, kissed his son, and, on his way out, deposited a fat pouch of silver pennies on the table in the main room to join the silver piece she had caught outside the cathedral earlier.

The dark winter morning was nowhere near dawn, and he thought he might doze in a chair for a couple of hours and then prepare for the archbishop's visit. As he set out for the Tower, his thoughts were all on the business of government, and Aelburgh was already pushed to the back of his mind.

## 2

### MANOR OF BERMONDSEY, NEAR LONDON,
### DECEMBER 1154

ALIENOR CONSIDERED THE MAN WHOM HENRY HAD JUST
appointed chancellor of England. Thomas Becket was
tall and thin with a lantern jaw, strong nose, and keen gray eyes
that even when focused on a particular matter missed nothing on
the periphery.

"You are to be congratulated, Master Thomas," she said.

He bowed with a small flourish. "I am grateful for the opportunity the king has given me, m-madam. I shall do my best to
serve you both to the best of m-my ability." He spoke slowly,
measuring the words. When she had first heard him, Alienor had
thought it was a ploy to increase his gravitas, but now realized it
was his way of controlling a speech impediment. Certainly his
diplomatic skills must be sound, for the archbishop credited him
with a large part in persuading Rome not to acknowledge King
Stephen's son Eustace as heir to England.

"Then we shall hope for great things, Master Thomas."

"Tell me what you require, and I shall do everything I can to
bring it to fruition." He tucked his hands inside his furred sleeves,
which were fuller than normal, serving to increase the space he
occupied. She had taken note of the ornate brooch pinning his
cloak and the gold rings adorning his manicured fingers. Master
Becket had the eye and the taste for luxury, but so did many at
court. A man of station had to support his dignity by his external

appearance—unless he was all-powerful like Henry and could do as he pleased. Nevertheless, it was an appetite to be watched.

"I am sure we shall work well together. It will be an advantage to have someone in the household who is familiar with the diplomatic business of the realm."

Becket dipped his head. "Indeed, m-madam. But there are always new skills to learn, and I look forward to doing so." As he spoke, his voice deepened its cadence. He was hungry for this, she thought. Eager to serve but keen to exercise his new powers.

Henry arrived, bright-eyed and ebullient. "Are you ready for the hunt, my lord chancellor?" He clapped an affable hand on Becket's shoulder. "My grooms have found you a fast horse, and you can borrow one of my hawks until you have time to fill your own mews."

Becket bowed. "Sire, I am yours to command."

"Hah, come then, time to go!" Henry swept his chancellor off, as enthusiastic as a child with a new playmate. The other men finished their drinks, swallowed last morsels of bread, and were off too, eager for the chase, keen to make an impression on their new king. Alienor watched them leave, feeling envious of their masculine freedoms. Entering the later stages of pregnancy, she was confined to narrow indoor pursuits. The men would talk the politics of the court interspersed with enthusiastic discussions about the sport. They would cement alliances, brag, show off, and vent their excess energy in vigorous exercise. Henry would learn more about Becket and the other lords upon whom his rule depended, and they would learn more about him—or as much as he wanted to show them.

Alienor's duty while the men went hunting was to talk with their wives, daughters, and wards and establish her own network. Feminine wiles were often more effective than male bluster, and there were subtle ways of attaining one's will that did not involve boasting contests and riding horses into the ground.

Among the gathering of ladies, Alienor took an instant liking to Isabel, Countess de Warenne, who was wife to Stephen's son William de Boulogne. She was an attractive young woman with glossy brunette hair dressed in two thick braids that showed beneath the hem of her veil. Her eyes, warm brown flecked with gold, sparkled with humor and intelligence. She took Alienor's small son under her wing and told him a simple story about a rabbit, which involved finger play and gentle tickles. Will squealed with laughter. "More!" he demanded, bouncing. "More... Now!"

Alienor noted the wistful expression on Isabel de Warenne's face. She had been wed to King Stephen's youngest son for six years, but the couple remained barren, which Alienor thought a good thing in political terms. William de Boulogne had abjured his right to the crown, but seeds of rebellion might still be sown in a new generation, and Henry was prudently keeping the young man under close watch.

Observing the rapport between her son and Isabel, Alienor decided to take the countess into her own household and cultivate her friendship. She would have invaluable knowledge about the English barons, particularly those who had supported Stephen. The more she could draw Isabel into her affinity, the better.

"You have some skill there, my lady," Alienor said warmly.

Isabel laughed. "It is not so difficult, madam. All children love these games." She put her arm around Will and made a rabbit shape out of the kerchief in her hand. "And men too," she added impishly.

Alienor chuckled, acknowledging the truth of the statement and thought that Isabel de Warenne would do very well indeed.

❖❖❖

"The queen has asked me to join her household," Isabel told her husband that evening as they prepared for bed in their lodging house near the Tower. She had thoroughly enjoyed her day. She had not had the opportunity to socialize at court with women of her own rank for many years, but now there was peace it would be different, and she had even begun to feel optimistic. Playing with the new queen's beautiful little boy and seeing Alienor's well-advanced pregnancy had given her a moment's sadness, but she had made the most of the moment and not allowed herself to dwell on her own situation.

Her husband lay on the bed, his back supported by bolsters and pillows while she rubbed his lower right leg with a warming unguent. He had broken his shin the previous year in an "accident" at court about which he refused to talk. The circumstances were murky, and Isabel had never unraveled them to her satisfaction. She suspected it had either been a warning to William to step aside from claims to his father's crown, or else a failed attempt at murder. Having no desire to pursue kingship, William had willingly yielded his entitlement, and the danger seemed to have faded, even though she knew he was still closely watched.

"I am not surprised," he said. "The king intends keeping me at court, and it is only logical that you should attend the queen." He looked wry. "One side of the coin is favor and friendship, and the other is polite house arrest. Henry does not trust us out of his sight."

"But that will ease in time?" Isabel asked with her need to have all right with the world.

"I hope so." He puffed out his cheeks. "I have never known anyone with so much energy. He hunted up hill and down dale today, and if his horse hadn't flagged, he would have carried on until nightfall and damn the rest of us. Only that half brother of his, Hamelin, and the new chancellor could keep up, and that was by sheer force of will and because they had the best horses. I have no doubt he will be off again tomorrow at the crack of dawn." He changed position, grimacing. "He plans to go to Oxford next week and then on to Northampton."

She gave him a sharp look. "Just the king's entourage or all the court?"

"Just the king. He did not mention the queen's household—be thankful!"

Isabel rubbed and pressed. "I shall miss you."

"I won't be gone long. Don't worry."

She concentrated on her work. The unguent was all rubbed in. Where the break had been there was a thick scar like a knot in a branch.

"Isabel."

He spoke her name in that gentle, melancholy way that made her want to weep.

"Come," he said. "Unbind your hair for me. It is so beautiful when it's loose."

She reached hesitantly to her luxuriant braids. Her fingers, moist with the remnants of unguent, clung to the heavy, elastic strands. She loved him deeply, but in the protective way an older sister might love a little stepbrother, and moments of intimacy were awkward. They had married at the decree of his father the king when she was sixteen and he was just eleven, and their physical relationship, as he came to maturity, had never truly blossomed. They lay together because they had a duty to provide heirs for the lands of Boulogne and Warenne, but thus far she had not conceived. She told herself there was time, and surely it would happen, but as each occasion proved unsuccessful, her doubts grew, as did her guilt at failure.

He set his hands in her hair and drew her close, but their embrace came to no more than strokes and gentle kisses, which, instead of intensifying, faded away as he fell asleep. Isabel lay at his side, trapped by his hand in her hair, which he gripped like a child with a comfort cloth. She listened to his slow, steady breathing, and her heart ached.

❖❖❖

At the end of February, a late snow fell, covering the land overnight in a thick white quilt. At Bermondsey, the hearth in the birthing chamber was kept well stoked, and although Alienor's lower body was naked during this later stage of labor, the covers around her shoulders were of insulating fur.

"Think," said Emma as she gave Alienor a drink of wine fortified with honey. "This child will be born in the ermine in more ways than one!"

Alienor was between contractions and so managed a wry smile. Her eldest son had been born to a duke and duchess whereas this new baby would be the offspring of the king and queen of

England. "Indeed, and his father will be here to see him this time." Henry had recently returned from his lightning travels around England. The deep snow had prevented him from hunting, so he would be closeted in his chamber with Becket and de Lucy, busy with matters of state. She sipped the drink, welcoming the sweetness of the honey. "When Will was born, Henry was away on campaign, and by the time he did set eyes on him, he was seven months old!"

The next contraction surged, stronger than the last, and with a gasp of pain, Alienor returned the cup to Emma.

The senior midwife performed a swift examination. "Very soon now, madam," she said with cheerful encouragement.

Alienor's face contorted. "Not soon enough!" she panted. "I tell you, men have the better part of the bargain in every way!"

It was almost noon before a baby's wail filled the birthing chamber, and Alienor slumped against the bolsters, gasping and exhausted.

"Madam, you have a fine, lusty boy!" Beaming, the midwife lifted the child from between Alienor's bloody thighs and placed him, all damp and squirming, on her belly.

Alienor laughed triumphantly despite her weariness. With two sons vouchsafed to the succession, she had more than accomplished her duty.

The midwife cut the cord and dealt with the afterbirth, tending to Alienor while her assistant bathed the baby in a brass bowl by the fireside. Once dried and wrapped in warm linen and furs, he was returned to his mother. Alienor cradled him in her arms, stroked his birth-crumpled little face, and counted and kissed his fingers. A glance toward the pale light shining through the window leads showed her silent feathers of green-tinted snow whispering past the glass, and she knew she would always remember this moment. The stillness after bloody struggle; the warmth of fire and pelts protecting her and her new son from the cold; the sense of hushed, enclosed peace that was almost holy.

❖ ❖ ❖

Alienor awoke from slumber to the sound of London's church bells and the closer peal from Saint Savior's ringing out the joyous news that a prince was born. The window showed quenched afternoon light fading toward dusk, and the snow had ceased. Henry was standing at the bedside, looking down into the cradle with a beatific smile on his cold-reddened face.

Alienor pushed herself upright against the pillows, wishing that her women had woken her before his arrival and given her a moment to prepare.

He turned at her movement, and she saw the shine of tears in his eyes. "He is beautiful," he said, and his throat worked.

Alienor seldom saw this vulnerable side of her husband. His expression, the way he spoke, filled her with aching tenderness, as if her maternal instincts were flowing out over him too. He lifted the swaddled baby from his cradle and sat down with him on the side of the bed. "You have given me everything," he said. "You have fulfilled every part of the bargain. I do not give my trust lightly, but I give it to you here. You are my dearest heart."

There was complete candor in his stare, and Alienor's own eyes filled because she knew how much courage it took for him to lower the shield and admit so much. Clearly the sight of his newborn son had had a profound effect on him. Yet she was wary, because she knew from hard experience that, with Henry, something meant sincerely now was open to change at a later moment.

Eventually, he rose to leave and with reluctance handed the baby to one of her women. "I will arrange for his baptism— Henry, as we agreed. The bishop of London will perform it in the morning. I'll leave you to your rest. You need to recover and grow strong again, ready for the next one."

He kissed her and departed in his usual flurry. Alienor smiled, but she was exasperated. A moment ago everything had been enough and "perfect" for him, yet already he was anticipating the next one, and it was not what a sore, bruised wife wanted to hear just hours after giving birth. The notion of growing strong in order to produce another baby for him caused her eyes to narrow. She had warned him at the outset of their marriage that she was more than a brood mare, and she would not be treated as one.

# 3

## WINCHESTER, SEPTEMBER 1155

*T*HE ARCHBISHOP IS PUSHING ME TO ORGANIZE AN EXPEDITION to Ireland," Henry said, pacing the floor with vigor and irritation. "The old fox wants to bring the Irish Church to heel under Canterbury's influence. He suggests I should make my brother king there, but if he thinks to use me and Geoffrey to work his will, he is mistaken."

Alienor sat by the window dandling seven-month-old Henry in her lap and watching his older brother gallop his wooden hobby horse around the trestle, shaking its red leather reins. "What does Geoffrey say?"

Henry wrapped his hands around his belt. "He likes the idea of a kingdom for himself, but not as distant as Ireland. I certainly do not want him left to his own devices on my seaward flank."

"You are right to stand your ground." Alienor was unable to warm to either of Henry's brothers. Geoffrey, the second born, was full of petulant bluster and resentful of Henry's primary position. Alienor did not trust him near her or her sons and avoided him when possible. She felt a similar but less strong antipathy toward Henry's youngest brother, William. He was less forthright in his sense of prerogative but sought to intimidate others as a way of bolstering his station. Henry's only decent brother was Hamelin, who was bastard-born and had to sustain his position at court through loyal service.

"I refuse to let the Church dictate to me," Henry growled. "Theobald may invoke Rome all he wants and play on how important he was in the past as a mediator. He can hint at how many favors I owe him, but it makes no difference. I shall deal with Ireland in my own good time, not his."

"Have you told him that?"

"Not as such." A sly look crossed his face. "I said that since it concerned my brother, it was a family matter, and I must consult our mother. I know for certain she will not agree. Like me she will see it as a waste of time and resources—and dangerous. Theobald will pursue it for a while, but I can outlast him."

"Clever," Alienor said. Henry's mother was his deputy in Normandy and ruled her roost from the abbey at Bec. She knew the archbishop well and would be a sympathetic intermediary, while still ensuring Henry's will was done.

"I think so," he said with a grin.

"Look, Papa, my horse can gallop fast!" chirruped Will, who had just begun to talk in sentences.

Henry's expression softened. "A man always needs a fast horse to be ahead of the game and outride his opponents." He caught and embraced his son, and their heads pressed together, Henry's fox-red mingling with William's brighter, ruddy gold, but both of the same coin.

"What does your chancellor say, being as he was once Theobald's man?" Alienor asked. "Has he sought to persuade you?"

"Thomas does as I command him." Henry flashed her a sharp gray glance. "He takes his instructions from me now, and his task is to raise revenues, which he is doing remarkably well. It must be his merchant blood." He set his son back down on the floor. "My mother will deal with Theobald, and that will keep the pair of them occupied and leave me free to attend to other matters."

Alienor handed the baby to his nurse. "You mean us. The matters are mine as well as yours."

A wary look entered his eyes. "That goes without saying."

"And yet I always feel I need to say it."

Irritation sparked in his eyes. "When I cross the sea to deal with matters in Normandy and Anjou, you will be my regent here; you are my proxy as I am yours. Rest assured I will always involve you."

Alienor had no intention of "resting assured," because she did not believe him. If he involved her, it was for his own ends. "But the business of Aquitaine is mine first," she said firmly. "And it is my choice to involve you, not yours to involve me."

Henry made an impatient sound. "Why are you arguing over words? You need the strength of my sword to keep your barons in check, and it is my sweat and striving that sees to the defense and protection of Aquitaine. Our son will one day inherit your duchy, and it behooves us both to do our best for him. I do not know why you fret about this."

"Because it matters to me. Do not take me for granted, Henry."

He made an exasperated sound before pulling her against him and kissing her forcefully. She gripped his arms, their embrace a battlefield, sparking with tension and pent-up sexual energy demanding release. "As if I would."

"I tell you it is more than your life is worth." She spoke close enough for her words to be part of the next breath he drew.

He laughed. "And yours, my love. Since it seems we are perfectly matched we should call a truce…" He kissed her again and led her to the bed, drawing the curtains around the canopy, shutting out the world. And as they undressed each other, short-breathed with lust, she had the thought that only opponents made truces, not allies.

❖ ❖ ❖

Alienor stood beside Henry in the great hall of Westminster Palace and studied the transformation with pleasure. The smell of fresh plaster and timber had replaced that of cold, damp stone and neglect. Craftsmen were still busy about their tasks, but they were cosmetic now rather than of structure. The final smoothing, the last touches of paint and varnish were falling into place. The hangings commissioned from Canterbury had recently arrived and were being suspended from poles beneath friezes of red and green acanthus scrolls that added detail and color. English embroidery was the best in Christendom.

"All will be ready for the council in three days' time, sire," said Thomas Becket with a sweep of his fur-lined sleeve. "The furniture will be here before dusk, and the napery is arriving tomorrow." One of his briefs had been to see to the refurbishing of the palace of Westminster ready for the great council and court gathering at Christmas before Henry's departure to Normandy.

Henry nodded his approval. "Excellent," he said. "A year ago this was an uninhabitable shell with water running down the walls and half the lead stolen from the roof. Now it is fit for the purpose intended."

Becket dipped his head and sent a glance of acknowledgment to Alienor. "With the queen's advice, I have done my best, sire."

"I am pleased to see my chancellor and my wife working together in harmony," Henry said with satisfaction. "I could not ask for a better result."

Becket bowed again, and Alienor reciprocated. She found Becket an enigma. He was unfailingly polite to her, never familiar. They could talk easily on many subjects and understand each other—he was cultured, observant, and sharp-witted—but there was no great warmth in their communication; she could never tell for certain what he was thinking, and that unsettled her. His goal seemed to be to provide whatever she and Henry desired of him, especially when it came to raising revenue, and that in its turn added to his luster.

Alienor had enjoyed working with Becket at Westminster—advising, designing, and selecting—but while her involvement was one of routine pleasure, he had been like a starving man let loose at a banquet; there had been moments when she had had to curtail his rampant enthusiasm. The subtle, textured hangings from the workshops at Canterbury were of her choosing, but the pink marble high table with its arched columns was Becket's contribution, as were the matching benches and the ornate fountain. She had not visited the chancellor's home yet but had heard it was sumptuous enough for the Greek emperor. It was ironic that Henry could as happily sleep on a straw pallet as a feather bed, whereas his chancellor had the tastes and inclinations of a potentate—or of a man striving to forget his common origins in a display of overblown grandeur.

From the great hall, Becket led them along a covered pathway. A bitter wind swept off the river, which was tipped with whitecaps as the incoming tide battled up the estuary. Alienor wrapped her cloak firmly around her body, sheltering her womb, where the child conceived in September was starting to thicken her figure. They came to a smaller hall that had been derelict the previous year and now stood proud in a coat of fresh lime wash, roofed in oak shingles gleaming like dull silk.

The warmth inside the smaller dwelling was like an embrace, and Alienor went to enjoy the heat glowing from the fire in the central hearth. Here too the walls had received new plaster and lime wash. An insulating layer of fragrant straw topped by reed matting covered the floor. Ceramic lamps hung from the ceiling on brass chains, and the exotic perfume of scented oil filled the chamber. On a sturdy chest under the window stood an exquisite little ivory box with ornate hinges. Henry pounced on it. "I remember this!" he cried. "My mother brought it with her when she came to fight for her crown. I haven't seen it since I was a child. She used to keep her rings in it." His face was animated as he raised the lid to reveal many small irregular lumps of opaque gray-and-gold resin resembling beach shingle.

"Frankincense!" Alienor looked over his shoulder and smiled.

"The bishop of Winchester left it behind when he fled," Becket said. "I am sorry there were no jewels inside, but the frankincense is worth its weight in gold."

"I am surprised it does not hold thirty pieces of silver," Henry muttered. He placed three lumps on a small skillet at the side of the hearth and held it over the fire until pale, fragrant smoke started to twist from the resin.

Henry, Bishop of Winchester, was King Stephen's brother. Unwilling to raze the castles he had built during the Anarchy, he had offered bribes and wriggled all ways to try to unhook himself, and when he saw that he was going to be brought down whatever he did, he had quickly and quietly arranged to send his purloined, amassed treasure to France, to the abbey at Cluny. He had followed, slipping out of the country on the ebb tide of a dark November night.

Henry wafted his hand through the smoke. Closing her eyes, Alienor inhaled the scent of royal power and of God. Memories coiled around her, many of them powerful and glorious even if not altogether happy.

When she opened her eyes again, Henry's half brother Hamelin had joined them. His grim expression and wooden posture were an immediate warning.

"It's Aelburgh," he said to Henry. "There has been an accident."

Henry rose from the hearth and swiftly drew Hamelin to one side. Alienor watched the latter stoop to murmur in Henry's ear and saw Henry stiffen. The English name meant nothing to her—she did not even know if it was male or female—but it clearly meant a great deal to Henry. Without a word to her or Becket he strode from the room, dragging Hamelin with him.

Alienor stared after them in astonishment and disquiet. She was accustomed to Henry's volatile flurries of energy, but not like this. "Who is Aelburgh?" She looked around at her ladies, who shook their heads. She turned to Becket, who was picking up the box of frankincense from the side of the hearth. "My lord chancellor?"

He cleared his throat. "I have no personal acquaintance, madam."

"But you do know who it is?"

"I think it best for the king to tell you when he returns, madam."

Anger flashed. She felt at a disadvantage—undermined. "You may 'think' what you like, my lord chancellor, but you will tell me if you know."

He looked down at the little box and secured the lid. "I believe the king has known the lady for many years," he said. "More than that I cannot say."

So it was a woman and of long acquaintance. Henry's sexual appetite was as intense as the rest of him, and Alienor accepted that he made arrangements to slake his lust when she was heavy with child or not by his side. There were nights when he did not come to her chamber. Much of that time he was working on matters of government, but she was not naive. Any court whore would leap at the chance to oblige him, and his position of power meant he would never be refused. But a woman he had known for many years was more than a passing fancy, and his behavior just now spoke of deep concern.

Everyone was avoiding her gaze. Standing tall, she gathered her dignity. "Thank you, my lord chancellor," she said with regal command. "The king has business to attend to, but you may show me what else has been accomplished here."

Becket bowed and took his response from hers. "Madam, I think you will like what has been done with the smaller hall." He gestured with an open hand.

Alienor followed him, and as he showed her the renovations with comments and flourishes, she replied as if she was interested, but when the tour was finished, she recalled not a word of what he had said.

❖❖❖

Henry gazed at the body of his mistress. With the sheet drawn up to her chin and her eyes closed, she might have been deeply asleep were it not for the waxen appearance of her skin, which lacked any warmth of color. Her beautiful hair still rippled with all the vibrant life that had left its owner.

"A cart in the street laden with barrels overturned and crushed her," Hamelin said. "By the time they pulled her out, she was dead. I am sorry." Words were inadequate; he almost felt foolish for saying them, but there had to be something to fill the void.

Henry grasped a hank of Aelburgh's hair and rubbed its softness between his finger and thumb, then leaned over and kissed her icy brow. "I was a youth of fourteen when we met." His voice caught in his throat, and he had to clear it with a cough. "She was a girl fresh from the country and sweeter than an apple blossom. There will never be another one like her for me."

"I am sorry," Hamelin muttered again. "I know what she was to you." He squeezed Henry's shoulder in sympathy and stood for a moment in silence. Then he said, "What about the child?"

Henry drew a shuddering breath. "I will bring him to Westminster to join the nursery. It was my intention to do so anyway at some point." He turned away from Aelburgh's broken body, leaving it to be made ready for church.

In the room below, his small son, Jeoffrey, sat on his nurse's lap fingering a scrap of blanket, his blue eyes big with wonder and anxiety. "Is Mama still asleep?" he asked.

Henry plucked him out of the woman's arms. "Your mama is sending you to live with me, because she cannot care for you anymore," he said. "You will have brothers to play with and people to look after you. Here, would you like to ride on my big horse?"

The child sucked his bottom lip but nodded gamely. Henry threw a look over his shoulder at Hamelin filled with a raw mingling of grief and anger.

Hamelin recognized dangerous ground. Henry never coped well when matters took away his control and made of him a straw in the flood. And he hated exposing his vulnerability to others. "I never knew my mother," Hamelin said. "She died at my birth—but I do remember our father's care and how he made me his son even though I had no rights of inheritance. I loved him for that and honored him all of his days, as you know."

Henry swallowed. "Yes, I do," he said and then looked at the little boy in his arms. "He is all I have of his mother." Abruptly he pushed his way outside. It had started to snow, and he protected his son within the thick fur folds of his cloak. Hamelin followed him out, closed the door, and directed their attendant guard to disperse the curious crowd that had gathered.

❖❖❖

As dusk advanced, Alienor set down her sewing to rest her eyes. The winter light was not conducive to fine work, but the repetitive act of pushing the needle in and out of the fabric, creating the design, always helped her to think.

"Madam, is there anything I may do for you?" asked Isabel de Warenne, who had been keeping her company throughout the afternoon. Heavy-eyed, little Will snuggled against Isabel's side, tucked in a fold of her cloak. He had been running around the room with his toy weapons earlier but had paused for respite and the comfort of a cuddle. His baby brother slept in his cradle, watched over by his nurse.

"No," Alienor said. "Other than bid the steward put bread and cheese under a cloth for when the king returns. He will be hungry. And summon Madoc. If I cannot sew, I will listen to music."

"Madam." Isabel tidied her sewing away with graceful, unhurried movements that soothed Alienor to watch and filled her with a glow of gratitude.

"Thank you," she said, lightly touching Isabel's sleeve.

"For what, madam?"

"For companionship without words."

Isabel's face turned pink. "I could see you were troubled but wished to keep your own thoughts. There is nothing I could say that would have been wisdom."

"And that is what makes you wise. If you had chattered, I would have sent you away."

"I learned discretion when I was at court before," Isabel replied with a small grimace. "Sometimes the silences have more substance than words." She started to rise, gently disturbing the little boy. "Come, my prince," she said. "Shall we find you some bread and honey?"

Will rubbed his eyes and grizzled, but Isabel cajoled him until he brightened and put his hand in hers, the other clutching his toy sword.

A sudden flurry at the hall doors and a blast of icy air heralded Henry's return. With mingled relief and exasperation, Alienor glimpsed his ruddy hair and the swirl of his short green cloak.

"Papa!" Will yelled, dashing from Isabel's side toward his father, brandishing his sword. He skidded to a halt in front of him, a look of surprise and consternation on his face at the sight of the other little boy standing at Henry's side. He was older than Will and taller, but the resemblance between the children was clear for all to see.

"This is Jeoffrey," Henry announced to Will and crouched with his arm around the newcomer. "He has come to live with us and to be your companion and playmate."

There was a sick taste at the back of Alienor's throat as she saw this cuckoo child standing in the curve of Henry's arm, while her own son stood outside of it.

The children eyed each other warily, and Isabel stepped into the gap. "Sire, I was just going to give my lord William some bread and honey. Perhaps Jeoffrey would like some too." She smiled and held out her hand, her movement flowing and natural.

Henry sent her a look filled with relief and gratitude. "That is kind of you, madam. Thank you."

Isabel curtsied and led the children off, one on either side.

Henry stood up, and his gaze followed Isabel and the boys for a moment before he advanced to warm himself at the fire.

Alienor felt raw, her pain exacerbated because she was containing words and emotions that could not be expressed before all these people who had seen him enter with the boy.

Henry's mouth was a set, thin line. He rubbed his hands together, and although his knuckles were red with cold, the action was tense rather than an attempt to warm himself.

A servant set down a glazed jug on a table near the hearth, along with platters of bread and cheese. Henry waved the man away and dismissed everyone from earshot before gesturing Alienor to sit down with him.

Alienor took the cup of wine he poured for her, sipped, and almost retched because the drink was sour and her stomach queasy. "Why did you not tell me you had a son?"

Henry shrugged. "It was none of your concern until today, but now I must make provision for him in the household." He swilled his mouth with wine and swallowed.

Alienor struggled for composure. "You say it is none of my concern, but for the security of our line, I must know these things." She felt like a lioness protecting her young. "You have kept this a secret from me for some time, to look at him."

"He was three years old in March," Henry said.

"And his mother?"

"She is dead." His voice was flat. "I have just been making arrangements for her funeral."

Alienor looked away. She would not let him put her in the wrong or make her feel small and mean by his words. "I know you seek elsewhere to slake your lust," she said. "I know you are not chaste when you are apart from me or when I am great with child. I would be a fool to believe you did not go rutting elsewhere, but you have dishonored me nevertheless by keeping a mistress and child under my nose without telling me."

"It was a separate part of my life." His face reddened with anger. "I did not keep her at court. There was never any insult or threat to you or our offspring. My grandsire had twenty bastard children in his household by numerous different mothers, and his queens accepted every one of them." He gestured out into the hall at his half brother. "My father raised Hamelin in his court, and Jeoffrey will be raised in mine. I acknowledge him. His welfare is my obligation, and it is your duty, madam, to welcome him."

Alienor tossed her head. "I would have done so without your command because a child is innocent no matter the sins of his parents, but I will not be kept in ignorance, Henry. That is my complaint."

He gave an irritable shrug. "And I would have told you, but I saw no need at this stage."

Alienor was tempted to dash her wine into his face. She could not believe he saw the matter as of no consequence.

"You must admit he is a fine little chap," he cajoled.

"I can see no wrong in him," she said stiffly and rose from the trestle. "Forgive me, I am not well. I need to retire."

Henry gave her a sharp look. "You are not going off to sulk, I hope."

"No, sire, I am not. But I am going to think long and hard… and so should you."

Without waiting his leave, she left the hall with all its fine new furniture and embellishments and went to her own adjoining chamber where she dismissed her ladies, sat on her bed with the curtains closed, and shut herself away. Once alone, she pounded the coverlet with her fists and let the tears and the anger surge through her body. It was betrayal of the worst sort. Even while she had been carrying and bearing little William, believing him Henry's firstborn son, he already had a male child out of this woman, and now the shine of her memories was forever tarnished. She did not blame the child, and yet she could not prevent feelings of terrible jealousy. She would have to see him every day in the nursery, his features a blending of Henry's and this unknown woman's. Having the advantage of age, he was already bigger and stronger than her legitimate sons and would be in a position to compete with them.

Eventually, she gathered herself together and wiped her eyes. Done was done and could not be changed, but the future was a different matter.

❖❖❖

By the time Henry arrived, Alienor was composed and sitting in bed clad in a fresh white chemise, her hair a golden ripple around her shoulders. Resting a wax tablet on her upraised knees, she tapped the end of her stylus against her lips as she pondered.

"To whom do you write?" Henry demanded suspiciously.

"To your mother," she replied. "To tell her she has another grandson—unless, of course, she already knows."

Henry shook his head. "It was none of her concern either." He wandered about the chamber, picking up a casket to examine the carving on it, putting it down and picking it up again. Eventually, rubbing the back of his neck, he turned to her. "I thought you did not want to know; otherwise, you would have asked."

She noted with weary inevitability how he had turned the

blame around. "Well then, I will ask you now: Are there any others I should know about?"

"None whose mothers have chosen to come forward. The child will be an asset to the household and a good companion to our boys. You will see."

Alienor's heart clenched. "I have no interest in the other women you bed; indeed, I do not wish to know about them. But if children are born of your rutting, that is different because they affect our affinities. I must know about them."

He shrugged. "As you wish." His eyes had the flat glitter in them that told her he was calculating how much he could keep to himself and how little he could give her.

"I do wish. I warned you once: I am not just your brood mare."

"So you keep saying, and so I well know, but I will not be dictated to or ruled by a woman's womb. Within two weeks I shall be in Normandy, and you will be regent here—I hardly call that treating you as a brood mare." He paced the room again, heeled around sharply, and then plumped down on the bed, uttering a hard sigh. "Let us be done with all this. I need your cooperation, and when measured against the governing of our lands, the fact that I have a son by another woman, and born before I wed you, is a trifling matter."

Alienor tightened her lips, still feeling resentful and insecure, but acknowledging the logic of what he said. He would never change his ways—there would always be other women, and the business of government mattered more than an argument over a mistress. It was the betrayal of trust that hurt. "Very well," she said shortly. "Let us be done."

Henry leaned over and gave her a kiss to which she responded with lukewarm enthusiasm before drawing away. "What do you intend for the child?"

He gave her a questioning look.

"You say he will be raised in our household, but what role do you intend for him later?"

He opened his hands. "That will all come in good time. I shall watch him and decide later what best suits him, be it the pen or the sword."

Alienor said nothing. It would be the priesthood if she had anything to do with it. That way, he would serve the family cause without being a threat to her own sons.

Henry began undressing. "There is no need to write to my mother about this. I will tell her when I arrive in Normandy."

Alienor set her writing aside and moved so that he could join her in bed. Usually on the eve of a great council he would have kept late hours with Becket, Robert of Leicester, and Richard de Lucy and then, for all she knew, gone elsewhere to slake his sexual energy. But tonight was for conciliation and mending broken bridges so that, although damaged, with care they might still be crossed.

# 4

## Windsor Castle, May 1156

Alienor paused in reading Henry's letter to press her hand to her womb as she felt it tighten around the child. By her reckoning she was not due for several weeks, but her body was making preparations. She had moved from Westminster as the spring advanced and settled in at the stronghold of Windsor for her lying-in. It was peaceful here but only twenty-five miles from London and within easy riding distance for messengers arriving from the south-coast ports.

A pleasant breeze ruffled the fresh green leaves on the apple trees, and the sun dappled the garden in coins of warm pale gold. Will and his half brother Jeoffrey were playing a game in the orchard, galloping around on their wooden hobby horses, waving their toy swords, and uttering bloodcurdling yells.

"Are you well, madam?" Isabel gently touched her arm.

"It is just a twinge," Alienor reassured her. "There is no need to summon the midwives yet, although I shall be glad to be free of the burden." She heaved a regretful sigh. "Henry will not be here for the birth unless circumstances change, which I doubt." She looked at the letter. They were still besieging Mirebeau and not expected home this side of summer. "I knew Henry's brother would foment rebellion the moment they crossed the sea. He was biding his time and paying lip service to loyalty while he was in England." She had never warmed to Geoffrey FitzEmpress. The fact that he had tried to abduct her just days after the annulment of her first marriage had colored her opinion of him, but independent of that he was a boor, not stupid by a long way but lacking the wit and charisma that made Henry shine. He claimed that their father had bequeathed him Anjou as his inheritance portion and had already incited one uprising in an effort to overthrow Henry's rule there. This was his second attempt, and Henry was about the business of putting down the challenge once and for all.

She lowered the letter to her lap. "I shall go to Henry immediately I have recovered from the birth. England is at peace, and my mother-by-marriage has grandchildren she has not yet seen." Her gaze followed little Jeoffrey FitzRoy. Over the past several months she had come to terms with his presence in the household and had achieved a state of detachment. She was still determined that his path would lead to the Church, but for the moment he was just a small boy. She had deliberately not sought to know more about his mother and what she had been to Henry. It was easier that way. "I must also go to my own duchy." She smiled at Isabel. "You have never seen Aquitaine, have you?"

"No, madam," Isabel said, "but I would like to."

Alienor glanced around the garden. "Today bears a resemblance, but the light is different there—brighter. Here the fruit is sharp and the wine is sour from lack of sun on the grapes. In Aquitaine, both are as sweet as honey—or perhaps I have just been absent for too long." She made a rueful gesture. "It is time I visited my people again and showed them their heir." She cast a fond look at Will who had flopped down in the shade to rest, his face pink from all the running about, and her heart flooded over with ocean-deep love.

❖❖❖

That evening, Will was quieter than usual. Heavy-eyed, he toyed with his supper of bread sops in milk. Jeoffrey devoured all of his and a second helping and then was ready to dash off and play again with the other castle children.

Alienor brought Will to sit with her and had her harpist play a soothing ripple of notes while Isabel told him a story from the fables of Aesop about a fox and a crow. Leaning against Alienor, he listened quietly and sucked his thumb while she stroked his hair.

Once the story was finished, Alienor beckoned to Pavia his nurse. "Bed for you, little one," she said tenderly.

Hands and face washed and prayers said, Will clambered into the small bed arranged beside his little brother's crib. Alienor came to check on the sleeping baby and to kiss her children good night. Will's clean chemise, which she had finished stitching yesterday, was as white as a bellbind flower in the gloom. Once again she stroked his bright hair. "Good night, God bless you," she murmured.

"Mama." He yawned, turned on his side, and in an instant was sound asleep.

Alienor and Isabel sat down to a game of chess, and the harpist continued to play softly for them, the notes as gentle as rain. Jeoffrey's nurse brought him in from his game and put him to bed, ignoring his protests that he was not in the least sleepy.

Alienor moved one of her knights and stifled a yawn. "I should retire too," she said. "I have no stamina these days."

"Even so, your wits are still sharp," Isabel replied, screwing up her face. "I do not know how I am going to escape from this trap you have set."

Alienor flashed a smile. "I am practicing so I will be ready for Henry. He's always so determined to win, and I like to prove him wrong and keep him on his mettle."

The women played for a while longer, drank wine, and listened to music while the candle burned down on its pricket. Alienor grimaced because her back was aching. Even sitting down with cushions against her spine there was no respite.

"Shall I rub your back for y—" Isabel's question was interrupted by piercing screams from Will.

"Mama! Mama!"

With one accord Alienor and Isabel shot to their feet and dashed to investigate. Will's nurse Pavia was already leaning over him. "I fear he has a fever, madam."

Alienor pressed her hand to Will's brow. He had been a little warm earlier, but no more than might be attributed to sun flush. Now he was scalding, and his eyes were glittery and half closed against the lantern light. "My head hurts," he whined.

"Hush, hush. All's well. Mama's here," Alienor soothed, her voice calm, although she was sick with fear. "Fetch Marchisa," she said to the nurse and lifted Will out of the bed. He wrapped his arms around her, and she felt his shudders ripple through her own body. There was a sudden gush of heat against the front of her gown as he spilled his bladder, and his wails increased, high-pitched with pain. The noise woke baby Henry, who began to howl in tandem, and Isabel hastened to soothe him.

Pavia returned from her errand. "Madam, let me clean and change my little lord. I have fresh linens here." She held up a folded pile of cloth.

Alienor gave him to his nurse. Will's urine had left a gleaming dark stain on her gown that soaked through her chemise to her skin. The moisture was clammy on her body below her heart and over the swollen mound of her womb, and she felt a terrible sense of foreboding.

Pavia removed Will's shirt and then stepped back, stifling a scream against the back of her hand.

Alienor stared, and her breath caught in her throat as she saw the dark red pinpricks blotching her son's torso and arms. "No!" She shook her head. "No!"

Marchisa put her head around the curtain. "Madam?" And then she saw Will, and her look of worried inquiry turned to shock. "I will fetch the physician," she said and was gone.

Alienor took Will from Pavia and brought him into the main room to examine him in better light. The blotches did not resemble the blisters of pox or *la rougeole*, both of which could be killers, but that was no cause for comfort. The contagion was burning through her son's tender body like wildfire.

Marchisa returned, Master Radulf at her side. He was disheveled from his bed, his hair sticking up in tufts around his skewed cap. His satchel of nostrums was slung over his shoulder.

Alienor berated him for his tardiness while weeping with relief. "Do something!" she cried. "In God's name, help him!" The physician took Will in his arms and called for more light to examine him. Will wailed and tried to hide his eyes from the blossom of the fresh candle flame. Master Radulf's lips compressed as he saw the rash.

Alienor gripped her hands together. "You can do something, can't you?"

He gave her an impassive look. "My best," he said. "I can do no more. I will not lie to you: this is a serious condition. We are in the hands of God, and we must pray for his divine mercy."

❖❖❖

Throughout the night Alienor sat at Will's side, powerless to do anything as his condition worsened despite everything Master Radulf tried. He vomited up the potions administered to ease his pain; he was bled to cool his raging blood but to no avail. At first he kept up a constant high-pitched wail like a citole bow sawing across a string that was about to snap. But toward dawn that stopped, and instead, he flopped in her arms as unresponsive as a hot rag doll. The blotches melded together, becoming a livid purple patchwork covering his arms and torso.

Alienor prayed in desperation, asking God's mercy and knowing that, as her son deteriorated further with each frail breath, God was not listening. For whatever reason, he was choosing to punish her and Henry by taking their child.

Every single member of her household from knight to slop boy knelt in prayer, and the chamberlain's lad flung the shutters wide to admit a bright May morning, the fresh air bursting with the scent of growing life.

Alienor's chaplain, Father Peter, administered the last rites to the limp, barely breathing scrap in Alienor's arms. She held him to her and watched the erratic rise and fall of his chest. A day since he had hurtled from his bed, his toy sword in his hand, ready to seize life with every particle of his being.

Hearing snuffling and sobs, she rounded on her women. "Cease your noise!" she hissed. "If he can hear us, I will not have him subject to such sounds!"

Emma detached herself from Alienor's ladies and, choking, fled the room, her hand pressed to her mouth. Alienor pushed the matted hair away from Will's brow. "Come, little one, my brave one," she said. "Mama is here. Hush, don't fret. All is well, all is well."

The little boy's chest rose and fell, rose again, shuddered, and was still. Alienor stared, willing him to take another breath, but the moment drew out, stretching into eternity. His eyes were almost closed, just a faint glitter under the lowered eyelids. The dreadful patches of fever had not touched his face, which was pure and perfect, but the rest of his body looked as if it had been ravaged by a demon.

"Madam." Her chaplain gently touched her shoulder. "He has gone to join his Father in heaven. God will care for him in his mercy."

Alienor was numb. Somewhere within her, grief was gathering, waiting to rend her apart, but this moment was the space between the slice of the knife and the realization of a mortal wound. "Why could he not stay with his mother on earth? Why take him?" Anger sparked through the numbness. Why not take the other child, who was the fruit of fornication? It was a dark and terrible thought, a sin, but she could not prevent it.

"It is not ours to question," the chaplain said gently. "We cannot know God's plan."

Alienor pressed her lips together before she uttered blasphemy. Her child's soul was on its journey, and she dared not hinder his path by railing against God. She continued to hold him against her, folding him into her body. Even though she knew it was over, she kept waiting for him to draw another breath. He had been hers to care for and protect, and it was all her fault that his bright little life had been snuffed out. But what more could she have done? What would Henry say? He had left the children in her care as her responsibility, and she had proven unequal to the task. She gave a low moan and would have doubled over, save that the child in her womb made it impossible. The new life kicked within her, even while she gazed on death.

"Madam…" She felt the gentle pressure of Father Peter's hand on her shoulder. "Come, I will send for someone to wash and prepare him."

"No!" Alienor thrust him off. "It is my duty and my right. No one else shall have this task and do what must be done. I am well enough for this."

The following hours lasted for an eternity to Alienor, and at the same time the passage of light to dark seemed as swift as the blink of an eye. There was so much to do to arrange the funeral rites and decide on the burial. To dictate letters so that messages could go out to those who had to know of the tragedy. All the practical details setting the seal on the brutal fact of Will's death. The letter to Henry was the hardest. She was too shattered to find the words, and the letter she sent was that of a queen to a king, not of one grieving parent to another.

Washing her son's lifeless, blotched body with rose water, she remembered the joy and triumph of his birth on an August morning in Poitiers. All the joy, all the hope and expectation. Cradling him in her arms, and later presenting him to Henry as a wonderful gift when he returned from campaign. A golden child bouncing on her knee, vibrant as the sun with life, arms around her neck in a tight squeeze. All now to become corruption and dust. She whispered under her breath as she worked, telling him she was here, that everything was safe and all right, even though it wasn't.

Isabel and Emma took the baby and Jeoffrey elsewhere lest whatever ill vapors had invaded Will's body affected them too. Father Peter and Alienor's advisers tried to make her leave, but she refused, growing angry when they persisted. Let the room be fumigated with incense and let the shutters remain open to allow the spring day to flood the chamber, because she wanted to remember her son as a being of light, far removed from the suffocating night hours and the terrible fever that had burned him up before her eyes. Alienor's numbness intensified as the hours passed until it was like a heavy iron lid covering a cauldron simmering with grief and guilt and fear. She dared not lift the lid because she knew the resultant burst of emotion would kill her too.

By the time evening came around again, Will had been stitched in a shroud of the finest linen, double-wrapped, and then enfolded in a length of red silk, with his face exposed. A small coffin had been swiftly prepared, and he was placed in it with rose petals and his favorite toy sword that only a day since had been killing imaginary foes in the garden while death waited its moment in the shadows.

Will lay in state in Windsor's chapel surrounded by a blaze of candles and lamps, in order to hold the light as the sun went down. Alienor insisted on kneeling in all that hot shimmer to keep vigil throughout the night. Isabel and Emma stayed at her side throughout, and neither woman spoke out to try to dissuade her because they loved her and they knew the strength of her will.

At dawn, following a requiem Mass, Will's coffin was borne from the chapel and placed in a cart decked with royal shields and rich cloth to be taken the seventeen miles to Reading Abbey where he was to be buried at the feet of his great-grandsire, the revered King Henry I.

Father Peter tried to dissuade Alienor from accompanying the cortege, saying she had already endured too much, and for the sake of her unborn child she should remain at Windsor and let others attend to the burial, but Alienor was adamant. "I will be with him when he is buried," she said. "I am his mother, and he remains my responsibility, even if he breathes no more. You will not sway me from this course, so do not try."

Heavily pregnant, unable to ride a horse, she traveled in a litter. The road between Windsor and Reading was sound, and they made steady progress. With the litter curtains drawn shut, Alienor tried to rest and gather herself for what had to be done. Her womb continued to contract and relax at regular intervals, although without pain. The journey was a risk, but she could not have let her little boy go alone into the dark. It would have been different had Henry been here, but he wasn't, and the responsibility was hers—all of it. She had to see it through, on this bright spring morning, to its bitter end.

❖❖❖

The weather changed for the return to Windsor the next day. Clouds covered the sky from horizon to horizon, and heavy rain turned the road into a patchwork of sludgy puddles. The going was slow, and behind the litter curtains Alienor counted her prayer beads through her fingers and saw images of the candles ranked around the tomb of King Henry I, and the darkness of the hole into which they had lowered her son. Not three years in the world and already finished with it. The chanting of monks, the scrape of a shovel tip on slate and soil, the weeping of her women. Alienor had not cried. That response was buried under a slab of numb disbelief.

Two days ago people had run to line the road to watch the funeral cavalcade pass by in brilliant sunshine, expectant of receiving alms, curious but respectful. On the return only a few hardy or desperate souls braved the waysides, bundled in hoods and cloaks, hands outstretched. Alienor did not part the hangings to investigate, but she heard their voices raised in supplication. The rain thudded on the roof of her litter, and a few cold droplets splashed in her lap, almost like proxy tears for the ones she could not shed.

By the time they arrived at Windsor, the sporadic contractions of her womb had become regular cramps, and she knew that she was in the early stages of labor. Marchisa took one look at her as she stepped from the litter and summoned the midwives.

❖❖❖

The pangs of full labor crashed over Alienor, and she clenched her fists, certain she was going to burst. The midwife bathed her forehead with cool herbal water. "Madam, all is progressing as it should," she said in an encouraging voice. "Soon you will hold your new babe in your arms, and he will take away the pain and ease your loss."

The seal over Alienor's numbness weakened and cracked, allowing rage to boil through. "How dare you say that to me?" she panted. "No child will ever take my son's place! He was everything!"

The woman curtsied and dropped her gaze. "I only sought to comfort you, madam, forgive me."

Alienor was incapable of reply as the next pain surged through her and with it the tears in gut-wrenching spasms. The baby slithered from her body in a welter of blood and fluid, and as it drew its first breaths and began to bawl, Alienor convulsed and howled her own grief to the rafters. She didn't want this child; she wanted Will.

"It is a girl, madam. You have a daughter." The midwife's tone was subdued as she held the squalling infant aloft, still attached to Alienor by the umbilical cord. "A lovely baby girl."

Alienor's body convulsed in a fresh paroxysm of grief. Looking worried, the midwife cut the cord and quickly gave the baby to an assistant. "The queen's womb has displaced itself. She is in grave danger," she said. "We must return it to its rightful place immediately, or there is no hope." She rummaged among her nostrums, emerged with an eagle feather, and thrust it into the flame of the nearest candle until it began to smolder. Swiftly she turned and wafted the acrid smoke under Alienor's nose.

The powerful, bitter stench made Alienor choke and recoil. The terrible spasms became a fit of coughing interspersed by retches, and when finally she was able to breathe properly again, she lay gasping like the mauled survivor of a shipwreck washed to shore. Her tears became a softer weeping, and Isabel de Warenne folded her in a firm, sympathetic embrace and rocked her like a child.

The labor pangs began again, and the afterbirth slithered into the midwife's waiting bowl. Alienor was no longer numb but wretched and sodden with grief. Even as she bled from the birth, it seemed to her that she was bleeding for her lost son too.

The baby, freshly bathed and wrapped in a clean towel, was presented to her. A daughter. In a way it was a blessing because no one would ever see her as a replacement for Will. Even with the marks of her birth still upon her, she was beautiful with a heart-shaped face and a quiff of soft, dark hair that reminded Alienor of her sister Petronella, who was in fragile health and being cared for at the convent of Saintes in Poitou.

"How is she to be named?" Emma asked.

"Matilda for her grandmother the empress," Alienor replied in a fractured voice. "That was the king's wish should it be a girl." If a boy he had told her she could have the naming, but it was a moot point. The messengers would bring him the news of his daughter's birth, following on the heels of that of Will's death.

A sense of failure swept through her. There would be no bells rung in joy for this child, for they were all occupied in tolling the demise of the heir—and it was all her fault.

# 5

## CHINON, JUNE 1156

AT CHINON ON THE LOIRE, HENRY WAS IN A GOOD MOOD. He had finally brought his brother Geoffrey to heel and seized the castles of Mirebeau, Chinon, and Loudun that had been in rebellion against him. Chinon had capitulated at dawn that morning, and Geoffrey had bowed his head and accepted the inevitable, if not with good grace, then with dour resignation. It was the second time he had rebelled against Henry. The three castles were a bone of contention between the brothers that was not going to go away. Geoffrey insisted their father had willed them to him, but in using them as centers of rebellion, he had made it impossible for Henry to let him keep them.

"Sire, if I may make a suggestion?"

Henry turned around from the embrasure and eyed his chancellor. Thomas had proven invaluable during the weeks on campaign, dealing with routine matters and keeping the coffers full. He was also a convivial and cultured companion with a shrewd eye for an advantage. "By all means."

"It seems to me that your b-brother will continue to be a thorn in your side for the foreseeable future. The moment you turn your back, he will be fomenting rebellion."

"I do not intend turning my back," Henry said, "but go on."

"Perhaps if he were to have lands of his own—something he can carve out of another estate that might benefit you also?"

Henry rubbed his forefinger across his beard. "You had in mind?"

"Brittany, sire. They have recently rebelled against their count and with a little persuasion might be prevailed upon to consider your b-brother to replace him? He would be occupied keeping the Bretons in check, and at the same time he would bring B-Brittany into your sphere of influence. It would also fulfill his desire for a title and elevate his standing."

Henry's eyes gleamed. "An interesting notion. On the margins, but not Ireland."

Becket made an elegant gesture of agreement that emphasized the garnets and pearls jewelling the cuff on his sleeve.

"It needs some thought, but I can see the possibilities." Henry clapped his shoulder. "You are to be commended, Thomas."

"I do my best to fulfill my duty, sire."

"Ah, no, it is more than just duty. You enjoy this," Henry said with a knowing smile. He glanced toward the door where a messenger had just been admitted. With Chinon newly taken, the bustle of envoys in and out of the keep was at full tide, but he recognized the man as one of Alienor's. His immediate thought was that the child had been born, and he beckoned the man to come forward. As he approached, however, following the usher, Henry realized something was wrong. There was no smile on the messenger's face, no anticipation of a reward for joyful news.

"Sire." The man knelt and from his satchel produced a single thin package to which was attached Alienor's seal. And then he bowed his head and looked at the ground. Henry took the letter and broke the seal, not wanting to open the thing but knowing he must, and immediately, lest he needed to act.

The words were Alienor's but written in the formal tone she used as queen, and what she wrote was so immense and devastating that he could not take it in. It was like being presented with a rock to swallow. Everything seemed to stop inside him. He lifted his gaze and stared around the room. At the stones in the wall, the hangings, at the texture of his chancellor's jeweled cuff, the glitter of light on the chips of rock crystal. They were all real because he could see them and reach out and touch them, but this letter spoke of something he had not seen, something so terrible that it couldn't be true, yet the fact that it might be took him to silence.

Becket was eyeing him in consternation. "Sire?"

Henry handed him the letter. He would not read it again because the words were indelibly branded on his brain. He left the hall and almost ran to his chamber, where he ordered everyone to leave before slamming and barring the door. Turning, he leaned against it with his eyes closed, shutting everything out, so it would not be real. Other men's children died, not his: his were strong and blessed. This one would follow him to the English throne. He could see him dashing about, full of vigor, waving his small sword and shouting, could remember the wet baby kiss on his cheek, and the trusting soft hand gripped in his as they crossed the icy yard at Westminster, with all the candles shining for the Christ child's birth.

Henry put his face in his spread right hand, and rare tears welled. Many times he had been ill himself as an infant, sometimes seriously, but he had survived. Why hadn't William lived? Why hadn't he possessed the constitution to win through? Wiping his face on his cuff he cursed and wept some more, while anger burned in his belly.

Surely something could have been done to save him if his protectors had been more vigilant? Why had Alienor allowed it to happen? She should have kept him in a place where the air was cleaner. Now there was no air in his son's lungs, only dust. The thought of Will, a fresh little child, surrounded by corpses and decay made him sick. He had left Alienor to guard and care for their son, and she had failed in her duty. Probably too busy meddling in politics and matters best left to men, as was her wont. When he thought that he had not been there to rescue his son, the dark feelings became unbearable, and he locked them away because he knew, if he gave them the opportunity to grow, they would break him. He knuckled his eyes and swallowed his tears because all the grief in the world would not restore his son to life.

Will was gone. He should go and pray that his soul had found its way swiftly to heaven, but he was not sure he could enter a church just now.

A hand rapped on the door. "Henry, let me in."

He palmed away his tears and went to draw the bar. Hamelin stood on the threshold, his brow wrinkled with sorrowful concern. He cleared his throat. "I grieve to hear the tragic news from England—Becket told me. I came to see if there was anything I could do, if there was anything you needed."

"No one can give me what I want or need," Henry said hoarsely but stood aside to let Hamelin enter the room. "Nothing will bring him back." He closed the door and leaned against it again. His chest heaved convulsively.

"Do you want me to say anything to the court?"

"No. I am my own spokesman." Henry swallowed. "I will not have the business of the court interrupted for this. Let masses be said for my son, and let us all pray for his soul, and then let us move on with business that applies to the living. I refuse to make a meal of my grief, and I will not let others make a meal of it for me. Do you understand?"

Hamelin frowned. "I am not sure I do, but if that is your wish, then let it be so. I am truly sorry. He was a fine little man."

"Yes," Henry said grimly, "and now he is no more, so I must needs beget more sons to ensure the succession." That was the way to deal with the matter. To be hard and pragmatic until the shell toughened and nothing could ever pierce it.

"Will you write to Alienor? She must be distraught."

Henry's mouth thinned. "We shall speak soon enough. For now I have nothing to say to her that I want to commit to a scribe or bleed onto parchment."

# 6

## Bec-Hellouin, Rouen, Summer 1156

*H*ENRY'S MOTHER, EMPRESS MATILDA, HELD HER SWADDLED namesake in the crook of her arm. A half smile deepened the lines surrounding her mouth. She had already greeted her grandson of sixteen months before hastily handing him over to his nurse to have his wet swaddlings changed. "I never bore daughters," she said to Alienor. "Perhaps it was no bad thing, for, strive as we may, it is men who rule the world, and they do not have to face the trials we do."

"No," Alienor agreed, "they do not." She had been churched two days ago, almost seven weeks since Will had died. The pain remained raw and desperate, but she dealt with it moment by moment, hour by hour, and day by day. Each mark of time took her further away from his death, but also distanced her from the time when he was alive, and she clung to his memory and painted it in her mind anew each day, knowing it would fade in slow increments until his bright presence dwindled to a shadow on her soul.

The empress had greeted her with a tender embrace and tears in her eyes—and this from a woman who never wept. Alienor had feared that Henry's mother would blame her for Will's death, but Matilda had been compassionate and concerned for her welfare.

"You look tired," she said. "You should not be about so soon after childbirth and your terrible loss."

Alienor shook her head. "Had I stayed in England, I would only have spent my days mourning things I cannot change." She bit her lip. "I have to talk to Henry, and he has his daughter to greet." She was dreading that moment. Not only was there the death of their son to be navigated, but she feared his response to the new baby because it was a daughter and not a boy to stand in the place of the one they had lost. She reasoned if she went to him now that she was churched, she might conceive again swiftly, and perhaps if she did bear another son, Henry would forgive her, although she was not sure if she could forgive herself.

"But you will stay here for the rest of the week at least." The empress patted Alienor's knee with her free hand.

"Yes, madam, of course."

"Good." She jogged the baby for a moment. "It is fitting that you chose Reading Abbey for the burial, and at my father's feet. He was a great king. My grandson would have been one too, had he lived."

"I did everything I could." Tears scalded Alienor's eyes. "But it was not enough."

The empress gave her a sharp but not unkind look. "I said that to myself on the day I sailed away from England. I spent nine years striving to win the throne that was rightfully mine. There were times I thought I would die in the attempt or be broken forever. Whatever your grief you must absorb the blow and continue because it is your duty."

"Yes, Mother, I know." Alienor tried not to feel resentful. Matilda meant well and offered sound advice, but she did not fully understand. She was the patronizing matriarch showing a younger subordinate how much she still had to learn despite the fact that the younger one had been ground through just as many mills.

"I shall write to Henry and tell him to be gentle with you."

"Thank you, Mother, but I do not need your intervention." Alienor had been going to say "interference" but changed the word in time. "I can speak for myself."

The empress's lips pursed as if she was going to take issue, but then she too hesitated and modified her words. "I know you can,

Daughter," she said. "But you should consider carefully what you say. My son is like my father and expects the world to do his bidding without question. But he has much of my husband in him too, and that means he will not always deal directly when faced with the needs of others. You must not let him push you too hard, especially when you are not yet in full health."

Alienor inclined her head. "Thank you for your concern, Mother." She knew Matilda would probably still write to Henry. "I do want to ask your advice on another matter."

Her mother-in-law immediately sat up a little straighter. "Indeed?" Her eyes brightened.

"It is about Henry's bastard-born son." Alienor indicated the small boy sitting with his nurse at the side of the room. She had to steel herself to look at him because he so resembled Will and was a constant living reminder of what she had lost.

The empress nodded. "I had heard rumors that my son had a child born of a common whore. I thought the tale unreliable—who knows the father in those circumstances? But I can see with my own eyes that whatever her occupation, the boy is of my son's siring."

Alienor grimaced. "I know little of the mother, nor do I wish to, but I have been told she was with him before he wed me and that she was English."

"A boyhood paramour then." The empress gave a dismissive wave. "What do you want to ask me?"

Alienor played with a beautiful pearl ring the empress had given her, turning it right and left on her finger. "Henry has taken responsibility for the child. I will do nothing to harm him, nor will I be hostile toward an innocent whatever the circumstances of his birth, but I will not permit him to undermine my own children in any way."

The empress handed the baby to the wet nurse. "Henry's father sired Emma and Hamelin on his mistress. She died in childbirth, and Geoffrey had them raised in his household. They were of no concern to me; I was fighting for a crown and had little time to worry about such things. Besides, my own bastard-born half brothers were the absolute backbone of my cause. Without them, Henry would not have his throne. I expected from the outset that Hamelin would grow up to support Henry, and indeed, he is more help to him than Geoffrey or William will ever be. Hamelin depends on Henry for his position. You need not fear that this child will usurp your sons. Raise him to his duty, and he will be an asset."

"It is the way Henry looks at him," Alienor said and could not prevent her lip from curling. "And now Will is dead and our little Henry still an infant…" She closed her hands into fists. "I desire to have my own children recognized and ranked as first in their father's heart." She felt miserable as she spoke, for she could not make such a thing happen for the willing of it.

"Then what do you want from me?"

Alienor leaned forward. "I ask you to take him into your household to raise and educate. I know it would be for Henry to decide, but the boy is your grandson." It meant he would not have to be under her roof, a constant reminder of the son she had lost, but still suitably placed within the family. "Would you consider doing so?"

The empress looked thoughtful and then slowly nodded. "Yes, I would be willing to think about it."

*More than willing*, Alienor thought, seeing the gleam that lit in the older woman's eyes.

The empress turned in her seat and beckoned the nurse to bring little Jeoffrey over to them.

The boy knelt respectfully when prompted by his nurse and then rose and faced Alienor and his grandmother with his legs set apart in a pose exactly like Henry's. There was no fear in his blue gaze, but he was wary.

"Can you say the Lord's Prayer, child?" the empress asked.

Jeoffrey nodded and did so, with barely a stumble, his Latin fluent.

"Good," she said and dismissed him, having first made him kneel again, while she patted his hair in blessing and gave him a small honey cake from the tray at her side.

"He has the aptitude," she said to Alienor once he had gone. "If his father agrees I will take him."

"Thank you, madam." Alienor was unable to conceal her relief.

The empress gave her a wintry smile. "If I can ease your burden I will. You have a heavy load to bear, and it will grow no lighter with time. I do not say this to discourage you, but it is always best to confront the truth."

Alienor forced a smile. At least her mother-by-marriage was honest. There was never any dissembling with the empress. Having resolved what she was going to do with young Jeoffrey FitzRoy she could now focus on dealing with Henry.

❖❖❖

Alienor was two miles from Saumur when she met an entourage traveling in the opposite direction. The sun blazed in a sky of naked blue as the first strong heat of summer struck the Angevin heartlands like the beat of a hammer on a new anvil. Drawing rein, Alienor waited for the approaching troop to pull aside and give her right of way in respect of her rank. The other party halted in the road too, refusing to give ground, pale dust sifting around the hooves of their horses and pack animals.

A young nobleman on a muscular gray palfrey rode to the front and glared at Alienor's troop. His gaze then lit on her, and with an irritated shrug of his body, he commanded his men to draw aside. "Madam my sister," he acknowledged curtly.

Alienor eyed her brother-in-law with distaste. Geoffrey was the main reason Henry was still here in Anjou when he could have been back in England long since—indeed, could have been with her when their son took ill. If Geoffrey was free and on his way though, it meant that he and Henry had come to terms.

"Brother." She managed to be civil. "I thank you for yielding the road."

"What else am I to do but honor the privilege owed to my brother's wife?" His voice was edged with disdain.

Alienor raised one eyebrow. "I take it you and my husband have mended your differences?"

Geoffrey brushed at a speck on his cloak. "Rather say that for now we have interests in common. The people of Nantes have asked me to be their count. I am to rule Brittany with Henry's blessing—and that is something I never thought to have." His tone intimated cynicism rather than gratitude.

"That is excellent news," Alienor said and meant it. She even smiled. Such an undertaking would keep Geoffrey occupied, prevent him from making trouble in Anjou, and meant that she would not have to be in proximity to him except on rare occasions.

"It remains to be seen, but for now I agree." He gathered the reins as his restive palfrey sidled. "I was sorry to learn of my nephew's death." The remark was perfunctory and insincere.

"I am sure you were," Alienor replied stonily. "I wish you a safe journey, my lord." *And never to see you again.*

"And I wish you the best of fortune with my brother." He gave her a sour smile. "You could have been wed to me if you had taken a different road."

"Indeed," she said smoothly. "I thank God for guiding my path that day."

Geoffrey gave her an ironic salute. "Are you sure it was God? It is claimed that line of Anjou is descended from the devil." He reined over to join his men at the side of the road and let her ride on to Saumur.

❖❖❖

Despite the heat of the day warming the castle walls, Alienor felt shivery—as if she had a fever. She walked back and forth across the chamber to which Henry's steward had shown her. Henry himself was absent, hunting, even though he knew she was expected. She felt too sick with apprehension to be angry; indeed, she almost welcomed the delay.

She had changed her dusty traveling gown for a court robe of gold silk embellished with pearls, the lacing pulled tight to emphasize that once more she had a waistline between the curves of breast and hip. Her women had dabbed her wrists and throat with precious scented oil and dressed her hair with a jeweled net, but not all the gems and perfume in the world could make this moment any better or easier.

Isabel, who was attending her, turned from the window where she had been watching the courtyard. "Madam, the king is here." She too was strung with tension because her own husband was among the entourage.

Alienor joined her in the embrasure and looked out on a court-yard filling up with hard-ridden horses, panting dogs, and ebullient men, all jostling and milling. Thomas Becket and Henry were laughing together, arms clasped across their horses in camaraderie. Henry was sweating almost as much as his horse.

Isabel made a soft sound of concern as she located her husband amid the throng. "He looks thinner," she said, "and he's limping."

"I shall not need you when I speak to the king." Alienor touched her arm. "Go down to him. You have my leave."

Cheeks flushed, Isabel curtsied, rose, and hurried out on light, swift feet. Alienor turned to her other women. "Find things to do elsewhere," she commanded. "I will summon you if needed."

The women left, and Alienor returned to the window. Henry had gone. The hound keepers were rounding up the last of the dogs and returning them to the kennels. She wondered if she should go and find Henry, but he would still be surrounded by the boisterous melee of the hunting party, and she would be exposing her vulnerability to the world.

The sun shadow had changed angle on the castle walls, blocking one side in gold, shading the other in ash gray, when Henry finally arrived, entering the chamber in his usual brisk fashion. He had recently washed, for his hair was dark auburn and sleeked back, and he wore a clean tunic imbued with the scents of rosemary and spikenard.

For the time between one step and another he hesitated and then came on, arms wide. She started to curtsy, but he seized her by the waist and pulled her into a hard embrace. "I have missed you," he said and gave her a hard kiss. "You look good enough to eat!"

Alienor gasped at the vigor of his greeting. His tone was open and jocular, as if he were still talking to his hunting cronies—as if nothing had happened and nothing was wrong. His smile was open and broad. Whatever she had been expecting, it was not this, and she was dumbfounded.

"Henry—"

"Where is my daughter?" He overrode her before she could speak, a sharp gray glitter in his eyes and his jaw taut. "Let me see her—and my son."

Filled with unease, Alienor went to the door and summoned the nurses to bring the children for his inspection.

Henry's keen scrutiny fixed on the baby girl in her nurse's arms, a round little face and the rest bound in swaddling bands. "We shall make a fine marriage alliance for you," he said, chucking her chin. "The king of England's firstborn daughter, eh?" He gave Alienor a stiff smile. "I have no doubt she will grow into a beauty." He crouched to be at eye level with his namesake, now sixteen months old and clad in a long linen smock. Little Henry's hair was dark blond rather than red-gold, and his eyes a mingling of blue and gray.

"Walking now," Henry said with a grin. "Aren't you a fine little man?" He picked him up and tossed him in his arms until he squealed. Having handed him back to the nurse, he focused on the third child who stood on the threshold, half in the sun ray slanting through the window, his coppery hair glittering. For an instant a look of surprise widened Henry's gaze.

"I have kept my word to you," Alienor said. "And I have brought him with me. Your mother has expressed an interest in fostering him."

"Yes, she said so in her letter."

So Matilda had written to him. Alienor wondered what else she had said.

Henry beckoned the nurse and child forward. "I think it a good idea, but not quite yet." He rumpled Jeoffrey's curls. "You have grown tall since last I saw you—almost a man!"

Jeoffrey puffed out his chest, making Henry chuckle. "While you are here, we can spend some time together. Perhaps some riding lessons, hmmm? Do you have a pony of your own?"

"No...sire."

"Would you like one?"

Alienor's throat tightened. This interaction should be Will's, not this little cuckoo's.

Jeoffrey's eyes shone. "Yes, sire."

"Good. Then we'll find you one and I will teach you, and when you are older you can come hunting with me, eh?"

"Yes, sire," Jeoffrey said, his expression wonderstruck.

Henry smiled and dismissed the nurses and their charges. His gaze lingered on Jeoffrey before he turned around to Alienor, clapping his hands and rubbing them together. "We shall have a feast to welcome your arrival, and tomorrow we can go hawking along the river. We have a fine troupe of players from Quercy you will enjoy, and Thomas has some bolts of cloth for your inspection."

Alienor listened to him in stunned silence. He was filling his mind with loud and superficial things so that there was no opportunity for the deeper issues to leap upon him and take him where he did not wish to go.

Before she could speak, he was at the door, shouting for Becket, calling for musicians and courtiers. "Come," he said over his shoulder, looking at her but through her. "We must celebrate your arrival, and I am not the only one you must greet!"

❖❖❖

The hours until retiring were an endurance test for Alienor. She spoke and smiled; she mingled with the court. She received polite condolences, murmured outside of Henry's hearing, and she saw the sidelong glances people cast in his direction. Thomas Becket was sincere and solicitous but also eager to show off the yards of glorious silk damask he had bought at a bargain price from a Venetian merchant. While she was politely examining the cloth, he was at pains to inform her that the idea to make Henry's brother the count of Nantes had been his.

"It is well thought of," Alienor replied, giving praise where it was due.

"Better than Ireland," he agreed. "Now we must find a similar position for my lord's youngest brother."

Alienor raised her brows and wondered how much responsibility Henry had delegated to Becket. One did not have a dog and bark oneself, but at the same time the animal could not be allowed to dominate the owner.

Alienor looked at the young man Becket had mentioned. William FitzEmpress stood among a group of young knights, ostensibly listening to their conversation but taking his time to gaze around the chamber, measuring and assessing, never still. Alienor did not particularly like Henry's sandy-haired youngest brother, but he was less of a threat than Geoffrey, and at only twenty years old, there was time to decide his future. He caught her watching him and lifted his cup in acknowledgment. She returned the courtesy, and he looked away.

Hamelin arrived to speak with her, kissing her on both cheeks, holding her hands, and facing her without evasion. "My condolences on Will's loss," he said. "I cannot imagine what it is like to lose a child, especially one as precious to you both as he was."

Alienor swallowed, suddenly tearful that Henry's half brother could mention Will while Henry could not. "No, you cannot imagine, but thank you," she said. Drawing a deep breath, she steadied herself. "How has Henry seemed to you? He will not even speak Will's name."

Hamelin glanced across the room to where Henry was talking with Alienor's chamberlain Warin FitzGerold. "He does not speak of him among us," he said with a shake of his head. "We have learned to avoid the subject because he either deflects it in rage or, as you see now, he diverts himself with other matters. He will not think about it because if he did, the grief would unman him."

"And he blames me. I know he does."

Hamelin looked uncomfortable. "No one knows what my brother thinks and feels. Even those of us who are close to him cannot fathom his mind." He touched her arm. "I do know he is pleased to see you and the other children, and I believe it will make all the difference to him."

"You are kind," she said with a wan smile.

"No, I am truthful. He has missed you. Your presence will help him deal with the wounds he licks in private."

She wondered if it would. After a hesitation she said, "I have brought him the son born of his concubine. Do you have any insights for me, Hamelin?"

His expression grew wary. "I was raised under my father's roof, and Emma was sent to Fontevraud. The empress was indifferent to me and Emma, but she was always fair, and I respected her for that and still do."

"And how did you feel?"

He shrugged. "I resented Henry because I was the firstborn but he had all the privileges, and that only worsened when his other brothers arrived. I was always at the bottom of the pile because I was the count's bastard. I would lie in bed wishing things had been different, but as I became a man that changed. I learned to accept I would never be a king or a count. Indeed, would I want it? With the position I hold now, I can work for the good of the family and be rewarded for it. I am an important part of Henry's web, but I do not have to spin the thread of policy and worry about catching flies."

Alienor smiled at the comparison and kissed his cheek. "You have given me things to think about," she said. "Thank you." But she still intended Jeoffrey for the Church.

❖❖❖

Alienor watched Henry raise his foot onto the bed and unwind his leg binding. They were alone—finally. She had feared he might find somewhere else to sleep in order to avoid her, but he had come willingly enough to her chamber.

Removing her rings and dropping them into her enameled jewel casket, she said, "You have so many plans and you are not still for a moment, but you have not told me how you are faring yourself."

He kept his focus on his task. "I do not know what you mean. I am well; you can see I am. You do not need to ask."

"Henry, I do. You refuse to speak of Will, as if he never existed, and the more you do not speak of him, the deeper the wound cuts. It will never heal, no matter how many bandages you wrap over it." She came and stood in front of him, forcing him to look up.

He put the leg binding down with a sigh. "Speaking of it is pointless; it will not bring him back," he said in a rough voice and pulled her into his arms. "Rather look to the future, and the new lives we shall create."

"Henry…"

"No more." He set his forefinger against her lips. "It is over now, I have told you." He kissed her, silencing her with his mouth over hers and the probe of his tongue.

He took her to bed and made love to her with long slow thoroughness. Alienor gasped and sobbed beneath him as the languorous sensations grew into exquisite torture. She dug her nails into his upper arms and opened herself to him. He pinned her down as he thrust into her for the final moments of giving her his seed, and she welcomed his forcefulness and the tight throb within her body because she wanted to conceive another son, and for that to happen, the man's seed had to dominate the woman's.

Henry took her twice more that night and then, drained, slept curled into her, his arm across her body, the last thing he murmured as he fell asleep, "I meant it. It is done. We shall not talk about it—ever."

She curled on her side, feeling wretched. Henry might think he was smoothing the path between them by refusing to discuss the death of their son, but he was just burying stones under the surface. If he would not allow her to speak of it to him, then how was she to shed the burden of her grief and remorse, and how was he to bear his? They would just stumble along that stony path bent under the weight of their baggage until eventually it brought them down.

# 7

*I*T HAD SNOWED EARLIER IN THE DAY, A SCANT DUSTING THAT lay like crushed sugar over rooftops and turrets. Dark foot-prints patterned the courtyard of the Ombrière Palace and left an ephemeral record of activity across the open ground to and from the buildings.

"This was always my summer home when I was a child," Alienor told Isabel as they walked side by side in the gathering dusk, bundled in thick, fur-lined cloaks. "We spent our time in the gardens, and sometimes we had our lessons there in the shade of the trees."

"My lessons were held at our castle at Acre in Norfolk," Isabel reciprocated. "I never imagined then what fate had in store for me."

"Nor me," Alienor said ruefully. "I would have told my younger self to run for her life had I known. Perhaps that is why God keeps us in ignorance." She glanced fondly at Isabel. Had her husband been more robust and chosen to dispute the throne, they would have been rivals for a crown. Instead, they were compan-ions, cut from different cloth but still with a pattern in common. "You must have heard tales of Aquitaine though."

Isabel smiled. "Oh yes, we often heard stories and songs about troubadours and handsome knights who sought to seduce women away from their husbands—and told them to one another too. Our nurse would warn us to be on our guard against the blandishments of young men, while we secretly prayed to be objects of their affection. How innocent we were."

"I was never innocent," Alienor said with a grimace, "except in believing that I might have what I wanted, and that belief withered on the day I was told I must wed Louis of France. I was thirteen years old, and my father had recently died, leaving the instruction in his will without telling me."

"I was sixteen when my father died," Isabel said. "I was his only child, and King Stephen arranged a marriage with his son. William was eleven on our wedding day." She gazed into the distance. "While I was marrying him, my mother was taking Patrick of Salisbury for her second husband, so we found ourselves wedded into opposing factions and no say in the matter."

"That must have been difficult."

"It was, but we found a way, as women must always do." Small white flakes started to drift down out of the dusky blue. Isabel looked at her. "You and the king seem content in each other's company of late. I am glad for that."

"For the moment, yes, although who knows how long it will last," Alienor said with a brittle smile and did not elaborate. She and Isabel had come to know each other well, but she did not want to speak of her troubled relationship with Henry. Matters had indeed improved between them as they spent the summer and autumn together, progressing through their lands. The awkwardness of that first night at Saumur had healed over, like a deep wound that had closed but left a thick scar. The flesh was whole but not smooth and would never be the same. She and Henry had gone forth from that moment as if the past was a blank and Will had never been born.

Their daughter Matilda was almost seven months old. Two weeks ago Alienor had bled yet again, a sign that the seed in her womb had not taken root, and she was anxious lest God had indeed turned against them.

The snow began to fall more swiftly, and the women abandoned their walk and returned indoors. Folk gathered around the hearth to roast chestnuts and eat small, tasty morsels that had been cooked earlier before the kitchens lost the daylight: spicy pastries, fruits, and marchpane subtleties. A troop of musicians performed songs in the *lenga romana* of the Bordeaux region, and people played games, danced, and took time to laugh and socialize, forgetting serious matters for a while.

Accomplished in her role as queen and duchess, Alienor set out to beguile, to weave her spell. She felt Henry's brooding gaze upon her as she talked, laughed, and flirted with her courtiers. When she glanced his way, she detected both wariness and desire in his expression—like a lion observing dangerous prey.

They danced together, duke and duchess, and when they touched, the erotic charge between them reminded Alienor of their wedding night. The pupils of Henry's eyes were wide and dark, drinking in the light as they joined hands and circled. The dance was progressive, and they were separated for several verses, but when they came together it was like fire. Alienor's breath shortened. His hand cupped the curve of her hip, and his fingers angled inward. She gave him a languorous look and moistened her lips. At least here, if nowhere else, they were very compatible.

❖❖❖

The January weather was bright but bitterly cold on the morning that Alienor arrived at the convent of Notre-Dame de Saintes to pay her respects to her aunt Agnes, who was the abbess, and to visit Petronella, her sister, who was in delicate physical and mental health and had been in the care of the nuns for more than five years.

The chestnut trees wore a lacy foliage of hoar frost, and the convent sparkled in the hard winter sunlight as if dusted with powdered rock crystal. Alienor dismounted at the gatehouse, her breath puffing in white clouds and her hands numb from holding the reins despite the insulation of fur-lined mittens. A groom took the horses, and a nun led Alienor to the abbess's chamber while her attendants waited in the guesthouse.

Her aunt left the lectern at which she had been reading and hastened to embrace Alienor with tender affection. "It is so good to see you, Niece!" Her wrinkles deepened as she smiled. "It has been a long time."

"Four years," Alienor replied with a tremulous smile of her own. "So much has happened, and so much has changed."

"Indeed." Compassion filled her aunt's shrewd dark eyes. "Come, sit by the fire. Warm yourself and tell me all." She gestured to a cushioned bench by the hearth. Grooming its fur in front of the fire was a handsome ginger tomcat that put Alienor in mind of Henry. She raised her brows at her aunt, who made an embarrassed gesture. "Tib earns his place by catching mice. It may be a worldly sin to indulge myself with a cat, but he is God's creature, and it gladdens me to see him content."

"And why should God not take pleasure at your kindness?" Alienor said. She joined the cat before the fire, as grateful as he was for the glowing heat on this raw day. A young novice brought her hot wine laced with ginger and cloves. Her aunt declined the wine and took a cup of water for herself while Alienor caught up with the years since last the women had seen each other, stitching all the stray threads into the tapestry of news until it was complete. Alienor did not feel any lighter for doing so, but having run the events through her mind in sequence, she had new perspectives to consider.

Her aunt gave her a thoughtful look. "And after your visit here, what then? Do you remain in Poitou?"

Alienor shook her head. "We have business in Normandy, and then I am to return to England to govern as Henry's regent."

"It is a pity you cannot stay longer."

"I have thought that myself," Alienor said ruefully.

The cat gave a long, sinuous stretch and yawned, exposing a jagged landscape of white teeth, before strolling to the door and uttering an imperious meow. Her aunt rose to open the door, and a cold draft swept around the room as he stalked out, ginger tail waving like a furry banner. Alienor rose too, shivering. "I should see my sister."

"I would have brought her to you here," Agnes said, "but she has not been well, and we are keeping her in the infirmary where it is warm and she can be properly nursed. Come, I will take you."

❖❖❖

The convent's infirmary was a well-appointed room holding a dozen beds, four of which were occupied by elderly nuns being ministered to by the infirmaress and her assistant. The fire was bright and clean-burning, with plenty of room at the hearth to cook nourishing meals. A cauldron simmered over the logs, the steam laden with an appetizing aroma of meat broth.

Huddling by the fire was a frail old lady. Gaunt-cheeked and hollow-eyed, she plucked at the squirrel pelts edging her cloak. Alienor stared in silent shock as the woman gave a deep, wet cough. The hand she raised to cover her mouth was skeletal.

"Petra, dear God!" Alienor hurried to her side and looked on, helpless to act, while the spasms tore through her sister. Eventually, Petronella spat bloody mucus into a cloth and sucked in a harsh breath. Alienor cupped the thin shoulders and kissed her forehead. "I grieve to find you in this state."

"Alienor," Petronella croaked. "I wondered if you would come. I've been thinking of you often of late." She coughed again, but not as harshly, and reached a shaking hand to the cup at the side of the bench. "Horehound," she said and took a swallow. "They say it will do me good, but I know better. They think I know nothing, but I am merely mad, not foolish."

Alienor looked at her aunt. "How long has she been sick like this?"

Agnes shook her head. "The cough began over a month ago and will not shift whatever we do. We are keeping her warm and tended. She has spiritual comfort and all of our prayers. Perhaps when the spring comes she will improve."

It was a platitude. Alienor could see how sick her sister was and knew it would take a miracle to pull her through to the warmth of a new season. She was thirty-one years old but looked like a crone. In her mind's eye, Alienor glimpsed beyond her desperate condition to see Petronella the child, Petronella the dancing young woman with lustrous brown hair and sparkling eyes. Her grip on reality had always been fragile, but to see her end her days like this was heartrending. So much promise never realized, like a rose that had begun to open and then withered on the stem.

Petronella tilted her head as if listening. "Is Papa home from Compostela?" she asked. "He has been gone a long time."

Alienor looked at Agnes. "No, my love," she said. "He is not back yet." And never would be because he had died there twenty years ago and was entombed at the feet of Saint James.

"She spends much time in the past," her aunt said. "What is before her eyes is not what lies before ours. She never speaks of her marriage or her children."

"That is probably for the best," Alienor replied bleakly. Petronella's marriage had been a volatile, passionate disaster that had caused more trouble than it was ever worth and had ended in ruin for all concerned. Now her husband was dead and her children in French wardship. If she had blotted it from her damaged mind, so much the better.

"Papa is coming for me," Petronella said. "I will see him soon." She gripped Alienor's hand. "We should go up to the battlements and watch for him."

"No, stay here by the fire," Alienor said, her throat tight with tears. "He would not want us to get cold. There will be time later. Here, drink your tisane." She sat down beside Petronella and wrapped her cloak around both of them, drawing her in close.

The fire caught on a knot of wood and sent up a shower of swift red sparks. "Do you remember watching fireflies in the garden at Poitiers?" Petronella whispered. "And making wishes each time we saw a new one glow?"

"Of course I do. It was our favorite thing." All the possibilities, all the hopes and dreams. Alienor's eyes filled, and the firelight became a single golden blur.

"They are gone now," Petronella said sadly. "Every last one."

# 8

ROUEN, NORMANDY, FEBRUARY 1157

ALIENOR RETURNED TO HER CHAMBER FROM THE LATRINE where she had been sick for the third time that morning. Her stomach rolled as if she was already at sea rather than waiting out the rough weather before embarking for England.

Henry eyed her with predatory speculation. "Are you unwell, or is there another reason?"

She rinsed her mouth with the ginger tisane Marchisa had prepared to combat the nausea. "I believe I may be with child again." Speaking the words made her feel queasy with hope and fear. She dared not smile, for this was a serious undertaking and she would not have God think she was being frivolous.

"That is good news indeed!" Henry drew her into his arms. "You must rest and look after yourself." His tone was solicitous as he stroked her brow with his fingertip. "Let others do the work." He glanced at her ladies who were packing the traveling chests ready for the return to England.

"Do not worry on that score." Alienor swallowed her irritation. If Henry had his way, he would confine her to her chamber, her sole occupations those of embroidery, keeping the nursery, and writing occasional innocuous letters to men of the Church to further diplomatic relations.

Little Henry toddled over to his father and threw his arms around his legs. Henry picked him up, turning him in a somersault on the way, eliciting squeals of delight. "What a brave little knight you are," he said. "Be a good boy for your mama while I am busy in Normandy with the king of France, hmm?" The look he sent Alienor filled her with guilt and unease, for it warned her that he had not forgiven her over the matter of Will's death. They would never speak of it, Henry had made that clear, but what need was there for words when looks said everything?

"Papa!" Jeoffrey, his bastard son, dashed into the room holding his toy sword in one hand and a miniature shield painted with two gold lions on a red background in the other.

Alienor strove to maintain a neutral expression as Henry laughed and tousled the child's hair. Each time she saw him, she saw Will, and she knew Henry saw it too. And while to her it was as gall, to Henry that resemblance was a joy and comfort—as if this little boy was Will made whole again. Perhaps too his affection was for the sake of the mother, but Alienor did not want to dwell on that either.

"Here is another fine little knight come to defend the house-hold with his mighty sword!" Henry declared. "Well met, Sir Jeoffrey FitzRoy, slayer of dragons!"

Alienor compressed her lips. If she had her way, the boy would not have a secular career as a knight and baron because such a path led to virility and power, and who knew how far he might try to take his ambition. He was remaining in Normandy with the empress, but that meant for the moment he would still have access to his father. It was only for a few weeks, she told herself, and could not be helped, but even so, she struggled with her misgivings.

❖❖❖

Alienor put her hand on her womb as she felt a series of flurries and kicks. She had thought her other offspring busy little souls, but this one outdid them all. He—as she had determinedly decided his sex—was never still, and he had quickened early. She felt pleasure at this show of vigor and did not bid him be silent. She needed a strong child to rule Aquitaine, and she prayed regularly to Saint Radegonde and Saint Martial that this was the one.

Despite her pregnancy and Henry's warnings, she had been busy about her duties all that late April morning. She had issued authorizations of safe conducts and permissions to leave the country under her seal to several merchants and two deacons on Church business. She had notified a sheriff to desist cutting down trees in woodland belonging to Reading Abbey and had instructed her chamberlain to order more oil for the lamps in her chamber. The tasks were routine, but she was looking forward to talking with two envoys from Navarre over dinner.

"I think I shall name the child Richard if it is a boy, which I know it will be," she told Isabel as her ladies made her ready to perform the duties of gracious hostess.

Isabel gave her an inquiring look. "Why Richard?"

Her women slipped a gown of patterned red-and-gold damask over her head. "It means 'hard ruler,'" she said, "and when he is a grown man, he will need to be to control my barons." She stroked her womb. "It is not a name from either side of the family except in the distant past. This one shall stand in his own light."

"Will the king not wish to call him for his own father or perhaps his grandsire Fulke, king of Jerusalem?"

"It is not Henry's choice," Alienor said curtly. "It is for me to do the naming, because this child is my heir."

"And if it is a girl?" Isabel asked with a half smile.

"Then she will be Alienor, and she will still be mine." Alienor raised her chin and a fierce look entered her eyes. "But I know it will be a boy."

❖❖❖

Henry arrived in London a week later, having ridden hard from his landing at Southampton. "You look well," he said, greeting Alienor in the public chamber at Westminster. He kissed her on either cheek and then on the lips. His manner was more relaxed than it had been in Normandy, and his smile was sunny and generous. "And blossoming."

Alienor returned his smile, taking pleasure in his admiration. "I am, sire, very well indeed." While she was cautious, she too was less tense. The two months of absence had smoothed the rough edges caused by the friction between their personalities, and the sick exhaustion of early pregnancy had diminished. She was less irritable and having received advance word of his arrival had had time to make herself ready.

The children were presented for him to inspect. Little Henry was bright-eyed and full of wriggling energy. Matilda was more solemn as she considered her father from the safety of her nurse's arms, but she was rosy and chubby with health. Henry kissed them both and nodded brusquely to Alienor, indicating that he was satisfied she had kept them whole and safe. She did not know whether to feel relieved or resentful and drew back behind a facade of regal dignity.

❖❖❖

"You have done well," Henry said to her later in her chamber when the formal rituals were over and they were alone, their attendants dismissed. He poured them each a cup of spiced wine from the flagon on the chest.

"I am perfectly capable of overseeing the government of England while you are gone, even when I am with child," she said with asperity.

"I do not deny that, my love, but you must be careful of your health. You do not want your womb to go wandering around your body. That is what happens to women who overtax themselves—often with fatal consequences. I have heard you are susceptible."

"You leave your mother to rule Normandy—why should it be any different for me?"

"My mother's childbearing days are over. Why are you being so sharp with me when you have been acting regent here for the past six weeks?"

"But always under careful scrutiny from your administrators."

"Every ruler has advisers. Use them to good purpose and be grateful for their assistance."

Alienor controlled herself, aware that she was playing into his hands. "Sometimes 'assistance' feels very much like 'interference,'" she said.

"It is not intended to be."

"Is it not?" Alienor raised her brows.

"English laws need taking under advice, and it is only common sense that you have support." He made an exasperated sound. "You are making mountains where none exist."

He was blocking her with that look in his eyes that intimated he was being reasonable and she was not.

"So," she said, changing the subject, "did your discussions with Louis fare well?"

He shrugged. "They were as expected. He has acknowledged my rights as count of Anjou in the abbey of Saint Julian and is content to accept my brother as count of Nantes. For the moment we have a cordial truce, which leaves me free to deal with English matters." He contemplated his cup. "Indeed, he was in an unusually fine mood because his wife is finally with child—due in the late autumn, I gather. But his queen is delicate and narrow through the hips I hear, so she may not fare well at the birth."

Alienor's gaze sharpened. "But if she survives and bears a son, matters will change overnight."

"Indeed, but we can do nothing about it." He gestured to the curve of Alienor's belly. "Let us hope that Louis's queen births a girl and that ours is another son."

A soft knock came at the door. Henry went and opened it upon one of the duty squires and, standing behind him, Alienor's chaplain, Father Peter, his mouth set in a serious line. "Sire," he said with a deep bow, "madam, I am sorry to disturb you after you have retired, but there is news from Aquitaine."

Henry beckoned the priest into the room, and he entered, tall and somber, the cross around his neck glinting in the light. Alienor shivered. It couldn't be about rebellion or war, because that would not be the task of her chaplain to announce. Priests, on the other hand, were always the harbingers of family death.

"Madam." He presented her with a letter bearing the seal of the abbey of Saintes. "The messenger is in the hall, but I will have him summoned if you wish."

Alienor broke the seal tag and opened the letter. The parchment was shadowed with faint ripples where the animal's ribs had once pressed against its skin and was overlaid with elegant script in dark brown ink. "It's Petra," she said, putting her hand to her mouth. "My poor sister, my poor, sweet sister." She stared at the writing, assailed by a feeling of hollow shock. "I knew she was sick, I knew I would probably never see her again, but even so…"

"Madam, I am deeply sorry. I grieve with you," said Father Peter. "She was such a…fragile lady."

Henry took her in his arms, and she gripped his sleeves, hard, almost angrily. Her eyes were dry and burning.

"She was," Alienor whispered. The hollow feeling at her core spread outward, engulfing her. Petronella: in childhood their lives had been closely intertwined. They had slept in the same bed, played the same games, gotten into the same scrapes—had done everything together. When their mother died she had become the protective big sister and surrogate mother to Petronella and then watched her wreck her life on the treacherous rocks and undercurrents created by men. Now there was no one else in the world to carry those memories. She was their sole keeper.

"Your sister had been unwell for a long time," Father Peter said. "Now her suffering is over, and she is with God."

Alienor bit her lip. "I lost her years ago, but it was a comfort to know she was still in the world." She drew away from Henry and folded her hands under her heart. "I shall always think of her as a little girl. In fairness she never grew up, and when adult things were asked of her she did not have the ability to do them." She gestured to the chaplain. "Please make arrangements for masses to be said for her soul and a vigil. I will talk with you later."

"I shall do so immediately, madam." He departed, his head bowed.

Her throat was tight and aching. "I should write to my aunt."

"You can do that tomorrow," Henry said. "You must consider the child and rest."

She shook her head. "I shall not sleep."

"No matter." He made her lie on the bed and plumped the pillows and bolsters. "Shall I send for your women?"

She knew his solicitous behavior was in the interests of protecting their unborn child, and he had no part in this grief—it was hers to bear—but still she reached out to him. "Henry, stay with me...please."

He had been about to withdraw, but he hesitated and then, with a sigh, climbed onto the bed and lay down at her back, wrapping her in his arms and resting his chin on her shoulder. She felt the prickle of his beard against her neck, and the warmth of his breath, and it was at least some small comfort.

Enfolded in his embrace, she remembered when she and Petronella had cuddled together in their childhood bed. The scent of laundered linen and chemises, warm skin, tangled hair. Giggling under bedclothes festooned with bread crumbs and sticky smears of honey sneaked from the high table, and once a jug of wine. Whispered secrets, hopes, and dreams. Long ago and far away on the other side of innocence. Pressed against Henry's hard, masculine body, she daren't cry because she knew she would never stop.

# 9

## BEAUMONT PALACE, OXFORD, JULY 1157

"MADAM, I HAVE FOUND YOU A WET NURSE." ISABEL BECKONED to the heavily pregnant young woman who waited on the threshold of Alienor's chamber, her gaze modestly lowered and her hands clasped in front of her swollen belly. "This is Mistress Hodierna of St. Albans. She is of impeccable reputation and can be vouched for with references other than mine." She indicated the midwife accompanying them.

With an effort the young woman dropped in a deep curtsy. Her hair was respectably covered by a wimple of bleached linen. She had fine, clear skin and white hands with short, clean fingernails. A plain gold wedding ring gleamed on her heart finger, but she wore no other jewelry.

"You come highly recommended," Alienor said with a smiling glance to Isabel who, together with Dame Alice, had made it her task to find a suitable wet nurse from among the numerous candidates for the position. Thus far few had measured up to the exacting standards. "Your husband?"

"I am a widow, madam," Hodierna replied with quiet dignity. "My husband was a sergeant employed by the bishop of St. Albans, but he died of the stiffening sickness before I even knew I was with child. For now I am living with my mother."

That was good: no man was making claims on his wife's time and loyalty. "Let me see your body."

With quiet dignity Hodierna unpinned her dress and shrugged down her gown and chemise to expose her breasts, which were large and white with prominent blue veins, pale brown nipples, and large areolas. Her figure was well nourished but not obese, and her belly was a distended curve.

"Cover yourself," Alienor said with a gesture. "I can see no flaw in you and will be glad to take you into my household as a wet nurse when the time comes. My chancellor will see you paid."

Once Hodierna had dressed, she curtsied again and was ushered from the room by the midwife. Alienor turned to Isabel. "You did well to find her."

"I am glad you approve." Isabel screwed up her face. "We lost count of the number who came seeking the position. I have never seen so many women with child and none of them suitable. Hodierna was the gem among the dross."

Alienor's expression was wry. "There are many babies born as autumn arrives. The Christmas feast and the dark days of winter always result in a crop at harvest time."

Isabel said nothing. For other women that might be the case, but not for her.

She and Alienor took their sewing into the garden where they had the benefit of the full summer light. "Do you think the king will be home for the birth?" Isabel asked as they sat down.

Alienor took a hank of silk thread from her sewing box. "He said so, but I have learned that with Henry, saying is one thing and doing quite another."

Having received the submission of King David of Scotland, Henry was occupied with a campaign to bring Owain Gwynedd, Prince of North Wales, to heel and had taken an army to Rhuddlan to deal with the matter. Thus far there had been little news of his progress, but Alienor assumed all was well. They had parted amicably enough after traveling together and attending Mass at the great Augustinian abbey at Saint Edmund's with its altar front of beaten silver studded with gems. Following their progress, Henry had turned his attention to Wales, and Alienor had come to Oxford to await the birth of their fourth child. She had not missed the thread of anxiety in Isabel's question and was a trifle exasperated. "You fret too much over that husband of yours," she said. "Let him take responsibility for himself. You are not his mother."

Isabel gave her a startled look and then dropped her gaze to her embroidery. "For a while I was," she said.

Alienor raised her brows but remained silent, knowing that letting a moment extend was often more profitable than filling the gap with chatter.

Isabel sighed and spread out the altar cloth on which she was working. "My father rode away to war and never returned. I do not want to grieve for my husband in the same way."

"He is doing what men do. It is a risk they take, and we must accept that," Alienor said shortly.

"I know, and I tell myself that, but I still worry. He was just a boy when he stood at the altar with me. I was very young, but I was a woman in ways that he was not a man. I have seen him shed the tears of a child even when I have been his wife, and it is hard not to be overprotective."

Alienor was torn between compassion for her friend and the desire to tell her to let her husband be a man. In the end she settled for lightness and touched Isabel's sleeve. "I cannot tell you when he will return because that will depend on the king, but he will live to bring you his sack full of dirty baggage, steal the bedclothes in the middle of the night, and make you wonder why you ever worried!"

Isabel put on a brave smile. "I will hold that thought in mind whenever I turn foolish and begin to brood, especially the dirty baggage," she said, but her eyes remained haunted.

❖❖❖

Hamelin's shoulders prickled as if his mail shirt was lined with tiny thorns facing inward and stabbing through his gambeson. The stifling August heat was cooking him inside his armor, but his discomfort was also caused by an acute sense of unease. Henry had taken a mounted contingent on a shortcut through the forest of Cennadlog, leaving the main army and baggage train to follow the coast road. His intention was to come up behind Owain Gwynedd's Welsh forces at Basingwerk, encircle them, and force a swift surrender.

Their Welsh guides, enemies of Owain, were leading them along little used forest trails, narrow and winding. Oppressive heat bore down on them like an extra weight. The deep green light was suffused with sudden slashes of gold where fallen trees opened up a shaft to the sky and fresher air. It was almost otherworldly, and although Hamelin was accustomed to hunting through dense forests, this felt different, and dangerous.

In front of Hamelin, Henry's big bay destrier swished its black tail against the irritation of numerous blood-sucking flies. Sweat dripped from its hide and frothed along the line of the rein. Henry's constable, Eustace FitzJohn, rode at Henry's left-hand side, holding his skittish black stallion on a tight rein. FitzJohn turned frequently in the saddle, his vision hampered because he only had sight in one eye. Ahead and to one side rode Henry of Essex, bearing the royal standard.

Close to Hamelin, William de Boulogne leaned over to rub his bad leg. "The Welsh have an affinity for forests," he said with a grimace. "They are certainly more at home in them than I am."

"You have fought them before?" Hamelin blotted his face on his gambeson cuff.

"No, but people talk of them around the fire, and the border barons employ Welsh archers and mercenaries in their retinues. They do not have great cities; they live on their herds, on milk and meat. They will not stand and fight because they do not have the weight and power we do. Instead, they are wraiths with arrows. They are knives in the dark."

Hamelin arched his brow at William's poetic turn of phrase. "And we are swords in the sunlight," he replied with a fierce smile. "We are the weight of powerful warhorses and castles of stone."

"Indeed, and I shall be glad when we are within our walls of stone, because this is their domain."

A sudden crashing sound from the trees ahead had everyone reaching for their weapons, but then Henry burst out laughing and pointed to a pair of mating pigeons thrashing about in the leaves of an ash tree. The men relaxed, puffing out their tension, chuckling and exchanging relieved, sheepish glances. The laughter was still on their faces as with a swift singing of air an arrow punched into the face of Eustace FitzJohn, shattering his cheekbone and spraying blood. The scout who had been leading them screamed and fell, a shaft quivering in his chest. Another dart thudded into a tree, narrowly missing de Boulogne and causing his stallion to rear and plunge.

Hamelin scrabbled for his shield and brought it onto his left shoulder while drawing his sword and felt the impact of two shafts thudding into the linen-covered wood. Arrows sang all around like angry hornets, creating destruction and mayhem. Following that onslaught, the Welsh came in swiftly on foot armed with javelins and long stabbing knives, aiming to hamstring the horses and bring the knights down. Warriors leaped out of the trees, howling their battle cries, landing on saddles, swarming like ants.

As Hamelin tried to reach Henry, a Welshman sprang into his path, armed with a round shield and a nailed club. Hamelin pivoted his stallion and struck with his sword. His shield took the blow of the club, and his enemy fell away with a howl. That was one disabled, he thought grimly, and spurred forward, chopping down at another bare-legged snarling warrior. Aware of another Welshman attacking from his left, he twisted to strike, but there was no need because William de Boulogne had already felled the man with a well-aimed back swipe.

Before them they saw Eustace FitzJohn dragged from his horse and speared through the chest and throat by three of the enemy with javelins. There was no sign of Essex, and a Welshman had seized the standard and was wafting it with fierce triumph. Henry's big bay was bleeding profusely and, as Hamelin reached Henry, the horse's legs buckled. Henry fought free of the saddle and avoided being crushed by a hair's breadth. His complexion was bone-white save for a blood spatter across one cheek, and his eyes glittered with fear and rage as he hefted his shield and raised his sword. The Welshmen who had slaughtered FitzJohn advanced on him, javelin points thirsty for another kill. Hamelin spurred his stallion into them, striking and trampling. The hot tang of blood and spilled guts permeated the humid air. William de Boulogne dealt with the second warrior, and Henry fought off the third, ramming his sword under the Welshman's ribs. Hamelin seized the reins of FitzJohn's big black and handed them to Henry, who grabbed them and hauled himself into the saddle. Roger de Clare had retrieved the standard and was bellowing at the knights to hold hard and rally around the king.

For a time the fighting intensified, but Henry's mauled troop, fighting cohesively now, seized the advantage and turned on their attackers, who started to melt away into the forest.

"Hold!" Henry roared as some of the knights spurred in pursuit. William de Boulogne grabbed the hunting horn on his saddle and let out three sharp blasts to sound the recall. They could not go on but had to retreat as swiftly as they could and rejoin the safety of the main army, their plan in tatters.

The dead were hastily thrown across riderless horses, and the troop turned back through the forest. Hamelin rode as close to Henry as the trail allowed, protecting him with his shield and his body. The Welsh might still rally and pursue, hoping to pick off a few more as they retreated, and it only took a single arrow to strike home.

Eventually, they slowed their pace to conserve the horses. Their scouts had died in the first rush of the attack, but the trail back was marked by broken branches and the imprint of shod hooves in the soft mulch. Another hour of riding brought them into thinner tree cover, and the heavy, humid scent of foliage became mingled with the smell of the sea. A sudden movement through the trees ahead sent hands to weapons again, everyone fearing that Owain Gwynedd had in his turn come around and encircled them, but then a hunting horn blew a sequence of recognized blasts, and the knights slumped in their saddles with relief. William de Boulogne took his horn and raised it to answer with three powerful notes.

An instant later, soldiers from the rearguard of the army appeared on the path, together with Henry of Essex, whose expression was a mingling of horror, shame, and relief. "Thank Christ, thank Christ you are alive, sire!" he said hoarsely. "I thought you had been killed. I rode to bring help!"

"Indeed, I am alive, but no thanks to those who did not stand," Henry replied with icy rage. "FitzJohn and de Courci are dead, and many other good men besides."

"Traitor!" spat Roger de Clare. "You sought to save your own skin, didn't you, and let us bear the brunt!"

A red flush burned Essex's cheekbones. "I did not! I rode to raise the alarm. I am no traitor, and you shall not call me one."

"I will call as I see fit!" De Clare reached for his sword.

"Peace!" Henry bellowed. "This is not the place to argue. We are not safe yet nor will be until we join the main troop. Let everything stand in abeyance until then."

As they left the trees and headed out onto the firm open road, Hamelin breathed out hard, trying to let go of his tension. Beside him William de Boulogne leaned over his saddle and vomited.

"I'm sorry," he said, looking shamefaced as he wiped his mouth. "It always takes me like this afterward."

Hamelin gave him an assessing look and was aware of others glancing their way. "But you did not run. You stayed to fight."

William took his wine costrel from his saddle to rinse his mouth. "I wanted to, believe me I did, but a man who abandons his comrades is no man at all."

Hamelin gave a brisk nod. "Indeed." He was never going to be a close friend of King Stephen's youngest son, but he respected his honesty and his ability to stand firm when called upon, no matter that he puked and shook afterward like a green squire.

The troop rode swiftly to rejoin the main army, the forest on their left and the sea on their right. The green darkness of the trees cloyed the late-afternoon heat, and Hamelin could still smell the blood of the slain all around him.

# 10

*H*ONEYED SEPTEMBER LIGHT SHONE THROUGH THE OPEN SHUT-ters onto the bed where Alienor labored. The thunderous August heat had yielded to crisper, fresher air, but it was still pleasantly warm, and the sky was as blue as the Virgin's cloak. Alienor endured the painful hard work of travail with optimism. All was well, and she had made herself believe that the difficult times were behind her and that this child's birth would herald a new beginning.

The baby's head crowned between her thighs and, after another steady, controlled push, emerged from her body, followed smoothly by the rest of him. As the midwife laid him upon her belly, Alienor saw that his hair was a wet red-gold. He cried immediately, and his skin flushed with pink color.

"A boy," the midwife said. "A fine, healthy boy." She picked him up and wiped him with a towel, then, smiling, she gave him to Alienor. Gazing into his crumpled little face, Alienor felt something that was almost recognition. This newborn baby was God's sign that he had not forsaken her after all. This was the heir to Aquitaine, and now her work could begin.

"Richard," she said softly, feeling enhanced and strengthened. "My beautiful Richard."

The baby gazed at her as if already knowing his name. His tiny fists opened and closed, already grasping handfuls of the world he had so recently entered.

While Richard was bathed in a brass bowl before the fire, the midwives tended to Alienor, and by the time she was clean and comfortable, he was ready for her to take in her arms, wrapped in soft linen swaddling and folded in a blue blanket. Alienor was exhausted but resisted sleep. She just wanted to hold her newborn son because not only was he a hope for the future, but a blessing to heal the past.

❖❖❖

Henry returned from an energetic day's hunting to the news that while he had been pursuing heron and crane along the bank of the Thames with his white gyrfalcon, Alienor's labor had begun.

He had returned from Wales just over a week since, the campaign having taken longer and cost more in lives and money than he had ever expected. However, he had learned his lesson from the mauling he had received and had eventually made sufficient inroads on Welsh territory for Owain Gwynedd to come to terms and render him homage. For now there was peace, albeit uneasy.

"How's your horse?" Henry asked Hamelin as his half brother entered the room, plucking burrs out of his tunic.

"He is all right," Hamelin replied. "A leg strain but not serious. Any news?"

Henry shook his head. "No," he said and gave a sour grin. "It is the law of the land that men always have to wait upon a woman, didn't you know that?"

Hamelin poured himself a cup of wine and sat down on a bench, stretching out his legs. "I had heard it was courtesy," he said, "but not law."

"Wait until you have a wife. You'll learn." Henry glanced around. "Where's Thomas?"

"Still fussing over his hawk," Hamelin said. "He's not happy that it flew into a tree and he nearly lost it. Said he'd come in a moment."

Henry snorted. "Told him he should have waited longer in the training but he wouldn't have it. He had to fly it today."

The door opened, and Emma entered the room, her face bright with excitement and joy. "Sire," she said, curtsying to Henry, "you have another son, lusty and red-haired."

"Hah!" Henry raised his half sister to her feet and gave her a smacking kiss on the lips. "That is great news!" He felt expansive with pleasure, pride, and relief. The birth of another male child meant he could thicken the skin over the scar caused by Will's death and pretend it had never happened. "And the queen?" he asked. "How does she fare?"

"The queen is well," Emma replied. "She is tired because of the travail but joyous over the birth of another son, and she sends you her greeting."

Henry turned to the men gathered around the hearth, a wide grin on his face. "Prepare a toast for when I return, and we shall celebrate!" He looked up as his chancellor tardily entered the room. "Thomas, I have another son! What do you say to that?"

The creases in Becket's face deepened as he smiled. "Congratulations, sire, that is the best of news. I will present him with a silver christening cup when you bring him to his baptism. How is he to be named?"

"I will let you know when I return." Henry slapped his chancellor's shoulder. "How's the hawk?"

Becket grimaced. "In need of further training, sire."

"Hah, I told you not to fly her."

"Next time I will take your advice, sire."

"A man should always bow to superior knowledge—and his king," Henry said with a smug look. "You still have a great deal to learn, Thomas." He slapped his chancellor again and set out for the confinement chamber.

Alienor was sitting up in bed, her hair a skein of shining gold around her shoulders. She looked tired, as Emma had said, with fine lines around her eyes in the clear September light, but even so she was beautiful. She was gazing down at a swaddled baby wrapped in a soft blue blanket, an expression of such fierce love and tenderness on her face that Henry felt his chest expand with an emotion he was at a loss to identify, except that it made him want to weep. He stooped to kiss her lips and then gave the baby to the midwife to unwind the swaddling bands so he could look at his new son.

The infant's hair sparkled red-bronze like his own, and the brows were fine gold threads. The little fists were furled over like closed buds. He was long-limbed and strong, neither plump nor scrawny.

"What a fine little man," he said, taking him in his arms so that everyone in the chamber would see his pleasure and acknowledgment.

"I am going to call him Richard," Alienor said with the finality of a decision already made.

A frown twitched Henry's brows at such audacity. "For what reason?"

"Because he is the heir to Aquitaine and mine to name, and I choose it for him. He will make it his own, and he will stand in his own light."

Henry took a moment to think whether he would permit such a thing and decided it was not worth fighting over. "Have your will. Let it be Richard," he said. "The next one shall be Geoffrey—for my father."

"The next one?" A spark of indignation kindled in her eyes. "Why can't now be enough?"

Henry laughed softly. "But you accomplish the duty so well, my love. Because of me you are not a barren queen but the matriarch of a dynasty. I promised you that when we wed." He gave Richard to the midwife to wrap up again. "I'll return later. For now, I have to go raise a toast." He kissed her again and left the room, striding out as if he owned the world, which Alienor supposed that for now he did. She was a little annoyed, but she smiled too. The alchemy of her seed and Henry's had united to create this wonderful little being, who would one day grow into a fine, strong warrior: a prince of Aquitaine.

❖❖❖

Hodierna sat on the settle before the fire, cushions under her arms as she suckled two babies, one with downy hair of copper-gold, the other soft brown. Richard was latched onto her right breast and her own son Alexander on her left. The room filled with the sound of their guzzling, and it amused Alienor greatly to hear them. "Heaven help the cellars when they move on to wine," she said.

"At least I have an excuse to eat well at table, madam."

Alienor laughed. Richard was already much bigger than his milk brother, although both babies were thriving. He was going to be tall and strong: a long-limbed warrior like her father and her uncle Raymond, once prince of Antioch.

Alienor turned back to her seamstress. She was having some new gowns made for the Christmas feast, which was to be at Lincoln this year. Wearing their crowns, she and Henry would preside over a vast gathering of barons and clergy, and she intended to be magnificent in silk and fur, gold and jewels. The queen of an empire stretching from the Scottish borders to the foothills of the snow-clad Pyrenees.

Richard's birth had done much to improve her relationship with Henry. She had been churched just over a month ago, and their reunion in bed had been mutually satisfying. She did not resent Henry as much while they were both in England because this was his birthright, and she did not have the same ache in her soul when he took command of ruling it. She still had her own roles within the curia as diplomat and peacemaker, and she had a busy family household to oversee. The children had nurses and wet nurses to attend to their needs, but she had to oversee those women, and even if her duties took her away from her offspring at regular intervals, she was often in the same room and keeping a watchful eye on their development.

Little Henry had recently begun pointing to his chest and referring to himself as "Harry," which was often how the English servants at court rendered the name "Henry." He was a good-natured, charming child with thick golden-brown hair and striking gray-blue eyes. He was swift, intelligent, and vastly curious, his constant chatter punctuated by numerous questions. Where did the sun go at night? Why did dogs wag their tails? Why didn't babies have teeth when they were born? He had a particular rapport with Isabel, who was endlessly patient with his demands and would play games with him and tell him stories when he was tired.

He loved his siblings too and constantly wanted to kiss them. Alienor suspected that such behavior would change in time, but for the moment at least, all was sunshine, except when he poked the sleeping Richard and woke him up. She was relieved that Henry's bastard son had remained in Normandy with his grandmother. As yet no other by-blows had been presented at her chamber door, although she was constantly waiting for it to happen. Henry's sexual appetite was voracious, and he bedded other women in the same casual way he used food for sustenance.

She was studying a bolt of ruby-colored silk when Henry breezed into the room. Picking up his heir, he swung him in his arms. "Well, my young man, what have we here?"

Harry giggled, showing two rows of perfect baby teeth, and reached up. "I want your hat!"

Henry removed his blue woolen cap and plopped it over his son's head. "There, now you look very fine indeed, my boy. The apparel of a king suits you well." Turning to Alienor, he eyed the bolt of red silk cast across the trestle in shimmering ripples. "Fit for the queen of England herself!" With a beguiling grin, he seized Alienor around the waist and danced her around the room together with Harry, the latter wearing the blue cap covering his face as far as his nose. Alienor began to laugh, her emotions bright with pleasure.

"What has put you in such a good mood?"

Henry set his son back on his feet and lifted little Matilda instead. He swept her in a swift circle, kissed her cheek, and returned her to her nurse. "I have just heard that Louis's wife has borne a daughter," he said, grinning. "By all accounts the mother has survived and the baby is healthy, but it confirms that Louis cannot beget sons. Even given a meek and biddable wife he still cannot accomplish a man's task in her bed."

Alienor spared a brief moment of pity for Louis. He must be beside himself. The news made her think of the two daughters she had been forced to leave behind when her first marriage had been annulled. Children she had barely known, yet at the same time had nurtured in her womb, flesh of her flesh for nine months. Marie and Alix were being convent-raised until they were of an age to marry the men to whom they were betrothed—Theobald and Henri, brothers of the powerful house of Blois–Champagne. Alienor had schooled herself long ago not to think of the daughters she had borne to Louis, but occasionally the memories would surface and take her unawares.

"Does the baby have a name?"

"Marguerite," Henry said with the shrug of such a thing being of no importance.

"Saint Margaret is often invoked by women with problems in travail," Alienor said thoughtfully. "A child named in her honor might be a sign of gratitude for surviving a difficult birth."

"If so, then Louis is on the horns of a dilemma. He has to decide whether to bed her the moment she is churched and try for another son, or let her rest for a while longer and regain her strength. For now all that concerns us is that Louis still does not have a son, and we have two." He looked at her with a gleam in his eyes. "And after last night, perhaps three."

Alienor turned back to the red silk, a rueful half smile on her lips. She wouldn't be surprised either. Certainly he had not given her time beyond her own churching to recuperate, and he was always at his most eager in the weeks when she returned to her marital duties after leaving confinement.

Henry retrieved his hat from his heir, tucked it in his belt, and departed about his business. Alienor pressed her hand to the soft curve of her belly. Never again would it be as flat as a girl's. Sometimes she envied the narrow waists and high, firm breasts of nubile young women, but then fecundity had its own areas of advantage, and it was better to be an experienced doe in the forest than a youngster, easily chased into a trap by men and brought down.

# 11

FOR ONCE HENRY HAD TAKEN A MOMENT AWAY FROM throwing himself at life to sit and relax with Alienor in the domestic chamber. The morrow was Easter Sunday, and they were to attend a celebratory Mass in Worcester Cathedral followed by a banquet. Being a formal occasion, they were both obliged to wear their crowns.

Henry's remark in November about begetting another child had been wrong but only by a month. Once again, the Christmas celebration had resulted in a pregnancy, and yesterday Alienor had felt the child quicken. Richard would only be a year old and still taking sustenance from Hodierna when the new baby arrived.

"I have been thinking about the crown-wearing," Henry said. "About having to do this four times a year. All the expense and ceremony and the weight of the thing. Everyone knows I am king by now."

Alienor rather enjoyed the crown-wearing ceremonies, but Henry was always impatient, bored, and restless, tapping his feet, drumming his fingers. "So what do you propose?"

"That we leave our crowns on the cathedral altar in permanence and only wear them on exceptional occasions. I am tired of the fuss every time. The man should wear the crown, not the crown the man."

She could tell from his demeanor that he intended to push through the idea whatever the objections. She supposed it showed he was sufficiently secure in his authority not to need the physical trappings of kingship, but others expected it of royalty. "What will your mother say? You know how set in her notions she is. She won't be overjoyed to learn you are dispensing with the crown-wearing ceremony, especially since she fought so hard to obtain you that crown in the first place."

"My mother is not in England," Henry said dismissively, "and while I value her advice, I do not always take it. She has her ways of governing, and I have mine. I have no need of embellishment. Let others parade silks and furs in my stead. My chancellor has proven himself more than adept. He enjoys such spectacles. Why have a dog and bark yourself?"

Alienor made no reply. There was no point in arguing a decision when Henry had made up his mind. He was right about Becket. While many were uneasy at the sums the chancellor spent on lavish clothes, entertainments, hawks, and hounds, Henry was amused and indulgent, like a rich sponsor watching an impoverished child stuffing itself at his table. He teased him sometimes—once riding into Becket's dining hall all sweaty from the hunt and tossing a gutted hare on his trencher, and another time forcing Becket to hand over his new cloak to a street beggar—but mostly he saw the largesse as a just reward for what Thomas was able to do for him in terms of raising revenue and putting forward ideas. And, as he said, why should he bother with the fuss of ceremony when he didn't enjoy it and his chancellor did? A man who could indulge one of his servants thus was surely magnificent in himself.

❖❖❖

At Mass on Easter Sunday, Henry and Alienor placed their coronation crowns on Worcester Cathedral's high altar. The diadems rippled with gold-and-red reflections from candles and lamps, as if flickering with the energy of regnal power. A king and a queen side by side. Three-year-old Henry reached to grip the silver-gilt coronet on his own head, his bottom lip quivering and his eyes big with tears.

"What is wrong, my little man?" Alienor stooped to ask him. He had stood proudly at his parents' side, a symbol of their fertility and the secured succession, and had behaved beautifully, but Alienor knew the mercurial characters of small children and how everything might change in an instant. She cast her gaze around in search of Hodierna.

"I don't want to put my crown on the altar," he said, articulate and forceful. "It's mine."

Alienor's lips twitched at his possessiveness. "Well, then it is a good thing you do not have to. Only kings and queens may do that, and you are still but a prince." She shared a moment of suppressed laughter with Henry.

"A strong sense of possession never did anyone harm," Henry said. "But mark my words: you will have to wait a long time before you wear that crown, my boy, and then you will discover just how heavy it is."

❖❖❖

Henry sat before the hearth with his chancellor, drinking wine and fondling the ears of a dozing hound. Earlier he and Thomas had played chess together and satisfied honor by winning one game each—which meant losing one game each too. Now they were discussing the business of the realm and finishing off the flagon at the end of a highly agreeable day.

Thomas said thoughtfully, "Seeing your heir with that coronet at his brow today made me think."

"Oh yes?" Henry eyed him. Thomas had pushed back his sleeves as if preparing to do business. They were edged with a thin line of blackest sable, and behind the fur were stitched pearls and gemstones. Henry knew that if Becket had been king, he would not have put his crown on the altar. He would have taken it to bed with him and slept with it under his pillow and paraded it at every opportunity. "What scheme do you have in mind now?"

"I was thinking of the little princess of France, Marguerite, and wondering if it is too early to consider a marriage alliance."

Henry's gaze sharpened, and he sat up. He enjoyed these late-night talks with Thomas. You never knew what he was going to come up with. As a promulgator of ideas, and as a man capable of implementing them, he had few equals. "You mean a marriage alliance with my son?"

Thomas took a sip of wine from his silver cup. "You would b-be able to settle the matter of the Vexin territory by a marriage treaty, and it would foster peace between you and France. If Louis continues to beget daughters or has no other children, then in the fullness of time, Marguerite's husband could become very important indeed. You have nothing to lose, sire, and everything to g-gain."

Henry chewed his thumb knuckle and rose to pace the room while he considered. He imagined his eldest son riding out as a glorious young man, his standard-bearer carrying the double banners of England and France on his spear. Suddenly that moment in the cathedral earlier, when the child had desired to hold on to his coronet, seemed like a portent. "The idea has potential," he agreed, "but will Louis be willing to consider this, or will he reject it out of hand?"

"Sire, I would not have broached the matter if I did not believe it was tenable. If we go about the proposition in the right way, then the king of France will see advantages in the alliance just as we do. His daughter will be queen of England, and his grandson may well sit on the English throne, just as yours may sit on the French one."

Henry lifted one doubtful eyebrow at that, knowing French law, although he was smiling. "We would need to take her for fostering and raise her in our traditions so that she cleaves to our ways."

"Sire, that goes without saying. If we undertook such a scheme, it would also prevent the king of France from wedding her to someone who might cause damage to our interests."

"I am not blind, Thomas," Henry said, casting his chancellor a dark look. "It is a good plan. I put it in your capable hands to make overtures, but keep me informed."

Thomas bowed. "I shall do so, sire."

Henry paced the room and turned. "If we do go forward with this, I want discretion. There is no need to raise the issue with the queen or court her opinion until we know whether there will be a positive outcome to the discussions."

Becket's gaze was knowing. "I understand perfectly, sire," he said with a bow.

"You always do, Thomas." Henry clapped him on the shoulder and saw him out of the room. Then, rubbing his hands, he sent one of the doorkeepers to fetch the new girl he had noticed recently among the court whores. Her hair had a way of rippling like ripe wheat when she walked, and he had been saving her as a reward for himself. Tonight he would thoroughly enjoy harvesting her field.

❖❖❖

Alienor stood at her chamber window and inhaled the fresh May morning. In the fourth month of pregnancy she felt bloated and ungainly. There had been no time for her body to recover from bearing Richard before she was with child again, and it seemed to her that she was a plodding beast of burden.

Warin, her chamberlain, entered the room, bowed, and announced that the chancellor was here requesting an audience. Still facing the window, Alienor closed her eyes and sighed. "Show him in," she said and, after a moment, gathered herself and turned to watch Thomas Becket enter the room.

As usual his garb was immaculate—a fine robe with the large sleeves of a cleric so that he occupied twice as much space as his narrow body actually required. A white linen shirt gleamed at cuff and throat, and a ring set with a large green beryl shone on the middle finger of his right hand.

"Madam." He bowed to her. "I am sorry to impose on you this early."

"I am sure you would not do so merely to gossip, my lord chancellor. What can I do for you that my husband cannot?" Henry was conspicuous by his absence. There had been some talk of hunting, but she suspected his prey was of the female variety. She had asked Thomas to obtain some more lamps for her chamber, but that was a routine matter for one of his underlings and would not warrant a special visit.

"Madam, it is a delicate matter of the realm and foreign policy." He presented her with a letter that had been tucked up his sleeve. It had been opened, but the seal of France still dangled on a cord from its base.

"What is this?"

He clasped his thin, fine hands. "Madam, we thought that now was the time to tell you. We did not do so before, because matters might have come to naught."

Alienor read what was written and then read it again, unable to take it in because it was so preposterous. It seemed to concern a marriage proposal between her eldest son and Louis's baby daughter Marguerite. Louis wished to discuss the situation in more depth and was inviting Henry to Paris for talks on that and other matters of diplomatic concern.

Trembling, she struck the parchment. "Whose idea was this?" She was horrified that an issue of this nature could have been conducted behind her back and gone this far. "You and the king have discussed this between you and omitted to tell me despite the matter involving my son and having wide-reaching consequences?"

"Madam, you were unwell at the time in the first months of pregnancy, and there would have been no point in disturbing you if the proposal had come to naught," Becket replied in a reasonable voice.

"And you think I am not more disturbed by this?" She struck the parchment again. "That you went behind my back and chose not to tell me until you had to?"

He opened his hands in a placatory gesture. "Madam, truly we thought it for the best. There was no intent to deceive."

She glared at Becket, hating his obsequious smoothness. She knew it must be his idea, because he was always presenting schemes to Henry like jewels on a necklace, and Henry would seize on them with delight and further embellish them. "Do I look like a fool, my lord chancellor? Of course there was intent to deceive."

"Madam, I assure you there was not."

She needed time to think, to organize and regroup. She folded the parchment so that the blank sides were outermost. "I shall give you my reply after I have considered," she said with regal dignity. "You may go."

He cleared his throat and stirred his toe in a circle on the floor. "Madam, the reply has already been sent in anticipation. I am to travel to Paris to open negotiations." His expression was a polite mask. "The king will tell you more when he returns."

Alienor felt sick. She was being pushed out. They had not seen fit to tell her because they had known she would object. "Get out," she said in a choked voice. Turning her back on him, she went to sit in the window embrasure and fanned herself with the parchment. Becket did not ask her to return it, but he would have had copies made.

The revelation of what had been done without her knowledge had stopped her brain. She could not think, could not comprehend. There was no one she could turn to for support. Behind her she was aware of Becket taking his time to exit the room. He was talking to a scribe and collecting some parchments that needed dealing with, as if waiting for her to relent and summon him back, but she had no intention of doing so, because his words would be as smooth as syrup and make her sick. Eventually, he did depart, murmuring that he would return later, and she closed her eyes in blessed relief.

The shock had left her feeling limp and wrung out. She summoned her women to comb her hair and bring a basin of tepid water so that she could change her gown and cleanse away the stain of this news. She stared at the crumpled piece of parchment in her hand. For two figs she would have put it in the candle and burned it to ashes, but she needed this solid proof of treachery and disrespect.

"Lock this in my jewel box," she said, handing the letter to Isabel and suppressing a heave.

"Is there anything I can do, madam?" Isabel asked, her expression full of concern.

It would be easy to cry, but this was not worth the easy tears. "No," Alienor said. "This is for me to face by myself." She watched Isabel fold the note and place it in the jewel box without looking at it. Isabel was as trustworthy as gold. Not so much as a sidelong glance to try to steal a glimpse of the content, but still Alienor could not tell her. "I thank you for asking."

The scented water and change of clothes cooled Alienor's body and restored her sense of self, but she was still perturbed and distracted. Sipping from a cup of wine, she paced the room, pondering strategies and trying to deal with the bitter feelings of betrayal.

Her thoughts were interrupted as the door flung open and Henry strode into the room. His tunic was covered in dust, and he was still wearing his spurs. The defensive gleam in his eyes told Alienor he was well aware of her exchange with Becket.

Alienor dismissed her ladies and waited for the last one to leave and the latch to fall. Henry went to pour himself a cup of wine, his attitude so deliberately insouciant that it ignited her rage.

"What is the meaning of this preposterous marriage alliance you have been negotiating with France?" she demanded without preamble. "You could not even tell me but left it to your chancellor. That is rank cowardice." She spat the words at him. "You have betrayed me; you have betrayed my trust. How could you do this, Henry? How?"

He raised a warning forefinger from his cup. "You should not rile yourself; it is not good for the child. If I did not speak to you about it, it was because of your health, and the idea might have come to nothing anyway. Physicians say it is unwise for a woman with child to excite herself with political matters lest her womb become displaced and she miscarry."

Alienor almost choked on her fury. "You said you would not take me for granted, but you always do. It is as though I am but a marker on a bloodline with nothing for myself. A breeder of children."

"This is precisely the reason I did not want to involve you," he said self-righteously. "You lose all sense and reason when you are with child."

"You expect me to condone our son wedding into that bloodline? To marrying him to my former husband's daughter? Dear God, Henry, it is not my wits that have gone wandering but yours!"

His eyes brightened with anger. "This match is a strong way of achieving accord. Mingling our bloodline with that of France will make us more powerful. It will pave a path to peace and prosperity. You must put the past behind you and look to the future. Louis is agreeable to the match in principle. Bloodline appears to be no hindrance to him."

"How do you know how the girl will turn out? She is but a baby in the cradle."

Henry gave her a pointed look. "How do any of us know how our spouses will turn out? You always take that gamble."

"She is half sister to the daughters I bore Louis. Dear God, it is almost incest!" Her belly heaved. Turning from him she ran to the garderobe and was wretchedly sick.

"I will summon your women," Henry said implacably. "I told you this would make you ill, and I was right. Mark me, this is for the best and it will go forward. Accept it and be done, madam, because you have no other choice."

That was what made her sick: the knowledge that she was trapped without a choice. Six years ago of her own free will she had married Henry FitzEmpress, hoping to create a golden future, but all she seemed to have had from him was a dross of broken promises, sharp-edged and tawdry.

Her women clustered around her in concern. Alienor waved them away and took to her bed, ordering them to draw the curtains so that she could have privacy to think.

Obviously she could do nothing to influence Henry. He thought it an excellent notion and would not change his mind. He and Becket were of one accord, and the rest of the court would follow their lead above hers.

And yet she was the one who bore the heirs and controlled the nursery. The children were half hers and all in her keeping. A woman could wield power through her sons and daughters if she was astute. Even if little Harry was betrothed to a French princess, he would still be within Alienor's sphere of influence. Like a patient general she had to bide her time.

# 12

## WESTMINSTER, SUMMER 1158

*"L*OOK, MAMA, LOOK!"

Alienor raised her head as Harry burst into the room, his small face shining. His father and Thomas Becket followed more sedately. Perched on Henry's shoulder was a small brown monkey with a chain around its neck. It clutched a date in its dexterous leathery hands and was busily eating the fruit and glancing around out of intelligent dark eyes set beneath bushy brows.

Alienor stared, not knowing whether to laugh or be dismayed. A monkey in the chamber was the last thing she needed. Her women were all cooing and making silly kissing noises with pursed lips.

"Well, what do you think of this as a gift for Louis?" Henry asked, chuckling. "I thought it could sit on his shoulder and give him advice since monkeys are renowned for their wisdom."

"It's called Robert," Harry said earnestly. "I want to keep him."

"Ah no, my boy." Henry wagged his finger. "This is a gift for the king of France. When you are older, perhaps."

Alienor raised her eyebrows. "Indeed, what a good idea," she said. "You could replace your own advisers with monkeys, and all it would cost you would be a few bags of almonds and dates. Think of the saving."

Henry grinned. "What do you say to that, Thomas? What if I were to replace you with a monkey?"

Becket smiled with vinegar on his lips. "I am sure you would find it most enlightening, sire."

The monkey clambered onto Henry's shoulder, wrapped its tail around his neck, and began industriously searching his hair for lice.

Alienor burst out laughing. "Certainly it would perform more functions than you, Master Chancellor, and that would be a miracle!"

Henry grabbed the creature off his head, making it screech, and handed it back to Becket.

"Master Thomas has lots and lots of monkeys!" Harry's voice was high with excitement. He screwed up his face as he calculated. "Twelve! Come see them, Mama! Come see!" He seized her hand and tugged.

"Why twelve?" Alienor gave Thomas a cynical look. "Was one not enough?"

Thomas exchanged glances with Henry and smiled. "One to ride each packhorse bearing gifts when I enter Paris, madam," he said. "And then later they will be presented to select members of the French court."

"The intention is to show Louis how much wealth and power I have at my disposal," Henry said. "And also to make a spectacle for the French people." Henry slapped his chancellor's shoulder in the same way he would slap a horse's neck when it had performed well for him. "Thomas has been particularly inventive. Not only monkeys for wisdom, but also a parrot that can say the paternoster and two golden eagles." His eyes sparkled with mirth and pride. "Not to mention assorted packs of hounds, guard dogs, and enough furs, fabrics, and furniture to equip a palace."

"Is there anything left in the treasury, or are you giving it all to the French?" she queried in a biting tone. It sounded like a vulgar assemblage of unprecedented proportions. What Louis with his aesthetic tastes would think of it all, she dreaded to think, but perhaps the rest of Paris would marvel. It sat ill with her that all this money and effort was being spent on soliciting a match of which she disapproved.

Thomas performed a suave bow. "Rest assured, madam, I have not spent beyond the king's means."

"How good to know," Alienor replied disdainfully, but to humor Harry, and satisfy her own curiosity, she donned her cloak and allowed herself to be taken to see the fruits of Thomas's toil.

The noise and the smell of the menagerie Becket had assembled was overwhelming. Alienor had to cover her nose with her wimple. There were packs of dogs as Henry had said. Black and tan slot hounds with lugubrious features, floppy ears, and low yodeling barks. Curly-coated otter hounds from the Welsh borders. Darting terriers, yappy and energetic, and great golden mastiffs as big and muscular as lions for guarding the numerous wagons being assembled to carry the masses of gifts and baggage. Harry's eyes were as wide as moons as he moved from area to area, cage to cage, exclaiming at everything he saw.

Henry took Alienor's arm. "It will all be worth it, I promise."

"They do say that the more you pay, the more it is worth."

He gave her a hard stare. "You have to look beyond the personal things to the long term. This alliance with France will give us the lands of the Vexin when Henry and Marguerite marry. Making peace with Louis will enable us to take an army down to Toulouse and restore it to the duchy of Aquitaine. This is the means to achieve that goal."

Alienor compressed her lips. She still thought all this show was about Thomas Becket's desire for lavish gestures and Henry's determination to outshine and overwhelm Louis with a flamboyant display of all the resources he possessed and Louis did not. It was no more than one dog pissing higher up the wall than a rival. Nevertheless, if they did gain the city of Toulouse, which she had long coveted for Aquitaine, then this circus might just be worth it.

"Trust me," Henry said and smiled at her, with the broad, straight grin that she knew never to trust. Taking Harry in his arms, he went to look at the stable of horses Becket was assembling for the parade.

Henry's brothers Hamelin and William were already there, evaluating the beasts with John FitzGilbert, one of Henry's marshals. FitzGilbert was an experienced horse master whom Becket had delegated to help collect animals of the color and quality required. Two of FitzGilbert's sons had accompanied their father. The oldest was an adolescent—a handsome, gray-eyed lad of serious mien. The other, a couple of years younger, sat confidently astride a glossy bay palfrey while Hamelin peered in the horse's mouth, assessing its age.

"A fine animal," Alienor said, joining the gathering. The men made their obeisances, and the brown-haired boy in the saddle bowed deeply from the waist.

"It's to pull the wagons," Hamelin told her. "The chancellor needs five sets of two, all matching, and all of high breeding."

"He doesn't ask the impossible, just miracles," John FitzGilbert remarked sardonically.

"You know the traders to contact and the places to seek, my lord marshal," Henry said. "I have faith in you. You kept my mother in fine horseflesh when she was fighting her cause here, and in more difficult circumstances."

FitzGilbert bowed. "I still have my uses, sire," he said with a mordant smile.

Alienor was only a little acquainted with John FitzGilbert. In former days, it had been one of his duties to provide horses for battle campaigns, but now his work was fiscal and mainly at the Westminster Exchequer. He was sometimes present at court, but part of the background rather than a prominent player. The left side of his face bore thickened burn scars and a ruined eye socket from a terrible time during the war for the crown between Empress Matilda and King Stephen, when he had been trapped inside a burning abbey. The right side revealed that before his injury he had been a handsome man, his features strong and clear-cut. He was in late middle age now, his fair hair silvered with gray, but he was still tall and straight with an air about him that commanded respect and caused women to study him with interest despite his scars. Henry thought him an old warhorse who needed to be kept on a tight rein, but he esteemed him nevertheless.

Harry pointed at the big bay. "I want to ride!"

"Hup!" said the boy on the horse and, leaning down, held out his hand. "You can sit with me, sire."

Hamelin lifted Harry, and FitzGilbert's son grasped him with cheerful confidence and tucked him securely in front of him on the saddle.

"William has two younger brothers at home," the marshal said, looking amused and a little exasperated.

The marshal's son took Harry for a ride around the yard at a steady walk, while the adults talked, then returned him, handing him down to his nurse before leaping lithely from the bay's back. He fed the horse a crust of dry bread from the palm of his hand and patted its neck. Alienor decided that she approved of the lad; he was mischievous and lively, but he did not overstep the bounds.

In a sudden flurry, the monkey that Harry had been holding earlier swarmed up William's body, snatched a second crust out of his hand, and made to abscond with its prize; however, the boy was faster and seized its chain, apprehending the thief even as it crammed the bread into its mouth.

"No," his father said, emphatically shaking his head. "Before you ask, we are not having one of those at home. God knows, you and your siblings are bad enough. Your mother would take it to her heart, and there would never be peace in my chamber again."

Looking a little crestfallen, William handed the monkey to one of the chancellor's attendants.

Alienor and her women gathered the children together and returned to the bower, leaving the men to their business. Becket's circus, she thought scornfully. She gazed at Harry skipping along at her side. It was too hard to imagine him being betrothed when he was still so small and his bride barely out of the cradle. There was many a slip between now and adulthood, but she would still have to come to terms with the notion of a French daughter-in-law, the seed of her former husband and half sister to the daughters she had borne to Louis, and time was not going to render that notion any more palatable to her.

❖❖❖

On the appointed day, Thomas Becket set out from the Tower of London with his flamboyant entourage, bound for Southampton harbor and the sixty-six ships waiting to transport it across the Narrow Sea.

The parade was twice the size of the one at Alienor and Henry's coronation. The latter had taken place in midwinter. This was late spring dressed in new green, a warm breeze lightly swirling cloaks and wimples. The carts rumbled and clattered along the thoroughfare, pulled by their matching bay horses and laden with all the largesse of the Angevin empire.

Alienor watched the cavalcade pass before her, and her mind strained at the seams, unable to absorb all this visual brilliance. There were hordes of attendants clad in rich fabrics and furs usually reserved for the nobility. Everywhere the twinkle of precious metals, jewels, and silks. Somehow Becket had trained the monkeys to sit on the backs of the packhorses like small jockeys at Smithfield horse fair.

"Dear God, he is emptying England," Alienor said to Henry. "We shall be wrung dry of every drop of color in the kingdom when he has gone."

Henry chuckled. "But it will be worth it," he said. "And really, you wouldn't want to keep half those things."

Alienor pursed her lips. She would certainly have liked some of the fabrics, and the jewelry, not to mention a couple of the high-stepping palfreys.

"It proves my sincerity to Louis. I would not go to this trouble unless I was serious about the proposed match. Once Thomas has made his impression, I shall follow in due course."

"You can hardly hope to match him," Alienor said tartly.

"I don't intend to…it is like eating a peacock at a feast. First you display all the brightly colored feathers to catch everyone's attention and admiration, but then you discard them and come to the meat of the matter. Both Thomas and I are consummate players."

*Yes, you are,* Alienor thought. *And perhaps too clever for your own good and everyone else's.*

❖❖❖

Several weeks later Alienor sat sewing in her chamber. Her pregnancy had advanced a stage, and it was difficult to find a comfortable position in which to sit; she had already adjusted the cushion at her back half a dozen times.

The news coming out of France was a triumph for Henry. Becket had been received with huge acclaim. The roadside had been lined with people exclaiming at the spectacle and shouting the praises of the king of England as gifts of money and food showered upon them with profligate largesse.

"Apparently King Louis's brother was very taken with his namesake," Henry told her with a grin. He was playing with Harry, who clung like a limpet to his legs while Henry made a game of trying to shake him off without using his hands. His heir was maintaining a fierce grip.

Despite herself, Alienor laughed as she imagined Robert, Count of Dreux, with a monkey on his shoulder. "I expect he will find ways to train it to his advantage."

"Thomas says he overheard one courtier remark how great the king of England must be if he sends his chancellor in such magnificence."

"If only they could see you now," she said with a raised eyebrow.

Henry chuckled. "Hah, being ridden by my own son! I yield, you win!" Grasping Harry's hands, he rode the boy on his leg for a moment, making him squeal, and then perched him on his shoulders. "The victor!" he shouted and trotted him across the chamber floor. "Thomas says Louis is keen for the match and the way is clear for full negotiation. Now we have to hammer out the entitlements, and for me that means the territories of the Vexin must be handed over as the bride's marriage portion when the wedding takes place." He somersaulted Harry down his body to the ground. Richard escaped his nurse and crawled to his father, determined to have his share of the attention. Henry scooped him up, and Richard seized on the cross and chain around his neck, attracted by the bright gold and gemstones. Henry pried him off. "I love this one dearly," he said, "but I will love him better when he's older." Taking further stock of his offspring, he studied two-year-old Matilda, who was playing quietly and seriously with a straw doll.

"I hope that look means you are not thinking of betrothing our daughter just yet," Alienor said archly.

"Not unless the right offer comes along," Henry replied with an irrepressible gleam. "I…" He turned as Alienor's chaplain entered the room, followed by another cleric, mud-splattered from hard travel and hollow-eyed with exhaustion. With a jolt of anxiety, Alienor recognized her brother-in-law's chaplain, Robert.

"Sire, there is grave news from Brittany." Robert knelt at Henry's feet. "It grieves me to tell you that the count of Nantes has passed away while suffering a quartan fever." He held out a sealed letter. "There was nothing we could do. I was at his bedside when his soul left this world. I extend my deepest sorrow and condolence."

Alienor summoned the nursemaids to remove the children. She was shocked by the news but not grief-stricken. She had always avoided Geoffrey if she could; indeed, she had been relieved when he had left court to become count of Nantes, but she had never expected this. His health had always been robust. "I am so sorry," she said.

Henry's mouth twisted. "I should have expected no less of him. I put him in a position useful to all where he will benefit our family, and he has to go and die. He caused me trouble to the end, God give respite to his soul." He gestured to the kneeling chaplain to his feet. "You came straight to me?"

"Yes, sire." The man's expression revealed bewilderment and shock at Henry's brusque response. He heaved himself upright, stiff-kneed and wincing.

"What is happening in Nantes now?"

"Sire, I do not know. I left immediately to come to you."

"You may go." Henry waved his hand. "But stay close lest I need to ask more of you later."

As the two chaplains departed, Henry began pacing like a caged lion. "You know what will happen," he said. "Duke Conan will take this opportunity to seize Nantes, and I cannot let that happen. I'll discuss the situation when I visit Louis and see what can be done." He made an impatient sound. "Why in God's name did the idiot have to drop dead when all was going so well? I could almost think he has done it to spite me."

"I suspect he would rather have lived," she said. The loudness of his protest was a shield: hard, shiny, and dense like a scar. "You are angry because he is not there to push against and the landscape has changed."

He gave her an irritated look that warned her she was treading dangerous ground. "I need more information. The danger of what will happen in the space left by his death is what concerns me. Grieving will not bring him back."

"No, but it might help you to go forward."

"You prate women's nonsense," he snapped. "My grief is that he no longer holds the reins in Brittany. Let us hope that messengers with more than condolence are on their way."

Alienor quashed her irritation and tried again. "Your mother will have to be told."

Henry braced his shoulders as if settling a burden. "I'll visit her on my way to France."

"It is hard for a mother to lose a child whatever their age, and even without the years of contact," Alienor said softly. "They have still been flesh of your flesh, and you have carried them within your body for nine months." She paused to balance herself as she thought of Will, such a short time in the world. Henry would not countenance a mention of that particular loss. She came and put her hand on his arm. "Even if this is no great grief to you, I am sorry all the same."

He said nothing, but after a moment, he looked down at her hand and covered it with his own. And then he cleared his throat and withdrew, muttering that he had matters to attend to in the wake of the news.

Alienor called for her scribe, let out a deep sigh, and began to compose a letter of condolence to her mother-in-law.

## 13

*H*EAVY RAIN OVER THE PAST TWO DAYS HAD MADE THICK sludge of the roads. Although the weather was not cold enough to turn the rain to snow, the air was bitter, and even wrapped in her fur-lined cloak Alienor was chilled to the bone. She and her entourage were slogging their way through the mud toward the royal palace at Sarum on its lofty hill overlooking the windswept Wiltshire Downs. The vista was gray and forbidding with needles of rain stabbing into their faces, forcing them to squint at the rutted path through half-closed eyes.

Alienor's most recent offspring, two-month-old Geoffrey, traveled in a packhorse pannier that was cozily stuffed with blankets and fleeces. Cheeks as rosy as apples, he gazed around with interest, his little face sheltered by an overhanging section of waxed canvas. This third son to secure the succession was named for his paternal grandfather, Geoffrey le Bel, Count of Anjou. He was a quiet baby and although he had only been in the world since September, Alienor had already decided he was going to be a watchful character, a thinker and considerer.

Messengers had reached her from Normandy with news that Henry's business in France was proving satisfactory. He and Louis had agreed on a formal betrothal between Harry and the infant Princess Marguerite. Louis would yield the territory of the Vexin together with three strategic fortresses on the day that the young couple married, and in the meantime those castles were to be held in trust by the Templars.

Thinking on the matter as she rode, Alienor screwed up her face against more than just the rain. Louis had insisted as part of the terms that she was not to have any part in Marguerite's upbringing, and had stipulated the child must be raised elsewhere. Alienor wondered what pernicious influence Louis believed she was going to exert on the girl should she be left in her hands. Teach her that men were perfidious liars who would betray you at the drop of a wimple pin? Henry had agreed to the terms without protest, but Alienor was not surprised. No matter. She had Harry, Richard, and now Geoffrey to raise, and for the moment they were hers to influence. If she did her job well, then the ties would remain strong. When Harry and Marguerite did marry, Louis would be unable to keep her from the girl, and she could exert her influence as a mother-in-law.

The messengers also brought news that Henry had settled the situation in Brittany. Duke Conan had claimed Nantes on Geoffrey's death but had yielded when faced by Henry's army, sanctioned with French approval. An agreement had been reached whereby Conan swore fealty to Henry and for the moment kept his gains.

Judging from the letters Alienor received, Henry and Louis had become warmly cordial during the negotiations, even to the point of visiting the abbey of Mont Saint-Michel and spending the night in prayer together. Diplomatic relations were well and good, and peace between England and France was essential for longer-term policies, but Alienor was deeply suspicious of this accord between Henry and her former husband. It might all be a ruse on Henry's part, but she could not help feeling that she was being excluded and that it was a deliberate ploy by both men.

The white walls and towers of Salisbury drew closer through the murk, and the smell of smoke from domestic fires drifted toward the royal party. Alienor thanked God that they would soon be warm and dry. The scenery for miles had been dank grass, sheep and rain, and she had begun to feel that she was coming to somewhere at the ends of the earth.

The wind blew at a fierce slant as they took the slope to the fortified palace. On the higher ground, the rain was flecked with snow. The baby, who had been as good as gold until now, began to grizzle in his pannier, and she could hear Richard whining too and Hodierna trying to soothe him. She shivered. From somewhere she thought she heard the words *This is a godforsaken place.* But how could that be, when it was white and shining in the November murk, and she could hear the bells from the cathedral ringing the hour of nones?

They clattered through the gateway and into the courtyard where attendants waited to take her horse and escort her to the royal apartments. A glowing fire cheered the hearth and cast warmth into the room. On a table covered with clean white napery, jugs of hot, spiced wine and bowls of steaming meat broth with bread sops stood ready to nourish the travelers. Geoffrey's wet nurse, Edith, settled herself on a bench to suckle him, and Hodierna did the same with Richard, who barely needed the sustenance now but still took comfort.

Wrapped in furs, drinking a cup of the spiced wine, Alienor held her hands out to the fire and soaked its warmth into her being. Various documents awaited her attention on a side trestle, but she would look at them later when she had recuperated. The bolts of cloth she had sent for from Winchester had arrived, ready to be made into winter gowns for the Christmas court at Cherbourg. There was red wool, thick and heavy, woven damask from Italy, and white linen of Cambrai for chemises. Alienor ran her fingers over the fabrics, taking pleasure in their rich color and textures. If nothing else, these things she could have for the click of her fingers and a few words. She had wealth. She had people to do her bidding and see to her every comfort.

A command brought her musicians into the chamber to play and sing for her pleasure. The smell of incense rose from small braziers on wafts of silver smoke and the heat from the fire made her fingers tingle. Her life was like this fortress on top of its isolated, windy hill. One reality inside and another without. The wind howling against the shutters was a desolate sound, and she was out on the margins, far, far from Aquitaine.

❖ ❖ ❖

At another fire, in Rouen, Henry stretched out his legs toward the embers and eyed the king of France. Louis intrigued him. On the surface he seemed mild-mannered and easily dominated; however, there was another side to him that Henry couldn't quite grasp: a thin, razor-sharp sliver of steel hidden at his core. They had been sharing a flagon and company over a chess set, and each had won a game. A third one had not been played by mutual and diplomatic consent. They had been discussing women, and the subject had finally and convolutedly come around to Alienor, who had been wed to Louis for fifteen years until their marriage had been annulled. In all that time she had only borne Louis two daughters, whereas in six years, she had already given Henry four boys and a girl. It was a subject neither man mentioned, but the awareness charged the atmosphere between them.

"Alienor always had areas that she liked to keep to herself." Louis steepled his long, pale hands beneath his chin. "She had little liaisons and enclaves with others at court, and there were often small things she should have told me but which—in the way women do, whispering to one another in corners—she kept to herself. Things she did not share with me when she should have done." Louis tapped the side of his goblet. "It is in her nature to be wayward, and because of that, I could never trust her."

Henry said nothing. He had noticed the things that Louis mentioned, but he was not going to open himself up and agree: that would be giving knowledge and power to a man who, for all their camaraderie, was his rival. Besides, Louis was probably exaggerating in the interests of sowing discord. Henry would do the same if the situation had been reversed. He knew how to handle Alienor; he was not a fool in that department like Louis. "I think we understand each other," he said.

Louis nodded. "Then let it rest," he said with a satisfied glint in his eyes. "I have given you a word to the wise."

❖❖❖

In late December, the Angevin court gathered for the Christmas feast at Cherbourg. It had snowed on the eve of the solstice and the land wore colors of ermine and silver. The sky had cleared to a pure, winter blue, but it was bitterly cold and everything had a sharp, crystalline glitter. The water had frozen in the butts, icicle daggers hung from eaves and gutters, and straw and ashes had been thrown down to grit pathways and thoroughfares. Red-cheeked children made slides and held snowball fights, and the older ones strapped the shin bones of oxen to their feet and skated on the frozen fish pond. The elderly felt their way gingerly, walking sticks in either hand, and prayed for a thaw.

Henry was delighted when Alienor arrived from England two days before the Christmas feast, and was mightily pleased with his new son. "What a fine little man." Henry tickled him under the chin and smiled at Alienor. "You have done well, madam. Another boy for our dynasty."

She inclined her head, accepting the compliment graciously in public. Frozen from the long journey, all she wanted was a warm room and sustenance. But the courtesies and rituals had to be observed.

Henry turned next to Harry, who was also swathed in furs and red-lipped with the cold. "And here's our young bridegroom!" He patted Harry's head. "Let's see how much you've grown. Hah! As tall as my thigh now!"

Harry puffed out his chest. Alienor set her lips at the mention of the marriage between Harry and Louis's daughter.

Henry picked up Matilda, kissed her, and did the same to Richard, who was wriggling in Hodierna's arms. Then he turned again to Alienor. "I know you must be cold and tired," he said. "I am not ignorant of your needs, even though you think I am. I have had food brought to your chamber and the room prepared."

Alienor eyed him with surprise and almost asked what he

wanted but then gave him the benefit of the doubt. She had not seen him for almost a year, and if he was prepared to make an effort, then so should she. "Thank you." She gave him a genuine smile, which he reciprocated.

The chamber was indeed welcoming. The shutters were closed with a thick curtain drawn across them and the room flickered with warm golden light from fire and candle. The sensual perfume of the lamp oil she loved filled the atmosphere. She noticed two new books on top of a chest and glanced at Henry before going to study them. One had a cover bound with ivory panels set with small gemstones.

"I thought you might want something to read," he said. "I enjoyed the Geoffrey of Monmouth, and the other is a book of devotional songs in the *lenga romana*. You will have to let me know what you think."

She was torn between suspicion and delight. Perhaps this was his way of getting around her after all her protests over this marriage alliance with France. If so, it wouldn't work, but at least she could take pleasure in the fruits of his efforts. Knowing Henry, he probably had some scheme afoot.

Food and drink had been set out before the fire. There was bread, a variety of cheeses, small date and nut pastries dusted with sugar, curd tarts, and broth with bread for the children.

Henry sat down to dine with her, and while to Alienor it was a golden moment of domestic harmony snatched from the troublesome concerns of ruling an empire, it was unsettling too, because it was so different from Henry's usual way. Getting him to sit down was normally a mammoth task in itself.

Eventually, replete and warm, she dozed before the hearth, and sipped sweetened, spiced wine while Henry told the children a story about a king named Wenceslas and about the power and piety of ancient kings. Matilda climbed into his lap and curled up like a small dog, her fists furled beneath her chin. Smiling, Henry stroked the curve of her spine and looked at Alienor across the firelight.

The nurses eventually took the children away to bed, leaving their parents alone. Alienor was tired from the journey but sleepily receptive when Henry joined her on the bench and folded her in his arms. "Am I forgiven?" He nuzzled her throat.

She turned to him and felt his solidity and strength. "Why should I ever forgive you for going behind my back and betrothing my son to my former husband's daughter?" she demanded.

Henry nipped her earlobe and cupped a hand over her hipbone. "What if I were to say that by next Christmastide I would give you Toulouse? Would you forgive me then?"

The word "Toulouse" was like being burned by a stray spark, and she straightened in his arms, suddenly alert. Toulouse had belonged to Alienor's ancestors but had been lost during disputes in her grandmother's time, and she had always nurtured hopes of recovering it for Aquitaine.

"Yes," he said with a broad grin. "Since I have a peace accord with Louis, I can turn to the matter of regaining Toulouse and setting it as a jewel in our regalia. I'm summoning a muster on midsummer's day. Thomas has the details in hand. It will be the greatest army gathered since the one Louis took to Antioch when I was still a youth."

Alienor shivered at his words. She had been a part of that muster with all its fierceness, all its vainglory, and eventual bitter defeat. She had learned to hate her first husband on that journey. "Let us hope you have better success than he did."

"Ah, do not spoil it," Henry protested. "You are looking my gift horse in the mouth. And you have still not answered my question."

Alienor curled her arms around his neck and parted her lips close to his. "I would forgive you almost anything if you won Toulouse," she said into his breath.

"'Almost'?" He lifted her in his arms and carried her to the bed.

"I told you," she said. "Never take me for granted, Henry, and do not promise me Toulouse if you are not going to make good on that promise."

"Trust me," he replied, pulling off his tunic and shirt, revealing a muscular torso, marked with a pectoral cross of auburn hair descending to a thick bush at his groin. "I shall not let you down."

Alienor was eager to lie with him and enjoy the fierce strength of his lovemaking. It had been such a long time, and her own appetite was strong, but even as she responded to him with the eagerness of lust, she did not trust him an inch.

# 14

POITIERS, MIDSUMMER 1159

*E*ARLY-MORNING LIGHT STREAMED THROUGH THE OPEN SHUTTERS and reached the foot of the bed, brightening a section of the embroidered linen coverlet to dazzling white. Turning over, Henry kissed Alienor's throat and ran his hand over her bare hip and flank. Sleepily awake, she looked at him. His freckled pale skin had darkened to gold on face and hands where it had been exposed to the sun, a testament to the amount of time spent in the saddle, but the rest of him was the color of new milk. Her hair cascaded over his arm in a tawny shimmer. Of late she had discovered the occasional wiry strand of silver among the gold and was ruthless in plucking them out, preserving the perfection of sheeted gold.

Henry cupped her breast and kissed her mouth, running his tongue around her lips, but rather than foreplay, it was a taste before withdrawing, and he sat up with a sigh. "As much as I want to linger here with you, I have a city to claim in your name, and an army awaiting my command. I have no doubt my chancellor will be pacing the floor, fit to wear out his shoe leather by now." He gave a grunt of amusement. "The notion of being a soldier seems to have captured Thomas's imagination."

Alienor yawned and stretched. "He is like you—in some ways."

"Hah! What makes you say that?"

"He enjoys power. He likes to be in control and have authority over others."

"He has no authority over me," Henry said sharply. "He is my chancellor, and he does as he is bidden. I delegate to him, but I am the king, and the word is mine."

She realized that she had touched a sore edge. "Thomas thinks of himself as a king by proxy," she replied. "He bolsters his importance through extravagant spending and demonstrations of magnificence. He throws lavish feasts; even his ordinary tunics are trimmed with silk. All the things he feels you should do as king. He wants to make a gilded cover to throw over his humble beginnings so that people will not see them. But of course they do, because he draws attention to them."

"But that is not like me," Henry argued. Leaving the bed, he donned his braies and fastened the belt. "I care nothing for embellishment. I left my crown on the altar at Worcester Cathedral because I was sick of having to bear the weight of the thing four times a year. By all means let Thomas have his silk and wear it in my name, because it means I do not have to bother. If it bolsters his sense of importance, what does it matter?" He put his hands to his hips. "I am still the king whether I stand here in my braies, or in robes of ermine and silk. And he is still my servant."

Alienor gathered her hair in her hands and swept it over her shoulder. "Yes, but often Becket's ideas are the coin on which you strike your hammer."

"But I choose whether to strike or not." Henry kissed her again before leaving the room, but his gaze was thoughtful.

❖❖❖

The army assembling to advance on Toulouse was almost the size of a crusading force. Thomas Becket had seven hundred knights under his command and had cast off his cleric's robes in favor of a mail shirt, and a fine sword stood proud from the red leather grip of an ornate scabbard slung at his left hip. Fired with the same vigor he had brought to organizing the betrothal parade in Paris last year, he had levied taxes on England and Normandy to pay for the war, to the tune of nine thousand pounds.

Despite her words of caution to Henry, Alienor was delighted at the chancellor's achievement. This great gathering of resources made her heart sing with fierce pride and anticipation. Toulouse must fall to such an undertaking, and perhaps when she finally sat in state in the great hall of the Château Narbonnais as her ancestors had once done, and dispensed justice as Lady of Toulouse, she would know that everything had been worth it, and the world set to rights.

❖❖❖

In another chamber within the palace complex, Isabel de Warenne was bidding farewell to her husband as he prepared to ride out. The army bent on seizing Toulouse was leaving Poitiers in full martial array for the benefit of the townspeople and their duchess. Isabel had seldom seen William in full armor, which he usually reserved for the battle camp far from home, and it gave her a frisson of fear and pride to see him clad in his hauberk with his surcoat of checkered blue-and-yellow silk, his sword belt latched at his waist. He had recently lain with her, and she was praying that this time there would be a child.

"You look very fine," she said and touched his arm where warm flesh was now covered by hard steel rivets.

He gave her a drawn, preoccupied smile. "I am going to swelter in all this. I hope we don't have to ride too far before we stop to take it off. We haven't even set out and all I can think is that I'll be glad when this campaign is over."

She gave a small shudder. "I will be too."

"Yes." He looked down, his lashes thick and dark. Her heart turned over. She wanted to smooth the frown from his brows and make everything all right.

"I shall miss you," she said. "Take care of yourself until I join you in Toulouse."

He eased the neckband of his mail coif with a forefinger. "I dreamed of you last night," he said. "I knew you were there; I could feel you, and smell your skin, yet I couldn't see you or find you. And then I woke up and you were leaning over me with your hair tickling my cheek."

"I am here," she soothed. "I will always be here."

He took her in his arms and kissed her again, hard, almost desperately. When he released her, she staggered, moved and unsettled by his vehemence. While she was still regaining her balance, he left her, pausing at the door for a final look over his shoulder before he ran down the stairs to the courtyard.

Isabel went to the window arch, the imprint of his kiss still damp on her lips, and her stomach queasy. She hated the time of parting. She could remember her father setting out to join King Louis on the road to the Holy Land, and he had not returned. Indeed, he did not have a grave. His bones lay bleaching somewhere on the high slopes of a mountain in Anatolia where he had been slain by Turks and left to rot. He too had worn his armor as he bade farewell and marched out with that single last glance over his shoulder. Men and their wars. How she hated them.

❖❖❖

Henry set out for Toulouse in brave array at the head of a long streamer of armored knights, banners rippling on spears in the summer morning light. The townsfolk had lined the road to witness the spectacle and threw flowers, or leaned out from their balconies and spinning galleries to cheer their support. Others ran out with gifts of food for the soldiers: bread, wheels of cheese, chunks of smoked sausage. A sunburst of pride lodged in Alienor's heart as she watched Henry on his prancing white stallion, every inch the conquering hero before he had even left the walls of Poitiers behind.

Harry stood at her side wearing a coronet on his brow, his face shining at the sight of such martial pageantry. Hodierna held the infant Richard on high to watch his father ride out, and Richard waved his arms and shouted loudly.

"When you see your papa again, Toulouse will be ours," Alienor told her sons.

"When will that be?" Harry wanted to know.

"Soon, my love," Alienor said, drawing a deep breath and feeling equal amounts of exultation and anxiety. "Very soon."

❖❖❖

In the late afternoon, the summer day was airless and laden with heat. Flickers of dry lightning turned the clouds a strange shade of milky purple. Thunder had been rumbling since noon, but still there was no respite of rain. Henry's army was busy making camp within sight of the walls of Toulouse, and the city too was outlined in eerie flashes of light.

Hamelin felt the pressure of the thunderstorm as a thick headache, clogging his skull. It had been a long, hot day in the saddle and his shirt and tunic were sodden with sweat. Mosquitoes whined around his moist skin, and he batted at them with the back of his hand.

Henry stood gazing at the city with his legs apart and his hands clasped at his belt. The expression on his sunburned face was fixed and determined. At his side, Becket eyed the walls with the sharp gaze of a hawk intent on its prey.

Although there had been successes along the way, nothing had gone quite to plan. The hope that Raymond of Toulouse would be intimidated by the size and strength of the army riding against him and surrender had not been realized. Instead, he had dug in his heels and ignored all threats, demands, and gestures of diplomacy. Henry had continued to pressure him. Cahors had been pillaged and burned as a warning, but Raymond had just reinforced his walls and stocked his larders.

Louis had offered to mediate, but Henry had brushed that aside, knowing all Louis wanted to do was prevent the assault on Toulouse. Louis's sister Constance was Raymond's wife, and Louis had a vested interest. However, Louis himself had once tried to seize Toulouse twenty years ago when married to Alienor, and thus was caught in a moral cleft stick.

"Well, my lords," Henry said. "Here is the nut to be cracked."

Grimacing, Hamelin rubbed the back of his neck with a water-soaked cloth. The city supplied itself from the river, and the span of its walls meant it would be a massive undertaking to surround it. Even given the numbers they had, their time was limited. Despite all the gathering of provisions and the organization that had gone into preparing this campaign, Henry had only budgeted to pay his mercenaries for thirteen weeks. When that money was gone, so was the campaign.

"It can b-be done," Becket said, grim-faced with determination. "We came here hoping that Count Raymond would negotiate, b-but with the expectation that we would have to fight."

Hamelin glanced at him. All the organization had been Becket's, and his reputation was staked on the success of the undertaking. Henry demanded miracles and thus far Becket had performed them. But Hamelin had his doubts about Becket's ability to achieve this particular one. His stammer was prominent today and that was not a good sign.

"I shall give Raymond of Toulouse my ultimatum tomorrow," Henry said. "And unless he replies by noon, he will suffer the consequences." He turned aside to give orders to one of his engineers about the siege machines. Already they were being assembled from the component pieces in the supply carts. "I want them ready for Raymond to see when he rises in the morning."

The sky by now had bruised to the color of charcoal, and the dry lightning was like a hammer striking an anvil. A hot wind swept across the camp and blew the sides of the tents like bellows. Henry's adjutants had managed, with much effort and extra tent pegs, to raise and secure the royal pavilion, a great circular affair of red-and-gold canvas with enough room for Henry's bed and accoutrements.

"Come," Henry said brusquely, "we have a campaign to plan." He sent squires and heralds to summon the other lords of his advisory circle and entered the tent. From one of the chests that had recently been carried in, he removed a rolled-up plan of Toulouse and spread it on the table, weighing it down with a cup, a knife, and a large loaf of bread. Lamps had been lit because it was so dark, and the flames ghosted with each swirl of breeze from the tent flaps. Hamelin went to pour himself wine from the flagon standing on the chest. It was raw, fresh from the vineyard, but he gulped it down anyway.

One of Henry's scouts dismounted outside the tent in a lathered flurry, crying aloud that there was news.

"Sire." Panting with exertion, the man knelt and bowed his head.

"What is it?" Henry demanded. "Quickly, tell me."

"It is Toulouse, sire," he gasped. "The king of France has arrived and is preparing to defend the city against you."

"What?" A look of utter astonishment crossed Henry's face. "How can that be?"

"Sire, it is true, I swear it. One of our spies in the city managed to get a message to me. Even now Louis's banners are being raised on the battlements of the Château Narbonnais."

"By the bleeding hands of Christ, I do not believe this!" Henry shouldered out of the tent to stare through the purple gloom at the city walls, the lightning dancing over the crenellations.

"The whoreson," he spat as Hamelin joined him. "The poisonous, godforsaken, toad-eating whoreson. All the time he was pretending to mediate he was planning this…this treachery!"

Hamelin was not surprised. Louis was often mistaken for a pious, mild-mannered weakling who would rather back down than stand firm in a crisis, but that was far from the truth. Louis was the kind to survive through devious stratagems while biding his time. A man who would give ground, stepping back until his heels were on the edge of the battlefield, but who would never leave it, waiting his moment to lunge. A man who lost the fights but won the wars—the most dangerous kind of all.

Becket joined Henry too. "We should still lay siege to the city, sire," he said.

Henry stared at him. "Have you lost your wits?"

Becket looked bemused. "No, sire. We have this great army at our command and the full impetus to take Toulouse. If we stumble now, the enterprise will all have been in vain."

"Who is this 'we,' Thomas?" Henry sneered. "When last I looked, I was the king of England and you were my chancellor—my servant. I was not aware of any change in our circumstances."

Becket flushed but stood his ground. "Sire, I apologize if I offended. I thought everyone in this enterprise had the same goals." His gaze widened to include Hamelin. "Surely it is a waste to withdraw just because the king of France has taken up residence in the city."

Hamelin said nothing and buried his face in his cup. Even if Becket could not see it, he certainly could and was not about to get himself mauled in the lion's den.

Henry flashed Becket an angry glare. "I thought you had knowledge of the law, or are you being deliberately blind, Thomas? It is an act of treason for a vassal to attack his overlord, and that is precisely what I would be doing if I launched an assault on those walls now. It would set a dangerous precedent. Any noble with a grievance against me would see it as sanction to take up arms and claim he was only following my example."

"B-but you have fought Louis of France often before," Becket protested, looking perplexed.

"I have never been the first to draw sword. I have always defended myself vigorously against Louis and will continue to do so. What I will not do is attack my liege lord and risk the long-term consequences...and Louis knows that very well." Henry turned his glare from Becket to the lightning-battered walls of Toulouse.

"But if you attacked, Louis would not want to be your prisoner," Becket argued. "That would be a terrible humiliation for him. He would flee Toulouse rather than face capture, and we could always turn a blind eye and let him go if it looked as if he was going to be caught."

"And why would he do that when he is causing the most damage by staying where he is?" Henry curled his lip. "He knows what he is doing. He knows very well indeed."

"Perhaps if we drew him out from Toulouse?" Hamelin suggested.

Henry shook his head. "He would not take the bait. I wouldn't in his position. God's body, I should have seen this coming, or one of us should!" He turned a burning look on Becket.

Hamelin could sense the heat of Henry's rage and frustration flaring outward from his body. He was so seldom outwitted that he had no mechanism for coping with failure other than lashing out. That it was Louis who had done the outwitting was even more humiliating.

"Leave the siege camp assembled for now," Henry said brusquely. "We'll lay the countryside waste and take the castles where we can. Even if we do not draw Louis off, we'll make him and his brother-in-law pay dearly."

❖ ❖ ❖

Lightning flickered throughout the night but still without rain. An hour before dawn the sky splintered with dazzling white veins of light, one of which struck from heaven to earth and scorched the ground in front of the English tents, killing three sentries where they stood, and to the encamped men it was a sign of God's wrath, and a portent of things to come.

# 15

## POITIERS, SEPTEMBER 1159

*I*N POITIERS ALIENOR WAS ENJOYING THE GOLDEN WEATHER OF early autumn, mellow and fine. The sky was as blue as the coat on a shield, and all the colors were set and solid, as if painted in a church. Poitiers was beautiful at all times of the year, but this was one of Alienor's favorite seasons, with the last drops of the summer nuanced by the faintest melancholy of autumn.

There had been no recent news from the battle campaign, and she was waiting on tenterhooks. Reports received had been of the journey there, and the successful taking of Cahors, but information concerning the main objective had not been forthcoming.

This morning she had ridden her palfrey for exercise, imagining how it would feel to parade in triumph through the streets of Toulouse, her inheritance restored. She wanted this so much that it hurt like deep hunger, but there was nothing she could do to influence the outcome except pray.

Her sons were in the stable yard having their riding lesson and she was present to watch, encourage, and give advice. Harry's brown pony was sturdy and placid. Richard's shaggy piebald had short legs, and the toddler was being closely watched by an attendant, ready to grab him if he fell. Richard beamed like the sun and although he was only two, sat as straight as an arrow. "See me, Mama, see me!" he shouted.

The sight of him crowing like a little rooster, his ruddy golden hair floating in the breeze, gladdened her heart and made her laugh. "Ah," she said, "and everyone will indeed see you, my love, because one day you will be count of Toulouse and duke of Aquitaine!"

"And I will be king!" Harry shouted, not to be outdone.

"Yes, my heart," she said. "You will indeed."

The groom led Harry's brown pony by a halter rope, but Harry held the reins himself. Alienor took charge of Richard, walking his pony at a gentle plod, one arm ready to catch him. Richard sat his mount like a warrior, possessing a natural sense of balance that filled her heart with pride to see it in one so young. She loved Harry dearly, but her affinity with Richard was closer. He was her heir and she recognized her male ancestors in him, men whose legacy lived on in this bright, vibrant child.

A messenger arrived on a blowing horse as the children were being led back into the yard, Richard making a fuss because he wanted to stay out and ride some more. "Another time, my fierce little falcon," Alienor said and saw him into the care of Hodierna, who then had to deal with the ensuing tantrum.

Alienor summoned the man to her side. Usually she would have waited for the master of her writing office or her chamberlain to present her with the letters, but this was quicker, and she was impatient. The packet bore Henry's military seal of a knight on horseback, sword brandished. Queasy with anticipation, she broke open the letter and unfolded it. As she read, her hand went to her mouth.

Isabel was immediately at her side. "Is there something wrong, madam?"

Alienor looked at Isabel through a blur of tears. "Henry has withdrawn from Toulouse because Louis has gone there to defend it, and he refuses to attack his overlord." Her expression contorted with anger and frustration. "In other words, his great enterprise has failed and he has been outwitted by Louis. The worm has turned into a snake and Henry will not pin him by the neck." She raised her head to the sky. "All my life I have wanted to add

Toulouse to my dominions. All my life I have wanted to prove to my ancestors, my father and my grandmother, that I could do this for them and restore what was stolen. Louis could not take it when I was wed to him. He came prancing back from his campaign claiming victory when all he had was a handful of dust and a promise of homage that meant nothing. Now Henry has done even less, and with Louis resisting him. Dear God, I would laugh if I did not feel so betrayed."

"Is it certain Toulouse is lost?" Isabel asked tentatively.

Alienor crumpled the letter in her fist, feeling the sharp edges of the parchment buckle against her palm. "Henry would not have written this unless forced. He knew what it meant to me that he should be victorious. He knows he has let me down. All that is left to him now are petty deeds of burning and pillage while the great prize remains untaken and he is made to look a vainglorious fool." She wiped her cuff across her eyes. "There is no point waiting here for a victory parade now, is there?"

"But will not the king return to Poitiers?"

"No." Alienor shook her head. "It would be too humiliating. He will want to bury this deep—but it will always lie on the surface for me."

❖❖❖

The weather finally broke and the rain came in sheets, drenching the land until it was waterlogged. Henry had struck camp and was riding north in haste, burning and looting as he went. Louis had remained behind the walls of Toulouse, but his messengers had been busy, and even as Henry scorched the land around Toulouse, Louis's brothers had unleashed French troops on Normandy to do their worst. Caught in a cleft stick, Henry had had to abandon Toulouse and ride to deal with the situation. He had left Becket in command of the town of Cahors but, in a display of pique, had deprived him of men and the coin to pay them, blaming him for the failure of the campaign.

On the third evening of their journey, as the army halted to make camp at Montmorillon, Hamelin by chance drew rein beside

William de Boulogne. The young man was clinging to his saddle and shivering. Hamelin could not tell if it was sweat or rain on his face, but his teeth were chattering so hard that the motion of his jaw was a blur.

"You should have a physician attend you," Hamelin said. Bloody fluxes and quartan fevers were rife among the men, another reason Henry had chosen to withdraw. If they had stayed longer in the poisoned air of the camp, there would have been an epidemic.

William de Boulogne looked at him with fever-glazed eyes. "I intend to," he croaked. "Jesu, my head feels as if a thousand demons are beating drums inside it."

Hamelin made sure the young earl's men found a decent lodging in the town, and sent him Henry's own physician to tend him.

In the morning when Hamelin visited him to see how he fared, William's condition had worsened. His fever still burned like a furnace and he was fighting for breath. His chaplain had confessed him and the physician was dour and purse-lipped. "I can do no more for him," he said. "He is in God's hands. If his fever breaks he will live." He did not state the alternative, but it was there in his eyes, clear and certain.

Hamelin stood at the bedside. William's dark lashes flickered and he turned his head toward Hamelin, showing him the face of death with waxen flesh and woad-blue shadows in his eye sockets.

"I shall pray for you," Hamelin said, feeling pity and shock in equal measure. How swiftly the affliction had come upon him, and how fragile life was.

"When I am dead…make sure…the countess…receives this…" William raised a trembling hand and indicated a sapphire ring glowing on his middle finger.

"I do so swear." Hamelin crossed himself. "But you may yet live and give it to her yourself."

William's face contorted. "Yes…" he said, and tears slid from his eye corners. "I may."

❖❖❖

Hamelin found Henry about to mount his horse, cloak thrown back, foot in stirrup. Their youngest brother Will was with him, holding the stallion's bridle.

"I've just come from William de Boulogne," Hamelin said.

"How is he? Well enough to travel?" Henry asked.

Hamelin shook his head. "He is mortally sick. The fever will not relent."

"Is that so?" Will said with interest rather than concern.

"Unless God sees fit to spare him," Hamelin replied a trifle brusquely. He had little time for his youngest half brother, and the feeling was mutual.

"That is a great pity." Henry signed his breast, at least paying lip service. "I shall pray for him."

Hamelin knew that for Henry, it would be no tragedy if William de Boulogne did die, because it meant that Stephen's line in direct male tail would fail, and the demise would open all sorts of interesting possibilities when it came to the inheritance of his lands.

❖❖❖

Alienor too was on the road, journeying north from Poitiers, and had stopped for the night at Tours en route to Normandy. She was playing chess with Isabel and drinking a last cup of wine when Bernard, one of her chamberlains, announced that a monk had arrived with news from Henry's army.

"Admit him." Alienor was immediately on edge because monks were often the harbingers of tragic news. Dear God, for all that she was angry with Henry, she could not begin to envision a world without him in it.

The monk that Bernard ushered into her presence was a Benedictine, his habit and cloak mud-splattered and travel-stained. He had bushy silver eyebrows and deep-set dark eyes.

"You have news?" Alienor forestalled him as he started to kneel.

He bowed and produced a sealed parchment from a satchel slung across his body. "Madam, the king bids me say that he will see you at the Christmas feast in Falaise—this is a letter from him." He withdrew a second packet, together with a sapphire ring looped through a coil of blue ribbon. "It also grieves me to say that I bring sorrowful news for the Countess de Warenne."

Alienor turned to Isabel, who had been standing ready to support her but was now staring at the messenger and the object like a deer that had just been shot by a hunter's arrow. "No." She shook her head. "No."

Alienor turned and swiftly took her arm. "You had better sit down," she said.

Isabel thrust her off. "I do not want to know," she said in a voice brittle with panic. "Whatever you are going to say it is not true."

"Isabel…"

"No!" she cried and, pushing away from hands held out in concern, stumbled from the room.

"What happened? Tell me," Alienor said peremptorily.

The priest bowed his head. "It grieves me to tell you that the earl, William of Boulogne, died at the pilgrim hospital of Montmorillon of a virulent fever," he said. "The king had his own physician to tend him but to no avail. The ring is sent as proof."

Alienor took the item from him, so light to weigh so much. The sapphire cabochon gleamed like an oval of midnight sky. "Stay here," she said. "Warm yourself by the fire and take a cup of wine. I will need to speak to you later, and the countess may wish to talk to you when she has recovered from the shock."

Alienor went in search of Isabel and found her prostrate before the altar in the castle chapel. She had torn off her wimple and her beautiful brunette hair was spread around in a thick, disordered fan.

"Please God, please God, let it not be true, I beg you, let him not be dead!" she entreated, her body riven with shudders and her breath coming in harsh gasps.

Alienor knelt at her side and tried to embrace her. "Isabel," she said, "come now."

"I don't want to hear, I don't want to hear!" She thrashed in Alienor's grip. "It's not true. I won't let it be true!"

Alienor tightened her hold. "Hush, hush," she said. "Let it be." She remembered the day she had been told that her father had died on a pilgrimage to the shrine of Saint James at Compostela. The utter devastation had scooped out a hollow inside her as if dug with a jagged spoon. She had had to stand firm because she was his heir, the new duchess of Aquitaine, and she had a little sister to protect. In this moment, Isabel reminded her of Petronella, and it pierced her heart. "There is no door you can close against it and nowhere to run," she said. "Isabel, you must face it now, because if you do not, it will fester and bring you down."

"He can't be gone. He can't be!" Isabel sobbed.

"I know you do not want to believe it. I do not know your pain, but I remember my own when people who were everything to me left this world." Taking Isabel's hand, Alienor placed the ring in it.

Isabel stared at it, then gasped and doubled over with a howl, clutching her belly, crying out. Alienor rocked and soothed her while Isabel's grief rose to the vaulted ceiling, ringing out torment in place of praise. A priest came to investigate, and Alienor sent him in haste to fetch her chaplain and her maids.

Together they returned Isabel to the chamber. She was trembling and sobbing so much that she could barely walk, and she was bleeding. The shock had brought on her flux, which was several weeks late. It was far too early to know if this was a miscarriage, but the bleeding was heavy, and the knowledge that she might be losing her husband's child sent Isabel into fresh paroxysms of weeping.

The women cleaned her up and put soft rags between her thighs. Marchisa made her a hot tisane, holding the cup to Isabel's lips, coaxing her to take a few sips. Isabel refused to lie on the bed but huddled on a bench before the fire, shivering. "I cannot rest," she said in a ragged voice. "His soul still needs me even if his body does not. I want to know how he died, and then I must hold a vigil of prayers for him. That is my duty as his wife and his widow."

Alienor did not try to dissuade her from her purpose, but she was worried. Isabel had become a very dear friend. Running alongside her personal concern was the political awareness that Isabel had suddenly become a fine and eligible marriage prize. She was young, wealthy, and well connected. She had yet to bear a child. There was a chance she might be barren, but she was still of an age to make it worth the risk. Henry would want to match her with someone who suited his needs, but since Isabel was Alienor's companion and dear friend, she could bring her own influence to bear, and perhaps that was a glint of sunlight bordering a very dark cloud.

# *16*

## FALAISE, CHRISTMAS 1159

STANDING ON THE BATTLEMENTS OF THE GREAT DONJON AT Falaise, seat of the dukes of Normandy and the place where William the Bastard had been conceived and born, Alienor watched his great-grandson arrive.

"Mama, look! Papa's here!" Harry pointed excitedly to the cavalcade making its way through the snowy landscape toward them.

"Yes," Alienor said, "he is. The miracle is that either of us recognizes him." From her vantage point, the men were the size of toy knights. Henry wore a blue cloak lined with ermine and was riding a bright chestnut palfrey. Their paths had not crossed since he had ridden off to fail at Toulouse. He had not seen fit to visit her or the children and had barely written either. She cared that he had not, but it was a caring born out of anger and contempt, not thwarted affection.

She lifted Harry so he could better see the parade arrive, banners waving, the household knights glittering in their armor, the barons colorful in their thick woolen tunics and cloaks, and then she took him down from the battlements to the hall, collecting his siblings on the way.

By the time Alienor arrived, Henry was already in the great hall and had formally greeted his mother, who was holding court in her chair by the hearth. The winter cold had attacked her joints and although she refused to use a stick, the fact that she was content to sit by the fire was indicative. Henry's bastard son Jeoffrey stood at her side, now a sturdy freckle-faced seven-year-old. His tunic of dark moss-green brightened the copper tones in his hair. Alienor was irritated that he had been the first to greet his father when he should have been last, but she let it pass. It was not the child's fault.

Advancing to Henry, she made her obeisance. Harry knelt, little Matilda curtsied as she had been taught, and Richard gave a proper little bow before losing his balance and falling on his bottom. Geoffrey gurgled in his nurse's arms.

"Well," said Henry heartily. "What fine children. And you look well, madam."

Alienor inclined her head, playing the diplomatic role with aplomb. There were no chinks in her armor in public. "Indeed they are, as am I. And you, sire?"

"The better for seeing all my family gathered," he said with a fixed smile.

Alienor raised one eyebrow. In that case he could have felt better much sooner than now. "Will you come refresh yourself, sire? Your chamber is ready."

She saw his eyes flicker, and she wondered if he would try to extricate himself. But he stood tall and set his shoulders. "That would be most welcome," he replied, proving that he could play the diplomatic game too.

She led him up the stairs to the chamber she had prepared. His squires were still bringing in his baggage, but the room was warm and the bed freshly made. Scented water stood ready in a bowl and Alienor removed Henry's boots and attended to the customary ritual of foot washing. Little Matilda fetched a pair of warmed woolen socks and soft shoes and knelt to help her.

"You are training her well," Henry said.

"Indeed," Alienor replied. "She can also count to one hundred on a checker board, and recite her prayers in Latin, although she doesn't fully understand yet what they mean, but that will come in less time than you think."

Henry gave her an evaluating look but said nothing. He played with his offspring for a while, and, having satisfied himself as to their well-being, dismissed them to their nurses. Casting his glance over Alienor's ladies, he paused at Isabel de Warenne. "I am sorry for your sad loss, madam," he said. "Your husband was a fine man who always gave of his best."

"Thank you, sire. He was indeed," Isabel replied, her eyes downcast and her hands clasped as if in prayer. "I miss him every day." Her eyes filled. "I never realized when I bid him farewell that it would be forever in this life."

"Isabel, don't upset yourself." Alienor beckoned, and Emma came forward, folded Isabel in her arms, and led her away, murmuring softly.

"Good God!" Henry exclaimed, gazing after them. "The woman's become a bag of bones!"

"She mourns for her husband," Alienor said curtly. "I do not know if you understand that, but somewhere in your soul, I hope so."

"Of course I do, but it is unseemly and foolish to grieve like that. Better to build your banks steep than allow them to flood."

In part Alienor agreed with him because she knew what such grief was like and she had built her own defenses high over the years. But if you raised them too much, they became a prison and in the end you drowned with no one to hear you scream. "She felt guilty that she could not protect him."

Henry snorted. "How could she protect him on campaign? What a foolish notion."

"Mayhap it is, but I feel guilty every day that I could do nothing to save our son. Perhaps I did not pray hard enough. Perhaps the fault was mine."

Henry compressed his lips, resisting any mention of their dead child. "She must abandon her moping and remarry," he said. "She is a young woman of wealth and standing, and there is no shortage of suitors. Keep her close because competition will be keen and I want to control the choice of her next husband."

"She needs more time." Alienor kept her tone level. "She is not ready yet."

"It will be when I say."

She sat back and looked up at him. "Have you really grown so hard and lacking in compassion? She is in no fit state to be of use to any man as a wife and helpmate. Whoever you chose, you would be doing them both a disservice. Let her heal awhile, if not from your own sense of what is fitting, then as a favor to me—and after Toulouse you owe me a favor."

He returned her stare, his jaw thrust out in pugilistic fashion, but eventually he waved his hand. "Very well, let it lie for now and we'll reconsider in the spring." He spread his hands along the back of the bench and crossed his legs. "There was nothing I could do about Toulouse, not with Louis behind the walls."

"I know you could not, and Louis knew it too—which was why he did it."

"He would not rise to the bait when I tried to draw him out. He just sat there and mocked me while his brother ravaged Normandy. I had no choice but to abandon the siege."

She rose to her feet and sent Matilda away with her nurse. "Then it seems that you were outmaneuvered."

Henry's anger flashed. "It is but a single move in a game of chess. Yes, he outflanked me, but that does not mean I have been defeated."

"Then what does it mean?" she demanded. "Toulouse remains untaken, and there will not be another campaign for a while, will there, because all the money and impetus is gone."

"I thought you more sensible than to sulk and vilify me for it. Was I wrong?"

Alienor wanted to rage at him. She felt let down and betrayed, but ranting would only further his claim that she was a woman in the grip of hysteria. "What would be the point?" she said wearily. "Louis tried to take Toulouse and failed when I was wed to him. Now he defends it and denies us both. I am not content, but I must accept it." She gave him a challenging stare. "When we married, we both took a gamble. I want to think that it was a winning throw of the dice. Don't let me be wrong, Henry…"

He uncrossed his legs, rose, and came to take her in his arms. "Ah, Alienor," he said. "It is seldom I throw the dice and do not win. I will never let you be wrong."

There was something disturbingly ambiguous about the statement, but he covered her mouth in a searing kiss and ran his hand down her body with purposeful intent, and she set her misgiving aside to ponder a different time. Lust warmed her veins and she still desired him, and in bed, they were equals.

❖❖❖

Henry sat in his chamber before the fire, drinking wine with his brothers and his chancellor. Everyone else had retired to bed except the watchmen and the servants on duty, but Henry enjoyed keeping late hours. His mind was at its most lucid then; there was more space for his thoughts to expand and develop.

Hamelin, legs stretched toward the fire, was idly scratching the ears of a silver-gray gazehound, his other hand cradling his cup. Becket was preening, showing off his magnificent new cloak lined with Russian squirrel fur in shades of blue and cream. His own drink was boiled barley water sweetened with honey. He was suffering from an upset stomach to which he was intermittently prone.

Henry's youngest brother William was flushed with wine. His sandy hair stood on end where he had been rumpling it. "It is a great pity about the death of the count of Boulogne," he said. "What now becomes of his widow?"

Henry gave him an amused look. "Why, do you have a fancy to her? Shall I give her to you?"

"You could do much worse. All that land and influence of kin, and still young enough to bear half a dozen children."

"I take it you haven't seen the lady since our return?"

William shook his head. "Not yet, why?"

Henry grimaced. "She's in deep mourning and as bony as a starved cow. You'd have no joy or heirs out of her at the moment."

"But do I have permission to court her after she has finished mourning?" William pressed. "Starved cow or not, I'd still like to milk her lands."

Henry raised his brows. "You are eager, aren't you, lad? How much wine have you had?"

"I'm not drunk," William said, "and I'm not a lad."

Thomas Becket had been listening in silence, but now he cleared his throat. "The match would be consanguineous. The lady is related within the proscribed degree."

"What of it?" Henry waved an impatient hand. "So is my wife, but that didn't prevent the Church from joining us in wedlock. If necessary I can obtain a dispensation." He shot Becket an irritated look. "You are seeing trouble where there is none."

"I was merely making you aware, sire."

"I do not need reminding of bloodlines. Do you think I do not have the necessary information in my head?" He tapped his skull. "You don't legislate for everything, Thomas, even if you think you do."

Becket compressed his lips.

Henry turned back to his brother. "You have my full permission to court the Countess de Warenne and take her to wife, but leave it until her mourning period is over; otherwise, I will never hear the last of it from the queen, and she is already in a pet over the marriage between Harry and the French girl. Women cannot separate their hearts from their heads."

"I shall be the soul of discretion." William pressed his palm to his heart and flourished a bow. "Not a word until the time is right. With me she will discover what it is to have a real man in her bed."

"Then make sure you are one," Henry said with irritated amusement.

William reddened at Henry's put-down but then shrugged it off and called for more wine. Becket excused himself to see to matters of the chancellery before retiring to bed.

When he had gone, the tension that had crept into the atmosphere eased and mellowed, not least because Henry ceased to bristle. "God knows I love Thomas," he said, "but I love him even better when he's not being a self-righteous prig." He refreshed his own wine. "Don't worry about the dispensation, Will, you'll have it."

"Thank you." The young man lurched at Henry to embrace him. The latter stood up and adroitly avoided him.

"Sit down before you fall down," he said with indulgent scorn, and as his brother plonked down on the bench, making it shudder, Henry began to pace. "As well as leaving a widow, our cousin also left a grieving sister."

William blinked owlishly. "But she's a nun—abbess of Romsey."

"For ten years, yes." Henry rubbed a forefinger gently back and forth across his beard. "But I am thinking perhaps she might like a change now that she has inherited her brother's estate."

"Jesu God, Henry, you can't mean to take her out of the nunnery!" Hamelin was shocked out of his usual courtier's insouciance. "That makes consanguinity pale to nothing by comparison!"

Henry shrugged. "It is not unknown, and the pope will look the other way because he needs my support. I was thinking of our cousin Matthew, Aunt Sybilla's son."

Hamelin almost choked. "But to take her out of a convent when she's been there for the last ten years… Dear God, she's the abbess!"

"She'll thank me for it," Henry said. "As the last of her line, she has a duty to produce heirs."

It seemed a specious argument to Hamelin. And yet Henry was his brother and he owed him loyalty and allegiance. "What will you tell Alienor?"

"Nothing," Henry said. "She will find out soon enough." He gave a wry grimace. "No point in kicking over an ants' nest until you must."

❖ ❖ ❖

"How could you!" Alienor was so incensed with Henry that she was shaking. "You worthless snake! Of all the women in Christendom you could have married to Matthew of Alsace, you have to drag a bride of Christ out of a convent to satisfy your power-grubbing schemes? Your own kin too!"

He stood tall and puffed out his chest in that way of his she hated. It was as if he was forming himself into such a posture that her words would bounce off him without impact, and his expression said that her opinion on the matter was irrelevant. "It is to secure our lands and the lands of our heirs," he retorted. "I would not do this unless it was necessary."

She was disgusted. "And that mends everything and makes it right?"

He lifted and dropped his shoulders. "Rail as you will, madam, it makes no difference to my decision. Count yourself fortunate I am not insisting the Countess de Warenne remarry immediately. I have heeded your plea on that, but I can easily change my mind." He walked out, leaving her to fume.

It was always the same, she thought. When she confronted him, he either shrugged and walked away, or intimidated her with threats, the only opinion he listened to his own. There was indeed nothing she could do about Mary de Boulogne, but at least for the moment, Isabel was safe.

# 17

## ROUEN, AUTUMN 1160

ALIENOR CONSIDERED THE EMBROIDERY SHE HAD BROUGHT with her from England. She had not yet begun stitching, but the design of a hunting scene was drawn on the linen ready for that moment.

For the last three days she had been visiting Henry's mother at the abbey of Bec. Henry was due to arrive. She had not seen him since the Christmas feast at Falaise, nor had she particularly missed him and suspected that the feeling was mutual.

Alienor had not brought their two youngest children to Rouen. Richard at three was constantly into everything, and there was never a moment's peace even when Hodierna had charge of him. Combined with two-year-old Geoffrey's tantrums, the resulting mayhem would have been too annoying for the aging empress, who preferred children to be seen and not heard. Harry at five and a half and four-year-old Matilda had reached an age when they were more civilized.

Harry was outside having a riding lesson with his bastard half brother. Alienor was accepting of Jeoffrey because she had to be, but it still caused her anxiety. Each time she saw him he had grown taller, stronger, and more vital. Although he was ostensibly being prepared for a life in the Church, there was nothing monkish about him. Here was no studious little boy with downcast eyes, rather instead a vibrant and vivid little warrior. The empress was strict with him but at the same time watched him with fond eyes. She was having him trained in military and riding skills, and Alienor was beginning to wonder if she had made a mistake in sending him to be raised at her court. The empress had seen little of Henry's childhood because of her struggle to gain England's crown. Perhaps she was substituting Jeoffrey for the child Henry, and treating him as a prince, not a bastard side shoot.

Little Matilda was busy sorting through a basket filled with hanks of embroidery wool. She selected a green one with a needle stuck through it. "Is this the one you want, Mama?" Her hair shone in the firelight, thick dark gold like Alienor's but shot with subtle glints of copper.

"Yes, my love, the green will go very well." Encouraged, Matilda rummaged again and held up a pink one. "And this one?"

"Yes, that one too."

Matilda gave it to her and delved again, this time for blue.

"I think we have enough for now." Laughing, Alienor lifted Matilda onto her lap. Then nothing would suffice but her daughter had to sew on the blank canvas. Alienor indulged her, letting her take a threaded needle and put a few laborious stitches into an area that did not call for detailed work. Eventually, Matilda grew bored as Alienor had known she would, and went off to play with her doll.

"I can unpick these later if necessary," Alienor said to her mother-in-law who had been watching the scene without comment, "but they are neat for a child of her age and I shall keep them if I can."

"She is very able," the empress said.

"Indeed, madam, she is." Alienor let out a pensive sigh. "I pray to God that men do not take too much advantage of her, for that is the way of the world. I know I must prepare her for hardship too. Good needlework is but an embellishment of daily life."

"Have you and Henry considered her marriage yet?" the empress asked her, eyes shrewd.

"In passing. I have a few years with her yet." Alienor's voice developed a bitter note. "Unless Henry suddenly decides otherwise, of course."

The empress shifted in her chair to ease her joints. "I know it is difficult for you to come to terms with this match between your son and your former husband's daughter, but you must see what a strategic move it is for our dominions."

"I do see, madam," Alienor replied. "My mind accepts it; my heart does not and never will. It disturbs me that Henry has no such qualms." In fact no conscience at all, she sometimes thought, after what he had done to poor Mary de Boulogne.

"He cannot afford to," the empress replied. "He is the king, and he must often make unpalatable decisions for the good of all. I agree it is difficult when your head and your heart are not in harmony, but as my son's queen, you cannot let yourself be ruled by tenderness in matters of state."

"I know that, madam." Alienor began threading her needle in order to avoid the empress's perceptive stare, and in the meantime, she mastered her irritation.

The empress folded her hands in her lap. "Has Henry spoken to you concerning the marriage of the Countess de Warenne?"

Cold shock ran down Alienor's spine. Dear God, what had Henry been doing behind her back now? And after he said he would leave Isabel in peace to mourn. She would kill him with her own hands! "No, he has not," she said. "Forgive me, madam, but why would he speak to you on the matter and not me since the Countess de Warenne is my companion and a dear friend?"

The empress patted Alienor's knee. "It is unfortunate that he has not done so, I agree, but calm yourself. My youngest son has expressed an interest in the countess, and that is why Henry broached it with me."

Alienor gazed at her mother-by-marriage in horror. "Has he indeed?" She had no love for William FitzEmpress. Like Henry, he had a tendency to ride roughshod over others in order to get his own way.

"Naturally the countess is in mourning and must be given the opportunity to complete that with all dignity," the empress said with regal hauteur.

"As Mary de Boulogne was allowed to grieve for her brother at Romsey Abbey?"

The empress firmed her lips. "Indeed, I agree with you. That decision was not well made, but I have spoken to Henry about that."

"And you probably received the same reply that I did—that it was necessary and that I was being squeamish and unrealistic because I am a woman."

The empress sighed. "There was a time when I thought I could change everything. I have learned the hard way that we only have so much strength: better to use it for fights where we stand a chance of winning."

"And if you had thought that way when Stephen took your crown?"

The empress gave her a hard look. "But I did win that one for my dynasty. I warn you to be very careful in choosing your battles with my son." She rubbed her thumb over a gold ring on her index finger. "Henry told me he would give the Countess de Warenne time to mourn, but it might be useful for you to prepare the ground."

Alienor had no intention whatsoever of promoting William's cause. Henry had already given his youngest brother valuable English estates and monetary wealth, but Isabel's lands would make him a powerful magnate. While she would welcome Isabel as her sister-by-marriage, the thought of having Henry's youngest brother frequently in her chamber was unbearable. Besides, she was toying with the idea of wedding Isabel to one of her Poitevan barons, thus increasing her own influence at court.

The empress narrowed her eyes. "You say nothing, Daughter?"

Alienor gathered herself. "It has come as a surprise, that is all."

"Well, when you have recovered, think on it well. A judicious word from you could make all the difference in this matter."

"Indeed, Mother." Alienor decided she would do nothing for the moment. Henry had not broached the subject to her, so she had the excuse of ignorance. If he was hoping that the matter would be successfully carried forward by "women's talk" in the bower, he was very wrong.

The women worked at their sewing in ruminative and slightly strained silence until a clerk arrived from the empress's writing office bearing a message from Henry. The empress set aside her needlework, took it from him, and read the contents, holding the letter away in order to focus.

"There is news from France," she said. "Louis's queen has died bearing a daughter." She passed the letter to Alienor.

Reading the message, Alienor was sad for the loss of Louis's young wife in the common lot of childbirth. Every time a woman opened her legs to a man, she risked her life. Politically she was relieved that the infant was a girl because it meant she and Henry continued to have the upper hand. Raising her eyes to the empress, she saw her own thoughts mirrored in the older woman's face.

"God rest her poor soul," said Matilda. "I know too well the perils a woman faces in childbed. I almost died bearing my Geoffrey."

Alienor set her hand to her own womb. She had not conceived at Christmas so had a momentary respite but knew she must face that arena again and again until her muscles grew slack, her breasts drooped, and her body ran out of seed. It was the foremost duty of a queen to bear children, preferably enough sons to secure the succession, and then a plethora of daughters to create affinities. "Yes indeed," she said. "God rest her soul." *And God help all women.*

❖❖❖

A fresh autumn breeze bustled Alienor's cloak and tugged at her wimple. The court had ridden out for a day's hunting, men and ladies together, and thus the pace was brisk but merry, rather than hard with competitive purpose.

The sky was an intense deep blue, populated by a few wind-chased clouds. Twirls of ruddy leaves from ash and beech showered upon the riders as they trotted through light woodland and hunted over soft tawny fields, fallow after the harvest.

Alienor was enjoying the fresh air, her white gyrfalcon on her wrist and her spirited chestnut palfrey dancing beneath her. Isabel rode beside her on the dun palfrey that had been her husband's favorite mount. She was still in mourning, although Alienor suspected that her grief had become a mantle, protecting her from suggestions of a new marriage. William FitzEmpress kept trying to strike up conversations with her and sidling his horse close, but Isabel responded with indifferent courtesy. Alienor endeavored to keep Isabel as near to her as she could and squeeze William out. Henry had said nothing as yet about betrothal plans. Alienor had been waiting for him to broach the subject and had no doubt he was waiting for his moment.

The hunting party stopped to picnic on the edge of the trees where a natural hollow created a windbreak and shelter. Servants had ridden ahead to prepare food, cooking it over the hot coals in shallow-dug fire pits. There was griddled fish with piquant sauce, coneys cooked in wine and honey until the flesh was tender with a sticky, sweet-sour coating, and skewers of pork interspersed with chunks of roasted apple. The bread was white, soft, and plentiful, and the wine for once was as smooth and rich as a silk curtain.

Chancellor Becket dismounted from his white Spanish stallion and gave the reins to his groom. The horse was trapped out like a beast from a song of the troubadours, gold thread twinkling on the saddlecloth, which was dyed with Tyrian purple. Becket's robes were in forest colors but of expensive hues, rich and deep, and his belt was punctuated with silver studs in the shape of crosses. In contrast, Henry wore serviceable hunting gear of plain madder-dyed wool, and his mount was a broad-rumped bay with unembellished harness. Becket might easily have been the king, and Henry his servant, both in terms of appearance and behavior, the one high-handed and finicky, the other sitting on a tree stump, sucking sauce off his fingers.

Sitting with Isabel, Alienor bit into a chunk of the skewered pork and apple. Becket chose the fish and, as usual, cut his wine liberally with spring water because of his delicate stomach. Alienor had heard a rumor to the effect that Becket had himself scourged before he went to confession and she was trying to decide whether to believe it or not. He seemed at ease among the gathering, and he hadn't ridden like a man suffering from the effects of a whipping.

Henry's younger brother William joined her and Isabel. He was eating a piece of the sticky rabbit and a red smudge of sauce bedaubed his upper lip. The napkin in which he held the meat was smeared and blotched too.

"Have you tried the coney?" he asked Isabel. "It's excellent. Would you like some?" He indicated a spare portion in the cloth.

Isabel gave him a swift glance and shook her head. "It is kind of you but I have enough."

He bit into his own piece, chewed with vigor, and swallowed. "That dun of yours," he said. "He is too big and strong for a woman. You should change him for a daintier mount. I will find you one."

"I am content with him, sire," she said, her expression setting like stone. "He belonged to my late husband, and he is dear to me."

"But still I think you should—" He broke off as a messenger galloped up to the line of tethered horses, dismounted at speed, and went to Henry, who was sharing his rabbit with his favorite gazehound.

Henry wiped his hands, took the letter presented to him, broke the seal, and read what was written. "Hah!" he cried. "The conniving weasel!" He jumped to his feet and thrust the parchment at Becket. "Louis," he said. "He's arranged a new marriage for himself already, the skinny old goat."

Becket studied the document with narrowed eyes.

"To whom?" Alienor asked, annoyed that Henry had shown his chancellor the document before her.

"To Adela of Blois–Champagne, madam," Becket said. "There is no doubt whose influence rules at the French court now."

Alienor recoiled. The brothers of Blois–Champagne, Theobald and Henri, were betrothed to Marie and Alix, her daughters by Louis, and that was influence enough, but for Louis to marry their sister Adela meant that they had truly nailed the royal banner of France to their mast. It was like a gleeful smack in the face to Henry's policies. Furthermore, the Blois bloodline was that of England's former King Stephen, and that made Louis's choice of wife even more undesirable and dangerous.

"He intends to do it immediately," Henry said. "He's not even allowing time for the earth to settle on his wife's cold corpse before he is climbing into another consanguineous marriage bed. Hah, so much for his vaunted piety and godliness!"

Alienor gave an involuntary shudder. Louis projected himself as a golden king and the champion of Christendom, but she had been married to him: she knew what he was like. God help his new wife—whatever her affinities.

❖❖❖

Henry paced the chamber like a caged lion, back and forth, back and forth. The tread of his boots raised the scent of crushed herbs strewn over the floor rushes, and the candles flared with each pass he made. It was very late, but he was still awake and restless, worrying at the problem of the new French queen and what it would mean to him and his heirs to have a Blois wife as Louis's consort.

The empress had retired to bed long since. Alienor's eyes were tired and sore, but Henry showed no signs of slowing down. Becket's expression was controlled and stoical.

"Pope Alexander needs support while there are disputes over the papacy," Alienor said. "In return for your goodwill he might be prevailed upon to ban the match on grounds of consanguinity. At the least he could force him to wait awhile and undertake a proper time of mourning."

"You think I had not considered that?" Henry growled. "It is like striking an enemy with a cushion; it won't have any impact because the pope will be seeking support from France too and playing us against each other. It will be as easy to issue a dispensation as a ban."

"But better than nothing. I know Louis: his life as a man is perilously tangled with his relationship to the Church. Papal condemnation will unbalance him."

Henry gave her a speculative stare tinged with suspicion. "Such a detail can hardly be taken for granted."

Becket said, "Sire, what if the betrothal between your son and the Princess Marguerite was advanced into marriage immediately instead of waiting ten years? You would gain the castles promised by the treaty and the lands in the Vexin."

Henry stopped pacing and turned.

"No!" Alienor was appalled. She looked between Henry and Becket and saw the collusion. The twitch of a smile on Henry's lips, the gleam in the chancellor's eyes. "You should leave this to the allotted time, no good will come of it!"

Henry shot her a swift glance. "Why court the wind when you can have the leaves that fall now?"

"Wedding a five-year-old boy to an infant barely out of the cradle is neither reputable nor honorable. People will vilify you for this."

She saw Henry exchange a glance with Becket, as if to say, "See, this is what I have to deal with in my chamber," and she clenched her fists.

"Some may do so, I agree," Henry said, "but others will say I am merely being astute. The pope will have to give a dispensation because of their youth, but since he needs my support and Rome is always eager to listen to entreaties from Saint Gold and Saint Silver, I am sure it can be arranged without difficulty. Louis can hardly cavil when his own intended marriage is not following a pious route. He will need a dispensation too so cannot turn on the pope no matter how displeased he is."

"The Templars are holding the dower castles in trust," Becket said. "Are they likely to yield?"

"The agreement has nothing to do with them beyond the fact that they are custodians of those keeps. When the marriage is accomplished, their part is over." Henry clapped his hands and rubbed them together. "We can set matters in motion first thing in the morning."

"I shall prepare letters, sire." Becket bowed and left the room.

Henry turned to Alienor. "Come," he said. "Put your anger aside. This is a fine plan and it gives us a way out of the dilemma."

"You and Thomas Becket are too clever for your own good,"

Alienor retorted. "I still stand by what I said: you should not do this."

"And I have heard you, but Thomas is right. A betrothal can be broken, but it is far less simple to unforge a marriage. The Vexin will be ours." He pulled her against him. "Come," he cajoled, kissing her temple and then her lips. "Leave it for now and come to bed. There is no point talking about it any more tonight."

There was no point any other time either, Alienor thought, because he would not listen. He never did. She might as well be part of the wall.

❖❖❖

On a freezing, rainy day in early November, Alienor looked down at the infant girl who had been brought to the women's quarters to be shown to her. Marguerite, princess of France, was three years old with a chubby face and shiny brown eyes. Her cheeks were rosy with cold and her nose was streaming. A stolid, plump child, she bore no resemblance to the dainty, blond-haired, blue-eyed daughters Alienor had borne to Louis, and it was impossible to think that this was the future queen of England and mother of Harry's heirs.

"What a sweet child," Isabel said, wiping the infant's streaming nose with a square of soft linen cloth.

Alienor shook her head. Isabel thought all children were sweet. "She must resemble her mother. I can see nothing of Louis in her. Let us hope she does not have any of his traits."

Harry's nurse brought him to be introduced to his future wife. He had had the details explained to him at a superficial level, and did his part by bowing to Marguerite and reciting a little speech of welcome, to which his bride responded by turning around in a circle and falling over. Harry regarded her the way he might regard a puppy that had just pissed on the bed, and, the instant his duty was done, made his escape to run off and play vigorously with his toy sword, cutting and swooshing with it in a frenzy. His sister Matilda, her sense of duty already honed at the age of four, showed Marguerite the bed of straw she had made for her cloth doll and gave Marguerite another doll she didn't like quite so much to play with.

"All will work out well," Isabel said to reassure Alienor.

"I hope so," Alienor replied dubiously. "But I feel as if I have traveled a long way and gone nowhere."

❖❖❖

Harry and Marguerite's marriage was celebrated the next day in Rouen Cathedral. The rain had stopped, but it was still overcast and bitterly cold, and everyone sported thick, fur-lined cloaks over their finery. Alienor wore a close-fitting gown dyed a dark bloodred with subtle gold embroidery swirling at the hem and banded at the cuffs. The color and the effect made her look long-limbed and elegant, if a trifle austere.

Watching Harry do as the archbishop told him, and speak his part without a stumble, made Alienor proud, even through her disapproval. She loved Harry with all her being for behaving so well while he was the center of attention. He looked every inch the prince in his tunic of red silk edged with purple. His golden-brown hair curled around a jeweled coronet that glinted in the light from the cathedral windows.

She had explained to him all about the marriage and the land, and that he must be a big boy and do his duty for his family. Living with Marguerite would come later; it was just a formal ceremony to settle everything. There would be a feast afterward with special food and entertainment, and if he was a good boy, he could sit at the high table under a silk canopy. He need not bother with his bride beyond being formally polite in public because she was smaller and younger than him and would not understand what was happening. He was to be a little man and protect her. All this she had told him, feeling utterly heartsick, knowing she could do nothing about it. Perhaps as a polit-ical matter Henry was right and it was for the best, but it would never be something she would have chosen of her own accord. How much Harry understood she did not know. How could he? He was only five years old.

Once the marriage had been solemnized, Marguerite was

returned to the nursery, being too young for the wedding feast. Her part was over. Harry, however, occupied the place of honor at the high table, where a special wooden block had been made for his chair to boost him to table height. By now a hectic flush of exhaustion flared on his cheeks and his eyes were glassy. Henry gave him a sip of sugared wine to revive him, and Harry sat manfully through the speeches and the first course of the feast, designed to whet the appetite for more to come. Alienor kept a close eye on him, and as he began to droop once more, she beckoned his nurse. Henry forestalled the woman and lifted Harry in his arms. "I will take him," he said. "He has done well and it is only fitting I should do him this honor, as he has honored me."

Alienor signaled the feast to continue and within a short while Henry returned, a satisfied smile on his lips. "Asleep before his head touched the pillow," he said and, taking Alienor's hand, kissed her knuckles. "You will come to see that this was the best course."

"Do not seek to cozen me," Alienor replied frostily. "You have your marriage. Let that be enough."

"As you wish, madam." Henry's tone was equable. He leaned back in his chair, full of indulgent bonhomie because now he legally had the Vexin and its most powerful castles under his belt and there was nothing Louis could do about it because it was all legal.

When they retired, Henry came to Alienor's chamber and made love to her with ardent force. She had been determined to lie passive beneath him and not give him the satisfaction of a response, but instead, in the moment, she found herself responding with fierce vigor of her own, because whatever he gave, she could take and return double measure, and even win, because when a man was finished, he was finished, but a woman had no such limitations on her flesh.

# 18

## LE MANS, CHRISTMAS 1160

*H*AMELIN MADE HIS WAY DOWN THE NAVE OF THE CATHEDRAL of Saint-Julien, his path to the north ambulatory illuminated by swords of bleak winter light. Walking at his side, eyes wide and alert, was his bastard nephew Jeoffrey, a sturdy red-haired boy, freckles standing out against his pale complexion. The soft sound of their footfalls mingled on the flagstones.

Whenever Hamelin was in the vicinity of Le Mans, he made a point of visiting the cathedral to pray, give alms, and pay his respects to his father, Geoffrey le Bel, Count of Anjou. Today he had taken it upon himself to show Jeoffrey the tomb of his paternal grandsire.

It was so cold that Hamelin's breath clouded the air, and his knuckle joints were stiff. A brass lamp above the tomb glinted soft light on the representational enamel plaque illuminating his father's likeness. At Hamelin's side, the boy shivered. Using his cloak to cushion his knees from the icy stone flags, Hamelin knelt at the side of the tomb and unfastened his prayer beads from his belt. Jeoffrey copied him, clasping his hands and closing his eyes.

The sounds of the church echoed around them. The soft footfalls of the attendant clergy, the murmur of other worshipers, the rattle of a censer on its chain. Jeoffrey's lips moved, reciting in flawless Latin: "*Requiem aeternam dona eis, Domine, et lux perpetua luceat eis. Requiescant in pace.*"

When they had completed their prayers, Jeoffrey tentatively touched the small enameled effigy plaque, admiring the detailed workmanship and vibrant colors. The hair was the same copper-gold as his own and his father's and the eyes were a piercing aquamarine blue.

"He was my father and I loved him," Hamelin said with reverence. "He did not forget me when he begot me. He took me into his household; he fed and clothed me and raised me to manhood under his protection."

The boy's attention sharpened with interest. He eyed Hamelin's rich apparel, the gilded belt and the rings on his fingers, the cloak of smoke and silver vair. "Can I be a knight in your household?" he asked.

"That depends on what your father intends for you," Hamelin said. "I know it will be a role that gives you honor and prestige. Being the bastard of a highborn man is a privilege, not a shame." Gazing at his father's effigy, he clenched his fists. He had not always felt privileged when his sire was alive. There were times when he had wanted to murder Henry for being the legitimate heir when he was the firstborn son. And there were times when he had felt the least, and little more than a whipped dog. Even now whenever he and his brothers were together, there was always that divide. And this child must learn to live with that kind of division. There was shame too, whatever he said to the boy. A bastard child was born not from the sober needs of duty and dynasty, but from the sin of lechery and lust, even if some called it love.

"Do you have any bastards?"

Hamelin's mouth twisted and he shook his head. "No, lad, I do not." There had been women in his life; he had taken no vow of chastity, but he was always careful, and thus far that care had paid off. "But if I did, I would acknowledge him, or her as my child and make him my responsibility as my father did to me."

Hearing a sudden movement behind him, Hamelin turned to see the Countess de Warenne accompanied by her maid. She had clearly been at prayer elsewhere in the church but had paused to acknowledge him. Her face was pale and sapped of color against the dark wool of her cloak and white wimple; indeed, she looked almost like a nun. "Madam." Hamelin bowed.

Her smile of greeting was reserved but genuine. "My lord vicomte," she said, turning to Jeoffrey. "And Messire FitzRoy. It seems we are on similar errands—praying for the souls of dear ones departed."

"That is so, madam," Hamelin replied courteously. "May we escort you back to the keep?"

She inclined her head. "Your company would be welcome." Dusk was falling as they set out in the sharp, frosty cold from the cathedral to the donjon. "I heard what you said to your nephew," she said. "That was kind of you, and wise."

Hamelin shrugged. "I know his position, because I have been in it too. The life of a royal bastard is both privileged and cruel. Jeoffrey will have a difficult time of it, but he's a spirited lad. If I can help him from my own experience, I will."

They walked in silence for a while and then Hamelin asked with careful tact how she was faring.

"I am well, sire," she said with quiet dignity. "It is the season of Our Lord's birth and I am ready to rejoice in it."

Hamelin gave her a swift smile. "My father often told the story of how he went to Mass in the cathedral here one Christmas Day. He saw a clerk outside the door and called out to him, asking if he had any news. The clerk answered, 'Sire, there is great news indeed!' My father was excited and said, 'Quick, tell me!' So the clerk replied, 'Jesus Christ the Savior is born today!'" Hamelin chuckled. "My father was rightly humbled by those words and rewarded the man for his timely reminder by taking him into his household as one of his chaplains."

"It is a fine story," Isabel agreed. "Indeed, it reminds us of the true meaning of the Nativity."

On arriving at the castle she left him with a graceful curtsy and her thanks for his escort. Watching her walk away, Hamelin noticed a small sprig of red-berried holly tucked in the band of her wimple, and it made him smile. She was a lovely, gracious woman, quiet, but by no means a mouse. The notion of her being married to his brother gave him a feeling of distaste, like seeing a fine sword being used to scrape mud from shoes, but since it was the way of the world and Henry's will, he knew he had to be pragmatic and detached.

❖ ❖ ❖

Three months later on a brisk March morning, Henry greeted Alienor with a hearty kiss on the lips. She had returned to le Mans, having visited England in January to deal with matters of state on Henry's behalf. Their time apart had served to ease the abrasiveness between them while not being long enough to create the diffidence of strangers. Henry flicked a glance at her waistline. "Either you dined very well while in England," he said, "or you have some good news for me, my love."

"You left me with another gift at Christmas," she answered wryly. "And I will deliver it back to you in the autumn."

Henry drew himself up with masculine pride and looked smug. "Hah, there is no sign of Louis's new queen being similarly blessed. It takes a man after all." He kissed Alienor's cheek. "I have to go, but I will come eat with you later." He breezed off in his usual manner, and Alienor shook her head with exasperation but smiled despite herself.

❖ ❖ ❖

Several hours later, she and Henry sat at a long trestle in her chamber. Beeswax candles gave off a warm golden light, and a cozy fire glowed in the hearth. Alienor wore a dress of silk damask, the colors flowing into each other, red and gold like the fire. In the privacy of her own chamber, she had dressed her hair in a simple loose braid twined with gold ribbons. She knew that in the muted light she looked alluring, and with the new life growing inside her, she felt powerful.

Henry considered the slight curve of her belly. "Dare I hope God will grant us another daughter?" he said.

"Men usually wish for sons," she replied with a smile.

He looked amused. "Only those that cannot beget them. Louis would have an apoplexy if he could hear me wish for a girl. A seasoning of daughters is not to be sneered at. A father can make some very useful marriage alliances." He smiled and leaned back. "I think if this one is a girl, we should name her Alienor for her incomparable mother."

"Yes, we should," she said, her light tone matching his. They were like partners in a dance—or opponents stepping purposefully in a sword fight.

Henry suddenly raised the tablecloth and peered down. "Child, what are you doing under there?" he demanded of little Matilda, who was busily working away at his feet.

Matilda peeped up at her father. "I'm a shoemaker, Papa," she said seriously. "Would you like a new pair?"

Diverted, Henry chuckled. "My chancellor is the one who sets store by such things, but yes, why not?"

Matilda removed his shoes and sat cross-legged like a little tailor to study them. She fiddled about, folding and unfolding the vamp and chattering to him earnestly as she pretended to make his shoes. Henry raised his eyebrows. "So this one's future is as a leather worker," he said to Alienor.

"It runs in the family, does it not?" Alienor replied and Henry gave a shout of laughter because William the Conqueror, his great-grandsire, had been the grandson of a common Falaise tanner. He was secure enough in his own manhood to find the detail a source of grand amusement.

Matilda trotted off to a corner with the shoes, saying she had to attend to them in her workshop.

Henry drank his wine, and when he and Alienor looked at each other, it was with reciprocal mirth. Children as well as dividing a couple could bring them together.

"Ho, mistress, are my shoes ready?" Henry shouted.

"Nearly, Papa! You have to wait!"

"You don't know how impossible that is for your father," Alienor said. "I don't think anyone has ever dared say that to his face before."

Henry raised his goblet in a sarcastic toast. "I can bide my time if I must."

Matilda returned to him, pink in the face. Each shoe now had a large green cross stitched in embroidery wool to the vamp strip down the front. "Here you are, Papa," she said. "They're all new now."

Henry's chest heaved with suppressed laughter. "I can see that they are. No one else will have any quite like this."

"No, Papa, they cost five marks."

Henry choked. "Who have you been taking lessons from, mistress? You should ask my chancellor to buy them if you're demanding that sort of sum!"

"But they're special, Papa!" Matilda explained. "You can wear them this way, or that way." She folded the vamp over to demonstrate the attractions. A long trail of green thread dangled from one of the shoes. She knelt and placed them back on his feet with comical seriousness.

"She gets her shrewdness and powers of persuasion from me," Alienor said, her shoulders shaking.

"Oh, very well," Henry capitulated. "But you will still have to ask my chancellor for the money because he has the keys to the strongbox. But you may have this as a token of my faith." He tugged a small gold ring off his little finger and presented it to her.

Matilda took it from him with a curtsy and then backed away with a mercantile flourish that made Henry snort. He signaled to her nurse and the woman came from her seat near the door to take Matilda off to bed.

Henry readjusted his shoe but made no attempt to remove the awkward big green stitches. Alienor's heart was warm that he should do that and not mind; indeed, that he should take time to play with his daughter.

"If only you were always like this," she said softly.

He raised one eyebrow. "You likewise, my love."

The door opened to admit a chamberlain, ushering before him a chaplain from the household of Theobald of Canterbury.

Alienor marked their progress across the room. The chaplain's expression was grim, and his face gray with tiredness. She also noted the mud-splattered hem of his cloak.

With an effort he knelt to Henry and Alienor. "Sire, madam, I bring you grave and sad tidings. It grieves me to tell you that my lord the archbishop of Canterbury gave up his soul to God at sunrise on the feast of Saint Apollonius."

Alienor was saddened but not surprised by the news. The elderly archbishop had been ailing during her last visit to him in England before she returned to Anjou. The difficulty now would be finding someone wise enough to replace him from the candidates who would hope to be chosen. The bishop of Hereford for one, and Robert of London for another. She was not particularly fond of either man, but then again, the see could be left vacant for as much as a year while candidates were considered. What they needed was a primate who would serve both church and state with a tactful and even hand, and that was not going to be easy.

❖❖❖

Isabel was sitting in a window embrasure, her sewing tilted toward the light, when William FitzEmpress strolled up and sat down beside her. She shifted on the seat to put space between them, her stomach clenching. She had noticed him looking at her recently like a cat biding its time at a mouse hole.

"You spend a great deal of time at such toil," he commented.

"I enjoy the work," she replied, "and it is practical."

"But surely it is not all your life."

"Indeed not." Isabel was flustered. "My life is full. I attend upon the queen and I have my own duties as a countess."

"But surely not full enough. It must be empty for you without a husband to protect and advise you—and give you heirs for your earldom."

Isabel lowered her gaze to her needlework, worried at the course the conversation was taking. "I mourn my husband deeply, even now," she said. "And since I am under the queen's protection and have loyal people to serve me, I have not considered the matter."

He shrugged. "But you must turn thought to it in the near future. It is a year and a half since you were widowed."

Isabel pressed her lips together. His words had formed a knot of fear in her belly as she remembered what had happened to her sister-in-law. The former abbess of Romsey was now wed to Matthew of Alsace and pregnant with his child. The king could do anything he desired and no one could stop him.

Across the hall a sudden vicious sibling fight broke out between three-and-a-half-year-old Richard and six-year-old Harry. The small boys rolled about on the floor, punching, kicking and yelling. Their sister Matilda tried to pull them apart and was sent flying by a wayward blow.

Hamelin FitzCount, who was on his way through the hall, diverted to drag his nephews off each other and stand them at arm's length, giving each of them a good shake. "Enough!" he roared. "Is this the behavior of royal heirs?" Their sister sat on the floor crying and rubbing her arm.

"I must see to my lady Matilda," Isabel said, relieved to have a reason to leave her place. "You will excuse me, sire."

William rose to his feet, taking his time. "We shall talk again, my lady," he said.

Isabel murmured an inanity and eased past the small space he afforded her, making her focus the sobbing little girl and not his predatory smile.

"Come, come," she soothed, stooping to Matilda. "Brothers are not worth shedding tears over, and this is but a graze." She kissed the angry red stripe on Matilda's forearm.

Having confiscated the toy sword over which his nephews had been fighting, Hamelin stuck it in his own belt.

"You make a good nursemaid," William sneered, sauntering over with folded arms.

"I learned from my childhood mistakes," Hamelin said and turned back to Richard and Harry, who were both glaring at him, united against a common enemy. "You can have this back when

I see fit. Now go, and if you must fight, do it somewhere you're not going to be a nuisance to others."

Isabel folded a comforting arm around Matilda and took her upstairs to Alienor's chamber to find some salve for the graze. Halfway there she realized she had left her needlework behind, but wild horses could not have dragged her back to retrieve it while William FitzEmpress remained in the hall.

Alienor was busy dictating a letter to her scribe when Isabel and Matilda arrived.

"Richard and Harry were fighting over a sword," Isabel told her, "and Matilda tried to stop them."

Alienor sighed. "Harry and Richard would fight over anything, and it won't be long before Geoffrey is joining in. I sometimes believe the tales about Angevins being born of the devil are true. The males of the line certainly seem to have the devil in them." She stroked her daughter's hair as Isabel searched in a casket for a pot of salve. "It is the task of a woman to be a peacemaker," she told Matilda, "and a very important one it is too. Kingdoms have been won on the diplomacy of a woman's work, but she should also know when not to waste her time on a lost cause."

"Richard and Harry are lost causes," Matilda said, putting her nose in the air.

"Yes, they are."

Isabel had just finished rubbing salve into Matilda's grazed arm when Hamelin arrived to take Emma to visit their father's tomb while the court was still in Le Mans. Isabel eyed the disputed toy sword still stuck through his belt. Hamelin followed the direction of her gaze and gave a dry smile. "I shall keep this safe for the time being," he said. "I'll think about returning it later if my nephews are polite to me. In the meantime I have something for you, my lady." He produced her sewing from under his cloak. "I don't mind wandering the court with a toy sword stuck through my belt, but a piece of lady's needlecraft holds its own set of dangers. You left it behind and I thought I would spare you or your maid the trouble of fetching it."

Isabel felt her face grow warm. "Thank you, that was kind of you."

"I could see you were done with the company," Hamelin replied with a quirk of his eyebrow. He bowed to her and departed with Emma. Isabel saw to Matilda and then took her sewing away to a quiet corner. She felt unsettled and a little weepy. All the feelings about losing Will washed over her again. The guilt that she had been unable to help him, that she had failed as a wife. She didn't want to think about making another match but knew she was on borrowed time.

Alienor joined her on the bench. "You have come here to hide," she said. "This corner is far too dark for sewing. What is wrong?"

Isabel shook her head. "I was thinking of my husband," she said. "The king's brother came to me in the hall and said it was time I thought about remarrying." A tear plopped onto the fabric. "But when I try to imagine myself as another man's wife, I cannot."

Alienor set a gentle arm around her shoulders. "You will have to wed again at some point. It is inevitable; you know that. You have a duty to your lands to give them an heir."

"But not yet!" Isabel's voice grated with panic. "Let me stay in your household a while longer."

"Oh, now you are being foolish," Alienor said with exasperation. "I will make sure you are not pestered, but it cannot be forever." She gave her a firm look.

Isabel swallowed. "I understand that, madam," she said, but her heart quailed at the thought of being tied to William FitzEmpress. "I just need a little more time."

❖❖❖

Holding a bowl filled with gobbets of raw rabbit flesh, Alienor fed the white female gyrfalcon perched on the hawk stand in her chamber. La Reina was old and no longer ruled the skies as she had done in her prime. Alienor had a new young gyrfalcon in training, but she kept La Reina as a pet, and still flew her in the exercise yard on bright days when the sun was warm on the bird's gleaming white feathers. The falcon seized a lump of meat from Alienor's fingers and gulped it down. In spite of her years she still had a voracious appetite.

Alienor glanced around as Henry arrived. "Your brother is paying court to Isabel de Warenne," she said. "I assume he has your permission. When were you going to tell me?"

"I thought you knew," he said blandly.

"Your mother dropped hints when last I saw her. I suppose you were using her as your filter to avoid broaching the matter with me in person." She pursed her lips and made a smacking sound to the bird. "Perhaps I have someone else in mind. She might settle very well with one of my own barons."

"But her keeping is not in your gift," Henry said. "It is for me to decide." He removed his cloak and tossed it across an oak chest. "My brother is the son of an empress and the grandson of a king, and that matches with what she had before. Why should I want to give one of your barons influence in England? My brother already has English estates and this will suit him very well." He picked up the toy sword lying on the hearth bench. Hamelin had earlier restored the weapon to Harry and Richard following a stiff lecture about actions and consequences.

"But you put your men in positions of authority in my household," she retorted. "My chancellor and my steward are both your choices. Why should I not reward one of my own? I am sure you could afford one switch of affinity. There are plenty of other women your brother could marry."

Henry scowled. "That is not the point. William will marry Isabel de Warenne. I have promised him. You will not fight me on this." He cut the air left and right with his son's sword. Swish, swish.

Alienor fed the gyrfalcon another gobbet of meat and stroked her snowy breast. "Isabel is not ready for remarriage. I cannot see the need for haste when the revenues stay in your hands while she remains a widow. No one is going to abduct her out of my household. She is safe and she will still be of childbearing age even if you delay another year. Let your brother bide his time a while longer and I will encourage Isabel to take a more active part in the life of the court."

Henry gave her a dark look. "I will not wait forever on this," he said. "When I give the command, it shall be done."

"Indeed, as you say." Alienor was prepared to be conciliatory now that she had at least the hint of a concession.

Henry gave a brusque nod, put down the sword, and went to pour himself a cup of wine.

"Your sons were arguing over that toy and Hamelin had to sort them out," she told him. "Brotherly love does not extend to sharing possessions."

"Brotherly love is rarer than daylight in December," he said with cynical amusement. "If it was over a weapon, I expect Richard started it."

Alienor wiped her bloodied fingers on a napkin. "He is very forward for his age. He learns swiftly and he is dexterous. He doesn't see himself as smaller than Harry." She felt a quiet glimmer of pride. She loved both of her sons, but Richard was the one she had marked out.

"But he will have to learn his place in the family nonetheless, and that is subordinate to Harry as the heir."

Alienor said nothing. Richard would not view himself as subordinate to anyone, and she had no intention of dampening his spirit.

Henry took a swallow of wine and after a long moment said, "What would you say if I told you I was thinking of making Thomas Becket the archbishop of Canterbury?"

Alienor turned and stared at him in astonishment, and then disbelief. "I should say you were utterly mad! He is already the chancellor. Why would you want to give him more power than that?"

"Because he performs the task of chancellor very well. If I make him archbishop, then church and state will work together hand in glove."

Alienor gave a vehement shake of her head. "You will be putting the power of church and state in the hands of a single man. There will be no checks and balances."

Henry's nostrils flared with impatience. "Of course there will. Thomas will do my bidding. He has been my chancellor for six years, and I know him well."

"Do you?" Alienor shook her head. "I do not believe anyone knows Thomas but Thomas. The face he shows to you is a charming front. He is a consummate politician and he will tie you in knots. And even if I am wrong and you do know him, Henry, he knows you better. He is not even a priest. How will the clergy take to his rule?"

Henry scowled at her. "You are always contrary. Why do you always have to oppose me?"

Alienor returned his look. "You asked my opinion and I gave it. Have you said anything to Becket about this?"

"Not yet." Henry bit his thumbnail.

"There are other candidates?"

"Yes, Gilbert Foliot and Roger of Pont L'Évêque, but neither would fit the shoes as well even if they think they would. They will act as checks to Thomas should it be required."

"I still think you are treading on dangerous ground. I counsel you not to act in haste lest you repent at leisure."

Henry shrugged and drank his wine. "I will not change my mind. The advantages far outweigh the pitfalls."

Alienor was less convinced but well recognized that stubborn look by now.

"I am also of a mind to put Harry into Thomas's household to be tutored."

Another shock jolted through her. "He is too young for that." She felt as if she were in a fight and being pummeled by blows from all angles. "He already has a tutor."

"Yes, a good one, but that only suffices for the moment. He needs more. Thomas employs learned men in his household who will take him a stage further. He is a future king; he must be prepared, and the chancellor's household is the best place." He made an exasperated sound. "Christ, stop looking at me like that. I did not mean immediately. These things have to be planned well in advance."

Oh yes, she thought. Henry always had everything planned, always one step in front. But sometimes being one step in front meant you were first over the edge of the cliff.

# 19

## FÉCAMP, FEBRUARY 1162

$\mathscr{E}$NTERING HER CHAMBER, ALIENOR WENT STRAIGHT TO THE cradle to look at her baby daughter. "How is she?"

Although it was not long past midday, the light was already failing and candles had been lit. Alienor had been at the cathedral attending a prestigious reburial ceremony for the bones of the dukes of Normandy but had hurried back to her sick child the moment she could escape.

"No change, madam," said Hela, the wet nurse. "She is still very hot. I have bathed her in tepid rose water, and she has taken suck from me once but not for long. Her little mouth around my teat was scalding."

Alienor touched the baby's cheek with a gentle forefinger and fear arrowed through her. This, her second daughter, had been born at Domfront on a golden morning in October and baptized Alienor but called Alie to differentiate her from her mother. She had been small at birth compared to her siblings, a dainty child, perfectly formed, but not a hearty feeder like the others. Her brothers and sister were recovering from a contagion of itching pox. Now little Alie had succumbed and was very unwell.

Alienor had been worrying about the baby throughout the reinterment ceremony, and although she had performed her role with grace and duty, her thoughts had been with her sick daughter. She could not be bothered with Henry's dead ancestors when their living child stood in peril of her life. It brought back all the terrible memories of Will's death, and the reburial ceremony seemed like a portent.

Henry arrived, broad-shouldered and stocky in his ceremonial ermine and scarlet. "How does she fare?" His gaze darted to the cradle and then swiftly away.

"She is in God's hands," Alienor said. "All we can do is pray."

A muscle clenched in Henry's cheek. "You are needed among our guests," he said shortly. "Do not be long." Turning on his heel, he almost ran from the room.

"I am needed here too," she said to the space where he had stood and been unable to hold his ground. She felt helpless and riddled with guilt. Angry with Henry, angry with God. What if he dropped Alie as he had dropped Will?

Eventually, she joined Henry among the great gathering in the hall. Harry accompanied her because he was over the rash and the itching, but Richard, Matilda, and Geoffrey were still covered in scabs and confined to the nursery. It would not do to have the heirs of the dukes of Normandy sitting at the table scratching their crusted sores.

Alienor played her role to the hilt. She was smiling and gracious to their guests. She made witticisms. She listened and nodded and wove a smooth social ribbon. She engaged in serious conversations, although later she was not to recall what she said. But the moment she could escape without seeming discourteous, she retired to keep vigil over her tiny daughter.

Harry remained with Henry so that all could witness the continuity of the line from father to son, and everyone remarked upon the boy's good looks, his charm and finesse, uncommon in one so young.

"The saying goes that the fruit never falls far from the tree," Henry said and patted his son's head.

❖❖❖

In the small hours of the morning, the baby's fever reached crisis point and her little body stiffened and convulsed in a seizure.

Alienor had been dozing at the bedside, but the wet nurse's scream shocked her wide-awake.

"Demons have entered her body—send for the priest!" Hela wailed. "Holy Mary, save us all!"

"Be silent!" Alienor smacked the girl across the face, the sound cracking like a whip. "I will not hear such stupidity. Get out, get out now. I do not want to see your face again!"

The young woman fled, sobbing, and Alienor turned to the baby, her heart pounding with terror. The convulsion ceased and Alie flopped like a rag puppet. She was still alive, but her little ribs flexed and fell like overworked bellows. Marchisa arrived with a bowl of fresh, cool rose water. "We must keep wiping her down, madam," she said. "I have seen this kind of thing before in babies."

"Did they live? Look at me, tell me the truth."

Marchisa met her gaze with a steady brown stare. "Yes, madam."

"All of them?"

For the briefest instant Marchisa hesitated. "Most of them," she said.

For the remainder of the night, Alienor wiped her daughter's body with a moist cool cloth wrung out in the rose water, and begged the Virgin to spare the baby's life. Her eyes burned with dryness because she dared not close them, lest Alie be taken in that moment of blinking. She would not even leave her to Marchisa; only her own hand would do. Another wet nurse was sought and found in one of the huts outside the castle, and when Alie would not take suck, Alienor dripped honey and water into her mouth from the tip of a twisted rag.

As the dawn rose in the east with tiny specks of snow floating in a gray-and-gold sunrise, the infant's fever finally broke and her breathing eased. Alienor watched the gentle rise and fall of the little chest, no longer frenetic, and felt as twisted as the cloth she had been using as a drip feed. She had no energy for euphoria. Uttering a sound midway between a sob and a sigh, she pressed her face into her hands. She wanted to cry, but the tears would not come. She had hoped that Henry could visit to see how their daughter fared, and had been disappointed but not surprised that he had not.

"Come, madam, you must sleep for a little while now," Isabel said. "I will see to everything." She put her arm around Alienor. "If there is a change, I will waken you immediately."

Alienor drank a cup of spring water while Marchisa combed out her hair and helped her remove her gown. She was achingly tired, and nauseous too. She fell into bed, barely aware of Isabel drawing the curtains, and Marchisa speaking softly to the sick baby. Within moments she was asleep, and it was a deep, dark slumber, bereft of dreams and heavy with exhaustion.

She woke late in the morning to the sound of Henry talking to her women, his voice husky and cheerful. She sat up, bleary-eyed and sluggish. There was a vile taste in her mouth and the nausea of last night was still with her. Pulling a loose robe over her chemise, she parted the bed curtains and looked at Henry, who was his usual robust and energetic self.

"You have finally come to see how your daughter fares," she said.

"I knew you would send for me if needed," he replied with a shrug. "What use would I be with a sick baby? That is women's business."

"You could have sent word to inquire."

He gave her a look that said she was being ridiculous. Anger bubbled up inside her, hot, vile, nauseating. She had to run to the garderobe, where she knelt over the hole, retching. Henry listened to the sound with a thoughtful look on his face.

She returned, hunched over, her stomach sore. "I am with child again," she said and felt drained just announcing it, for Alie was only a little over four months old. He had indeed turned her into a brood mare.

"I thought so," he said with a hard smile and kissed her cheek. "That is good news indeed, and meanwhile there is still no sign of an heir for France."

Alienor forced herself to straighten. "Are you going to look at your daughter now that you are here?"

Humoring her, he went to the cradle. Little Alie had developed a flush of red spots over her body but was sleeping obliviously. The new wet nurse assured Alienor that the baby had recently fed well.

"See," Henry said, "there was no cause for all this fuss."

Alienor said nothing because she was incoherent with rage and contempt.

"Go back to bed," he said in pacific tones. "You must rest if you are to grow us another healthy child, and in truth you do not look well."

"What do you expect when I have been keeping vigil all night with our sick daughter? One you have not bothered to visit until the crisis is over, and now you say it is a fuss over nothing?"

"Because it is," he said. "The evidence is before your eyes." He took her arm, his manner patronizing and solicitous, as if he was being kind to a half-wit, and led her to the bed, where he made her lie down and pulled the covers around her. Then he waved her women away and sat on the coverlet. "That is better," he said.

She did not answer. Henry picked at a piece of embroidery on the coverlet where a thread had come undone. She watched him unravel it and stifled the urge to slap his hand.

He looked at her from under his brows. "The Countess de Warenne has had more than enough time to mourn," he said. "I want you to speak to her before Easter about my brother's suit."

Alienor sighed, just wanting to be rid of his presence. "I will do as you wish," she said, "but she shall keep me company until the child is born. Let the wedding wait until then. She and your brother will have time for courtship in the meanwhile."

His eyes narrowed and she thought he was going to refuse, but he eventually nodded brusque assent. "Very well, but they will be wed the moment you are churched. I will brook no delay after that."

"As you wish," Alienor said and shut her eyes.

❖❖❖

The door closed behind the squire and Henry reached for his wine and considered his chancellor. They had been playing chess and honor had been fulfilled by a stalemate, although the satisfaction of a triumph had eluded both men.

"I want to talk to you, Thomas," Henry said. "It's about the vacant see at Canterbury, but I think you already know what I am going to say. You know I have not summoned you here solely for the purpose of taking my son into your household to educate."

Becket bowed his head. "Sire, I had wondered." His expression gave nothing away.

"Well then, let me put an end to your wondering. I desire you to take the position of archbishop. It seems to me to be the most practical solution."

Thomas inhaled and Henry raised a hand to stop him. "No arguments. You will be lying if you say you did not desire this or that you are incapable. I need you to accept this post and bring church and state together in harmony. I have thought the matter through, and you are the only man I trust to do it successfully."

"Sire, there are others who could accomplish this task who are already seasoned bishops of the Church."

Henry snorted down his nose. "Foliot or Pont L'Évêque, you mean? I want men who are going to look to the future, not the past."

Thomas's face had flushed, and Henry saw his fists curl in his sleeve like a cat flexing its paws. "If we are speaking straightly, sire, I am not sure I should accept," he said. "It will be difficult to unite the secular and the spiritual because one will always push against the other."

Henry brushed the detail aside. "Well then, it makes sense to have the two in harmony, not opposition. You will be able to blend them together. You can always delegate more tasks to others and have them report to you."

"Sire, you honor me…"

"Yes, I do." Henry's eyes brightened and he leaned forward in his chair to put over the full force of his will. "I expect you to take this up, Thomas. If you do not, I shall indeed have to consider the likes of Gilbert Foliot. Would you rather deal with him as head of the Church while you are chancellor, or would you wear both mantles and have him answer to your authority on all counts?"

"I think you know the answer to that one, sire," Becket replied, "b-but it is a big step to take."

"But one you want, despite your protestations. I know you, Thomas. I know your ambition and hunger. How great would it be for your family? A common London citizen raised to the pinnacle of church and government." Henry watched his chancellor's flush deepen. He knew how much Thomas hated references to his mercantile roots, and how he yearned after the power of privilege. "I need you in that position," he reiterated. "It is time for reform."

Thomas clasped his hands together as if in prayer, and pressed his fingertips beneath his chin. "You have raised me to the chancellorship and now you ask me to be your archbishop of Canterbury. I will do my utmost to fulfill those roles, but, by your leave, I must pray for guidance."

"As you will," Henry said, knowing he had caught his fish but content now to let it land itself.

❖ ❖ ❖

Harry wore a new blue tunic that enhanced his eyes, turning them the color of wild harebells. His cloak was of bright red wool banded with gold and his belt buckle carved from a piece of walrus ivory. Today he was leaving the care of his nurse, his mother and her women, and entering the chancellor's household to begin a more rigorous regime of education.

Alienor's throat tightened as she looked at him, so grown up yet still so much the little boy. "I want you to work hard at your lessons," she said, smoothing his dark golden hair. "One day you will be a king and a duke, and what you learn now will stand you in good stead for then. I want to hear good reports of you from the chancellor."

"Yes, Mama." Harry nodded manfully, his expression a mixture of anticipation and bravado. He knew Chancellor Thomas well because he was often about the household, speaking to his parents about matters of finance and government. He had wonderful clothes, much finer than Papa, and two muscular white gazehounds with red collars and silver bells. Harry knew from overheard conversations that Thomas was going to be the new archbishop of Canterbury, and that it would make him very important indeed. When he had asked his papa if Thomas was going to be more important than the king, his papa's eyes had hardened, but he had then laughed and said that no, the archbishop of Canterbury was still the king's servant and Thomas would have to do as he said.

Becket arrived wearing a magnificent cloak lined with squirrel fur and pinned with a round gold brooch.

Alienor steeled herself to be polite to him. "May I congratulate you on your new position, my lord chancellor," she said.

Becket's expression was calm, but his eyes were wary as he bowed to her. "Madam, I do not underestimate the importance and difficulty of the task I have b–been set and will attend to it as diligently as I am able."

"I am certain you will," she answered with diplomatic grace. Time would tell, she thought. He had many enemies among the barons and prelates, including the bishops of Hereford and London who had been passed over for the appointment, but he had friends too, several at the papal court, and that counted for much. She still thought Henry insane to give one man so much power, but for now she would hold her peace.

"I am counting on you to educate my son with integrity," she said. "Teach him what he needs to know in order to rule wisely and well."

"Madam, I shall do my utmost."

Alienor bade formal farewell to Harry. She had already said her heartfelt good-byes, and this was not the time for more beyond the official kiss of peace. But even so as she felt his child's lithe body and inhaled his scent, it broke her heart to know that never again would he be a small boy playing underfoot in her chamber. This was his moment of severance from the world of women, the time when he turned away from her toward manhood and absorbed different, harsher influences. Her chest constricted, but she held her head high as he left the room, Becket's arm sheltering him like a wing.

# 20

## Falaise, Normandy, April 1162

ALIENOR HAD BEEN FEELING EXHAUSTED AND QUEASY ALL morning. From the beginning of this pregnancy she had been unwell, and the sickness had continued beyond the early weeks. The usual remedy of drinking barley water with a pinch of ginger and taking more rest had done nothing to alleviate the symptoms. This was the seventh occasion that Henry's seed had taken root in her womb in nine years. She was thirty-eight years old, and the frequent pregnancies were taking their toll.

She brought her embroidery to the window seat and joined Isabel, who was working on a chemise. For a short while Alienor picked away at her own stitches, but the act of looking down increased her nausea. Raising her head, she looked at the light filtering through the lozenges of glass in their lead housings and tried to distract herself from her discomfort.

"You know that the king has marriage plans for you and his brother," she said to Isabel. "When I tried to broach it before, you said you were not ready."

Isabel's needle wove in and out, glinting with silver light. She said nothing and Alienor received the impression that she would have melted into her work if she could.

"I need you to consider it now. My lord is looking to make this match before the end of the year."

Isabel set her needle in the fabric without looking up. "You have been very patient, as has the king, and I am grateful."

"But that patience is finite. The king has agreed you may stay with me until the child is born. That will give you and my husband's brother time to become better acquainted before you are wed."

Isabel's expression was blank. "Yes, madam."

"Think on it," Alienor said. "I can do no more for you, even though you still have my protection. It is your obligation to do your duty, as we all must."

She picked up her sewing again, but before she could make the first stitch, a deep, squeezing pain struck in the small of her spine, and she doubled over with a gasp.

Isabel pushed aside her own work, put her arm around Alienor, and cried for help. Alienor's women came running and helped her to her bed, although Alienor was barely able to walk. Her belly cramped and she felt the first hot flush of blood between her thighs as the miscarriage began.

Someone ran to fetch a midwife, someone else a physician, and everything became a blur of frantic activity. Nothing could be done to stop the labor and save the baby. Alienor saw the fear in her women's eyes and it mirrored her own. This was not an early miscarriage, and there was a lot of blood. Her chaplain had been sent for too. She could hear his voice in the antechamber.

The midwife arrived, rolled back her sleeves, and set to work, externally massaging Alienor's womb and entreating the intercession of Saint Margaret, patron of women in travail. Isabel held Alienor's hand and, in between her own entreaties to the saint, murmured reassurance.

The baby was another boy, no bigger than the length of Alienor's palm, born still and dead, followed swiftly by the placenta. The midwife quickly covered the blood-splattered bowl with a cloth. "He died in the womb," she said. "It happens sometimes. There is naught to prevent you from bearing another child when you are well."

Alienor stared dully at the wall without answering. The midwife's pragmatic remarks, the soothing murmurs of her women, and all the looks exchanged across her body seemed to be part of someone else's experience and she a stranger watching it happen. Journeying in the Holy Land she had miscarried of a boy child on the road between Antioch and Jerusalem, and this experience had exhumed all those terrible memories. No matter how deep she buried them, they would always resurface, unquiet and crying out to be acknowledged. There was nothing to prevent her from bearing another child, the midwife said. That had to be a curse, not a blessing. No consecrated ground for this little corpse. No baptism, no resurrection—just the long void of limbo.

❖❖❖

Alienor passed the next several days in a state of pain and fever. The latter burned so high that her wits wandered and she thrashed in nightmare dreams. Isabel, Marchisa, and Emma attended her constantly, cooling her with rose water and soothing her when she cried out. Physicians came and went. Once Alienor saw Henry watching her at the bedside but could not be sure if it was real or just the fever dreams. She thought she heard his voice, hoarse with anxiety. "She is going to live, isn't she?"

"Sire, she is in God's hands," the physician replied gravely.

"I say to you again, she is going to live—isn't she?"

"What for?" Alienor heard herself ask in a scratchy, faded voice.

Henry leaned over the bed and she could smell the fresh scent of outdoors on his clothes, and the more pungent aroma of hard-ridden horse and sweaty man. "Because, my love, you are always contrary. You will not give up the fight, even if it is only to spite me."

"I could spite you by dying," she murmured. Across the darkness behind her lids, a white gyrfalcon soared into her vision, wings outspread like those of a fierce angel.

When next she woke, Henry was still at her bedside. Morning light filled the room, turning his hair to tongues of fire, and making the green of his tunic as vivid as new grass. His gray gaze met hers. "I told you so," he said.

"I am most certainly not in heaven," she croaked. "It remains to be seen whether I am in hell."

He lifted a sardonic eyebrow. "That is up to you, my love, but I am glad you decided to stay." He leaned over to take her hand and pressed his lips to her wedding ring.

A memory surfaced of blood and pain. "The child," she said. "I lost the child."

"Hush, it does not matter."

"But it does."

"You are still very weak. Rest now and grow strong. I do not want to lose you." He kissed her brow and left the room, his footfall quiet for once.

"He has been here every day, madam," said Emma as she tidied the covers and poured Alienor a cup of barley water. "He cares for you. Truly he does."

Alienor sipped the cold, cloudy drink. She felt frail and hollow, but she was hungry, and her mind was clear. "Yes," she said with weary cynicism. "He cares that I should live because if I do not, he will face upheaval and rebellion in Aquitaine. He cares for the prestige and the affinities I bring to our marriage, but he cares for me only in the way of pushing against a familiar obstacle. Should that obstacle suddenly disappear, it will unbalance him, at least for a while." She shook her head when Emma made to protest. "It is the truth. I know where I stand with him—better that than living with delusions."

❖ ❖ ❖

September sunshine bathed the walls of Chinon Castle, turning the stone to the same mellow gold as the surrounding harvested fields. Orchards hung heavy with ripening silver-green pears and red-flushed apples. In field and meadow, animals fattened on the last of the glut before the autumn slaughter.

Alienor had been slow to recover and only now was she beginning to feel strong and well. Recuperating, she had been glad to sit at her sewing and involve herself with her children, playing games with them, reading, listening to music. She had found peace of mind in taking time for contemplation and prayer. Let others see to the details of policy, government, and diplomatic striving. What did they matter?

She had been quietly indifferent toward Henry during this time. It was as if she was contained within a protective bubble and whatever he did had no impact on her. A favorite opinion of his was that women lost their wits when they were breeding and became as bovine as cattle. Alienor had felt that way throughout the long weeks of recuperation and only now in the mellow autumn days was she beginning to feel lighter in her being, and to look beyond the bower. The world was developing focus and color again, and her appetite for its caprices was sharpening.

Standing by the open window she saw Henry's brother William strolling toward the stables with Isabel at his side. A falconer walked behind, William's peregrine perched on his gloved wrist. William was gesticulating to Isabel and talking rapidly. She had her head down and slightly turned away. He had asked her to come riding with him, and although Isabel had agreed, she had left the bower with the look of someone going to their doom.

Out on the sward, Hamelin was practicing swordplay with Richard and Geoffrey, teaching them their strokes and defenses. Richard was hammering at his uncle as if he were on a battlefield and meant every blow, whereas Geoffrey's movements were more measured, lacking the killer fire.

Alienor looked around with a start of surprise as Henry burst into the chamber, disturbing the tranquil atmosphere. This morning, when she had seen him in the great hall, his humor had been sharp and cheerful, but now his lips were set in a hard, thin line, and his eyes were narrow with fury. "Whatever is the matter?"

"Becket." He almost spat the name and kicked a stool out of the way. "I cannot believe he has done this to me. How could he, after all the privileges I have bestowed on him, the lowborn ingrate."

"Why, what has he done?"

Henry's jaw worked as if chewing on gristle. "Resigned the chancellorship. Says he cannot in conscience dedicate himself to both church and state. God's teeth, he knew when he accepted the position he would have to deal with both."

Alienor raised her brows. "You took the risk when you appointed him," she said and forbore to comment that she had warned him against choosing Becket.

Henry glowered. "Why can he not delegate more duties as he agreed to do when I appointed him?"

"Perhaps he has more responsibility than he thought—more to learn and to do if he is to control the Church?"

Henry exhaled hard. "Hah, Thomas is capable of that with one hand tied behind his back."

"Then perhaps he prefers to give his full attention to the greater calling," she said. "As head of the English church, he is your equal, not a subordinate. He little needs to answer to you as archbishop in the same way he does as chancellor." She suspected that for Henry it was like having his favorite hawk fly off into a high tree from where he could neither retrieve nor control it. In his mind, it was one step away from betrayal, and even while he was prepared to break his own word as easily as washing his hands, it was unacceptable for others to mete out the same treatment to him. "What are you going to do about it?"

"I shall refuse and tell him to think again."

"I fear you may have sown a crop that will cause you a bitter harvest."

"There will be no harvest," Henry snapped. "If the crop is poisoned, then I shall uproot it."

Alienor eyed him with foreboding. She knew what he was like when thwarted. She saw the same behavior in her sons when they had tantrums. If the difficulty was straightforward and Becket was indeed just overtaxed, then perhaps matters would resolve themselves, but she suspected the issue was more tangled and difficult than that. It would not be as simple as uprooting. Anyone who tried to do that to nettles always got stung. "You will need a chancellor in the meantime."

"Geoffrey Ridel can take on the task. He's archdeacon of Canterbury and knows the working of the chancellery. He's competent—but still not what I intended." His tone became harsh, almost petulant. "Thomas knew. That is what sticks in my craw."

Alienor liked Ridel even less than Becket. An obsequious slug of a man with a sly gaze and dirty fingernails. Competent, but hardly an asset.

The children came hurtling inside from their outdoor play, several boisterous dogs leaping around them, with Hamelin following in their wake, tugging down his tunic, which had been stuffed in his belt. Richard was still at such a pitch of excitement that he chased Geoffrey around their father, yelling, and accidentally whacked Henry on his shin where a horse had recently kicked him. Henry roared with pain and rage and struck Richard across the face with the back of his hand, so hard that he felled him. Immediate silence fell, everyone trapped in the reverberation of the slap. Geoffrey was the first to move, running to hide his face against his nurse's skirts. Richard rose from the floor, a livid red mark striping his cheek. His lower lip quivered and then tightened. He shot his father a fierce blue look filled with hatred. Henry snatched the toy sword from him and snapped it across his thigh.

"Teach him some manners, madam," he snarled to Alienor, "or I will thrash them into him myself." He rounded on Hamelin. "And you, you fool, should know better than to feed such folly. You are worse than they are." He tossed the broken sword on the floor and stormed from the room.

Richard stared after him, trembling like a hound, but not with fear. Alienor wanted to take him in her arms but held back. From a very young age Richard had eschewed tears, and on the rare occasions he did cry, it was always hidden away, or on Hodierna's soft breast. With Alienor he was always manly and proud. "Come," she said. "Your father is angry about something else and you rushed in at the wrong time without thought or manners. You must learn to control yourself if you are going to be a great ruler and commander of other men."

Richard thrust out his lower lip. "Papa doesn't."

"That is not true. You should not have barged into my chamber like a wild animal."

"He broke my sword."

"Because you challenged him." Alienor did reach out now and lightly caress his hair. "I shall have one of the squires make you another one. Go now with Hodierna and she will put some salve on your face. We shall talk later about the responsibilities of princes."

When Richard and Geoffrey had been taken away by their nurses, Hamelin, who had remained silent throughout the exchange, asked, "Why is Henry in such a temper?"

Alienor told him about Becket's resignation. "What do you make of it?"

Hamelin grimaced. "A man cannot look in two directions at once, nor serve two masters with opposing needs. I fear we may be at the top of a slippery slope, but I pray not."

"Indeed, there is always prayer," Alienor replied cynically. Hamelin rubbed the back of his neck. "I had better find Henry and see what's to be done in the interim."

When he had gone, Alienor sat down in the embrasure, her expression thoughtful and troubled.

❖❖❖

In the stable yard, William FitzEmpress stood beside Isabel, close enough to touch cloaks. "I have been looking forward to riding out with you," he said.

Isabel looked down, feigning modesty. She did not reciprocate his sentiment, but he appeared not to notice, being more concerned with the sound of his own voice. "When I am your husband, we shall go hunting and hawking often."

She murmured a platitude.

His gaze became predatory. "I will show you a world your first husband never did. I will show you the difference between a boy and a man."

Isabel's expression set like stone. A true man did not need to boast at the expense of others. He had already been looking over the charters and terms by which she held her lands, had been cultivating her knights and retainers, speaking to them as if she was no more than his appendage, buying them with big talk and bribes. She had heard him issuing promises of grants and largesse to his own retainers too. Each time she imagined being wed to him, sharing the same bed, sitting with him in church and at the dining trestle, she felt sick.

William signaled and the grooms led out the horses, saddled and ready—a dainty black gelding for Isabel, followed by her deceased husband's favorite golden dun, Carbonel. She was horrified to see the palfrey because it was sacrilege that William FitzEmpress should ride him. The fact that he had given the order to have him harnessed when he was not entitled to infuriated her.

"Sire," she said, "the horse belonged to my first husband. I would rather you chose a different mount."

He gave an arrogant shrug. "I know full well this was your lord's palfrey. I would think you glad for me to ride the beast, for certainly it is no mount for a woman."

Isabel hated conflict but could stand her ground if she must. "We are not yet married, sire. I would have you wait until you have the right. And I have no difficulty handling him."

William's lip curled. "We would have been wed years ago but for you prevaricating, my lady. Since we are soon to be joined, I see no reason to wait longer for what is mine." He boosted her onto the black and placed her foot in the stirrup, his hand lingering on her ankle in a gesture that signaled possession. Isabel moved her foot. He gave her a narrow smile and turned away to mount the dun, deliberately wrenching the horse's head around with a vicious pull on the bit.

Isabel swallowed. She did not want to ride with him, but to refuse would be giving up too easily. Perhaps when he had finished showing off he would settle down. She made an effort to push herself through the moment but could not prevent a murmur of dismay as she saw the blood on Carbonel's bit, and the way the palfrey was rolling his eyes.

"You have to show a horse who is master," he said.

"My husband never had any difficulty with Carbonel's obedience," she replied. "He did not need to use spur and whip."

William arched his brows. "Then likely he was fortunate, my lady," he said. "And he is no longer your husband; you are his widow."

The barb cut Isabel to the quick and robbed her of words. He seemed to think he had put her in her place and, as they rode along, he talked expansively of the plans he had for the earldom. As Isabel listened, she became increasingly dismayed, not because the plans were outrageous or foolish, but because he was already taking it for granted that her property was his to do with as he chose.

They were taking a track through a hay meadow, blowing with daisies, dandelion, and speedwell, when a young hare flashed away from beneath Carbonel's hooves. The dun, already sweating and distressed, reared, plunged sideways, and gave several twisting bucks, the last one flinging William from the saddle, and then bolted. William landed hard, the air slamming from his lungs, leaving him struggling like a landed trout. Still fastened to his wrist, his hawk flapped and bated. Isabel clapped her hand to her mouth and stared at him in horror, although she had a desperate urge to laugh.

William's squire spurred after Carbonel's dust cloud.

"He never did that to my first husband," she said. "Are you hurt?"

Aided by another squire, William struggled to his feet. He handed his frantic hawk to the youth and then beat at his mud-smirched garments. "No, by the grace of God," he snarled. He took his squire's horse for himself but had to be boosted into the saddle because he was still out of breath.

The hunt aborted, they returned to Chinon, William in a thunderous mood and speaking barely a word to Isabel. She did not attempt to cozen him out of his rage but rode in silence. Her satisfaction at seeing him take a fall, the momentary urge to laugh, had gone. If he was like this now, how was he going to behave when they were married?

They were dismounting in the yard when the first squire caught up with them at a rapid trot, Carbonel on a leading rein. Sweat dripped from the trembling dun's coat and he was lame on his offside hind leg. Isabel was appalled.

William dismounted gingerly, and clutching his ribs, eyed the distressed horse. "That nag is fit only for dog meat," he spat and turned to a stony-faced groom. "Have it slaughtered and fed to hounds."

"No!" Isabel was no longer able to hold her peace. "The horse is mine and I say what is to be done with him." She turned to the groom. "Unsaddle him and see to his injuries. Do it now, I say."

The groom hesitated, caught like a grain between two millstones.

William glared at her. "He is not a fit mount to ride. He's worthless."

"Then no one shall ride him. I gave you no permission to do so, and even if he is worthless to you, he has value beyond gold to me." Again she gestured to the groom, and this time he obeyed her with downcast eyes.

William bared his teeth. "By God, when we are married, it will be different. You need someone to handle you and teach you to be a biddable wife. You have been too long in my sister's company!" His hand pressed to his side, he lurched from the yard.

Isabel drew a deep breath and strove to hold herself together. She followed the groom into the stables. The palfrey was dancing on his hooves and swinging his rump in a distressed manner. The groom spoke softly, seeking to calm him down. "Will he be all right?" she asked.

The man screwed up his broad, freckled face. "As far as I can tell, madam. He has a sore mouth and a strained leg, and he's been stirred up by a hard rider, but I reckon with a few days' rest and care he'll recover."

"A hard rider" was a tactful way of saying that the palfrey had been abused by a fool. "I have a mind to send him back to Norfolk," she said, "but until I can make arrangements, I do not want him ridden again without my permission, is that understood?"

"Yes, madam."

Isabel gave a firm nod, but inside she was shivery and upset. Returning to the keep, she went directly to the castle chapel and knelt before the altar to pray for strength. It was difficult to form the words and concentrate, because her mind kept flitting over what had happened. Whatever was decreed by the king, she could not wed this man. His treatment of Carbonel had marked the final turning point. But how she was going to extricate herself, she did not know.

❖❖❖

Alienor looked across to Isabel who was sitting in her usual seat in the embrasure, sewing as if her life depended on it. She had been very subdued since returning from her ride with Henry's brother and had kept her own company, speaking in monosyllables when addressed.

Bidding her other women continue with their duties, Alienor joined her. "Now then," she said. "Tell me, what is wrong? You cannot keep it all to yourself."

Isabel pressed her lips together, but her chin was wobbling, and she suddenly burst into tears and, grabbing a scrap of linen, pressed it against her face. "I am sorry," she sobbed. "I am so sorry."

"For what?" Alienor demanded with bewildered exasperation. "What have you to be sorry about?"

Isabel swallowed and wiped her eyes. "I cannot make it right that I should marry William FitzEmpress." She sniffed. "And yet it is my duty to do as the king bids. I have tried and tried, but I cannot bear to be in his presence and company for the rest of my days."

"Why, what has he done?" Alienor looked sharply at Isabel. "Did something happen on your ride?"

Isabel told her, pausing now and then to wipe her eyes and blow her nose. "I would stand in his path with a sword in my own hand before I would let him near Carbonel again." She was vehement through her distress. "I do not wish to let you down, because I know it is for the king's political purpose, but I cannot do this." She squeezed the damp scrap of linen in her hand.

Alienor was desperately concerned about Isabel but also dismayed, knowing how Henry would respond. She knew what it was like to have the wrong husband, and Isabel, although outwardly gentle and soft, had a core of steel, and she had to take what she said seriously. This was no whim.

"Do not worry," she said. "I am certain something will happen to remedy the situation. I will see what I can do."

Isabel shook her head. "But that will make it difficult for you, and what can you do anyway? I cannot put this burden onto your shoulders."

"Come, come, let us have none of that talk. I would not be a friend if I did not try to help." She patted Isabel's hand. "I am glad you have told me."

"But in truth, madam, I do not see how you can help."

Alienor kissed her. "You do not need to know the details, only that I will do what I can. A queen has certain ways and means open to her that may yield results." Calling for her scribe, she left the embrasure. She thought of Henry striking Richard across the face a few hours ago; she thought of the conversations she and Henry had had on the matter of Isabel's marriage; she thought of William's mistreatment of Carbonel and his threat to have him slaughtered. There was one avenue that might be of benefit, and she was sufficiently nettled to take it.

The scribe arrived, sheaves of parchment tucked under his arm, several quill pens behind his ear and an ink horn hanging from his belt. "Madam?"

"I want you to write a letter to the archbishop of Canterbury," she said.

# 21

## Barfleur, Spring 1163

THE STORM HAD FINALLY ABATED, BUT THE WIND REMAINED brisk; it was going to be a wild horse of a crossing to England. Alienor did not enjoy heavy seas, but neither was she a victim of seasickness. Bernard her chamberlain always spent the journey with his head in a bucket.

She and Henry had expected to spend Christmas in England, but the bad weather had prevented their voyage. Henry had been impossible to live with during the lack of communication with his kingdom. It was several years since his last visit to England, and he needed to attend to business there.

He was currently pacing the dockside like a leashed lion. Had he possessed a tail, he would have been lashing it from side to side. At almost thirty, the slender contours of youth had set into a more solid masculinity and the first fine lines etched the skin around his eyes. He was no longer the lithe young king, untried and fresh, but a man of power with a tread made heavier by a weight of suspicion and the burden of ruling a vast empire stretching from the Scottish borders all the way to the folds of the Pyrenees.

Alienor winced as she heard Alie wailing in her nurse's arms. The child was at the fractious toddler stage, too small to listen to reason and brimful of furious emotion. She was ready for a sleep too, but that would not happen until they boarded ship.

Well on her way to being seven years old, her older daughter was solemn and composed. Just now she was shaking her head at Geoffrey and Richard who were dashing about the dockside creating mayhem.

"Let them run off their wildness," Alienor said to her. "We'll be cooped up on board ship for several hours."

Matilda gave a superior little sniff. "Boys are not as sensible as girls."

"Indeed, that is true." Alienor gave her a woman-to-woman smile and a hug.

It began to snow, small, fine flakes little larger than scurf in a beggar's hair. Alienor looked over at Isabel de Warenne, who stood shivering among her other ladies. Her gray cloak with its sable collar exaggerated the pallor of her face and the dark circles under her eyes. Alienor had not received a reply from the new archbishop to her letter about Isabel's marriage because of the wild weather, but she would find out soon enough.

Eventually, the tide was right and everyone boarded for the voyage. With the disaster of the *White Ship* in mind, where the vessel had sunk with the heir to the throne on board, the royal children were divided. Richard, Matilda, and the baby sailed with Alienor, and Geoffrey accompanied his father on the sleek magnificent king's vessel with its double lion banner, which pleased him mightily and caused Richard to sulk.

The fleet sailed out of the harbor's calm water and struck the hard salt spray of the open sea. Alienor gazed out over the swell of marbled green water. It seemed a lifetime since she had first voyaged to England with all her hopes fresh and new, and a crown to be claimed. So much hope and anticipation. Today her feelings were gritty and edged with endurance. The nights were opening out and spring was on the horizon, but that sense of anticipation had trickled away like water through her hands.

❖❖❖

A welcoming party waited to greet the royal fleet in Southampton. Drawn up in serried ranks, the archbishop of Canterbury's knights and men-at-arms were polished and equipped to the last detail.

Becket shone in his robes like a winter morning of frost and gold. He held a crosier of silver gilt and rock crystal in his right hand, and his left rested benignly on Harry's shoulder. The lad was dressed in a dark red tunic and fur-lined cloak, a golden circlet gleaming on his brow.

At a gesture from the archbishop, his entourage knelt as one, the sound resembling the muted flapping of a ship's great sail. "Sire," he said, and he too knelt, drawing Harry down beside him.

Henry studied the display with hard eyes, and Alienor felt a deep sense of unease. Becket's attitude was that of a ruler greeting guests at his door, rather than a royal servant acknowledging the arrival of the country's sovereign and his consort. However, she hid her concern beneath a regal exterior and murmured platitudes. For now she needed Becket's support. Their eyes met for a moment in acknowledgment of their business, and then he looked away, and she turned to Harry, greeting him with kisses on his wind-chilled cheeks and exclaiming at how tall he had grown. "You are almost bigger than me!"

He gave her his beautiful sunray smile. "And my father too."

Henry had overheard and gave an indulgent chuckle. "Just as long as you do not grow too big for your breeches," he said, then shot his archbishop a piercing look that sat completely at odds with the smile on his face.

❖ ❖ ❖

Later that day, Henry and Becket sat over a cup of wine as they had so often done in the past, but everything had changed. Where there had been trust and cordiality, now distance and wariness held sway. "I refuse to accept your resignation," Henry said coldly. "That was not my intent when I made you archbishop of Canterbury."

Thomas looked regretful but resolute. "My bishops accuse me of paying too much attention to secular matters. There is a constant clash of interests and never enough time to sort out the needs of the chancellery and the archbishopric. I cannot do both tasks well."

"That is a paltry excuse and you know it. You could delegate more tasks and just keep an eye on matters. I do, so why can't you?"

"God does not deserve divided attention, sire."

"That did not concern you when you accepted the post. I appointed you, and it is for me to remove the chancellorship should I see fit, not for you to resign." That was what stuck in Henry's craw. That Becket should do something like this of his own accord.

"Sire, I confess that I believed in my pride that I could do my duty to both offices, but it is too much for one man to hold, even with delegation. I did not do this thing lightly—I gave it much thought—but in the end I concluded that service to God is the most important service of all—for any man."

Henry's chest expanded with anger. "It was not God who raised you from the dust but me. Do not think to aggrandize yourself at my expense because if you do, I will cut off your arms." He made a gesture of angry dismissal. "Do then as your conscience dictates, but be it on your own head. I shall appoint Geoffrey Ridel chancellor in your stead because he is accomplished at fiscal work and will perform his office with more faith than you have."

"Sire, I am sure he will serve you well," Becket said calmly, although a muscle flickered beneath one eye.

"Better than some."

A heavy silence ensued as the men drank their wine. Henry banged his cup down. "Since you desire to abandon your duties as chancellor and devote yourself to ecclesiastical matters, there is the business of the dispensation my brother needs to wed the Countess de Warenne. The woman is being difficult and insisting upon it. I want you to draw up the document so that we can hold the wedding before Lent."

Becket fiddled with the edge of one voluminous sleeve. "Unfortunately, I cannot do that, sire."

"What do you mean, you cannot do it? Don't be preposterous!"

"Sire, I did mention it to you once before. There is a matter of consanguinity. The couple is related in the third degree. There are too many close family ties to make their union viable."

"Well, of course there are family ties!" Henry spluttered. "That's why they need a dispensation, but they are hardly brother and sister, are they?"

Becket remained implacable. "Unfortunately, sire, the fact remains that the Countess de Warenne and your brother are too closely related. I cannot give a dispensation when it is against the law of God."

Henry leaped to his feet and stood over Becket. "By Christ, why do you balk me on this? You shall give me that dispensation. This marriage has been planned for years, as well you know! You are doing this to flaunt your own power. Do not think I cannot see through you."

Becket too stood up, tall and gray as a granite rock compared to Henry's volcano. "Sire, I do not do this to inconvenience or spite you, but b-because it is not lawful. After what was done to the Countess de Warenne's sister-in-law, I would have expected you to treat this lady gently. Mary de Boulogne has been petitioning me for an annulment on the grounds that she was a nun illegally dragged from her convent ever since you arranged that particular union. Surely it is better to show tact and yield to the laws of consanguinity. I am given to understand that the Countess de Warenne does not look favorably on the suit for those very reasons—there are concerns at court."

Henry's complexion, already bright, grew incandescent with fury. "You are 'given to understand,' Thomas? Who gave you to understand? Has the Countess de Warenne asked you to deny the dispensation?"

Becket shook his head. "No, sire, she has not."

"So someone else has done so, which suggests that I have spies and meddlers in my household." A nauseating sense of betrayal ripped through him. Treachery and disloyalty were what he feared the most, especially under his nose, and he could guess the source.

"The salient point remains: the match is consanguineous, and I cannot condone it," Becket said, making a shield of righteous dignity.

"Be careful, Thomas." Henry's voice was thick with rage. "Be very careful. You have damaged the bond between us. Push the boundaries one step further and you will harm it beyond repair. Do not fight me, because I will not let you win."

❖❖❖

Marchisa ran the comb through Alienor's hair and followed downward with her palm, smoothing gently. Finding a gray strand amid the burnished gold, she carefully plucked it out.

"Another one?" Alienor was rueful. "They are gathering apace these days. They say wisdom and experience are compensations for the aging of the body, but I am not convinced of that. It would seem to me more practical to have all those attributes at the same time." She was rubbing rosewater unguent into her hands. They at least were still smooth and without blemish but nevertheless belonged to a woman of nine and thirty, not a girl. Hands that had held an orb and scepter, that had touched Christ's crown of thorns in Constantinople and impressed seals upon letters of destiny. Hands that had gripped Henry's flanks in pleasure as they conceived a child, and then held that child as he died burning with fever.

Marchisa had just finished her task when Henry slammed into the chamber unannounced, his expression thunderous. Alienor dismissed her women with a swift word and rose from her chair, pulling a loose silk robe over her chemise.

"Have you anything to do with this, madam? I know it's you!" He threw the piece of parchment he had been clutching so that it landed at her feet in a crumpled ball.

"To do with what?" She feigned indifference, although her heart had begun to pound.

"You know very well! Thomas Becket has refused a dispensation for the marriage of Isabel de Warenne to my brother, on grounds of consanguinity. He could grant a dispensation with a flick of his wrist and yet he has chosen not to. Why should he do that unless someone has whispered in his ear?"

Alienor made no attempt to pick up the parchment. "Perhaps he followed his conscience," she said, her voice calm but forceful. "Sometimes I think you have lost yours."

"Christ on the cross, madam, I will not have you interfering in matters of state. This was a sound match and you have destroyed it with your foolish meddling!"

"As was the match with Mary de Boulogne?" She faced him with her chin up.

"Yes, it was! I will not have you pushing me on that. You have never liked my brother. Every time I mention advancing him you either look the other way or make a disapproving face. Do you think I have not noticed you hiding Isabel de Warenne in the bower and protecting her under your wing?"

Alienor stood tall and met his blazing stare with composure even though she was very afraid. She did not regret what she had done and she was not going to back down or apologize.

His expression contorted. "You are the woman I take into my bedchamber, the mother of my heirs. You are supposed to support me in what I do and be a haven of grace and trust. And yet you agitate against me and thwart me at every turn, and then wonder why I am angry."

"And you never listen to what I have to say," she retorted, her chest tight with anger and grief. "You ride roughshod over all needs but your own, and then wonder why everything falls apart around you. I have done nothing of which I am ashamed. You put Thomas Becket in the position of archbishop of Canterbury, and the final decision on the matter of a dispensation was his. Had he chosen to sanction the marriage, there is nothing I could have done to prevent it. It is my duty as queen to intercede when requested, just as much as it is yours to govern."

Henry clenched his fists. "Do not use your specious arguments on me. I will not have you interfering and going behind my back, do you hear me?"

"I hear you," she said, and it was a statement of fact that acknowledged without giving ground. He could bluster all he wanted; it did not alter the fact that Becket had refused the dispensation—and she had won.

"You will obey me…"

She bowed her head and said nothing. Looking contrite was not the same as being contrite.

Henry pulled her against him, cupping the back of her head in his hands. "...or I will break you," he added, his breath mingling with hers.

*Not if I break you first*, she thought but let her body flow against his like water. "As you say, sire." She reached her hand down between them to stroke him, and found him as hard as an iron rod. Henry made a sound in his throat, took her arm, and pushed her roughly onto the bed. She welcomed him and goaded him, urging him on, scratching him with her nails when he bit her shoulder, and wrapping her legs around him as he thrust inside her. No matter how many mistresses he took, only she was the vessel by which his heirs were begotten, and no matter how strong he was when he entered her, she would take that strength and leave him soft and drained. That he might plant a child in her body was both a challenge and a danger, and in this moment, she was ready to accept both, even if the light of day might bring regret.

When they had finished, Henry rolled over and pillowed his head on his bent arms. Coppery tufts of hair gleamed in his armpits and fuzzed a dark red stripe down to his groin. "This annulment," he said breathlessly, "I am not done. The Countess de Warenne will marry whom I say. If you were thinking to match her with one of your Poitevans, you may scrap your scheming now, because it will not happen."

"As you please, sire," she said with a twist of contempt.

"No, I don't please," he snarled, "but I will make the best of it." He left the bed and donned his clothes. She looked at the scratches on his shoulders before he covered them with his shirt and wished she had gouged them deeper.

❖❖❖

In the morning, after Mass, Alienor bade Isabel attend her and waved her other ladies out of earshot. Isabel was pale and somber, her hands clasped in front of her and her eyes downcast.

"You must know why I want to talk to you," Alienor said quietly.

"Yes, madam." Isabel bit her lip. "I am prepared for whatever you have to tell me."

"I am not sure you are."

Isabel gave her a wide stare, brown eyes full of dread, and Alienor shook her head. "You have the manner of someone waiting to hear terrible news, but in truth you should have a smile on your lips and be wearing that red dress that suits you so well."

Isabel looked bewildered. "Madam?"

"The archbishop has ruled that the proposed match between you and William FitzEmpress is consanguineous and he will not be issuing a dispensation."

Isabel gasped.

Alienor curled her lip. "Of course, the archbishop's reasons are mostly not concerned with accommodating my plea, but still, he has seen fit to block the proposed match." She smiled to see the change in Isabel as realization dawned and her face flushed with color.

"Thank you, madam!" Tears welled in Isabel's eyes. "Thank you! I dared not hope for a reprieve."

"I said I would do what I could." Alienor grasped Isabel's hand. "The king has not taken this defeat well; you must be careful around him. I do not think his brother will be sanguine either, so you had better keep to the bower until the storm passes."

Isabel nodded and wiped her eyes on her sleeve. "I owe you a debt I can never repay."

"Let there be no talk of debts. I did little enough but write a letter."

"Even so, madam, I am grateful—and even if you say there is no debt, I still hope one day to repay you," Isabel said stoutly.

"You can do that by living the opportunity you have been given to the full," Alienor said, a bleak look entering her eyes. "With all your strength and without looking back. So few of us are permitted that grace."

❖❖❖

"He cannot do that!" William FitzEmpress shouted in furious disbelief. "He cannot ban my match with Isabel de Warenne on the grounds of consanguinity!"

"He can and he has," Henry said, tight-lipped.

"Why?" William demanded. "And why didn't you stop him?" He crashed his fist down on the table, causing the goblets on it to leap and the wine to slop onto the board. "You said everything would be simple once Becket was archbishop of Canterbury, so why isn't it simple now?"

Henry's face reddened. "I was not to know that becoming an archbishop would addle his wits." He waved his hand impatiently. "You will just have to take a different bride. I will find you one."

"From where?" William spat. "Out of thin air? There are no other women with lands or connections comparable to hers. You promised her to me. Are you going to let an upstart like Becket get away with this? Appeal to the pope. Get a dispensation from him!"

"I have greater concerns than that with the archbishop," Henry replied. "It will be for the best if you do marry elsewhere. I have made up my own mind on this. Accept it and be done."

"I will never accept it!" William shouted. "Becket is a common huckster's son who winds us all around his precious archbishop's crosier, a crosier you gave to him. Mark me, he will bring you down if you do not stop him. You are his dupe, brother. Do not expect me in my turn to be yours!"

"I have heard enough," Henry said. "Get out."

"Enough, mayhap, but this is not the end." William strode to the door. "We shall see!" He banged from the room, yelling for his squire.

❖ ❖ ❖

Seated at the long dining trestle on the high dais, Alienor looked out on the gathered clergy and nobles. Archbishop Becket had blessed the bread, and servants were bringing the first-course dishes of roast venison, roast capon, and spiced frumenty to the high table. There was an empty place halfway along the board that should have been occupied by Henry's brother, but he had not been seen since storming out several hours ago calling for his horse to be saddled.

At a brusque gesture from Henry, a steward quietly removed the setting and everyone eased along on the bench so there was no gap to show that a place had been laid for the king's brother at the high table. Harry sat between his parents under the gilded canopy as a special honor. He was boosted to the height of the adult company with the aid of several silk cushions, and his eyes shone with pride and a certain smug pleasure. His siblings all had to sit with their nurses at a different table, their presence emphasizing the virility of the royal bloodline but keeping them separate. They could gain experience and learn their manners without being a nuisance to the adults. Richard kept glowering at Harry, his jealousy plain to see, and Harry responded to it by smirking and preening in his fine new clothes.

Henry's mood was dour, and he barely spoke to the archbishop. He tapped his fingers on the board. He fidgeted and ate his food with the deliberation of a soldier on campaign, champing through it without enjoyment.

Alienor could see that more trouble was brewing between the men. Henry intended to raise taxes and Becket had been objecting on behalf of the sheriffs. The archbishop had also been insisting that the barons still holding Church lands they had seized during the civil war, now ten years over, should disgorge their gains. There were numerous bitter disputes over the issue, with claims and counterclaims clogging the courts. Becket was insisting on observing the minutiae, and Henry thought there was no good reason for Becket's obstruction beyond high-handed power play.

There was the additional matter of criminous clerks, which Henry had hoped to tackle with Becket in the dual roles of chancellor and archbishop, but that strategy was now as defunct as a mill with a boulder thrown into the cogs.

Henry's opinion, widely shared, was that every crime in the country should be tried in a secular court. Becket, however, insisted that clerics must be tried in the Church's own courts, in keeping with current practice. Henry wanted the law restored to that of his grandfather's time, when everyone, whatever their occupation, had been tried by the ancient customs of the land. Too many concessions had been made to the Church in moments of need, and it was time for everything to be put back as it was. Henry and Becket were like dogs circling each other with raised hackles but tails still wagging; however, Alienor suspected that a full-blown fight was about to ensue.

The formal meal ended with a serving of ginger comfits, spiced wine, and sweetmeats. Henry retired to his chamber to drink hippocras and socialize with a select group of courtiers that did not include his archbishop, the strongest sign yet that all was not well between them.

The chosen group talked, played games of hazard and chess, and listened to Henry's Welsh harpist coax glorious rills of music from his instrument. Alienor moved among the gathering flirting lightly with a turn of her wrist and a gesture of her sleeve. Smiling, engaging in conversations, collecting impressions and information without being obvious. Promising to take someone's nephew into her household as a page, talking to a knight recently returned from a pilgrimage to Jerusalem. Alienor's diplomatic smile froze on her lips as Henry's youngest brother staggered drunkenly into the chamber, his hand clamped around the wrist of one of the more notorious court whores. She was drunk too, but less than he was. She was hanging back but unable to free herself from his vicious grip.

William reeled up to Henry. "I'm going to marry this one," he slurred, lurching and swaying. "No...consang...consang... consanguinity here. Thomas can't complain about her. She started out from the bish...bishop of Winchester's brothel in Southwark. What do you say? Will she make a good wife, d'you think?"

"You can't marry her, Will lad!" yelled a courtier who had also imbibed too freely that day. "She's already had the king in her burrow. It'd be incest!"

A horrified silence fell. Then someone stifled a guffaw. William let go of the whore and attacked the courtier with a roar of rage, fists flailing. The man, one of Richard de Lucy's household knights, lurched, blood bursting from his split lip. William pursued him and they grappled against the sideboard, knocking over flagons and cups. The whore took her opportunity and fled the room, and two of Henry's knights stepped in to drag William off his victim.

William stood swaying, barely able to stand. "All women are sluts and whores!" he panted. "Queen or countess or common Southwark bath girl. They are all faithless harlots who lead men on with their cunts!" He glared at Alienor and Isabel.

Henry made a sharp gesture and the knights dragged William, cursing and swearing, from the room.

"Well," Henry said, addressing the shocked gathering, "an interesting piece of spontaneous entertainment. I am sure the good archbishop's chambers are dull by comparison." He looked at the courtier with the bloody lip. "Let that be a lesson to you, Saer. It's what you get for spouting inanities—blood for your words."

Uneasy chuckles followed Henry's pronouncement, and conversation resumed, limping at first but gradually rising to a normal level. Isabel quietly retired, accompanied by Marchisa, but Alienor had no such option as Henry joined her and gestured to a vacant chessboard in the embrasure. "Madam, will you play?"

She was aware of everyone watching to see how she would react to William's outburst. To silence the gossips and deny them the satisfaction of seeing the king and queen at odds in public, she smiled at Henry and acquiesced with grace, although she felt far from gracious toward him.

She arranged her pieces on the board with elegant movements that emphasized the beauty of her hands. "That was interesting," she said, speaking quietly but with excoriating scorn. "I did not know you had added her to your tally."

"That is because I was not foolish enough to waft her under your nose. She is nothing, a slut from the stews who can as easily return there. What happened a moment ago was unfortunate but of no consequence."

"Ah, yes, of course. And now your brother has cast slurs on myself and Isabel and ranked us alongside the Southwark whores!"

Henry folded his arms and leaned over the board. "The Countess de Warenne is the cause of all the trouble in the first place, madam. If she had accepted my brother as was her duty, the situation would never have arisen, would it? She has been indulged and allowed to make a meal of her grief. She should have been married long ago."

"And what a husband your brother would have made for her," Alienor retorted. "Wearing bruises with dignity is always difficult for a woman because they make her feel ashamed, even while they shame the man." She took a silver coin from her purse marked with Henry's head on one side and an incised cross on the other. "Which side, my lord? King or cross?"

Henry waved his hand. "I yield my potential advantage, madam. You make the first move and I will watch you. I prefer to observe which way the land lies, rather than leave it to chance, contrary wives, and archbishops."

Alienor gave him a caustic smile. "Well then, do not complain when you lose." She made the first move.

"Vixen," he said with dour amusement. "William will be all right when he has sobered and has had time to consider. I am sending him back to our mother and she can talk sense into him for a while in Rouen."

Alienor raised her brows. "Or he might try to talk her into negotiating with the archbishop to change his mind? That is sly, my lord."

Henry shrugged and did not deny it. "My mother has a certain way with recalcitrant men of the Church."

Alienor contemplated her next move. "She won't succeed. The archbishop will break before he will bend."

"Then if it becomes necessary, I will break him," Henry answered, his mouth a straight, tight line.

The game ended in stalemate as Alienor had known it would. He was determined to defeat her and she was equally determined that he would not win. They retired to bed to continue the battle. When it was over with no one victorious, but both of them gasping and mauled, Henry got dressed and left her, and Alienor did not know whether to be thankful or depressed.

Leaving the bed, she went to the garderobe to clean herself with a damp cloth, and as she performed her ablutions, saw the blood. Her flux had begun. There would be no child from this sowing, and all she felt was glad that she had a reprieve from the battlefield for at least another month.

She sent one of her women to bring soft rags and donned a pair of old braies under her chemise. And then she went to find Isabel.

She was not abed but sitting over a candle hemming a chemise. It was servant's work but easy to see in the dark, and Alienor knew how soothing the repetitive action could be—a way of ordering one's thoughts, or of banishing them to limbo.

"Are you all right?"

Isabel nodded. "Thank you, madam. I am sorry the king's brother took the news so badly, but it only reinforces to me that I could not be his wife. Without the archbishop's intervention I might have had to wed him. I would have done my duty while praying for release every moment." Her face clouded. "I am sorry for what happened in front of the court. It was not seemly."

"And not your fault." Alienor's eyes brightened with anger. "Never take that blame on yourself. What William did is upon his conscience, not yours. Like a winter storm, it will blow itself out." She shifted on the bench in discomfort as her womb cramped. "What will be left is a new shore with clean sand, and you can make any footprint you desire."

# 22

## WESTMINSTER, OCTOBER 1163

ALIENOR LOOKED UP FROM THE LETTER SHE WAS READING AS her chamber door opened and Harry entered with his father. "What's this?" she asked in surprise, because Harry should have been at his duties among the archbishop's pages and squires.

"I am taking our son out of Becket's tutelage," Henry said, an angry glitter in his eyes. "That household is proving no fit place to educate a future king. God knows what seditious notions that man is planting in my son's skull."

Alienor stood up as Harry knelt to her and then raised her son to his feet and embraced him. "It didn't occur to you before that he might plant them?"

"Why should it?" Henry snapped. "He served me diligently until I made him archbishop. Now he has chosen to interpret his post as a challenge for power, not partnership." He stamped around the room, picking things up, banging them down. "If I could undo his office, I would, and give the responsibility to Gilbert Foliot, but since I cannot unless Becket resigns as archbishop, I must bring him to heel by other means. There are plenty of better tutors who can educate our son."

"I liked it in the archbishop's household," Harry said and then shrugged. "But it was boring sometimes."

"Did the archbishop say anything to you about me?" Henry asked suspiciously.

"No, Papa. He only said he was sorry he was not going to be tutoring me anymore and hoped I would return to him later when matters had been resolved."

"Well, that's just another of his vain hopes."

Harry went to greet his other siblings. Matilda gave him a huge hug, which he reciprocated, being very fond of his closest sister. Five-year-old Geoffrey, who had been playing a game with a ball and scoop, wanted to show him how good he had become at landing the ball in the socket. So then Harry had to have a go, adding small flourishes such as catching it under his raised thigh and while twirling around, his movements swift and dexterous. Richard said nothing. With Harry back in the family, no matter for how short a time, his own ranking immediately diminished. He watched, his arms folded scornfully, until Harry came over and gave him a friendly punch. It turned into a scuffle, and Henry bellowed at them to go and take their brawl into the garden.

"Brats," he muttered under his breath.

"They take after you, my lord," Alienor said sweetly.

Henry grunted. "Mayhap, but they need direction. Every tree requires pruning, whatever the stock."

Alienor said nothing. Henry's direction would turn them into versions of himself, and that was not what she wanted.

"I have decided to spend Christmas at Berkhamsted," he said.

Alienor eyed him in surprise. Becket had been granted the use of Berkhamsted Castle as a concession when he had first been appointed chancellor. He used it often and had refurbished it magnificently for his own comfort.

"I have revoked Thomas's privilege to use it," Henry said. "Why should he have such honor when he defies me and refuses to listen to reason? We shall stay there and make it clear who is master. I want you to gown yourself in full array and we shall hold a great court."

"As you wish, my lord." Alienor was rather pleased because Berkhamsted had been hers to use as queen, and she had been accepting but not overjoyed when Henry had lent it to Becket.

She doubted ploys such as removing Harry from Becket's household and curtailing the archbishop's privileges would bring him to heel though. Henry was only hitting back, not dealing with the problem. She had no obligation to speak out on Becket's behalf. Even if he had done her a service over Isabel's marriage, that particular issue had been a matter of mutual interest. She had no desire to become embroiled in Henry's quarrel with his archbishop, which was of the men's own making.

"Your mother sent a letter about William," she said, changing the subject. She brought him the parchment she had been reading when he arrived.

Henry gave her a sharp look. "What of him?"

"She says he has no appetite and has lost his interest in hunting. All he wants to do is sit by the fire and curse his bad fortune. He complains of gripes in his stomach, but whatever the physicians do has no effect."

Henry grunted and read the letter himself. "She also says she has written to Becket and cannot understand why he has suddenly become so concerned about a matter of consanguinity." He gave her a dark look. "If she knew you had meddled, I doubt she would be pleased."

"Of course she would not be pleased," Alienor answered calmly. "You may tell her if you wish, but I do not see what purpose it will serve. Becket could as easily have granted a dispensation as not, as you well know. I will pray that your brother makes a good recovery from whatever is troubling him, and I will pray for your mother's comfort and succor."

"How charitable of you," Henry said.

"No, how dutiful," she replied with a sarcastic dip of her head.

❖❖❖

Following a lavish, ostentatious Christmas at Berkhamsted, the court moved to the royal palace at Clarendon where magnates, barons and clergy alike, were summoned to a great conference to debate the laws of the realm. Once again Henry and his erstwhile chancellor turned archbishop locked horns and grappled over the rights of church and state, each becoming more entrenched until the talks ground to a halt. Becket had finally agreed to verbally acknowledge the ancient customs of the land but had refused to put his seal to any document that would bind him deeper than words. Henry had eventually handed him a chirograph detailing the proceedings of the conference and listing the disputed customs. Roger of Pont L'Évêque, Archbishop of York, had a copy too, and Henry had retained one for himself. Becket had chosen to see it as a mere written reminder; however, a chirograph, even without a seal, was a legally binding document.

In the sharp winter's morning, Alienor went for a walk around the palace grounds, accompanied by boisterous children and dogs. Snow had fallen heavily the previous day, but the skies had cleared overnight and the wind had dropped, leaving a world of biting, crystalline white, shadowed blue in the hollows. The pure air and fluffy humps of snow encouraged high spirits, and her companions flurried and bounded through the drifts, yelling and barking until Alienor could barely hear herself speak to her ladies.

Despite the thick snow, various bishops and magnates had begun departing from the failed assembly, Becket included, still muttering that the ancient laws and customs of the realm infringed on the rights of the Church and that Henry had had them rewritten to suit himself.

"What will happen now, madam?" asked Isabel as they watched another cavalcade of laden packhorses plod down the snow-rutted track on its way to the road. The men wore the livery of Gilbert Foliot, Bishop of Hereford. The latter rode behind his standard-bearer, his corpulent body enveloped in a sable-lined cloak. Bells jingled on the breast band of his dappled-gray palfrey, and his purple saddlecloth was embroidered with silk crosses in gold. Four sleek gazehounds loped alongside the horse, and they too had bells on their collars. Foliot was Becket's implacable enemy because he believed Canterbury should have been his. Since Henry had declined to sponsor him to that position, his relationship with the Crown was strained too. An influential and dangerous man.

"I do not know," Alienor said. "Henry may think he has gotten the better of the archbishop by issuing that chirograph, but it will not be the end of it. I suspect Becket will appeal to the pope."

"But the pope needs the king's goodwill and support too."

"Indeed," she said wryly. "They all argue and believe matters would be simple if only the others would see sense."

Wild yells broke out as Richard and Harry began a fight in earnest, laying into each other with kicks and punches as hard as they could. Alienor sent one of her household knights to pull them off each other. Richard stood panting, blood dripping from a cut lip. Harry writhed on the ground, clutching himself between the legs, and then he rolled over and retched. Geoffrey, observing with bright eyes, rubbed his nose with the back of his hand.

"What now?" Alienor demanded with exasperation. "You are the sons of a king and have futures as rulers ahead of you. How are you going to govern your lands if you cannot govern yourselves?"

Droplets of blood splashed from Richard's lip and landed in the snow like scarlet berries. "He said I had to kneel to him because I was his vassal, and younger than him, but I will never bend my knee—never!"

"It is not worth a fight to the death at your age," she said wearily, and gestured one of her escort to pick up Harry and set him on his feet. "And hopefully by the time it is, you will have resolved your differences before you are both the death of me. Far better to find common enemies than tear each other to pieces." She sent Richard off with a squire to have his lip tended and had one of her knights bear Harry back indoors.

"I despair sometimes," she said to Isabel, her breath puffing out in clouds of vapor. "It is good that my sons are competitive and ambitious, but the way they are constantly at each other's throats is fit to turn all my hair gray."

"I don't fight, Mama," Geoffrey piped up.

"No," she agreed wryly, "you don't. But you often say things to start them, so don't pretend to be innocent with me."

Geoffrey gave her a look from wide, dark blue eyes, but Alienor was not fooled by his blameless expression. As the youngest of the three boys and only by a year to Richard, he constantly strove to carve out his own niche and undermine the other two.

"I suppose it is the price of raising eaglets," she said to Isabel with a pained smile in which there was still pride. "They all want to be king of the birds."

❖❖❖

Henry looked up from the parchment he was reading as he became aware that his five-year-old son was standing before him holding a large book bound in leather with an ornate clasp. It was too big for him and he was struggling to hold it.

Henry set aside his work. "Where did you get that, my boy?" he asked with amusement. With all the difficulties concerning Becket and his perfidious, ridiculous behavior, Geoffrey's appearance was a refreshing diversion.

"It was in Harry's chamber," he said, "but he doesn't want it because he just left it on the window seat, and I thought a mouse might make a nest of it like it did of one of Mama's letters."

Henry's lips twitched with malicious amusement. The book must be from Becket's library and have been among Harry's baggage when he left that household, because certainly he had not seen it before. It looked like a costly volume too. "And what are you going to do with it, my son?"

"I'm going to read some of it to you, Papa," Geoffrey said as if it were the most obvious thing in the world.

"Are you indeed?" Henry lifted Geoffrey onto his lap. "Let me see how good you are." Henry unfastened the clasp and opened the thick, creamy parchment pages. "What does this say here?" He pointed to a large red letter embellished by the illumination of an eagle flying toward the sun, which was depicted in brilliant gold leaf with rays flashing out.

Geoffrey screwed up his face and very laboriously began to read to his father. "'The eagle can look directly into the sun… As a test of the worthiness of its young, the eagle holds them up facing the sun. The birds that cannot stare into the sun and turn their eyes away are cast out of the nest.'"

Henry studied the boy as he struggled doggedly through the text. Geoffrey, in comparison to Harry and Richard, was a quiet child who made little fuss and was often overlooked. He never became embroiled in fights between his brothers, although he was not above setting the two older ones against each other. He was obviously intelligent, to be reading at this kind of level at so young an age. Henry decided that perhaps he ought to pay him more attention.

When he reached the end of the piece about eagles, Henry praised him and gave him the lump of amber in his pouch he had been intending as a gift for his current concubine. "Do you think you could look into the sun if I held you up?" he asked.

Geoffrey pondered. "It would make me sneeze," he said after a moment, "and see spots before my eyes, but it would be better than being thrown from the nest." He held the piece of amber to the light.

"I suppose it would," Henry said, grinning at his son's logic. "I will look after the book now. You can come read it to me again another time."

"Yes, Papa." Geoffrey started to run off but then turned around in midstride and bowed to Henry. "Thank you, Papa," he said and then dashed off again.

Chuckling to himself, Henry closed the book and gave it to one of his attendants. He was pleased and proud. Not many children could read so well at that age and of their own accord. He would have to remember to tell Alienor, although, knowing her, she'd make some preposterous claim to have taught him.

"A proper scholar, sire," said his justiciar, Richard de Lucy. "Perhaps he will have a great career in the Church?"

"Hah, I could make him the next archbishop of Canterbury," Henry said with a sour grin. "I do not have the Church in mind for him. There are far better uses to which he can be put." He glanced across the chamber and saw Hamelin talking to a travel-stained cleric who had just arrived. Henry's cheerful mood dissipated, his first thought being that Becket had done something else outrageous or against everything he was trying to achieve. Already he had heard from his spies that Thomas had declined to take Mass and donned a hair shirt in mortification because he had agreed to the ancient customs against his will. He had appealed to Rome too. If this was more bad news concerned with Becket, Henry did not want to hear it. However, as Hamelin approached with the cleric in tow, Henry realized the man was one of his mother's chaplains from Bec, and his heart kicked in his chest, because this could only be news of a personal and more difficult sort.

The chaplain knelt at Henry's feet. "Sire, I grieve to tell you that your brother, William FitzEmpress, has died of the wasting sickness in Rouen and been buried in the cathedral, God rest his soul. I have a letter from the empress." He extended a sealed parchment.

Henry's first emotion was relief that it was not news about his mother, but that was fleeting and was replaced by a sensation like a lump of ice settling in his stomach. Both his legitimate brothers were gone. His only sibling kin now were Hamelin and Emma, born of his father's concubine. Was this God's plan, and if so, what was the point of it all except perhaps to prove God's omnipotence—that he could take anyone at any time? It made him feel naked and vulnerable…and angry. He could not rely on anyone, God least of all.

"How is my lady mother?" He broke the seal and read the contents of the message. The words were formal and reserved and what he expected. His mother would not break her heart in a letter or in public. She would grieve in private and show a stern, proud face to the world.

"She mourns deeply, sire, but is taking comfort from the Almighty."

Who had done the taking in the first place, Henry thought.

The chaplain cleared his throat. "People are saying in Normandy that the lord William pined away because he could not have the Countess de Warenne to wife."

Henry snorted. "My brother would not pine away over a woman, or even over losing the lands. Eat himself up with bitterness about it certainly." His eyes narrowed. "Who do you mean by 'people'?"

"His knights," the chaplain said. "Those who knew him best, especially Robert Brito."

Henry shrugged. "It will do no harm to promote the tale and discomfort the archbishop, although I suspect the real cause of Brito's woe is that his hope of carving his own comfortable little niche from the de Warenne estates has been dashed. He will have to take his chance elsewhere, as will the rest of them." He waved his hand in dismissal. "Leave me. I will talk with you later when I have had time to reflect and prepare a letter for my mother."

Hamelin saw the chaplain out and returned to Henry. "I am sorry," he said.

"You were never fond of him."

"But we were born of the same father and he was my—our brother. We shared the bond of kinship, and for that I regret his passing."

A muscle worked in Henry's jaw. How easily death happened; how suddenly life was taken away. He couldn't trust anyone not to leave him, and that caused him to feel sick. He looked at Hamelin, who returned his stare before crossing the space between them and embracing Henry.

Henry was frozen with surprise and shackled by his inability to deal with grief. But some shard of emotion pierced his restraint, and for an instant he dared to open himself and grip Hamelin tight and close in return. Abruptly he drew away before the chasm in his defenses became any wider. He sniffed once and took a deep breath. "I may have some more news for you later," he said gruffly, "but I need to think on it first, and I want to be alone for a while."

Hamelin gave Henry a long look but did not question him. Swallowing down his own emotion, he bowed, and then, adjusting his cloak to settle himself, went to the door.

Henry watched him leave. One moment on this side of the arch and in full view, the next lost from sight. That's how easy it was.

❖❖❖

Alienor glanced at Henry, who was sitting by the fire in her chamber. He had not attempted to move, and she had made preparations for him to stay the night. Everything was quiet and soft so as not to disturb him. The children had been warned to be on their best behavior, and even Richard had been subdued for once. The nurses had taken them off to bed, and she and Henry were alone save for two dozing hounds. She came to rest her hand lightly on his shoulder. She no longer believed that their marriage was a haven against the world, but she wanted to offer him comfort.

"I have heard the rumors," she said, "that he pined away because he was denied the de Warenne lands, but I do not believe them."

"Neither do I," Henry said, grimacing. "My brother was of stronger mettle than that."

"I am relieved to hear you say so."

"Why, because it will make you feel less guilty?"

"Because it is a foolish argument. In some ways it is fortunate that the marriage did not take place—Isabel would have been widowed scarcely before becoming a wife."

Henry raised his brows. "I dread to think what you would consider unfortunate," he said. "Outside this chamber, I want to let the rumor spread that my brother died of a broken heart."

She looked at him in surprise "Why?"

"Because Thomas Becket denied him, and men will blame him. Even if they do not think it now, they will come to do so, and that suits my purpose."

It was a clever ploy. He would do whatever he must to win.

"At least my brother is proving useful for once," he said.

She recoiled at the flippancy of the remark, but then she saw the tension in his jaw and the tightness around his eyes and realized he was struggling. She suspected he had a raging headache but knew if she suggested he call for his physician, he would snarl at her to mind her own business.

"Still," he said, "I now know what to do about the marriage of

Isabel de Warenne." He rose to his feet and paced the chamber, dissipating his emotion.

Alarm jolted through her, but her expression remained impassive. "Whom did you have in mind?"

He sent her a fierce look. "After Lent, she will wed Hamelin. I will brook no argument."

Alienor was fleetingly disappointed because she would have preferred someone of her own affinity, but it was a decent choice and a fair one. She noted that once again Henry had succeeded in snubbing Becket. His choice meant that the de Warenne lands would still come under royal influence. "I will give you no argument on that score," she said. "I think it a fine idea."

"Well, that at least deserves praise and celebration," Henry said with an ironic twist to his lips.

"I am always amenable to reasonable suggestions," Alienor retorted. "Perhaps you do not make them often enough. I shall tell her on the morrow."

"And she will do as she is bidden. I will not have her hiding behind your skirts this time."

"I think you will find her compliant," Alienor said. "It is late, sire. Will you come to bed?"

He walked back across the room and set his hands around her waist. "It is a long time since you asked me that."

"It is a long time since you have been in my chamber at night." She reached to his belt buckle. "Perhaps we should both make the most of such a rare opportunity."

❖❖❖

The next morning, after Mass, Alienor drew Isabel to the embrasure seat in her chamber for a quiet word.

"I am sorry about the king's brother," Isabel said. "I have prayed for him, and I hope he is with God in heaven now. I did not want to be his wife, and I disagreed with him on many occasions, but I did not wish this end for him." She bit her lip. "I know what people are saying about his death—I have heard the rumors."

"Foolish gossip," Alienor said briskly. "I could imagine nothing less likely than him pining away. He didn't have that kind of nature." She took Isabel's hand. "Listen to me. The king has chosen another man to be your husband, and this time I think you will approve."

Isabel's eyes filled with trepidation, and Alienor shook her head and smiled. "Do not be alarmed. Henry has his other brother Hamelin in mind for you."

Isabel covered her mouth with her hand.

"I know it is sudden, but it is a good match. You have known Hamelin for many years, and I have never seen you ill at ease with him. He has Henry's favor; he is dependable—and handsome into the bargain," Alienor added with a smile.

Isabel took a deep breath. "It is all so unexpected. A moment ago I was praying for the welfare of William FitzEmpress's soul, and now you say the king desires me to wed his remaining brother."

"He does, and he will not be gainsaid," Alienor warned, steel entering her tone. "It is a good offer, and I advise you to take it."

Isabel shook her head. "I have never allowed myself to look at the vicomte of Touraine in that way. I have to adjust, but I do not think it will be difficult." Her lips curved in a tremulous smile. "If it be the king's will, I shall obey with a glad and joyous heart."

Alienor kissed her. "You would be a sheep if you said otherwise," she said with a relieved laugh. "Hamelin may not be a prince by birth, but he is certainly a prince among men. And an honored one too, to have you to wife."

Isabel blushed. "I hope he thinks so," she said. "I will be sorry to leave you, madam."

"And I shall miss you," Alienor replied, "but you will visit often and we still have some time together because the wedding will not take place before Easter. We have time to plan your nuptials and you and Hamelin can better acquaint yourselves before you share a bed." Her eyes sparkled mischievously and Isabel's flush deepened, traveling all the way from her throat to her forehead.

"I have long thought of you as a sister," Alienor added, "and now we shall be sisters-by-marriage—and that pleases me most of all."

❖❖❖

Isabel accepted Hamelin's help to dismount from her black palfrey and walked with him a little way until they came to a wooden bridge, hunching over the River Wandle with a water mill beyond. The spring sun was almost warm, but it had rained recently and the water rushed under the arch at tumbling silver speed. Hawthorn leaves had begun to show the tips of pale green buds, and yellow celandine flowers starred the upper reaches of the riverbanks.

Hamelin leaned on the bridge to watch the racing water and she was intensely aware of him at her side, as if they stood together in an illuminated reality that separated them from all but their immediate surroundings.

Yesterday the announcement had gone out that they would marry, but since it was Lent and the court was in mourning for William FitzEmpress, the celebration had been muted and the toasts formal and serious. Nevertheless, she and Hamelin had become the center of attention and there had been no time to talk alone until he suggested going out for this ride and leaving London several miles behind. Isabel had almost declined because the last time she had gone riding with a suitor, the enterprise had ended in disaster, and that suitor was now untimely dead.

Hamelin clasped his hands loosely together. "I brought you here so we could talk without being overheard."

"That is an excellent idea," she said with a tense smile. It was also proof that he had been thinking ahead.

He fixed her with a steady gaze. His eyes were hazel in the sunlight: a blend of pale amber and gray like fine shingle. "We are to marry, and I want us to be able to talk openly and honestly. I see a lack of it elsewhere at court. The truth is as difficult to find as a fleck of gold in six feet of mud, and I do not want that to be the way of our match."

Isabel's feelings tumbled at the same speed as the water. She returned his gaze with candor, because he had used the words "openly" and "honestly," but it was a hard thing to do. She did not know him well, and did not want to appear improper. "Neither do I, my lord."

"I want you to know that although this match has been agreed for political purposes at the king's behest, I enter it willingly and with a whole heart. I will put no other above you, and you will be my wife in love and honor for the rest of my life."

It was as if he had plucked a resounding note on her heart-strings, and for a moment Isabel almost reeled. It was the stuff of romantic dreams. These were words that young girls imagined handsome young knights saying to them in courtship, but they were not the coin of everyday life. Did she take them for kindness, for falsehood...or for truth? The latter was like daring to stare into the sun. She was thirty-two years old and Hamelin similar. They had both weathered the storms of life and were not naive.

His stare had that same intensity of focus as his royal brother's, but rather than fierce, it was patient. "What do you say?"

Isabel shook her head. "I do not know what to say. Whatever my words they will not be adequate."

He set his hand over hers and smiled. "I am the only one to hear them. I truly mean what I say about openness and honesty: never doubt that."

She inhaled deeply. "Then, in honesty, I will endeavor to content you and honor you through the blessed times and those of hardship too—and come to you with a whole heart." Her face was burning, and she had to look down.

"Then we have an agreement and all is well." He put his arm and his cloak around her, drawing her against him, and the symbolic strength of his protection filled Isabel with a delicate but growing happiness, like a bubble of light in her hands.

# 23

## Palace of Westminster, Easter 1164

"YOU ARE BEAUTIFUL," ALIENOR TOLD ISABEL AS THEY PREPARED to leave the queen's chamber at Westminster and parade to the abbey for Isabel's marriage to Hamelin.

Isabel smiled shyly at the compliment and adjusted her embroidered gold belt. The wedding gown of blue silk, damascened with gold, clung to her body before flaring at the hips. Her brunette hair, woven in two thick plaits, was secured in a net of gold thread, forming a base on which to pin a silk veil and a coronet set with sapphires. "Do you think Hamelin will like it?"

"I think that you will take his breath away," Alienor replied. "He is not a fool; he knows his good fortune."

"This is a new beginning," Isabel said, "and I have you to thank for it."

"You can best repay me by living your life with Hamelin to the full," Alienor said. "Do not waste a single moment."

"I don't intend to." Isabel stooped to accept a posy of spring flowers from little Matilda, recently picked in the palace garden. "Bless you," she said, kissing her cheek.

Alienor's other children had gathered in the chamber, waiting the moment to go to the marriage. For once Richard, Harry, and Geoffrey were behaving themselves, handsome royal princes of nine, rising seven, and rising six. They were strong, long-limbed, and sturdy for their ages and made Alienor deeply proud. Their sister Alie at two and a half had just begun to wear proper little dresses. Her hair was a mass of smoky-brown waves, and she had the striking green-blue eyes of her grandsire Geoffrey le Bel, Count of Anjou. She was a dainty child, fine-boned and delicate in all her movements, but her will was as fierce as fire and, despite her fragile looks, she was robust.

"Are you ready?" Alienor adjusted the clasp on Isabel's cloak of soft red wool.

"Almost." Firming her lips, Isabel removed, after some tugging, her first wedding ring and handed it to her maid to put in her jewel casket. "Yes," she said, raising her chin. "Now I am."

❖❖❖

Isabel looked around the comfortable chamber at Westminster Palace where she and Hamelin were to spend their wedding night before setting out for Acre in Norfolk the next day.

The women had removed her beautiful blue wedding gown and underdress, and all she wore now was a white chemise of delicate linen chansil. Alienor, who had been helping her disrobe, playing the part of lady's maid to honor the bride, started to unpin the headdress, but Isabel stopped her.

"That is my new husband's privilege," she said, pink-cheeked. "My lord has never seen my hair unbound. I do not come as a virgin to our marriage bed—but it will be the first time he sees my hair loose, and the first time we sleep in the same bed, and that is as sacred as virginity."

Her words humbled Alienor and almost brought tears to her eyes, because she remembered her wedding night with Henry when she had experienced those kinds of feelings for a mate, and gloried in the protection and strength of a virile man lying at her side. Sometimes she still caught glimmers of that emotion, but these days they were like motes in a sunbeam, briefly glittering and then gone. "Indeed, you are right," she said softly.

The men arrived, jostling the groom in their midst. Hamelin was laughing and taking the jests in good part, while Isabel presented the face of a modest, embarrassed wife, although her eyes were sparkling.

Gilbert Foliot, the new bishop of London, attempted to bring sobriety to the proceedings, but the guests, intent on merriment and full of ribald advice for the couple, were reluctant to cooperate. Thomas Becket pushed himself forward. Being more sober than most because of his delicate stomach, he set about controlling the proceedings, which earned him glares from Foliot and amused contempt from Henry.

"Is there any area where you will not stir that spoon of yours, my lord archbishop?" he asked.

"I would prefer not to sup with the devil, sire," Becket replied, "but ofttimes in this world it seems I must."

Henry arched his brows.

Becket continued smoothly, "For now I desire to wish the bride and groom well and leave them in peace, as I am sure we all do." He raised his voice on the last few words.

"And we are all capable of doing so without your instruction, Archbishop," Henry said.

"Sire." Becket bowed and stepped back with a flare and swish of his gilded cope.

The guests finally brought to order, Hamelin and Isabel were placed side by side between the sheets and liberally sprinkled with holy water by Gilbert Foliot, who had reclaimed his role. Once blessed and exhorted to be fruitful, they were finally left in peace.

"As far as weddings go, I think we escaped rather lightly," Hamelin said. "I've attended bedding ceremonies far more boisterous." He went to bar the door and knelt to peer under the bed and make sure there were no surprises. "I've known people to tie bells to the frame, so that every movement rings a carillon, or else put powders in the piss pot to make it foam over." He climbed back into bed and turned to her. "My brother can be vile and ride roughshod over everyone to attain his own desire, but I will love him forever for this gift. He promised me a great heiress many years ago before he was king, but I never thought it would come about like this."

"I too am glad," Isabel said. "I owe the queen a great debt too, but I will not be sorry to leave court and live on my…our lands for a while."

"Indeed, I will not be sorry either. I am looking forward to having time to explore all that I never thought to have." He touched the golden hair net. "Will you…will you unbind your hair for me?"

Isabel slanted him a look. "No, my lord, I will not."

He stared at her askance until she smiled. "It is your right to unbind it now—a husband's privilege. No other man has seen my hair loose since I wed my first husband. Not your brother William and not the king."

Hamelin swallowed, almost undone by her words. With trembling hands, he removed the fine metallic mesh and then one by one plucked out the gold pins securing her plaits. Slowly he unwound the heavy, dark braids, each as thick as his wrist, and inhaled a wonderful aroma of nutmeg and spices. He ran his hands through the strands to loosen them until he was looking at a shining brunette sheaf that spilled over her body like a second cloak and left him speechless with awe. This was all his: this woman, her beauty, her status, her virtue. What he had felt earlier when told he was to marry her, what he had felt on the bridge when he settled the terms of their relationship, was as nothing compared to now. It was like having a beautiful box and then opening that box and finding a sacred and precious jewel within it.

He unfastened the ties on her chemise and stroked the smooth shoulder that gleamed through her abundant tresses. She was like Eve in the garden. Her wide hazel-brown eyes, those slightly parted pink lips. She had never borne a child, and even while she was knowing, she was virginal too. He pulled off his shirt and laid her down, and her hair spilled beneath them like a sable blanket.

"This is sacred," he said. "This is for the rest of our lives."

Isabel put her arms around his neck and drew him close. "It is forever," she said, and her voice was fierce. "You are mine, and from now on, you come first above all."

# 24

PALACE OF WOODSTOCK, OXFORDSHIRE, SUMMER 1164

THE ROYAL HUNTING LODGE AT WOODSTOCK, EIGHT MILES from Oxford, had been a favorite domicile and retreat of Henry's grandfather. He had feasted and entertained his barons here, gone hunting in the park, and pleasured himself with his mistresses. The complex had also housed a menagerie of exotic animals that had been his whim to assemble. Alienor was not a frequent visitor, but she enjoyed the comfort and the idyllic surroundings.

The children loved Woodstock. There was plenty of room to play and ride their mounts in its rambling grounds. The menagerie, although a ghost of its glory during the old king's time, was still a huge attraction. Richard was especially taken with the lions and loved to listen to their belching roars and lean over their enclosure to watch the keeper feed them bloody chunks of beef and venison. The stench was choking, but the children barely noticed. Alienor warned Richard not to lean too far over to watch but smiled to see his affinity with these great beasts, the emblem of his bloodline.

"When I am king, I am going to have a collection bigger than my great-grandsire had," Harry said, leaning beside Richard. "He had camels and a porcupine."

"You could ask Papa," Matilda said, tucking a strand of golden-brown hair behind her ear. "He might get some. What's a porcupine?"

"Like a hedgehog but a lot bigger and its spines come out and stick in your hand," said Geoffrey, who had been reading again.

Harry shook his head. "Papa would say no. He's not interested in things unless they are useful."

Alienor listened to her children with amusement. Harry certainly seemed to have his father's measure.

"You have to ask him in the right way at the right time," Matilda said in a superior tone. "Animals are useful to show off to your guests or as gifts—like the monkeys Papa gave to King Louis. And people are always giving Papa hawks and hounds for his hunting."

Alienor approved of her daughter's reasoning. And the child did have a way of getting around her father that no one else did, herself included.

Richard dismissed her with a wave of his hand. "You should rely on yourself to get things," he said. "If you wait for others it puts you in their power."

"I was relying on myself," Matilda retorted. "There is no harm in asking to start out." She made a face at him. "You don't have to use siege weapons for everything."

"Mama." Geoffrey touched Alienor's arm and pointed toward her constable Saldebreuil de Sanzay, who was approaching them at a brisk walk.

Alienor braced herself. For Saldebreuil to come in person, rather than sending a squire, the message was more than routine.

On reaching them, he bowed. "Madam, the archbishop of Canterbury is here asking to see the king, but he is out hunting and has left no instructions. What shall I say?" His intelligent dark eyes were full of speculation.

Alienor gnawed her lip. The trouble between Henry and Becket had continued apace since Clarendon. Becket had come to Woodstock to speak with Henry following their most recent quarrel, and Henry had ordered the guards to turn him away, saying he did not wish to see him. Becket had then tried to leave the country but had been forced to turn back when the crew of his ship had thought better of incurring the royal wrath.

Since being a bridge and a peacemaker was one of a queen's most important duties, it was incumbent upon her to act. "Admit him," she said, "and bring him to my chamber."

"You are certain, madam?" Saldebreuil had been with her long enough to be permitted the leeway of a question.

"No, I am not, but admit him."

"Madam," de Sanzay said neutrally and went to see the order carried out.

"Papa will feed him to the lions," Richard declared with a gleam of relish.

"Your papa will do no such thing," Alienor answered sternly. She hoped not anyway. She handed the children into the care of their nurses, all save Harry. Since he was being groomed as Henry's heir, he needed to observe diplomacy and government at work.

Looking at Thomas Becket as she entered her chamber, Alienor was shocked by the change in him since Clarendon. The lines on his face, superficial before, were deeply carved, and his eyes were guarded and hard, lacking their glint of humor. His skin was gray and his bone structure sharp, as if he was in the act of turning to stone. He reminded her of the fanatical Bernard of Clairvaux, whose intensity had always frightened her. There was no peace to be had here. As Henry's chancellor, Becket had resembled a polished gem set in gold, shining and complacent. Now that he had found God instead, he was like a hard black flint, with razored edges that would cut to the bone.

He bowed and she kissed his bishop's ring with its large blue sapphire. Harry followed her example and for an instant Becket smiled. "I have wondered about you, sire," he said. "Are you well and attending to your lessons with your new tutor?"

"Yes, my lord archbishop," Harry replied, his tone polite but guarded.

"I am pleased to hear it. To become a king as great as your father you must apply yourself with diligence."

Harry raised his chin. "I shall be greater," he said.

"Then you will be mighty indeed, sire."

Alienor shot Harry a warning glance. "Wine, my lord archbishop?"

Becket shook his head and touched his stomach. "Just barley water, if you have it."

Alienor sent a maid to fetch the requested drink and gestured Becket to a bench near the hearth. "The most I can do for you is grant you entry here," she warned. "Beyond that I cannot intercede between you and the king."

Becket inclined his head. "I understand, madam, and I thank you. I deeply regret the quarrel between us, but if I compromise, I am failing God, and he is the greatest authority of all."

"Spare me your justifications, my lord archbishop. This is not about God. It is about men's desires and stubborn will to have the last word."

Becket looked affronted. "Everything is about God, madam."

Alienor was saved from having to find a diplomatic answer as Marchisa returned with a small crystal flagon filled with barley water.

Alienor took it from the maid and served Becket herself, presenting the cup to him together with a small napkin of fresh white linen. "The water comes from the spring at Everswell," she said. "I think you will find it palatable."

"Thank you, I have tasted the spring water before and it is always refreshing."

The door opened and Henry arrived, muddy and flushed from his morning's hunting. He had clearly received the news of Becket's arrival, for there was a glitter in his eyes that boded ill for the likelihood of cordial discussion. That swift, hard glance flicked over Alienor and then back to Becket.

"My lord archbishop," Henry said. "What a surprise to see you. Here I was thinking you wanted to leave my kingdom because you thought it not big enough to contain us both."

Becket rose and bowed, and Henry kissed his ring. Neither gesture was conciliatory. "Sire, my only wish is to have peace and understanding between us."

"Well, that is a fine wish for a beggar to ride," Henry snapped.

"I too desire to see church and state work together in harmony, and I thought when I appointed you to the primacy that it would happen, but I was wrong." He took a gulp of wine from the cup Alienor handed to him. "You do not look well, Archbishop. Perhaps your newfound piety is taking its toll on you."

"Indeed, I am not well, sire," Becket responded. "My conscience troubles me deeply, as does this dispute between us. I have a duty and responsibility to my office and to God and I must do it to the best of my ability whatever the consequences."

"If that is all you have come to tell me, then you might as well leave," Henry said. "You have a duty and responsibility to your king also."

"Indeed, sire," Becket said. "It is of that duty and responsibility I would talk."

❖❖❖

Alienor sat in her chamber as the long, summer dusk grew into soft nightfall. The windows had oiled linen stretched across them to keep out mosquitoes and night-flying insects, although several moths had managed to blunder their way in to flutter around the lamps. A young Poitevan troubadour was singing a plangent lai about unrequited love in the blossom days of summer while making eyes at her. She was amused and vaguely diverted. He was a good-looking youth with fair curls and blue eyes, and she had employed him to teach her children the musical arts. She enjoyed flirting with him, but he was no challenge, nor of particular interest; she only kept him for his delightful music and his looks.

The notes from the lute dropped on the evening air in liquid sweetness and, closing her eyes, she was transported to her chamber in Poitiers on a soft, spring dusk. She needed to be back there. It was like craving wine and knowing there was none in the barrel. North of Bordeaux, so few people played the lute. It was an instrument of the south, imported like precious rock crystal from the lands beyond Christendom.

The last note fell on the gathering darkness and the youth

looked at her from under his tumble of blond curls and gave her a dazzling smile.

"Beautiful," she said about both the boy and his music, and dismissed him with a smile and the gift of a small pouch of silver as Henry arrived to interrupt her dreaming. Earlier, he and Becket had been locked in deep argument that had looked as if it might continue all night.

Henry eyed the young man's departure with a slight sneer and muttered under his breath about "pretty boys." Having unfastened his belt, he slung it across a chest.

"Well?" Alienor said. "I assume you are here to speak to me and not just to hurl your clothes about and cast insults at my lute player."

Henry glowered. "He will not budge an inch," he said with frustration and disgust. "He refuses to yield over the matter of my right to try criminous clerks in my own courts. He is also refusing to cooperate on land claims made on the Church by my barons, even though he agreed at Clarendon they should go through my courts." His tunic followed his belt onto the chest, and there was a tearing sound as a seam gave way. "Now my new chancellor tells me he has discovered evidence that Becket was milking funds from the Toulouse campaign to line his own coffers. The man is not fit to be an archbishop! Small wonder he wants to flee the country."

"What kind of sums?"

"Three thousand marks of silver!" The pungent scent of sweat wafted from his shirt. "I will have him answer to me in a secular court for that one."

"The pope may well uphold him."

"Hah! I do not care what the pope does; he is not the king of England. Becket will confirm and obey the ancestral rules of this country and answer to me in my court for what he owes."

"And if he does not?"

"Then I will crush him."

Hearing the harshness in his tone, Alienor said nothing. He had declined her advice when he made Becket his archbishop and he would not be interested in her opinion now. As he said, all he wanted to do with the opposition was either bend it to his will or crush it.

He took her to bed and his attentions were vigorous. It was not lovemaking but a venting of fury and frustration, and an effort to subjugate her to his will too. On other occasions she had fought back, biting and scratching, but this time she yielded and did nothing, because her passivity was another form of defiance. She went elsewhere and thought of other things—of a warm summer evening in Aquitaine with the scent of roses on the breeze—and knew that he could not touch her.

# 25

*I*N THE FADING LIGHT OF A DANK NOVEMBER AFTERNOON, Isabel finalized her preparations for traveling to court. She had barely worn her elaborate gowns since her marriage seven months ago because she and Hamelin had been riding from manor to manor, castle to castle, visiting her lands, and that called for practical garb except for formal feasts and oath taking.

Hamelin had been absent at a council in Northampton, but his outriders had arrived, announcing he would be here by nightfall. Isabel carefully folded two chemises of fine white linen that were a gift for Alienor and placed them in a chest layered with sweet herbs. She had stitched the garments herself, including the smocked pleats which were her specialty. There were small gifts for the children, now her nieces and nephews by marriage. A fine antler-handled dagger for Harry, black leather belts with silver pendants for Richard and Geoffrey, each with different buckle shapes, a leather-bound psalter for Matilda, and a soft doll with yellow braids for little Alie.

Her packing complete, she checked that the fire in the main chamber was stoked up to give off lavish heat because Hamelin was bound to be chilled after his long ride. She changed her working gown for one of dark red wool that particularly suited her and pinned her hair so that it would cascade down her spine with just a few light touches when her veil was removed.

Moments later there were brisk footsteps on the stairs and Hamelin entered the chamber with a handful of knights and retainers.

Her heart quickening, she performed a formal curtsy. "My lord husband."

"Madam, my wife," he replied with equal gravity.

She gestured the servants to take his cloak and he handed it to them before throwing propriety aside, pulling her to him and soundly kissing her. His lips and hands were cold, but she didn't care. "I have been thinking of this all day," he said. "You and the welcome of this chamber."

She caressed his face. "That is passing strange because I have been thinking of you also. Will you wash and eat?"

Hamelin nodded and sat down on the bench at the foot of the bed with a heavy sigh of burdens released. He unlatched his belt with attached sword and dagger and handed it to his squire with a wave of dismissal.

Isabel brought him a cup of hot wine and then knelt to remove his boots.

Hamelin chuckled. "Before I was wed my squire accomplished the task well enough, but you are a far more rewarding sight to look upon," he teased.

She shot him an upward glance. "I should hope so." He had beautiful feet, well formed with high, smooth arches. She began to wash them, performing the formal duty of a wife on a husband's return. It was also a good opportunity to talk. "How did you fare at the council? Has there been a resolution?"

"No," he said. "My brother and the archbishop are riding runaway horses and spurring them on." He drank his wine. "I lost my temper. I am not proud that I did, but done is done."

Another glance showed Isabel that something had upset him. His hazel eyes were muddy and he was no longer smiling. In the months since their marriage, she was coming to know the man beneath the courtier's mask. He had a plentiful seasoning of Angevin flash and fire if he was caught on the raw or passionate about a subject, but it was a generous anger, quick to burn itself out. Right was right, wrong was wrong, and fair was fair. At court he had immense self-possession. "Lost your temper with whom?"

"The archbishop. It's a long tale."

"I am ready to listen if you want to tell me."

He considered and then nodded. "It is best you should know before we go to court. What I said that day on the bridge holds true. We should be able to talk openly and honestly."

Isabel flushed with pleasure. Hamelin had his notions about the place of men and women in a marriage, but he was not hidebound by them.

He changed his traveling attire for a soft linen shirt and loose tunic and slipped his feet into comfortable sheepskin-lined shoes. Isabel poured him more wine, and they sat down to eat at a trestle table placed near the fire. There was fresh white bread, wheat frumenty, and a warming dish of beef in ginger and cumin sauce.

Hamelin broke a piece off a small loaf and dipped it in the spicy stew. "The archbishop arrived in Northampton to answer a summons brought by John the Marshal about a land dispute. He expected to stay in the castle as he usually does, but Henry made sure those chambers were already occupied, and Becket had to lodge instead in the Priory of Saint Andrew outside the walls."

"Oh dear." Isabel replenished his cup. "That would not have pleased him."

"It didn't," Hamelin agreed. "Henry was making the same point he did at Berkhamsted. Becket took for granted what he should not and was justly put in his place." Hamelin ate a mouthful of stew. "The next day Becket was summoned to appear accused of contempt of court in the matter of denying John the Marshal justice in the business of a dispute over lands. The marshal never arrived to make his case. Henry gave out that he was busy at his exchequer duties, but the truth is that his horse cast a shoe, and he was unable to reach Northampton in time and turned back." Hamelin shook his head. "It was a specious excuse, but I do not blame him. Between my brother and the archbishop he would have been ground to dust."

Hamelin paused to eat more of the beef and then wiped his lips. "Becket told Henry he had no right to try the case anyway because it was a matter for the ecclesiastical courts. Stood there with his spine like a poker and banged his crosier on the ground and told us he was the archbishop of Canterbury and none of us should presume to judge him because only God had that right. Hah!"

"That does seem high-handed," she said, still none the wiser as to why Hamelin had lost his temper. What he had told her thus far was a catalog of irritations.

"And not the worst of it." Hamelin lifted his cup. "Henry ordered the bishops to pronounce a sentence of contempt of court on Becket and demanded he repay the money owing from the Toulouse campaign. Becket insisted the amounts had been written off when he became archbishop; Henry said they hadn't. And unless Becket could account for every penny he had spent as chancellor, he would confiscate his lands in lieu."

"It sounds to me as if the king is determined to bring Becket down." Isabel was worried at the wider repercussions. Whatever Becket had done, she owed him her gratitude for refusing to grant a dispensation of marriage between her and William FitzEmpress. Hamelin owed him gratitude too, but clearly he would not see it that way.

"No more so than Becket is determined to make his righteous stand as archbishop," he said. "The bishops encouraged him to resign, but he refused and took to his bed with the bowel gripes. Some said fear had caused his upset belly, and others thought he was playing Henry like a fish on a line. Henry chose to see it as falsehood and prepared to arraign him for treason."

Isabel listened with increasing dismay. As chancellor, Becket had been a consummate politician—urbane, charming, powerful, never putting a foot wrong. But if he had changed, then so had Henry. In the early years of the reign, he too had been flexible and less harsh. His treatment of Becket was that of a tyrant, and she had witnessed him exert that tyranny on Alienor, and on poor Mary de Boulogne.

"You said you lost your temper?" she said to Hamelin. "What happened?"

He rubbed his forehead. "On the last day Becket recovered enough to say Mass and preached a long sermon about the despotism of kings. Henry accused him outright of treason and ordered the Earl of Leicester to pass the sentence. Becket said he would not be judged by the likes of Henry's whoremasters, common servants—and lowborn bastard hangers-on."

Isabel gasped and put her hand to her mouth.

Hamelin's face contorted. "He said that were he a knight he would strike us all down, but since he was a man of God, he would leave. He was like a hissing cat, cornered by dogs but scratching with its claws. I am not proud of myself that I shouted in his face and threatened to silence him by wrapping his crosier around his neck."

Isabel was incensed. Becket's words were a slur intended to attack Henry, but the insult to Hamelin was inexcusable, even if Hamelin had let his anger get the better of him and responded inappropriately to a man of God. "So has he retreated to Canterbury?"

Hamelin snorted. "The archbishop would not call it a retreat, but no, he has not gone there. He left the priory in stealth late at night through an unlocked gate in the town that some sympathizer had left open. No one knows where he is. Henry has put a watch on all the ports. If he absconds abroad he will appeal to the pope. He is indeed a traitor to his king and his country—but of course not to his God, if you can believe that. Henry has written to France, asking Louis to refuse succor to the archbishop, but I cannot see Louis passing up an opportunity to cause trouble in Henry's domains."

Isabel bit her lip. "What will happen now?"

"Who knows?" Hamelin shrugged. "It depends what the pope decides. If fortune favors Becket, England may end up under interdict. If fortune favors my brother, Becket will resign and Gilbert Foliot will become archbishop instead." He gave a humorless laugh. "It is coming to something when everyone is looking to Gilbert Foliot to save us! For now I am home and I have never been more pleased in my life."

"Neither have I," Isabel said, supporting him with every iota of her being. "Put this incident behind you. To me you are a fine man and husband, full worthy to be the Earl of Surrey and Warenne, and father to the future heir." She took his hand and brought his hand to her belly.

His eyes widened.

"I am with child," she said.

Hamelin looked at his hand against her body, and slowly a smile lit up his face and continued to brighten. "That is the best of news! When?"

"In the summer I believe. Late May or early June."

"Well, that brings summer into my life immediately, and a plague on Becket and his doings. You have put everything into perspective and back in its place, my clever, beautiful wife!" He kissed her tenderly.

Isabel stroked his face. "Then I have succeeded in my duty," she said and wished Henry and Becket would attend to theirs and make peace.

❖❖❖

Alienor looked up from her needlework as her usher announced the arrival of the Countess de Warenne. Moments later, Isabel entered the room, her cheeks red with cold and her eyes alight with pleasure.

Alienor rose and greeted her friend and sister-by-marriage with a warm embrace. "You are blossoming!" she said, holding her away to look at her. "Marriage certainly suits you!"

"I expect it is the freezing sleet that has put color in my face!" Isabel said with a laugh. "But I am indeed blossoming. Hamelin and I expect a child in the summer."

"That is good news indeed!" Alienor drew her to the fire and saw her comfortably settled on a cushioned bench with a cup of hippocras. Outside the wind flung fistfuls of sleety rain against the shutters. Marlborough Castle stood upon a great mound that legend said had been built in the pagan times and belonged to the same age as the great circles and avenues of stone that strewed the Wiltshire landscape. The castle had been held by John the Marshal in the days of the war between Henry's mother and Stephen of Blois, but Henry had taken it back into his own hands six years ago as part of the reclamation of royal castles and estates.

"I am pleased to see you looking so well," Alienor said. "I have sorely missed your company, but I suspect you have missed mine less." She was amused to see Isabel blush.

"Indeed, I have missed your company, madam," Isabel tactfully replied, "but from the news coming out of court, I am glad to have been absent."

Alienor waved her hand in irritation. "Henry is like a bear with a sore head. He asked Louis not to succor Becket and is affronted because Louis will not take his part and supports the archbishop. What did he expect? Louis might agree to marriage arrangements and smile and extend the courtesies, but if he can tear Henry apart, he will." She sighed. "Henry's mind is as sharp as a new knife when it comes to the law; he understands all things that work with cogs and stratagems. But he does not know how to deal with people when they behave with their guts and their hearts, and all the places inside themselves that are not governed by cogs and logic, and that is because he cannot control those things inside himself except by locking them away." She gave a short laugh. "You see how I have truly missed you. You are the best listener of all my ladies."

Isabel picked up her wine. "I like to listen and I am glad to serve you," she said. "I think you have the measure of the king."

"Indeed," Alienor said with a wry look, "but having the measure does not always mean being able to do something about it."

"Has there been any word from Rome about the archbishop?"

"No," Alienor said, "but envoys are expected daily."

"Hamelin told me about Northampton."

Alienor was surprised and a little curious. "He talks to you of such things?"

"It helps him to settle his own mind and put his house in order." She smiled. "I am a good listener for him too."

A pang went through Alienor that was almost envy. "Then I hope he has the wit to use your talent for your benefit and his," she said. "What happened at Northampton consumes Henry. All I hear about from dawn until dusk is the perfidy of Thomas Becket and what a traitor he is. Henry cannot deal with being defied. I pray that Becket will withdraw from the brink and resign."

"Do you think he will?"

Alienor shook her head and looked pensive. "I do not know," she said. "I suspect not."

❖❖❖

In the late afternoon of the eve of the Nativity, Henry's envoys returned from their petition to Rome and were ushered to Henry's personal chamber to make their report. Alienor was with her household in the hall, watching an entertainment but alert to the happenings in the background. Everyone was on edge but pretending to enjoy themselves, and the entertainment was apt, if incongruous.

A man walked on stilts, another man perched on his shoulders. A voluminous robe covered both players from neck to ground, so they appeared as a single giant. The "giant" held a monkey dressed in a miniature archbishop's robe and miter. The creature had been trained to make the sign of the cross on its breast in exchange for almonds. Harry loved that one, the sight doubling him up with laughter. Another entertainer juggled with swords, the blades gleaming blue-silver where the light caught the razor-sharp edges. Richard was fascinated, and Alienor made a note to keep an eye on him; it was obvious he was desperate to attempt the trick and would likely cut himself or someone else into the bargain.

Glancing to one side, Alienor noticed one of Henry's scribes, two writing tablets under his arm, following a messenger through the chamber. Ranulf de Broc, the doorkeeper, accompanied them, his stride heavy and brutish like the man. By the time the next entertainer had finished making his fluffy white dog jump through a series of hoops, de Broc was back, cloaked and booted for a journey, spurs at his heels, a sealed packet clutched in his meaty hand. A few brusque commands brought sergeants and henchmen from their posts.

Alienor abandoned the entertainment and went to Henry's chamber, where she found him prowling the room with clenched fists. An open letter lay on the trestle and the scribe was writing busily on a fresh piece of parchment.

"What has happened?" she asked.

Henry spun to face her. "Becket tendered his resignation but with all the tricks and dramas you'd expect." He indicated the letter on the table. "He arrived to petition the pope on a prancing white stallion with an escort of Louis's French knights, if you please." Henry kicked the floor rushes in disgust. "Proclaimed himself the defender of the rights of the Church and told the pope I was trying to emasculate those rights. Oh yes, he calculated it to the last degree. I should have known what he would do. He's always had a taste for the grand gesture."

"What did the pope say?"

Henry curled his top lip. "The pope is a two-faced weasel," he growled. "Thomas went down on his knees, handed him his archbishop's ring, and begged that he be allowed to resign. But the pope put the ring back onto his finger and refused to accept it. If that was not all prearranged, then God's a monkey."

Alienor's heart sank at the implications. "So Becket is to return to England?"

"No, the pope has sent him to the abbey at Pontigny with instructions to consider his position and come better to know God." Henry snorted down his nose. "In other words, he has placed him out of my jurisdiction and in Louis's, where Becket can continue to subvert me and there is nothing I can do about it." He launched a vicious kick at a stool and sent it crashing over.

Alienor bit her lip. That was certainly not good news. Everyone had been hoping Becket would resign and Gilbert Foliot succeed to the primacy, but as Henry said, Pope Alexander was a weasel. In sending Becket to Pontigny, he had put him where Henry could not get at him, but by saying Becket was in need of spiritual guidance, he avoided the accusation that he was taking Becket's part.

Henry kicked the stool again. "If the pope believes everything will pass over like a headache on the day after a feast, he is mistaken. Anyone who trifles with me swiftly discovers that I return the favor fourfold. As from now all revenues to the papacy shall cease, and since Becket is going to dwell at Pontigny, his dependents can go there too and let him care for them. I won't have them in England on my soil."

Alienor stared at him. "You mean to exile his family?"

"Every last one," Henry said grimly.

"If you do that, there is no way back."

"Becket's behavior has put him outside the pale. I didn't start this quarrel. He is the one who has made diplomatic moves against me. I will not suffer a single relative of his to remain on my lands. Let him have them all and find homes and livings for them. It is no good rooting out only one rat from a nest. All must go."

"But surely not all to Pontigny? There will not be room!"

"That is Becket's problem, not mine. The Christ child was born in a stable; let Becket's kin sleep in one. Ranulf de Broc has gone to clear them out." He wagged his index finger at her. "If any of them come crawling to you seeking succor and requesting intercession, do not seek to meddle by helping them. I know your habit of going behind my back, and I shall be watching you."

Alienor drew herself up in regal dignity. "Has it come to this then?" she demanded. "Is this all there is left? Suspicion and spying and being so consumed by the desire to win that everything else falls away?"

"I do not need your advice or your lectures, madam, only your compliance. I trust that is understood?"

Alienor came very close to loathing him in that moment. Frequently these days she was reminded of her first marriage to Louis and the battles she had endured with him. There was a familiar ring to the argument. It was a man's place to go his own way and a woman's to do as she was bidden unless the man asked for advice or gave her permission to speak, and she was sick of it. "Yes, sire," she said icily. "Completely. Do I have your leave to go?"

He gave her one of his bright looks, sharp enough to cut, and she returned it, full on, meeting edge to edge.

"Yes," he said, "you have my leave, but expect me later in your chamber, madam."

So, he intended to use her bed to further exert his authority. Alienor disengaged and turned away. If she had had a dagger in her hand at that moment, she would have used it.

❖❖❖

Alienor had read the medical treatises of Salerno, which said that a woman should wash and perfume her body, including her private areas, if she was going to lie with a man. Waiting for Henry, she was disinclined to prepare herself, yet the political, logical part of her mind told her that a show of compliance would make matters easier. Overcoming her reluctance, she bathed and had her maids comb her hair until it shone in a heavy sheaf to her waist. She dabbed oil of roses at her wrists and throat and between her thighs. Her chemise was soft linen with delicate embroidery, and the sheets were fresh and tight.

When Henry arrived, she greeted him with dutiful courtesy. He gave her a suspicious look and she returned it blandly, and, behind the facade, wondered how far Ranulf de Broc had galloped on his way to London to roust out Becket's relatives.

"I have thought again about what you said," Henry remarked as he removed his clothes. "About turning Becket's relations out. It is not practical for all of them to make the journey, so I have decided some may stay."

Alienor stared at him, taken by surprise. Henry seldom went back on his decisions, and was even less inclined to heed her advice.

He pulled her down onto the bed and nuzzled her throat. His breath was warm, his beard raspy and soft at the same time on her tender skin, and despite having expected the encounter to be a duty, her body moistened with lust, and she gasped with pleasure as he entered her. When he gave her his seed, she climaxed with him and gripped him fiercely.

He kissed her mouth and patted her hips as he withdrew. "There now," he said. "That was good, wasn't it? I don't know why you fight me." He turned to dress, making it clear that, deed accomplished, he was not proposing to stay the night.

"Have you sent a message to de Broc making your intentions clear?"

"Yes, and by fast horse." His tone was cheerful. "He has instructions to let anyone stay who wishes to pay a fine of two hundred marks."

Alienor's softened opinion of him vanished on the instant. "Hardly any of them will be able to afford to pay that!" As well he knew. The infirm and those least able to cope would still lose their homes.

"That is their problem, not mine," he replied with a shrug. "Let Becket and the Church help them out. They're a merchant community; they are bound to have money hidden under the hearthstone. Becket embezzled thousands of pounds from me when he was chancellor; I am only recouping my losses." He pinched her cheek hard, kissed her mouth, and left the chamber.

"Bastard," Alienor said softly. Donning her cloak, she left the bed, poured a goblet of wine, and went to sit by the fire. From Henry's point of view, she could see how everything fitted together perfectly. Becket was punished whatever happened, and Henry stood to gain financially from it. She could not condone Becket's behavior, but Henry's was as bad.

Gazing into the hot embers, she acknowledged that she and Henry had been riding along parallel roads for a long time, but those roads were gradually pulling apart, and soon they would be unable to see each other at all.

# 26

## ROUEN, APRIL 1165

"WELL, MY DEAR," SAID THE EMPRESS, A TREMBLE IN HER voice, "another one to add to your brood. You have surprised me indeed, because I did not think you and my son would engender more children between you." She sat at the fireside, wrapped in a fur-lined mantle. A jet-topped walking stick leaned against her chair. She had been sick with a fever and congestion of the lungs, and was only slowly recovering her physical strength. Her mind was as keen as ever, though, and she was conducting business from her fireside with all her usual imperious will.

"Yes, Mother, I had thought so too." Alienor placed her hand on her womb, which was swollen with the child conceived at Marlborough. She had not been overjoyed to find herself pregnant again, but it proved to everyone that Henry was still sharing her bed and that she remained fertile and capable of fulfilling the duties of a queen.

Not that Henry had visited her chamber very often since. She had remained in England while he crossed to Normandy, and her arrival in Rouen for the Easter court was recent. She had also been making wedding arrangements for her eldest daughter. German envoys had visited England earlier in the year with various proposals. Delicate negotiations were still being conducted, and Alienor had yet to speak with her daughter about the match but knew Matilda must suspect something; she was an astute child, quick to understand nuances.

"Perhaps it will be another daughter," the empress said, "to be your companion and consolation when this one goes." She nodded at her namesake who was weaving blue-and-red braid on a small loom and telling her little sister a story.

"I do not know if that is a thing to wish for or not," Alienor said. "To raise another girl child and watch her beat her wings against a closed window."

The empress nodded, but her eyes, deeply set with age and ill health, were guarded and reminded Alienor to be careful about criticizing Henry. His mother was permitted to do so but not his wife. However, the empress would sympathize with her about a woman's lot in society. "But," Alienor added, "only a woman can bear sons. A man sows the seed, but it is the woman who makes it flesh and endangers her life in the bearing. It is the woman who raises the child until it is old enough to leave the nursery. She has the more enduring strength, because she must."

"That is true." Her mother-in-law nodded again, this time positively. She continued to observe her granddaughters. "I left England for Germany when I was eight years old, the future bride of a grown man I had never met. I was married to him at twelve and became his consort, by which time I spoke fluent German and had been taught the ways of his court. I had come to know him too. She will tread a similar path."

A pang of loss very close to grief surged through Alienor. "I will prepare her as best I can. She will begin learning German—she knows some words already, and she will have a magnificent trousseau and a household of people she knows and likes." She bit her lip. These were all practical concerns, but she was going to miss her eldest daughter terribly. It worried her too that the bridegroom was almost thirty years older than Matilda. It was an enormous age gap to cross. She was confident Matilda would rise to the challenge. She had no qualms about her shirking her duty, but her heart still ached at the burden being laid upon shoulders so young.

"I was deeply unhappy to leave behind everything I had known," the empress said as if reading her mind, "but I knew my duty. I did not weep when I bade farewell to my parents because I did not want to shame myself or them, and they did not weep either. I never saw my mother again. My husband was kind, and I became fond of him. Indeed, I came to be happy with my life there." Her face tightened with remembered pain. "If I had a choice, I would not have returned to wed Geoffrey of Anjou, even if we did make Henry between us—and two other sons, God rest their souls." She made the sign of the cross on her breast and clutched the ruby crucifix around her neck. "They made little of their lives, and I grieve that they left the world untimely, but Henry has achieved all that I hoped and more, and begotten a generation who will follow and increase his fame. It is to the future we must look."

Alienor gave an appropriate murmur. Whatever their disagreements, Henry was a determined and remarkable man, and their descendants would straddle the world. The empress had never spoken about her childhood before. From the way she was looking at her eldest granddaughter, Alienor suspected she saw herself in the little girl, and it had awakened old memories. Indeed, Matilda resembled her grandmother in many ways, being strong-willed and intelligent, with a rigid sense of right and wrong. But she was lively and limber too, and her husband would be many years older than the empress's had been.

The empress gazed at the ruby cross. "The years have flown. There are few left to me now. Many things in my life I would have done differently and I regret, but they gave me my son and my grandchildren. Had I stayed in Germany after Heinrich died, I would never have borne Henry and seen him become a great king."

"Indeed not, madam," Alienor said and lowered her gaze when the empress gave her a sharp look.

"I hope my son can count on your loyalty and support."

"Always, madam," Alienor replied. "Just as much as I can count on his."

"I admit he is difficult. Even though I bore him, I know his faults, but you must both rise above the troubles between you for the greater good."

Alienor was spared from answering as one of the empress's chamberlains arrived with a message from a contact at the French court. The empress opened the letter and squinted at the lines. "My eyes," she said impatiently. "Time was when I could see a fly on the wall hangings even from the other side of the room; now I can barely make one out if it lands on my skirt." She gave the letter to Alienor. "Read it to me."

Alienor's own eyes were not as sharp as they had been and she had to hold the letter a little away to focus. "The queen of France is with child," she said. "Due in the late summer." She read out the rest of what was written and returned the letter to the empress.

"They kept it quiet for a long enough time." The empress made a sound of contempt and struck the letter with her hand. "And Becket is being cited as a miracle worker because it was after his arrival at Pontigny that she became pregnant—how foolish!"

"I expect he got Becket to bless the marriage bed," Alienor said flatly.

The empress looked at her askance.

Alienor made a face. "When I was married to Louis, he had trouble when it came to the procreation of heirs."

Matilda raised her brows.

"Not at first when we were very young. He was eager then, but after I miscarried of a son, he struggled to play the man's part. It came to the point where he could only become aroused when the Church was involved. Marie was conceived after the dedication of Saint-Denis when Abbot Suger and Bernard of Clairvaux interceded on our behalf. Alix was begotten in a bed blessed by the pope at Tusculum. In between were long gaps of time when he either did not visit my chamber, or was incapable when he did." Alienor leaned forward to emphasize her point. "Louis can only perform the act with his wife when the Church gives him sanction. It would not surprise me if Becket's arrival in France gave him that impetus."

The empress looked stern for a moment, as if the subject was too unsavory to discuss, but then a glint of wintry humor entered her gaze. "Well, if this debacle is to blame for an heir to France, it is an unfortunate result of my son's dispute with his archbishop, but there is nothing to be done about it."

The women looked up as Henry arrived, returning from a day's hunting with his vassals and retainers. Close by his side was his bastard son Jeoffrey, his boots and tunic mud-splattered like Henry's. He was just starting his journey from boyhood into adolescence and had begun to grow like wheat in May. His face glowed with the pleasure of masculine camaraderie and a swipe of bright blood painted his right cheek to show that he had been in at the kill for the first time. Henry tousled his curls and, bidding him stay back near the door, crossed the room to join the women. The smell of the hunt was a pungent miasma around him, a combination of hard-ridden horse, sweaty man, and a faint tang of the butcher's stall. Dark blood rimmed the fingernails of his right hand. She did not have to guess who had smeared the boy's face.

"Good hunting?" asked the empress.

"Why, yes, Mother, indeed it was," Henry replied, eyes gleaming. "We cornered a great boar in his full prime. There is some excellent feasting in prospect. I hope the cooks have a big enough apple for his mouth."

The empress clucked her tongue. "Should you have taken the boy on a boar hunt? Is he ready?"

Henry looked affronted. "He is my son. I was barely older than he was when I crossed the Narrow Sea with an army to challenge the king of England."

"Yes, I remember," she said, looking up to heaven. "And it wasn't an army; it was a band of adventurers whom you couldn't afford to pay."

"But it made everyone take notice, did it not? And it put fresh heart into our supporters. I am not going to coddle the boy, Mother. He played his part in the hunt the same as the rest of the squires, and he is a natural on the back of a horse. He holds a spear well too," he added with a teasing grin.

Alienor said, "Is it wise to encourage him in such pursuits, sire, when he is intended for the Church?"

Henry sent her a taut look. "There is time enough to train him for whatever vocation he comes to, and even priests hunt. For now there is no harm in him accompanying me. Our own sons are either still too young or else not here. I will take them hunting when they are of age." He turned to leave, saying he had to wash away the grime and gore.

"Before you go, you should know that news has come from France," Alienor said. "Louis's queen is with child."

"Is she, by God?" Henry grimaced and then gave a hefty shrug. "Well, the last four have been daughters. God willing, both our luck and his will hold and she'll birth another girl. If not, our sons have the advantage over his because they're already half-fledged." He continued on his way, his arm across young Jeoffrey's shoulders in a man-to-man fashion.

"You will have to accept the boy," the empress said quietly. "I have done my best to prepare him for a life in the Church, but in the end it is Henry's choice what happens to him. He loves him and will do his duty by him, but it does not mean he loves his heirs any less or lacks care for them."

"Perhaps not," Alienor replied, "but I know he sees in him our firstborn son who died and the mistress he had who also died, and that makes the boy precious to him. When he takes him hunting before he has taken his legitimate sons, then it hits me here, and here." She pressed her hand first to her heart and then to her abdomen.

"Then you take the blows," the empress said curtly. "That child has the potential to be a firm ally to your sons, not an enemy. Without the aid of my own brothers, born of my father's mistresses, Henry would not now be king of England and duke of Normandy. I counsel you to use your head, not your heart in this."

"And I shall do so, Mother," Alienor said, "but it still does not prevent my heart from being wounded. I have shields for many things, but not this. You must have those places yourself, no matter how you hide them from the world."

The empress said nothing and instead held her gnarled, age-spotted hands to the fire.

❖❖❖

That evening, Alienor dismissed her women and sat to comb her eldest daughter's hair herself. It was beautiful, the glossy golden-brown tresses so long that Matilda could sit on them.

"I have some news for you, my love," Alienor said after a while. "I know how grown up you are, and I want you to listen carefully." She felt the cool silkiness of the hair under her palm. How difficult it was going to be to send this nestling out into the world, to know that there would never be moments like this again.

Matilda looked around, her clear gray eyes wide with question.

Alienor took a deep breath. "We have had a marriage offer for you, from a very important family in Germany. A cousin of the Emperor Frederick no less. Henry, Duke of Saxony, very much desires to marry you."

Matilda's eyes remained wide, but they were assessing rather than afraid. "Is that why that bishop was in England before, Mama?"

"Yes, my love, it is. The envoys from Germany came to discuss with me whether a match might be made. Your father thinks it a very suitable liaison."

Matilda chewed her lip. "I know I have to make a good marriage, Mama," she said steadily. "I know I must help my family and that you will choose well for me."

The words were adult, but they emerged in a little girl's voice, and Alienor's heart caught with pain. "Your future husband is a great knight," she said. "A man of whom you can be justly proud and who is strong enough to take care of you. You will have your own household and you will go with everything you need, including people you know."

Matilda folded her arms protectively around her body. "When do I have to go? Will I have time to say good-bye? Will I be able to see the new baby?"

"Of course you will!" Alienor put down the comb and hugged Matilda to her breast, unable to bear any more. Dear God, dear God. "For now it is but an agreement for the future. You will not be leaving for a while yet—perhaps two years. We have to set up your household and arrange your trousseau. You will have lessons in German and learn the customs of their court to prepare you. By the time you do go, you will be bigger and stronger and ready for your duties."

Matilda relaxed when she realized she was not about to be packed off at dawn, but a frown lingered on her brow. "After I go, will I ever see you again, Mama? It's not forever, is it?"

"Of course you will see me!" The words were bitter in Alienor's mouth because the truth was that she probably never would. Her heart bled. She opened her jewel box and poked among the pieces until she found a small gold ring with a dove incised on the flat top. "I want you to have this," she said. "You are old enough now to look after it. It was mine when I was your age, and my father gave it to me and told me it had belonged to his mother when she was a girl." She slipped it onto Matilda's middle finger, and it was a perfect fit. "There," she said. "Now we shall always be close."

"Thank you, Mama." Matilda rubbed the surface of the ring and blinked hard.

"Come," Alienor said briskly and kissed her cheek. "No more now. It is past time you were asleep." She took Matilda to her small box bed and, when she had said her prayers, tucked her in.

"May I wear the ring tonight?" Matilda asked.

"Of course, but you must put it away safely first thing in the morning." Alienor kissed Matilda again and watched her snuggle under the covers so that only the top of her head was showing, and then she tiptoed away from the bed. Her throat ached with grief. It didn't seem a moment since she had held her daughter in her arms, a snuffling newborn baby, and now her marriage was being arranged and she had to prepare to bid her the long farewell. Little Alie was not yet four, still a baby, but in another four years was she to lose her too to some distant land?

And this new child growing in her womb. Son or daughter, flesh of her flesh, barely quickened and already with a future carved in the shape of a broken heart.

# 27

## CASTLE ACRE, NORFOLK, JUNE 1165

HAMELIN CHECKED THE BAGGAGE CHEST WAITING TO BE taken from his chamber to the cart in the bailey and made sure he had packed his favorite hunting dagger. He knew very well that it was in there, but being certain helped to take the edge off his tension.

Outside it was the high morning of a perfect summer's day, and he should have been riding to join his brother on campaign. War had broken out along the Welsh borders, and Henry had planned a summer campaign to bring the troublesome Prince of Gwynedd to heel once and for all.

Hamelin had intended to leave at dawn, but Isabel had begun her labor in the small hours, and since it did not matter to a day when he joined Henry, he had chosen to wait. Now time was passing like the slow drip from a leaky spigot. The birthing chamber was barred to him, and although Isabel's women constantly brought him news and told him everything was progressing well, he remained agitated. His own mother had died bearing him; he dared not think about losing Isabel like that. She had become as dear to him as his own life.

Puffing out his cheeks, he took himself to the stables. Carbonel turned his head and nickered. Hamelin stroked the palfrey's soft taupe muzzle. "Well, my beauty," he said, "surely it cannot be much longer."

Carbonel butted him and lipped his hand. As a child, jealous of Henry, hurting, Hamelin had once lamed a horse that had been passed down to him after Henry had finished with it. He hadn't wanted yet another of his golden brother's castoffs. Their father had never realized what Hamelin had done and had given him a replacement—a well-upholstered plush white creature suitable for a staid matron and worse than the first horse because Hamelin had become a laughingstock. At the time he had raged at the unfairness of it all, but as he matured, he had come to be deeply ashamed of the deed committed by a foolish, resentful boy. The guilt still burdened him, although he had confessed the sin long ago and been absolved. He would never tell anyone beyond the priest, especially not Isabel, who trusted him. One of the reasons he had no bastards was because of his childhood, even if he was the brother of a king. His new family was his sustenance, and he would work himself to the bone to see it become illustrious, without taint or tarnish.

"Sire." Thomas, one of the lads who worked in the hall, hastened up to him and bent the knee. "Sire, you are sought by the midwife."

Hamelin's stomach wallowed. He started to ask a question and then shook his head. "Never mind, boy, tell her I am coming." He gave the horse a last pat on the neck and returned to the hall, trying not to run. Conscious of his dignity, he took measured steps and walked as if he was unconcerned.

The midwife was waiting for him, a squeaking, snuffling bundle cradled in her arms. Her expression was anxious, and Hamelin was immediately on edge. Something must be wrong with the child, or with Isabel. He gave the woman a hard look, anger masking fear, and she recoiled briefly before gathering her courage. "Sire, the child is born, but it is a girl."

Hamelin experienced an instant of weak, almost debilitating relief. A son was the goal that all men strove for, but he didn't care just now. "That is of no consequence," he said. "Is she healthy?"

"Indeed, sire," the midwife swiftly reassured him. "She has all her fingers and toes and cried the moment she entered the world." Her expression still tense with worry, she placed the baby in his arms.

The child had been loosely wrapped so that he could check for himself that she was healthy in all her limbs. Her hair was dark and damp, either from her birth or a recent bath. Feeling the little head in the crook of his elbow, Hamelin felt such a flood of joy and gratitude that tears stung his eyes. "I acknowledge her of my house," he said. "She shall be called Isabel for her mother." He looked at the midwife who was now smiling tentatively. "How fares the countess?"

"She is well, sire. There were no difficulties at the birth."

"Good." He swallowed to try to clear the tightness in his throat. "Tell her I shall visit her when she is ready." He gently gave his daughter back to the woman and turned to receive the congratulations of the household. Ordering two tuns of the best wine to be broached to drink the baby's health, he decided to defer his journey to Shrewsbury until the morrow and spend today at home in celebration.

Once everything was in hand, he sought solitude to have a quiet weep, releasing the heavy weight of emotion he had been holding back. Later, he visited Isabel and found her sitting up in bed, their swaddled daughter in her arms and her face radiant with joy. Going to her, he kissed her tenderly.

"You do not mind that it is a girl?" she said with trepidation.

Hamelin shook his head. "I care only that you are both well and whole. She will be a beauty like her mother. Men will vie for her hand, and her besotted father will think none of them worthy."

Isabel gave a teary laugh. "I never thought to bear a child. She is precious to me, and I cherish her because she is such a great gift from God." Her hazel eyes were almost golden. "I am so pleased you stayed to see her."

"The Welsh are not going to run away," Hamelin said with a shrug. At the moment he barely cared about them. "I shall see to her baptism tomorrow before I leave. I would rather stay here but needs must, and I hope to be home soon. When I return, we shall hold a great celebration for your churching."

"Just come back to us whole," she said and stroked his face. "We will be waiting."

❖❖❖

In the morning Hamelin took his daughter to be baptized in the font of Acre's castle chapel. Isabel, daughter of Hamelin the king's brother, and forever a princess to her father. Riding out from Acre, his heart was overflowing.

The weather started out bright, but by the time Hamelin reached Shrewsbury four days later, the sky wore heavy swatches of gray cloud and he had to pull up his hood and bend his head against the driving rain.

Eventually, the light darkening toward a wet dusk, he splashed into the sludgy stable yard of Shrewsbury Castle and dismounted from Carbonel uttering a heartfelt groan. The palfrey's head was hanging with weariness, and Hamelin felt the same. "See that he's dried off properly and given plenty of dry bedding," he told the groom.

"Sire."

Hamelin wished the same for himself and grimaced. He did not know whether to rub his aching back or knees first. His men would have to find lodging in the town and somewhere to pitch the tents, but his harbinger had that in hand. For himself, there would be sleeping space in the castle, even if he had to bed down in the hall with a host of others.

A squire escorted him from the stables to the castle and they squelched along straw paths, half buried in mud, before entering the keep. Henry was ensconced in a large chamber on the upper floor, the latter heaving with activity. By lamplight and candlelight, scribes worked frantically under the direction of Robert of Leicester and the new chancellor, Geoffrey Ridel, pieces of parchment piling up at their sides.

Henry sat at a trestle working through a sheaf of documents and talking to one of his shipmasters. Perched on a stool at his feet was an exquisite young woman, little more than a girl, with an apple-blossom flush on her cheek and flawless, creamy skin. A light veil did little to conceal her waist-length honey-brown braids. As Henry worked, he lifted her hand to his lips and kissed her knuckles. The latest mistress, Hamelin thought, but he was shocked by Henry's blatant behavior and the girl's youth.

Henry glanced up and saw Hamelin. For an instant his lips remained on the girl's hand before he raised his head. "Here at last," he said. "I expected you yesterday. Married life is slowing you down."

Hamelin bowed. Water dripped from his wet hair where the hood had not protected him and trickled down his face. His feet felt clammy and cold inside his boots. "My apologies, sire. The countess was in travail and I waited to see my daughter safely born and baptized. I thought you would not mind a day's delay."

"You are becoming presumptuous for the sake of a girl-child," Henry said, but there was wintry amusement in his eyes. "Better if your wife had borne you a son."

"I do not mind," Hamelin said. "I am just pleased that both mother and child are in good health. We have named her Isabel and she is already a beauty."

Henry snorted with affectionate scorn. "I would never have thought to see you so fond."

"Nor you, brother," Hamelin retorted pointedly.

Henry sent him a bright look filled with challenge. "You have not asked, but I will tell you. This delightful young lady is Rosamund, daughter of Walter de Clifford of Bronllys and Clifford Castle."

Hamelin knew Walter de Clifford, although not well: a pragmatic marcher baron of stature and backbone. "My lady," he said. De Clifford would need that pragmatism now. Perhaps he was looking forward to seeing his family's advancement through Henry's attachment to his daughter.

"Sire." Henry was still holding her hand, but she acknowledged Hamelin by inclining her head.

"A rose of the world," Henry said, "but only for me."

The pink in the girl's cheeks deepened. She flicked him a shy but coquettish look, to which Henry responded with a doting smile. "There are no thorns on her anywhere—or none that I have yet found."

Embarrassment burned Hamelin's face. He was long accustomed to Henry's infidelities, but this was a step further. "I came to report the moment I arrived," he said stiffly, "but I can see you are busy with other matters. Do I have your leave to go and get dried out?"

"As you will," Henry said with an insouciant wave. "We can talk later at dinner."

❖❖❖

When Hamelin returned to eat with Henry, he found him feeding the de Clifford girl from his own dish, holding morsels of chicken for her to bite daintily from his fingers. On Hamelin's arrival, he dismissed her with a pat on the bottom, telling her to wait in his chamber, and as she left the room with a maid in tow, he gazed after her with lust and longing.

"Are you mad?" Hamelin said. "I know you have your casual mistresses, but how old is she, Henry? Dear God!"

"Don't go all sanctimonious on me," Henry snapped. "She brings innocence and freshness into my life; she has not been corrupted by the ways of the court. I know I will have the truth from her without any politicking behind my back. She brings me to life in ways you could not begin to understand."

"I do understand," Hamelin replied, standing his ground. "Isabel does that for me, but she is my wife and of an age and awareness. You cannot afford to flaunt this...this child as your paramour."

Henry's expression took on a stubborn cast. "She is probably the only person in my life who has not beggared or betrayed me in one way or another. She is mine, and I look after what is mine."

"Have I ever beggared or betrayed you?" Hamelin could not keep the anger and hurt from his voice.

"You know I did not mean it like that."

"Sometimes you make it very difficult to do so."

"You are mine too," Henry said. "Stop scowling."

"What of Alienor?"

"What of her?" Henry gave an impatient shrug. "She is in Angers and she knows I take my comforts elsewhere when she is breeding. Our worlds do not mesh save in matters of state and business that concern us both." He leaned toward Hamelin to emphasize his point. "When you lack something in your life, you go out and find it. Rosamund is my finding, and I will not hear a word said against her."

Fixed by Henry's bright stare, Hamelin felt a jolt of recognition. There was an expression on his brother's face he had never seen before, and that expression was love.

❖❖❖

Standing on top of the high sandstone rock, Hamelin filled his lungs with the cold, salty air. On his left the sun sparkled on the Dee Estuary, on the right the sea was a series of blue-and-gray pleats running to a horizon of scudding storm clouds.

Far from teaching the Welsh a lesson they would never forget, the campaign had been a disaster. Hamelin had never experienced such rain before and thought this was how it must have been at the start of the great flood. Streams had become raging torrents; rivers had burst their banks and raced more swiftly than galloping horses, surging with brown foam and swirling with vicious currents. He had seen men and baggage beasts swept to their deaths. There had been sudden landslides where supplies had disappeared down mud slippages into ravines. There was no escaping the constant rain, and fires could not be lit to cook or to dry out saturated clothes and equipment. Men went hungry and sickened. Everyone had phlegmy coughs and aching lungs. Welsh snipers had attacked them all along the route, shooting arrows, setting traps, and melting away once damage was done, to become no more than wraiths in the forest.

The army had retreated to the Wirral peninsula to await their supply ships, which would aid them along the coast, but there was still no sign of them. The only glimmer of light in the whole boggy morass of this campaign was that it had finally stopped raining, and the sun was pleasantly warm on his body. He had heard mutterings among the men that God had turned against them because of the way Henry had treated his archbishop, and because the life he lived was one of sin and debauchery. There were times Hamelin thought it might be true.

Turning at a noise behind him, he was surprised to see the de Clifford girl emerging through the trees. When she saw him, she hesitated but then folded her arms inside her cloak and continued, a determined set to her jaw.

"Are you looking for the ships?" she asked. "Henry says they should have been here by now."

Hamelin was perturbed, almost shocked, that she should refer to his brother as casually as "Henry." The fact that he had confided in her about the ships was unwise. For now her power was naive and uncalculating, but that would change. Henry indulged her far beyond wisdom.

"They should," he said, "but we are at the mercy of winds and tide. Does my brother know you are wandering around unescorted?"

Rosamund returned a smile to his frown. "No, and he will scold me, but he is never angry for long." She slid him a mischievous look. "I shall say I was with you."

Hamelin recoiled and she laughed. "He won't be jealous. Do not worry."

"I am not worried," he snapped, "but I wonder if you know the depths in which you are swimming."

She sobered and gazed out over the water. "What choice do I have, my lord?" Suddenly she was not a girl barely old enough to bleed but a woman fully grown. "My body has bought my family favor and given me a life beyond them and the nunnery at Godstow. I am fond of both, but this is a taste of a different feast, and while it is mine, I intend to enjoy it. The king is my dear lord. I please him—and he is good to me." She gave Hamelin a steady look. "That is all there is to it."

Hamelin was nonplussed. This chit of a girl had just spoken to him as if she was a queen. "You are wrong," he said. "There is far more to it than whether or not you and the king please each other. There are matters of what is right and seemly. You are both treading a precarious path."

Her cheeks grew pink. "Sire, I know that. But the king has chosen me, and I will tread that path for him and with him whatever the consequence."

And, like a cat, would probably not lose her footing, Hamelin thought.

Suddenly she narrowed her eyes and pointed. "Look!"

Hamelin followed her finger and saw several long shapes the size of earwigs bisecting the sea and sky on the Dee side of the horizon. "The king's ships," he said. "We should return to camp."

Rosamund walked beside him, her eyes downcast and her manner demure. He supposed she must have acquired that from the nuns at Godstow, and it was incongruous when he thought of the way she behaved with Henry, leaning on him, letting him feed her lover's titbits. She was lithe and dainty, no taller than his shoulder. She was nothing like Alienor, yet she possessed a hint of that same core of supple steel.

❖❖❖

The ships, when they docked, proved to be only half the number Henry had expected, and many of the supplies they carried were salt-ruined and useless. The vessels had been blown off course, and when they tried to land at Anglesey to make repairs, they had been set upon and mauled by the locals.

"A whole summer wasted!" Henry raged. "An entire campaign scuppered. Why am I surrounded by dolts and incompetents who cannot do their duty?"

"Sire, the weather was against us," one man was foolhardy enough to venture. "There was nothing we could do but run before the wind."

"I do not want your feeble excuses." Henry shoved away from the table against which he had been leaning and threw up his hands. "Time and again I have sailed in gales and storms and still made landfall ahead of time with all intact."

Hamelin stood near the door flap of Henry's great campaign tent, listening to him flay the shipmasters with his tongue. In their childhood Henry had often thrown spectacular tantrums where he would thrash on the floor, drumming his heels and screaming at the top of his lungs. Such an episode looked imminent now.

A young man arrived at the royal tent clutching a sealed parchment. Hamelin eyed John FitzJohn, who had recently succeeded to the position of royal marshal following his father's death and was still settling into his new official role. He was tall and broad-shouldered, but whether those shoulders would bear the burden of his office remained to be seen.

"News?" Hamelin asked.

John FitzJohn eyed the raging king with trepidation. "Yes, sire. The queen of France has given birth to a living male child."

"I see." Hamelin took pity on the discomforted young man. Bearers of bad news were frequently blamed for it, and John FitzJohn was trying to establish his position at court. "I will deal with this," he said. "Go and see to your other duties."

"I am willing to do this, sire," the young marshal protested to his credit.

"No, you are not, even while I know you will do your duty. Go." Hamelin gave him a dour smile. "I shall call in the favor another time."

He waited until FitzJohn had gone, relief in his step, and then he approached the pacing Henry. "It is a night for bad news, Brother," he said and handed him the letter. "Perhaps you should swallow it all at once."

Henry snatched it from him, read what was written, and then crumpled the parchment and tossed it in the brazier where it caught light and burned up in a cloud of pungent blue smoke. "I don't care a fig," he growled. "Let Louis beget a dozen sons; none of them will ever be a match for mine! Get out, all of you!"

"Henry…" Hamelin began.

"And you too, you sanctimonious prig!"

Hamelin stepped back as if Henry had punched him in the face. Any other man he would have grabbed by the throat, but this was the king upon whose favor he was dependent for his every privilege; he had no choice but to swallow the insults. Turning on his heel, he swept out.

He could hear Henry crashing around the tent like an angry bull. Rosamund arrived and Hamelin caught her back. "You should not go in there."

"He did not order me to leave, sire," Rosamund said. "I am not afraid of him." She shook free of his grasp, entered the tent and tied the flap behind her. Hamelin waited for a furious bellow, but there was nothing beyond a single, cut-off expletive. And in that moment, he truly realized the power that this little girl had over Henry, and that was frightening indeed.

# 28

ALIENOR PAUSED ON HER WAY TO THE BATH TUB TO GAZE AT the baby gurgling in her cradle. The infant gazed back from sea-blue eyes and smiled. Everyone said little Joanna was going to be a beauty, and Alienor was so proud of her new daughter. The birth, two months ago, had been exhausting but Alienor had weathered it and her vitality was finally returning.

The Christmas feast was being celebrated in Angers this year, and Alienor was waiting for Henry to arrive. He had sent a brief letter in answer to the news of Joanna's birth, courteous and political in tone and accompanied by the gift of an amethyst intaglio ring. Alienor had been concerned but had blamed his response on his failure in Wales and the continued quarrel with his archbishop. He would delight in Joanna when he saw her at Christmas, she was certain.

Marchisa had prepared a saffron dye to brighten Alienor's hair and restore its golden sheen, and various pots and unguents were arrayed on a chest for rubbing into the face, feet, and hands.

Alienor removed her chemise and stepped into the tub. No longer proud and firm, her breasts carried the weight of years in their softness. Her belly had sagged from decades of childbirth and was mapped with numerous silvery striations where her flesh had stretched to accommodate growing babies. Her hand mirror showed her lines of age where once was firm, clear youth. She was forty-two years old, and Henry would be thirty-three in the spring. At times in their lives nine years had seemed no gap at all, but now she sensed the chasm. He was the king. He could have as many nubile young women in his bed as he desired. The only things she could give him that they could not were heirs and Aquitaine. Legitimate heirs to wed into other families and cement alliances. Girls to live the kind of life she lived herself. If she thought about it, she might cry.

Once she had bathed and her maids had anointed her with lotions and perfumes, once her nails were buffed to a soft shine and her hair tinted a warm and glossy gold, all strands of gray concealed, Marchisa helped her dress in a gown of golden damask with lacing at the sides that held in her waist and supported her breasts. Alienor decked herself with gold and jewels until she glittered like a treasure chest, but then her mind filled with the image of the empress, overblown with embellishment, and with a grimace she took everything off again. No amount of adornment would compensate for youth and beauty; rather, she would resemble a gaudy matriarch. Impatient, she discarded the dress for one of plain dark red with gold embroidery banding the upper sleeves and donned a ring of bloodred ruby on the middle finger of her left hand. Finished by a wimple of soft cream silk with fringed edges, one end trailing over her shoulder, it felt more truthful.

Richard arrived with his lute, its neck festooned with a bunch of scarlet ribbons. He had started lessons the previous year and was already proficient. He had a tuneful singing voice, clear and pure, a passion for fine music, and a talent for composing it. He tilted his head to one side. "Mama, you are beautiful," he said with a smile and a courtly flourish.

Alienor laughed. "You will go far, young man! That is what a woman always wants to hear."

"I have composed a song for you. Do you want to hear it?"

"Of course I do!" Alienor gestured her women to gather and listen. Richard sat on a chair before them and checked that the lute was in tune. He handled the instrument with confidence and his hair was a gleaming tumble of copper on gold as he leaned over the strings and sought the tune. The song, in praise of the Virgin Mary, was a simple one in a minor key, but its pared-down clarity was an exquisite performance for a child just eight years old. Alienor's eyes welled with tears of love and pride. "That was very well done, my heart," she said. "You are a true heir of Aquitaine." She gave him a ring from her little finger as she would any troubadour, and Richard flushed with pleasure. "You must play for your father at the Christmas feast."

Richard's smiled dimmed. "When is he coming, Mama?"

"He won't be long," she said. "A few more days."

Richard ran off to play a fighting game, needing to exert himself after the discipline of concentrating on the music. Alienor turned her own attention to preparing for winter banquets and sent instructions to the huntsmen to mark some good game for the men to pursue during the festivities.

Joanna started to wail in her cradle, and her wet nurse lifted her out and put her to her breast. Richard returned in search of his practice sword, which was made of whalebone and was his pride and joy. Following on his heels was a messenger from England with a letter bearing Henry's seal.

The note was short and to the point. Henry hoped she and the children were in good health. He bade her remain in Angers to keep the Christmas feast and entertain his vassals. He regretted he was unable to come because the difficult Welsh campaign had caused too much upheaval and he was still dealing with unfinished business. He had to settle the matter of knightly service owing to the Crown and would be spending Christmas at Oxford. He would join her at Easter, bringing Harry with him, but for now he bade her farewell.

Alienor gazed at the words with contempt, scorn, and feelings more ambivalent. She was angry and concerned that he was not coming, that she and their new baby daughter did not matter enough for him to make the effort. However, it would be more peaceful without him and she would not have to live in an atmosphere of tension bordering on hostility. "Your father will not be here for the Christmas feast," she said to Richard. "He has too much business in England."

Richard had found his sword underneath a tunic on the chest, and now he swished it about as if cutting at an enemy. "He has business here too, Mama."

"Indeed, but not as much as in England. Do not concern yourself. We shall celebrate the feast well enough without him, and Easter is not so far away."

Richard's look was as bright as a knife. "But it dishonors you, Mama."

His observation was as sharp as a cut. "The business of state comes first—and he will be here at Easter, I promise you."

"What if something else stops him?" He swiped repeatedly at the air, making a low thrumming sound.

She realized that for all Richard's loyalty to her, he had a jealous and covetous eye to his father. It would not have escaped her golden son's perception that Harry was spending Christmas with their father, basking in his attention and playing the prince to the hilt.

"It won't," she said firmly. "And Easter is far better for making journeys. It is not long away. I know you are disappointed, but it cannot be helped."

"I am not disappointed." Richard's face was a mask, the flesh taut on his bones and his cheeks starred with red. "I hate him. I hate the way he treats us. I don't care if he comes at Easter or not. Why should I want to see him when he doesn't want to see me!"

"Curb your tongue," Alienor snapped. "When you come to rule Aquitaine, you will understand that some things take priority. Your father would come if he were able."

"Would he?"

Alienor met his hard blue stare. "You have my leave to go."

He whirled and ran from the room. She bit her lip, knowing he would vent his anger in aggressive military play. He was big and strong for his age, and his playmates would suffer as a result.

Going to the hearth, she held out her hands to the fire. The ruby ring winked on her finger like a wound. Henry could have come if he had really wanted. Matters might be urgent in England, but they were also excuses. And where Henry was, the court was too; thus, she was pushed to the margins. By the time she saw him again, they would have been apart for a year, and he would not have seen their children either, except for Harry.

Alienor lifted her head and compressed her lips with determination. It did not matter that Henry was not joining her to hold the Christmas feast. She would hold a great celebration of her own, here in his heartlands, and she would make sure that while people might notice Henry's absence, they would not miss him.

❖❖❖

"I had not expected you home from court so soon," Isabel said to Hamelin. He had sent word ahead and she had hastily prepared for his arrival with the hour's warning his outriders had given.

Hamelin went to look at his baby daughter, who was asleep in her crib, all rosy pink and contented. The sight made him smile and softened the tension in his shoulders. "Henry gave me leave for a fortnight," he said, "although I shall have to return before long."

She marked the tone of his voice and prudently said nothing more until he had washed and changed and they were sitting together by the fire over a meal of bread, cheese, and a flagon of good red wine. "What is wrong?"

He took her hand and squeezed it. "Ah, nothing," he said. "Henry is making a fool of himself."

"Why?" She looked at him in concern. "What has he done now? Is it to do with the archbishop?"

"No, it's not that kind of matter." Hamelin grimaced. "He became involved with a new mistress when we went to Wales in the summer—Walter de Clifford's daughter Rosamund."

"He always had women when I was at court. He only kept a faithful bed when he was busy getting the queen with child."

"You do not understand. This is not one of his casual amours," Hamelin said with distaste. "He has bought her a little dog and gowns and jewels—and a ring, if you please, that she wears on her wedding finger. He has her sit beside him at table and feeds her from his own dish." His face flushed as he warmed to his theme. "He even seeks her advice above that of his courtiers and spends hours in his chamber with her. Even when the chamber is open to others, she will be there, sitting in his bed, wrapped in one of his cloaks. He is besotted to the point of folly."

Isabel gazed at him in shock and her thoughts flew to Alienor. "Oh, that is not right; indeed, it is disrespectful."

"The girl herself... I do not know what to think." Hamelin tossed his crust to a hound dozing by the fire. "She is convent raised and gentle but knows her worth. She was a virgin when he took her and no brazen harlot, and that makes a difference too."

Isabel was appalled. "How old is she?"

"Grown but not yet a full woman. Fifteen, at most. He has always liked girls of that age. I am gladder than you know to be away from the court just now."

"Does Alienor know?"

Hamelin shrugged. "I do not know, but she will find out. That kind of news always travels. Henry was supposed to be spending Christmas at Angers, but he has chosen to stay in Oxford to deal with English business, and Harry is with him."

"What must he think, seeing his father sporting with this young woman? It is no example to set."

Hamelin's mouth was down-turned. "My brother is as he is and nothing will change him. Standing in his path is like being an ant in a thunderstorm."

Isabel poured him more wine. "I suppose this passion will burn itself out. He was always keener on the chase than the capture from what I saw at court."

"It may, but for the moment he is smitten. She does not fear him; she is gentle and sweet, but she has a core of steel—and she is lovely to look upon."

"I could almost think you are smitten yourself," Isabel said, not entirely in jest.

Hamelin gripped her hand more tightly. "There is only one woman for me, and I am married to her," he said. "And for all that it was a match for political gain and we were directed to wed, I thank God every day for his great blessing." He lifted her hand and kissed her knuckles. "I want to forget court. Tonight there is just you, me, our daughter, and the children within us still to be born. Let that be all that matters."

# 29

THE APRIL SUN SHONE FROM A SKY OF RAIN-RINSED BLUE AND warmed the castle battlements with primrose-pale light. Wearing the red dress and an ermine cloak, Alienor stood on the battlements with the children and watched Henry's entourage approach the gates. Once her heart would have swelled with anticipation and grown so light that she could have flown it from the battlements on a silken ribbon, but now it stayed in her chest, beating in solid, turgid strokes, and she was full of dull tension because she knew how their reunion would go.

Among the banners and the glittering array of knights and sergeants, she fixed her gaze on her eldest son. Even from a distance she could see how tall and straight he sat on his horse. He had turned eleven during Lent. She could not believe he was standing on the last stepping stone of his childhood, and that added a tender pain to her heart, blended with an uplifting of pride.

❖❖❖

Henry held his chubby baby daughter in his arms and tickled her under her chin. "A fine little girl," he said, smiling.

"She entered the world with a cry fit to raise the rafters," Alienor replied. "It was not an easy birth. Perhaps we both realized our lot in the world."

"I am sorry I could not be here any earlier." He busied

himself handing the baby back to her nurse rather than meeting Alienor's gaze.

She withheld the comment that he could have been had he wished. "I am sorry too. Your children have missed you, and there are matters for your attention. Your men refuse to obey my orders, and there is disruption in Brittany and Northern Poitou. They probably thought they could rebel because you were looking the other way."

"I am here now and I shall deal with everything," Henry said, his voice level but irritation in the set of his shoulders. He rubbed his leg and grimaced.

"Just a few more years and Richard will be old enough to be my sword hand in Aquitaine, and then I shall not need to ask."

Henry's expression tightened, but he let the remark pass. "I may have been occupied in England, but I have been considering policies in the wider field," he said shortly. "Brittany can be solved by bringing Conan to heel and making a marriage alliance."

"A marriage alliance?" She eyed him warily.

"Duke Conan has a daughter, Constance. If we match her with Geoffrey, he can govern Brittany when he comes of age. That will provide him with lands and bring Brittany into our sphere."

The proposal made sense, and Alienor gave a guarded nod. She would have to know more about it first but on the surface had no cause to cavil.

Henry grunted with bleak amusement. "It seems we have an accord for once."

She inclined her head. "Perhaps," she said, refusing to be too impressed.

Henry greeted the other children, presenting them with gifts he had brought from England. Geoffrey gave him a serious look when told he was going to be count of Brittany. "Thank you, sire," he said, holding the beautiful ivory writing tablet Henry had presented to him, carved with lions, their eyes set with chips of ruby.

"Always the quiet one," Henry said. "What is happening inside that head of yours? I shall expect great things of your rule,

Geoffrey the Thinker." He ruffled his son's hair and was rewarded with a considering smile.

Richard was not to be cozened by the hunting horn and baldric that Henry gave him and was sullen and sulky, barely muttering his thanks, so that Henry eventually lost patience and dismissed him from his sight.

❖❖❖

"I dislike the boy's attitude," Henry said to Alienor when they were alone together. "You have been indulging him."

"He was angry when you did not come to Angers for Christmas," she replied. "He had been expecting you."

"Then he will have to grow up and understand his role in the world," Henry retorted. "He is a king's son, not a spoiled child."

"Indeed, but that king has not been here to set an example." And even when he had been present in Richard's life, that example was not always to the good. Yes, she had indulged Richard, but she had not spoiled him. Henry was only reaping what he had sown.

"You know my reasons for that, madam. It could not be helped." He rubbed his leg again and winced.

"What's wrong?"

"Nothing. My horse kicked me, the contrary nag."

Henry's horses were always kicking him. He was not gentle with them, and they tended to lash out.

"Let me see." She half expected him to push her away and tell her not to fuss, but he unfastened one leg of his hose and rolled it down to expose a livid hoof-shaped bruise on his thigh. Alienor gasped. She could see where the nail studs from the shoe had macerated the flesh. "You should have a physician tend to this!"

Henry waved her away. "He can look at it in the morning. I've taken worse. Rub some salve into it and stop fussing!"

Alienor shook her head but did as he bade. There was no point in arguing. "You are a fool," she said as she hunted out a pot of marigold salve and began gently rubbing it into the affected area. "You should get rid of a horse like that."

"Perhaps I shall," he said. "But the beast has its uses." He took her hand and drew it higher up his leg. "I will have him know who the rider is before I am done."

They went to bed for the first time since Joanna had been conceived. Alienor blew out the candles, because the dark was a kindly cloak concealing the ravages wrought by time, and without sight the other senses were heightened. Henry's own body was no longer that of a lithe and limber youth but of a solid, mature male, broad, stocky, and powerful. They had to be careful because of his injured leg. Alienor had to play the greater part, which was much to her taste. "What were you saying about being the rider?" She laughed breathlessly, as at last she climbed off him and lay down at his side.

"Ah," he said, "but it was of my will as much as yours. I gave you permission to play that part; you would not have done it without."

"And I played to win."

He gave a huff of amusement. "I'll grant you the victory this time."

She felt him gathering to leave, and put her hand on his arm. "Will you stay? Please?"

He hesitated, then gestured assent and lay back on the bed. "As you will."

She suspected he was too sore to argue. She did not want him to stay because of desire or to comfort her slumber but because in the morning their children and the courtiers would find them in the same bed, and it would bolster her position and power as queen. But as she settled against him, she received the impression that even though he was present in body, his mind had gone far from her, closed off and unreachable.

❖❖❖

The next morning there was a commotion at the forge. Richard had taken an unfinished sword blade from the armorer's supplies, had heated it in the fire until the tip was a glowing red, and had gone charging about with it, swiping it in the air and declaiming that he was the knight of the firebrand. He had attacked Harry in earnest, singeing his brother's fine new cloak, and the armorer had thrown a piss bucket over him to put a stop to his wild outburst.

Henry was furious; it was no way for a prince or indeed any man to behave. Richard said nothing and stoically accepted the thrashing Henry administered.

"That boy is a reckless fool," Henry roared at Alienor. "How is he going to rule Aquitaine if he cannot rule himself?"

"What boy is not wild at times?" Alienor rushed to defend her cub. "It is passing strange that his behavior is always angry and unpredictable when you are here."

"Meaning?" Henry snapped.

"Meaning I indulge him less than you have neglected him. He will do very well for Aquitaine when the time comes."

Henry narrowed his eyes. "That remains to be seen, madam."

However, that afternoon, Henry took it upon himself to spend time in weapons training with his sons, showing Richard, Harry, and Geoffrey various tricks and moves. Alienor watched him with the boys. For Henry it was all about control and supremacy. He kept correcting their stances and grips, as if they had not been receiving lessons in weapon play since they were small. Each blow that Henry struck in demonstration was forceful and dominant. He was never going to relinquish power to any of them. He might give them titles and plan their futures on the map of his empire, but they would all remain his subordinates, and since Henry had been such a young man when he begot his heirs, their flowering would only clash with his prime.

# 30

## WINCHESTER, AUGUST 1166

ALIENOR HAD BEEN TRYING TO SEW BUT HAD TO PAUSE AND press her hand to her womb as the child within her sent out a frantic flurry of kicks and punches. Her reunion with Henry at Easter had resulted in another pregnancy. Since the child was due at Christmas, she had to stay in England until after the birth. That it was the role of a queen to provide heirs, and that she had actively encouraged Henry to her bed at Angers, did not prevent her from feeling like a trapped animal. It was unfair that a man could sow his seed and then go about his business unencumbered.

She had quickened a few weeks ago, but this new babe was never still and she was exhausted. The others had all been busy infants in the womb, but this one kept up a constant pummeling. A couple of times she had thought she might miscarry—her womb had cramped, and there had been a few spots of blood, but the danger had passed and the pregnancy had continued.

Henry was still in Brittany dealing with matters, and she had to stay near the port of Southampton, ready to send Geoffrey across the sea to his father the moment he was summoned. He was to be betrothed to Conan of Brittany's daughter Constance and made heir to the province. They were all so many chess pieces on Henry's board, although Geoffrey was delighted by the arrangement because it would increase his standing and assure him lands of his own when he was older.

An attendant approached and murmured that the Countess de Warenne had arrived.

Alienor immediately brightened. "Admit her, and bring wafers and sweet wine," she commanded.

Isabel was shown into the chamber and knelt to Alienor, who hastened to kiss her and raise her to her feet. "It is so wonderful to see you!" She noticed with a quick sweep of her friend's figure that Isabel too was with child. A nurse had followed her into the room, a chubby baby in her arms.

"And this is little Isabel?"

"Yes, this is Belle." Isabel took the baby from the nurse and kissed her cheek. "Hamelin dotes on her."

"She looks like you. And another on the way, I see. When are you due?"

"The end of November. And you?"

"Christmas," Alienor said flatly. "I shall be in Oxford, and Henry in Poitiers."

The wine and wafers arrived as well as a platter of almond paste balls wrapped around a date stuffing. Alienor had the refreshments carried to the window embrasure overlooking the gardens, and the women sat down to gossip in the breeze from the open shutters.

"Oh, I have missed these!" Isabel popped an almond ball in her mouth and closed her eyes to savor the taste. "My cook has the recipe, but they are still not as good as yours."

"But in all other ways you are content. It shines out of you."

Isabel smiled. "Indeed I am. I have to pinch myself sometimes to know I am not dreaming."

"I am pleased for you." Alienor was wistful, even slightly envious. "Such a bond is rare and precious."

Isabel looked down and fussed with her sleeve. Alienor immediately recognized the signs. "So, if all is right in your world," she said, "what is troubling you?"

Isabel folded the cuff over and then turned it back. "I am unsure about broaching this with you—perhaps you already know. But if not, you should."

Alienor's stomach sank. "Know about what?"

Isabel raised her head, and her brown eyes were full of chagrin. "Hamelin...Hamelin says the king has a new mistress."

Alienor shrugged, relieved but weary and a little puzzled that Isabel should think this news of any import. "What of it? I know he is unfaithful; he has the urges of a tomcat."

"It is more than that," Isabel replied. "I would not have spoken if this was one of his usual paramours, but she has been with him for over a year and he dotes on her. Hamelin says he is making plans to build her a manor at Woodstock." Isabel returned to pleating her sleeve. "I am sorry to be the one to tell you."

Alienor shivered. She thought of the other mistress who had been more than a passing fancy and had given him a son. Aelburgh. The name was still branded on her mind. "Who is she?"

"Rosamund, daughter of Walter de Clifford. He took up with her during the Welsh campaign last year. Her family members are marcher lords, and she is no more than sixteen years old."

Alienor put her hand to her mouth and gave a dry heave.

Isabel set her arm around her. "I am sorry, I am sorry! I knew this would hurt you, but you had to know, because everyone else does and it's not right."

Alienor swallowed and gripped Isabel's arm until she regained control. "It does not surprise me," she said bitterly. "A house at Woodstock, you say?" She gave a cynical laugh. "I suppose it is fitting. He keeps his menagerie there, just as his grandsire used to do."

"Hamelin says it is outside the complex—at Everswell." Isabel brought her a cup of sweetened wine.

Alienor held the goblet between her hands and took a slow sip. "He once told me he was going to build a pleasure garden there... little did I think. Thank you for having the courage to tell me—I take it as a mark of our trust and friendship." She straightened her spine. "I am the queen and the mother of his heirs, and I will have his respect for that. Let him be the laughingstock." She gave Isabel a fierce look. "I will not see pity in anyone's eyes."

"No," Isabel said hastily. "I am indignant on your behalf, never pitying."

Alienor did not believe her; Isabel had too soft a heart. "Henry treads his own path these days, and I tread mine," she said wearily. "Once this child is born and the arrangements for Matilda's marriage finalized, I shall return to Aquitaine and raise Richard to govern it." She gave Isabel a wry half smile. "I have become adept at biding my time. Henry has never known how to do that—he has never had the patience. Indeed," she added with a curl of her lip, "he has never had to have the patience."

Their talk turned to the continuing difficulties with Thomas Becket, who had retaliated for the exile of his relatives by excommunicating the men Henry had sent to expel them and laying more people under interdict, including the justiciar.

"Do you believe there will ever be a reconciliation?" Isabel asked.

Alienor shook her head. "Fences will be difficult to mend, that is certain. And of course my first husband is joyfully stirring up trouble. It is a complete tangle, and I am sick of it." She sighed and placed her hand on her belly as the baby began kicking and pummeling again.

❖❖❖

Alienor sat at dinner with Harry, who was visiting her en route to join his father for Christmas in Poitiers. He was full of the adventure of the journey. At almost twelve years old, he considered himself very much the man, and a king in waiting. Watching his dexterity as he carved slices from the haunch of venison and placed them on her trencher, succulent with juices, Alienor was immensely proud. "You are going to be taller than your father." Strong, long-limbed sons of her womb who towered over Henry were satisfying images with which to feed her mind.

Harry preened. "I will be a better king than he is."

"You still have much to learn," she cautioned. "Have a care how you talk to him. Watch, and listen and learn. It does not mean you should behave in the same ways but observe how he treats people and how they respond to him. Watch how he deals with situations and think about what you would do in the same circumstances. Everything you learn will serve you in good stead later."

She felt his withdrawal and could almost see him rolling his eyes because he thought he was being lectured. "Of course I will, Mama. I know what his temper is like. And he always has to be right, even when he is wrong."

Her lips twitched. "Just so, my son," she said. "You must learn how to deal with that and how to arrange your own rule. Your father plans to have you anointed his heir, and there is more to kingship than wearing a crown. You will have to take on the responsibilities and duties and become a man."

Harry's eyes brightened. "Papa has the gold ready for my crown. He showed it to me two years ago." A petulant look entered his expression. "I would have been crowned then, if not for Thomas Becket."

"That is true, but at least by the time you are anointed, you will be older and more able to perform your duties." That was another bone of contention between Henry and Becket. It was traditional for the archbishop of Canterbury to crown the king of England, but Becket was refusing to do so. Henry had a dispensation from the pope, obtained five years ago, granting him permission to have his son crowned by any bishop he chose, but Becket had persuaded the current pope to declare that no bishop was to obey the dictate. Alienor suspected Henry would still find a way around it, and there was enough rivalry and aggravation among the bishops where Becket was concerned that some would ignore papal wrath and do the deed anyway. But for now the sacred gold remained in its coffer.

❖❖❖

On the following day, Harry continued his journey, heading for Southampton to take ship across the Narrow Sea. Richard was simmering with anger.

"Why is he going to Poitiers and not us?" he demanded. "I am the heir to Poitou, not him. Papa should have sent for me."

"I cannot travel that far with your new brother or sister in my womb," Alienor said with thin patience. "Your father is standing surety for me, and Harry is his heir and future head of the family. You are not yet nine years old."

"I hope he's seasick," Richard muttered.

"He is your brother and you will hope no such thing. You will go to Poitiers soon enough. I will make sure of it." She touched his hair, glinting like fine wire of blended copper and gold. "Curb yourself, my young lion. Your time will come."

# 31

## Beaumont Palace, Oxford, December 1166

*A*LIENOR STUDIED THE SILVER CUPS PRESENTED FOR HER approval. Most were intended for her eldest daughter as bridal goods to take with her to Germany, but she had ordered one especially as a gift for Isabel's new baby, a little boy, born a month ago and christened William. The cup sparkled in the sparse winter light from the high windows. Alienor was also sending a carved ivory rattle, and for Isabel a gold net and silk veil to dress her hair.

"This is beautiful workmanship," she said. "I am well pleased. See that the silversmith is paid promptly for his effort."

"Madam."

Alienor grimaced at a deep twinge from her lower spine. Her advanced state of pregnancy made walking difficult; whatever posture she adopted, she could not be comfortable. Throughout the Christmas celebration she had been exhausted and nauseous. There seemed to be no room within her save for this mass of baby and its constant activity that deprived her of sleep.

The weather was cold and sharp and the days so short that the candles remained constantly lit. What light there was filtered through the high windows, bleak and pale. Alienor could not remember when last she had been warm; perhaps it was a matter of the soul too. She wanted to be in Poitiers and the longing was almost pain. It did not help her situation that only four miles away, Henry's child-mistress was keeping Christmas as a lay visitor at the nunnery at Godstow. She had sent spies to find out what they could about the girl, her whereabouts and more of her circumstances. From all reports, the girl was lovely, sweet-natured, educated, intelligent—and she and Henry were besotted by each other. She was his love, and that made Alienor feel colder still. It was long since she had felt like that about anyone, and never about Henry, even when they had shared the passion and the glory. It had been like a fire made of dry tinder and parchment, swift to blaze up but with no red core to sustain the heart.

The presence of the young woman at Godstow gnawed at Alienor like toothache. She wanted to be rid of it, but it would not go away while the tooth remained. And while she kept this bleak winter feast in exile and waited to bear the child conceived on the eve of Christ's rising, Henry was in Poitiers, sitting in her hall, drinking the rich wine of her duchy and listening to the music of the south with their eldest son at his side.

The twinge came again, stronger this time. She glanced toward the sound of her daughter's voice. Matilda was reading aloud in German to Geoffrey and Alie. She stumbled over many of the words, but she had been practicing hard and had improved immeasurably in only a month. By the time she went to her marriage, she would be proficient enough to hold a simple conversation. Geoffrey, with his way with words, would probably be proficient in German by then too. Matilda's future husband had written to her saying how pleased he was that she was going to be his bride, and exhorting her to work at her lessons so that they would be able to talk as man and wife. He had sent her a Christmas gift of a silk bag containing ivory playing pieces, wonderfully carved with all different animals, and an inlaid checkerboard, which Matilda loved. He had also sent her a belt of pearls and gold wire, which she wasn't allowed to wear because it was to be added to her trousseau, but she kept opening the enameled box to admire it.

The pain came again, a regular pinching squeeze, and her belly tightened, harder this time, taut as a new drum. She called to Marchisa and bade her send for the midwives.

❖❖❖

Sitting on the birthing stool, her hair hanging down in loose straggles of gold and gray, her shift bunched beneath her breasts, Alienor did not know how many hours she had been in labor. The pains were excruciating, and she felt as if she was being torn apart by the infant within her struggling to escape. She feared for her life. The shadows of winter dusk were gathering, and still the baby had not come. She was bilious and tired, on the edge of exhaustion, and the midwives were exchanging glances with one another. A part of her wanted to give up, to close her eyes and let everything end here. The call was insistent, but more insistent still was her sense of duty to her other children. They still needed her guidance and protection. They still needed her to fight for them. If she died now, then Henry would have triumphed, and, by planting this seed inside her, he would be responsible for her death. Perhaps that was what he was hoping: that she would die in travail. And then he could marry an adoring, compliant wife. Perhaps the little nun at Godstow.

Another contraction surged through her. "Push, madam, you must push!" The senior midwife gripped her hands.

Alienor squeezed her eyes tightly shut and bore down. "I will not…let him be the death of…me! He shall…not win!" The last of her strength brought the baby's head to crown between her thighs, and she slumped, panting.

"Once more," encouraged the midwife, "once more and carefully, madam, lest you tear. Call upon the blessed Saint Margaret for help and she will assuredly aid you. The babe's head was in the wrong position, but it has moved now. Come, only a little more effort."

Alienor had been calling on the blessed Saint Margaret all day with little result. She was done with saints. "Damn you, Henry," she gasped as the head was born and then the rest. "Damn you forever."

"A boy," said the midwife as she caught the baby in a warm towel and an infant's thready wail filled the room. "A fine boy. Madam, you have another son."

Alienor was past caring beyond the fact that the child was out of her body. She closed her eyes and gripped the sides of the stool, enduring. The afterbirth followed swiftly and then, just as she thought it was done, she began to hemorrhage, a red stream of blood splattering the straw beneath the birthing stool.

"Blessed Saint Margaret!" The midwife thrust the baby into the hands of one of the other women and grabbed Alienor, issuing urgent commands to her senior assistant.

Alienor went away to another place while they desperately tried to stem the flow from her womb. Perhaps Henry was going to win after all. She imagined him in Poitiers with Harry, receiving the news that she had died in childbirth. Would he grieve even in the smallest part? And if he did, who would know, because he always hid his grief from the world.

"Madam, drink this." The midwife raised Alienor's head and urged her to swallow a bitter-tasting tisane. She drank and choked, then drank again. The world returned for a moment, swamping her in raw pain.

The woman stood back, one hand bloody to halfway up her wrist where it had been inside Alienor, compressing her womb. "Praise God and Saint Margaret, the bleeding has eased." Her voice shook. "But we must watch you lest it begin again. It is always a danger when a woman has borne many children."

"Too many," Alienor croaked. The shadows had deepened and although the maids had kindled the lamps and built up the fire, the room was heavy with darkness.

The youngest midwife brought her the baby, damp from his first bath and yet to be swaddled. He was small like Alie had been, and wiry too. His natal hair was dark with none of the coppery glint that she had seen straightaway in Richard, but his wail was strong and querulous, and his grasp on life surer than her own. Conceived at Easter at the rising of Christ, born in his nativity season. Surely this was a blessed child. But she could raise neither joy nor enthusiasm.

"I am pleased with him," she said for form's sake. He waved his little fists and legs with the rapid movements she had sensed in her womb, but now he had the space to flex his limbs.

"How is he to be named, madam?"

She could not think. Her mind was filled with fleece. They would need to know for his baptism, but it was almost too much effort. One more duty to perform. "John," she said. "Name him for the saint on whose day he will be baptized." Speaking the words exhausted her. Her eyelids seemed to have weights on them.

The women would not let her sleep for longer than an hour at a time. The midwife checked and changed the cloth between her thighs and made her drink more of the bitter tisane. The baby continued to wail and fuss. The wet nurse arrived, a buxom young woman named Agatha with a snub nose, thick flaxen braids, and milk-heavy breasts. She put the baby to suckle, and he latched on with a will.

"Knows what he likes," Alienor heard one of the younger midwives giggle. "He'll be one for the ladies!"

The other women shushed her with glances at Alienor. She pretended she had not heard and gazed toward the closed shutters, which were painted with dancers in a garden and a musician playing a citole. She drifted off to sleep and dreamed that she was with them in that garden. She could smell the roses and the sweet tarry scent of warm pine needles. There was a building like a cloister with arches open to the air. She was holding a pair of ripe cherries on slender green stalks, and she tasted intense sweetness as she bit down and pierced the glossy black skin. A warm breeze fluttered the sleeves of her green silk gown.

Her sister Petronella darted out from behind a cloister column and, with a joyful cry, ran to embrace her. She was young and carefree, her brown eyes sparkling and her hair flying loose. Then Alienor saw their father strolling toward her, his expression smiling and relaxed, and at his side a dark-haired small boy wearing a red tunic. Her brother Aigret. She became aware of other people in the garden, all turning to welcome her. A man with dark hair and hazel eyes, a baby in his arms, a man she had last seen on his deathbed when she had still been wed to Louis. She dropped her gaze at a tug on her gown, and met the blue eyes of another little boy with a mop of red-gold curls and a toy sword in his hand. "Mama," he said. Her knees weakened and joy poured through her like exquisite lightning as everything turned to white radiance.

Her next awareness was of voices talking over her in swift urgency. Calling her name, shaking her and exhorting her to wake up. She didn't want to. She wanted to go back to the garden, but it wasn't there. It was a vision glimpsed in a flash of light, and now there was only the grainy nighttime darkness of the birthing chamber, and the cramping pains from her abused, exhausted body.

"Let me be," she said in a rusty voice. "Let me return to the garden." Her throat was dry and they raised her to make her drink more of the tisane.

"There is no garden, madam," the midwife said gently as she lifted the covers to check that Alienor had not begun to bleed again. "You are here in your chamber at Beaumont Palace, safe and warm. The garden is all asleep under deep snow."

"There is a garden," Alienor insisted. Beyond the bitterness of the tisane, she could still taste the residual sweetness of cherries on her tongue. "I saw it."

"You were dreaming, madam."

Alienor turned her head away and closed her eyes, but the vision refused to come again, and she felt bereft.

She heard the women talking quietly among themselves, but not quietly enough. "This must be her last one," said the senior midwife. "She cannot sustain another child. It would kill her for certain, poor lady—if this one does not."

Alienor's eyelids tensed. Is that what it had come to—"poor lady"? Then indeed, she might as well die. She found the strength to raise her voice. "Do not pity me. I will not have it." The women immediately fell silent, and the atmosphere strained with tension.

"I am sorry, madam," said the midwife. "I should not have spoken thus in your hearing."

"Nor out of it. I am the queen, remember that, and I am the duchess of Aquitaine and Normandy and countess of Anjou."

"Yes, madam."

For whatever that was worth. Alienor closed her eyes as her son began to wail.

❖❖❖

Alienor was churched on the feast of Candlemas in early February, a few days short of the forty-day recovery period. The day celebrated the churching of the Virgin Mary and was auspicious. Alienor had not yet recovered from her ordeal; she was still bleeding, albeit scantily, and she tired very quickly. She had to pace herself as if she were an old woman and coddle what energy she did possess.

Isabel had come to attend her churching. Having made a full and swift recovering from her own travail in November, she was journeying from Lewes to Castle Acre and had taken a long detour to visit Alienor.

"I worry for you, for your health," Isabel said as they sat together after the obligatory banquet. Alienor was lying on her bed, her feet propped on an embroidered cushion.

Isabel's baby son slept in his crib, and she was gently jogging John in her arms. He was a fussy baby, but for Isabel he was being as good as gold.

"I am better than I was," Alienor said, "but I have been so slow to recover. The midwives say I should not bear any more children—that I will die if I do."

Isabel made a soft sound of concern.

Alienor gave her a tired smile. "Oh, I shall take their advice. We have four living sons and three daughters: let that be enough. I swore when I was in travail that I would not let my husband kill me this way or any other." She gave a cynical lift of her brow as she saw Isabel's shock. "Bearing a child is every bit as much a battlefield as the ones by which men set so much store—so is marriage."

Isabel stroked John's cheek with her forefinger. "But it is glorious too," she said softly. "And sometimes there are miracles."

Alienor suppressed the urge to call her a fool. Whether deluded or not, Isabel was plainly happy with her lot and besotted by her children and that husband of hers. She had wished the best for them and they had the best. If her own situation was a cup of poison, then she should drink from it herself and not expect Isabel to sip. "Yes," she said to humor Isabel. "Indeed, sometimes there are."

❖ ❖ ❖

A week later, the weather turned mild with pale blue skies and weak sunshine, harbingers of spring. Strong enough at last to sit a horse, Alienor decided to ride the four miles to Woodstock with Isabel and the three older children, leaving the others with their nurses. Richard was eager to be out in the fresh air, galloping his pony, waving his toy lance around, riding with the knights of Alienor's escort as if he were one of them.

Alienor watched him with amused pride. She could clearly see the warrior knight in him, and the imperious future count of Poitou and duke of Aquitaine. These were currently dominated by the eager, spontaneous child, but time would change that. Geoffrey rode after him, trying to keep up, but each time he came anywhere near Richard, his brother struck out at him and pulled away.

"It is a good thing they will all have their different spheres of influence," she said wryly to Isabel. "They are like young eaglets, all wanting to dominate the nest. Geoffrey will have Brittany, Richard Aquitaine, and Harry England and Normandy. And I know they will all look at what the other has and feel resentful."

"What of John?" Isabel asked. "What will there be for him?"

Alienor waved her hand. "The Church perhaps, or Ireland, or an heiress with lands and influence. For the moment it does not matter, save that he is another son to make the inheritance secure. That is how Henry will view him." Their last child. As everyone said, she could not sustain another pregnancy, nor did she desire to endure that ordeal ever again. A part of her was raw because it meant bidding farewell to an element of her femininity and her power to be the vessel that gave birth to the heirs. No mistress, no matter how exalted, could do that. She was losing precedence and prestige. That which had set her apart was now diminished.

"What did Hamelin say when you bore a son?" she asked Isabel.

Isabel laughed and turned pink. "The moment he heard, he ran into my confinement chamber and wanted to hold him! The midwives were horrified!"

Alienor was astonished. "I would never have thought that of him from the way he behaves at court!"

Isabel's blush deepened, making her radiant. "There are courtier's robes and there are the robes for every day," she said. "And then there are the moments without robes at all." She paused to guide her horse around a deep rut in the road. "He is a true and honest man, and I love him dearly."

"As he clearly loves you."

"I think so."

"I am glad for you," Alienor said. "Truly I am."

Approaching Woodstock, they crossed the path of another party riding out in the fresh February air. Curly-coated retrieving dogs and narrow-flanked gazehounds loped beside the horses, and a brace of hare hung from one huntsman's saddle. A young woman rode in the middle of the party. Her head was covered by a wimple, but long braids of soft golden brown showed beneath its edge. Her cloak was of costly blue wool, and small silver bells tinkled in the braids on her horse's mane.

"Make your obeisance to Queen Alienor!" shouted Saldebreuil de Sanzay, brandishing his mace of office.

The hunting party pulled off the road, dismounted, and bent the knee, although it took a moment to control the milling hounds. Alienor drew rein instead of riding on past. She knew most of the minor nobility in the area. They had come to pay their respects at her court at Christmas and then again at her churching. This young woman, barely out of girlhood, had not been present, yet she must dwell locally.

"Tell me your name, child," she said.

"Rosamund de Clifford, madam. Daughter of Sir Walter de Clifford," the girl replied, a red flush burning her brow and cheeks.

Alienor stared, bitterness welling up inside her. So this was what Henry wanted? She did not blame him, but taking it and setting it on high like a cherished precious jewel was a different matter. "And where are you going, Rosamund de Clifford, daughter of Sir Walter?" she asked. "And where have you been?"

The girl's gaze was wary, a touch resentful. "I have come from the abbey at Godstow and I am returning there, madam," she said. "I...we..." She gathered herself. "I rode out to enjoy the sunshine, and exercise the dogs."

Alienor raised her brows. "Godstow," she said. "I take it by the state of your garb and present company you are not a nun or a novice."

"No, madam, I have a corody there and so does my mother." The girl had weathered the initial shock and spoke in a steady, quiet voice.

Doubtless paid for by Henry. "Then you had better return there," Alienor said, "and fall on your knees and ask God's forgiveness, for you are sore in need of it." She shook the reins and rode on, her posture upright, and did not look back.

Isabel joined her. "Dear God, Alienor..."

Alienor's heart was taut with pain. "You told me she was young, but I had not realized. Small wonder there is gossip at court." She wanted to call the girl a slut and a whore, but she was nothing like the regular court prostitutes, and that made her dangerous. This was no practiced concubine; this was a gently bred girl, fresh and sweet. Someone Henry could dominate and who would not argue with him. Bile rose in her throat and she struggled not to retch.

"I am sorry. I do not know what to say," Isabel said, her expression filled with sympathy and disgust.

"What is there to say?" Alienor continued to stare straight ahead. "Henry has always liked younger women. They are easier to control and he can dictate the terms. When he married me, he hated that I was more astute than he was—that I knew more of the world and had a greater experience of life. He could put it to one side when we were both younger, but it is different now. I should not be surprised."

"What will you do?"

Alienor set her jaw. "Nothing. It is beneath my dignity as a queen to pay heed. I refuse to be undermined by this little girl just because she can lead my foolish husband by his ever-rampant member." She looked at the children, but they were all riding along without concern, so at least the scandal had not reached their ears yet; however, many of her entourage looked uncomfortable. In the adult world it was already common knowledge. She would armor herself in untouchable poise and self-possession. The more Henry lost his dignity, the more she would clothe herself in hers until nothing could touch her.

Alienor frowned as she pondered the direction from which Rosamund had come; there was only Woodstock nearby. She considered turning back, but something urged her on; she would know the worst.

At Woodstock's gates, the porter told her that the hunting party had passed that way but not stopped or entered.

Alienor frowned. "Do you know where they were going?"

The kneeling porter stared at the ground as if he thought the mud was fascinating. "No, madam."

Isabel said, "Hamelin told me Henry was building a house and garden beyond the palace—to make use of the water courses."

Alienor compressed her lips. She urged her palfrey through the gates into the Woodstock complex, but rather than riding to the palace gleaming through the trees, she took the path into the park, bidding all but Isabel wait behind. When Richard protested she ordered him with brusque irritation to stay with his attendants and ignored his scowl. She had no time for male fits of pique.

The path wove through the woods, the horses squelching in patches of pliable mud and disintegrated leaf mulch. As yet no buds showed on bush or branch and the tree bark was still winter black. The trail was lightly churned up; horses had been through here, but the tracks and the droppings were several days old, which told Alienor that today's group must have taken the long way around the perimeter of the complex.

They came to a wicker fence and a gate tied with a thin piece of rope. Isabel leaned down from her mount and unfastened the latter, giving access to an area of cleared woodland and signs of building activity, abandoned over winter but left ready for spring. Foundations for a hall were clearly marked out, and the felled area revealed just how ambitious the project was. Here were clear tracks and fresh dung, showing that horses had been here today, even if not at Woodstock.

Alienor gazed around with a set jaw. It was a muddy, bleak building site now, but in a couple of years it would be beautiful, a finely wrought setting for a favorite gem. "Bastard," she said, feeling contempt, hurt, and bitter anger as she imagined Henry riding up through the trees from Woodstock to indulge in cozy liaisons with his mistress.

Isabel reached for her hand and squeezed it.

Alienor shook herself. "Well, now I know," she said. "I have seen all that I need. Come." She turned her palfrey and rode away from the place without looking around, but her awareness of its presence traveled back with her as a dark burden.

On their return to Beaumont Palace, she ordered every candle to be lit and she called for joyous music, for lightheartedness and dancing. She donned a gown of April-green silk trimmed with gold, and she dressed her hair with a net of gems. Her smile was brilliant. She was witty, vivacious, and scintillating. She danced and flirted and lit the room beyond the light of all the blazing candles, putting on a facade for others, and herself, until that facade became the reality.

Isabel watched with compassionate anxiety that she dared not show as Alienor burned herself out. When at last she stumbled in the middle of a dance, Isabel caught her and summoned her ladies. Together, the women helped Alienor to her chamber, undressed her, and put her to bed. Marchisa brought her a tisane, and Isabel sat with Alienor, combing out her hair and gently rebraiding it to make it comfortable for sleep.

Alienor roused herself to drink the tisane, but only a flicker of vitality remained after the energy expended. "I had to do it," she said, her voice as thin as mist. "To remind myself of who I was and who I am…whatever happens."

"Indeed, but you did not need to do it all at once." Isabel stroked her hair. "You are not yet fully recovered from childbirth; you must ration your strength."

Alienor gave her a shadowed smile. "Yes," she said, "but tonight I had to know I was still alive."

"Even if you kill yourself in the act?"

"There are worse ways to die, but do not worry. I survived bearing John, and I shall not give up now. My children need me, Aquitaine needs me, and most of all I shall not give Henry the satisfaction." Her lids drooped and the tisane cup trembled in her hand. Isabel took it from her and set it on the chest. She removed her own gown and headdress and, clad in her shift, climbed into bed with Alienor and took her in her arms.

Alienor clung to her, rigors shaking her body, but there were no tears. Isabel shushed and soothed her, and Alienor eventually slept, and it was Isabel who silently wept for her friend.

## 32

### DOVER, SEPTEMBER 1167

$O$ N A PERFECT SEPTEMBER MORNING, THE DEEP WOAD-BLUE OF the sky was reflected in a sea bumped and hollowed by a gentle swell. Occasional clouds, fluffy as clean white fleece, were herded across the sky at the pace of peacefully grazing sheep by a westerly breeze.

A beautiful day, a farewell day. In the harbor beyond the castle walls, a small fleet of ships rocked at their moorings while the crew and laborers finished stowing the chests, barrels, and sacks that eleven-year-old Matilda was taking to her new life in Germany as the betrothed and eventual wife of Henry the Lion, Duke of Saxony.

For more than two years Alienor had known this day was coming, but having the time to prepare made no difference when it came to the parting. She was clenched inside, holding everything in. She did not know how she was going to bear this moment; she could not imagine her life without Matilda by her side. Her daughter was a companion and a helpmate, someone to talk to and share her days. Someone who understood. To lose all that was like having the umbilical cord severed all over again.

Henry had made no effort to see his daughter before their parting, although he had written a letter bidding her be a good and dutiful wife and obey her tutors. She was to remember she was the daughter of a king and uphold that truth in all she said and did.

He was proud of her and he would pray for her well-being daily. He had sent her a casket of jewels for her personal use. Alienor could not fault him for the gift, yet she doubted he had chosen them himself, and she could not let go of her bitterness and disillusionment toward him. Whatever Henry did now would be like scratches on once-clear glass.

Matilda had been chucking her baby brother John under his chin and kissing him farewell in his nurse's arms, but at Alienor's summons she joined her, and they walked down to the ships with Geoffrey and Richard, Alie and little Joanna. They all boarded the galley on which Matilda was to sail. Richard immediately set off exploring the vessel, tugging the halyards, running his fingers along the wash strake, ducking inside the canvas deck shelter to inspect it. The strengthening breeze carried a fishy tang of sea and shoreline. Gulls wheeled and screamed above their heads, and the vessels rocked on the rising tide.

Alienor tenderly adjusted Matilda's cloak and strove to control her sorrow. "If you need anything, write to me and I will send it," she said. "Do not think that distance will divide us."

"Yes, Mama." Matilda's gray eyes were steady and clear.

"Remember me in your prayers, as I will remember you in mine." Earlier Alienor had given her a small folding triptych for her personal devotions so that when Matilda opened and closed it each day she would be reminded of her family.

"Yes, Mama."

Alienor strove for composure while her daughter remained serene and sensible. She was fearless and Alienor was so proud of her.

The ship rocked under Alienor's feet and she heard the shouts of the crew as they prepared to cast off. "Until I see you again," she said, imbuing her voice with all the warmth and certainty she could muster as she embraced Matilda for a final time. In all likelihood she would never see Matilda again; even if she did, she would not be the child to whom she was bidding farewell, but a young woman who would have grown and learned from experiences in which Alienor had had no participation. She sent up a silent plea to God. *Keep my child safe on this journey. Give her your blessing and let her flourish.*

The courtiers escorting Matilda to Germany boarded the vessel. The tall, red-haired Richard de Clare, lord of Striguil, had been chosen to lead them. He wore a sword at his hip with casual grace and had a feline air, poised, elegant, and dangerous. "Look after my daughter," Alienor said, her voice tight and fierce. "As you value your life, look after her."

"Madam, my life would be worthless if I let anything happen to the Princess Matilda," he said with a bow. "She is my sacred charge. You can rely on me." There was a courtly smile on his lips, but the sharp candor in his eyes and the flexing of his broad shoulders conveyed that he took his duty seriously.

Alienor liked Richard de Clare a great deal. She enjoyed his flirting and banter when he was at court, which had been often of late as preparations advanced for Matilda's departure. Henry considered the de Clares overpowerful and had removed Pembroke Castle from their custody and demoted the family from the rank of earl. Richard de Clare had always sworn his loyalty to the Crown, but Henry deemed it prudent to send him on a diplomatic mission and have him out of the way for a while. He was good with a sword but eloquent of speech, and ideal for the task. The aging William D'Albini, Earl of Arundel, was attending too. As the father of several daughters, and the widower of a former queen of England, he was perfectly suited to the assignment. With strong young sons to rule his estates, he could afford to leave them and embark on this diplomatic mission. He had been showing Richard and Geoffrey how to tie a particular knot in a length of rope but now brought the boys over to Alienor.

"We shall be casting off very soon, madam; the tide is nigh." His gaze was compassionate and he exuded an air of solid dependability.

Alienor nodded. "God speed you on your way. You are all in my prayers."

She disembarked to stand on the wharfside. The vessel still

took a while to cast off, and she clenched her fists inside her cloak. Matilda stood at the ship's side, a brave figure in her scarlet cloak, protected by the powerful bulk of William D'Albini while de Clare strode about the ship, making sure everything was in order.

At last the galley eased from her moorings, together with her companion vessels, laden with the baggage and trousseau of a princess going to her betrothal and marriage. A gap of sea opened between ship and shore. Matilda raised her hand and waved, and Alienor waved in return, her eyes burning with the intensity of her focus as she took a last look at her daughter's pale face. *I love you, I love you, I love you.*

❖❖❖

Once back at the castle, Alienor buried herself in preparing to move to Winchester, but as she chivied the maids and spoke to her officials, her mind was constantly on Matilda as she waited for the turn of the tides to receive news that she had made safe landfall in Normandy.

She eyed a gown that Emma had laid out on the bed. A wine stain had gone unnoticed on the apple-green silk and looked almost like the mark of a deep wound.

"It is ruined, madam," Emma said. "What shall I do with it?"

The gown had been a favorite, but the last occasion Alienor had worn it was on discovering the building at Everswell. Since then it had lain in the bottom of the chest. The stain might be remedied by dabbing with a solution of vine ashes steeped in water, but even if it were cleaned, she would never don it again. Nor would she cut it down and make dresses for her two remaining daughters; every time she saw it, she saw Rosamund de Clifford. "Give it to the Church," she said. "They will find a use for it." The Cistercian monk Bernard of Clairvaux had always said no one should clad themselves in the work of worms, but vast numbers of the clergy did not subscribe to that view and she had no doubt the silk panels could be reworked.

Emma laid another robe on the bed, gold silk this time, with a weave so fine that it was almost possible to believe it had been created by angels. Alienor had brought it with her from Constantinople, a gift from the Empress Irene. She thought of the marble columns and pavements of the Blachernae Palace in the Greek capital, the gilding and the resinous perfume of incense. Every piece of cloth, every garment had its history, and this silk had traveled on sere desert roads from the lands of the Zin peoples.

And now here was her coronation gown, catching radiance from the September light gleaming through the window. A promise that had turned out to be a lie. Little Alie was awed by the sight of the shimmering silk lozenges and stroked it with a pale, tentative hand. "May I wear this when I'm grown up?" she asked.

Alienor gave a wry smile. "You will have such robes of your own one day, when you are a queen in your own right."

"When I go away to my marriage?"

The words cut Alienor to the quick. She didn't want to think of that now. Losing Matilda was already a struggle. "When you are a bigger girl," she said. "Not yet...you are mine for a little longer at least."

Alienor's chaplain entered, followed by a messenger, his garments stained by salt and sweat, his expression tight and grim. Alienor's first horrified thought was that Matilda's ship had foundered and sunk.

The messenger knelt and handed her a sealed packet from which dangled the seal of the archbishop of Rouen. "Madam, I regret to tell you that the Empress Matilda died two evenings ago in Rouen. She was at peace with God and all has been settled as she wished."

Alienor's knees almost gave way because she had been preparing to hear the worst. This was momentous and sad indeed; it made her heart lurch, but there was also a euphoric surge of relief.

Alienor took the letter and, fumbling, broke the seal. The archbishop sent her the sad news and offered his condolences. He had written to Henry too, but he was dealing with rebellion in Brittany and unlikely to attend the funeral. He would not deal with it well. Death was just another form of betrayal to him, and grieving about it a weakness. Yet despite everything, her heart went out to him.

"There was another message on the same ship," her chaplain said and handed her a second package. "The lady Matilda has landed safely in Barfleur and is continuing with her journey."

Relief and gratitude flooded through her at the confirmation, and she put the packet aside to read later because she could not deal with both at once, and the situation with the empress was more pressing.

"Go and refresh yourself," she told the messenger. "Be ready to carry a letter to Normandy within the hour." She turned to her women and clapped her hands. "Pack the small baggage chest," she said. "I am going to Rouen."

❖❖❖

The abbey of Bec blazed with torches and candelabra, creating crowns and flowers of light to illuminate the passing of an empress from her mortal life. Alienor inhaled the scent of incense and dust and felt the heat from the candles reflect on her skin. The empress's sealed lead coffin stood before the altar, the fringed silk shroud surrounded by wax tapers in a radiant palisade.

The Latin inscription on her tomb read: "Great by birth, greater by marriage, greatest in her offspring. Here lies the daughter, mother, and wife of Henry." The empress had worded that epitaph before her death, and indeed, all her hope and pride had been invested in her golden son who was too occupied in dealing with war and politics in Brittany to attend her burial. There was no mention of his father, Geoffrey le Bel of Anjou; rather, she had chosen to recall her first husband, Heinrich, Emperor of Germany, to whom she had been wed for eleven years from girlhood to young maturity.

As Alienor knelt and prayed, stood and bowed, she deeply mourned the empress's passing. Something great and noble had gone from the world. All that hard-won wisdom now silent in the tomb. Her different ways of solving problems had given Alienor fresh perspectives. Matilda had always defended Henry fiercely, but she had not been unsympathetic to Alienor and had often taken her part and offered support.

The empress had been a restraint on Henry too. He might not always have taken her advice, but he had been willing to receive it, and she had been a bridge between church and state, respected by both. Now he would no longer have that resource to call upon, and it would only diminish him.

The empress had bequeathed vast amounts of treasure to the Church. Gold chalices, portable altars, a magnificent cross set with gems, various crowns that she had commissioned throughout her life. She had liked her crowns, had thought them vital to her standing. Alienor's lips curved in a sad smile. And Henry had put his on the altar at Worcester and left it there.

Alienor's chamber for her stay in Rouen had belonged to the empress: the place from which she had governed Normandy, and where she had died. That did not bother Alienor, for Matilda's soul had departed in peace, and it was a space that had seen courage and loyal service. She drew strength from it and was not afraid.

Entering the room in the evening shadows, she saw a movement in her peripheral vision, and for a moment her heart clenched. A youth turned in haste from the table beside the hearth, and she found herself gazing at Henry as he must have looked in the space between boy and man. He had Henry's wide brow and strong jaw; his hair gleamed with coppery tints in the light cast by a cresset lamp. He held a box of carved ivory that contained the empress's chess pieces and seemed unable to decide whether to hide it behind his back, or brazen it out.

"Jeoffrey," she said in a level voice. "What are you doing here?" Removing her cloak, she draped it over a chest. Emma, who was attending her, went to light more candles.

"Nothing, madam," he said stiffly.

"Indeed?" Alienor raised her brows.

He gave her a wary look, not exactly hostile, but it could easily turn that way and was all Henry's. He would have to be found a new household, and that meant either taking him into her own, sending him to Henry in war-ravaged Brittany, or leaving him in the care of his tutors at Bec.

"Sit," she said and gestured to the bench by the hearth.

He swallowed. The large knot in his throat revealed his change toward manhood, and with the increased light, she could see a sparkling line of gilt hair on his upper lip.

"Sit," she repeated. "I will not bite."

Still clutching the box, he lowered himself onto a bench.

"It seems a strange thing to risk sneaking in here to steal." Alienor poured a cup of wine and gave half a measure to him.

A flush mottled his face. "I wasn't stealing it."

"Then what were you doing?" She gestured and reluctantly he handed the box to her. It was surprisingly heavy and for a moment her hand bowed under the weight.

"My grandmother... I... She used to play chess with me in this chamber." He sent her a defiant look. "She said one day the pieces would be mine in her memory. But I do not think she had it written in any will."

"So you came to take them without asking?"

"I...I wanted to stand in her chamber again before it was all changed and remember how it was. And then I saw the chess set on the table."

"And if I had not walked in at that moment, what then would you have done?"

"I do not know, madam. I suppose I would have taken it—no one would have noticed."

"You think not? Where would you have hidden such a thing about your person? You were bound to be discovered."

He made no reply. She considered him thoughtfully. Henry's bastard son. What sort of a man was he going to make? She was ambivalent toward him. When her children were younger she had regarded him as a threat, but with four sons to her name, the danger had diminished and she could view him objectively. His upbringing with the empress had given her that distance. It would still be for the best if he entered the priesthood—a bishop or two in the family was always useful—but it would be expedient to bring him into her sphere all the same.

"You were fond of your grandmother?" she said.

"Yes, madam." A forlorn note entered his voice. "She was kind to me, and she taught me a great deal."

Alienor wondered at the bond between the empress and her grandson. She had seldom been present in Henry's childhood, her focus concentrated on fighting for her crown. Perhaps she had compensated for that lost time by lavishing her attention on this boy who looked like Henry and was her own flesh and blood.

"So," she said. "What is to be done with you? Did your grand-mother ever speak of your future?"

He looked down. His eyelashes were like Henry's—short and stubby, and dusted with gold. "She said it was for my father to say, but in the meantime I was to receive an education fit for all purposes."

"Well, for now you shall come with me to England and dwell in my household," she said, deciding as she spoke. "And I will bring you to your father at Argentan for the Christmas feast—should he complete his business in time to be there." She could not keep the cynicism out of her voice.

"Yes, madam." He drew a steadying breath.

She gestured to the chess box. "Perhaps you will play with me now to honor your grandmother. I think she would approve."

Jeoffrey swallowed again, bowed to her, and, fetching the board, set it on the bench between them, his movements so commonplace that it was obvious he had done this many times before. He removed the pieces and arranged them with reverent precision. He resembled Henry and had some of his mannerisms, but his movements were less restless and he had an air of reserve that was certainly not his father's.

She won the game but had to concentrate, and on a couple of moves he almost caught her out. He had been well taught and had a quick mind, but he was indecisive, and when faced with a choice under pressure, he hesitated and made the wrong one.

And then he became cross and frustrated, and that indeed was like Henry.

"You must trust yourself," she said as he returned the pieces to their box. "Do not let your opponent see you are ruffled, and take your time. There were moments when you could have pressed your advantage."

"Yes, madam."

She could see that he was irritated and did not enjoy being criticized, but he was obviously absorbing the lesson too and storing it away for later digestion. "You may go," she said. "The chess pieces and the board are yours. Tomorrow I will have a writ made saying so and you may collect them then and do with them as you choose."

He thanked her with genuine gratitude and departed to wherever he kept his bed.

Alienor leaned back in her chair to finish her wine. It had been an interesting encounter. The youth had layers she knew she was not yet seeing. She had a desire to understand him but not to come any closer than that in terms of an emotional bond. She intended to keep a very close eye on him and monitor his progress, because she recognized ambition when she saw it.

# 33

ARGENTAN, CHRISTMAS 1167

ENRY BREEZED INTO THE DOMESTIC CHAMBER OF THE GREAT donjon at Argentan and then stopped midstride and stared at the infant boy who was wobbling across to him on unsteady legs.

"John?" He crouched, opening his arms. The child gave him a comical, quizzical look and crowed with delight as he reached him. Henry steadied the infant before he turned his wriggling little body this way and that to examine him from head to toe. "Aren't you the fine little man?" He ran a stubby forefinger through John's hair, which had lightened to sandy-blond since his birth.

Henry's expression was so full of genuine delight that Alienor almost softened toward him. She had arrived in Argentan with trepidation and a heart heavy with anger and disillusionment. Even setting eyes on Henry was like being punched. She had written to him following his mother's funeral and had received a curt, formal reply that told her nothing of his mood, save that he had made himself too busy to attend a beginning in the birth of his son and an end at his mother's requiem.

"It is a pity you could not have found the time to visit sooner," she said. "You have missed seeing your last child—or your last legitimate one—as a baby in the cradle."

John tottered away from his father, making his way determinedly to Alienor. Henry's face tightened. "What is that supposed to mean?"

"That I almost died bearing him, and it took me months to recover. Physicians and midwives tell me that if I quicken again, neither I nor the child will survive. I cry enough. I have done many things for you, Henry, but I will not die for you." She caught John and lifted him in her arms, sitting him on her hip in the age-old pose of motherhood.

Henry stood up and planted his hands on his hips. "I had expected a warmer greeting to begin a family gathering after so long apart, but I see I was being optimistic."

"It sets out where we stand," she replied. "Your mother, God rest her soul, produced three sons and no more. I have given you six, four of whom still live, and three daughters. It is beyond me to bear you more."

She saw anger flicker in his eyes and she did not care. He turned away from her and went to stand in the embrasure, facing the narrow window that looked out on the gray waters of the River Orne. "So be it," he said. "You know why I could not come to England. You know why I could not attend our daughter's leave-taking and my mother's funeral."

"Yes, I know," she said wearily. *Because you are indifferent to your wife and because you are too damaged to face parting from your daughter and your mother. And besides, we are only women.*

"Duty and the business of state always come first, as my mother was well aware, God rest her soul."

"I realize it more than you will ever know," Alienor said with quiet scorn. "I have spent the last fourteen years either with child or recovering from bearing one. You have often said that women's minds turn to fleece when they are breeding, but since that will no longer be the case, it is time I took an active part in other arenas."

"Such as?"

"Aquitaine," she said. "I was the duchess of Aquitaine before I was the queen of England. I should return before people forget who I am. Richard is no longer a small child and he must be introduced as my heir. I have been in exile for too long."

He turned to look at her. "In exile?"

"Sometimes that is how I feel," she said. "I need to reconnect with my heartland."

A look both calculating and pleased crossed his face. "For once, my love, we are in agreement," he said. "I was going to suggest that you go to Poitiers in the spring and take Richard and the others with you. It is indeed time that people saw their lady again." He stroked his close-cropped beard. "Since your barons are so volatile, you will need protection and a man of experience to help govern that element with a sword if necessary. I have Patrick, Earl of Salisbury, in mind for the task."

Alienor eyed him with shrewd awareness. Patrick of Salisbury was an experienced soldier and courtier. She had had dealings with him when she had visited Salisbury and Winchester. He was pleasant company, but he was Henry's man to the core and would always do his bidding. It would be like having a guard dog set over her to ensure she behaved herself. She had no doubt he would report her every move to Henry. Perhaps fortuitously, his wife, Ela, was Isabel's mother, which might play to her advantage. "I shall do my best to work with him," she said.

"Well then, all to the good." Henry's expression was both relieved and wary, as if he could not believe she was yielding so easily. He crossed the chamber and chucked two-year-old Joanna under the chin. She eyed him solemnly and clung to her nurse's skirts, plainly unsure as to the identity of this strange man who had invaded the domestic chamber. Henry moved on to Alie, who, at six, had more awareness and swept him a proper curtsy, calling him "my lord father," which amused him greatly.

"What a fine and gracious lady you are going to grow up to be," he said. "Just like your mother." He shot Alienor a sardonic look.

"Pray God she marries a husband worthy of her love and respect," Alienor replied, meeting his gaze steadily. "Richard and Geoffrey are busy with their riding master. Your other son is with them."

"Yes, I saw them as I rode in."

"What will you do with him?"

Henry wrapped his hands around his belt. "He may serve in my household as a squire while I take his measure."

Alienor nodded and did not push him. If she suggested the Church, Henry would only argue in the opposite direction, and she had learned since the early days. Jeoffrey's half brothers had accepted him with an air of cheerful superiority, and he had fitted himself into the mold of subordinate, although she suspected deep undercurrents were at work beneath the smiling exterior. After all, he was Henry's son and his mother had been a concubine. And that brought her to another point she needed to raise with Henry.

"Just after I was churched, Isabel and I rode over to Woodstock," she said.

That elicited a brow raised in mild curiosity. "What of it?"

"I saw the work being undertaken at Everswell—a 'Sicilian garden' is it called?" She curled her lip. "And I met your concubine on the road—the 'fair Rosamund,' so sweet that if you cut her she would bleed honey."

He said nothing, but his expression turned to granite.

"I know you take women to slake your lust and that you have had particular favorites in the past. I have borne with it because whatever the Church says, men are the ones more susceptible to weaknesses of the flesh. Women have far more reason to abstain. But when you flaunt her before the court, when you behave like a besotted fool and build her a fine house and gardens, when you pluck her from a convent…then it becomes a scandal. It weakens you, and it shows a lack of respect to me and your heirs. If you must have your whores, do not make yourself a laughingstock. Did you think I would not hear about it, or did you just not care because you consider me of no consequence?"

His complexion had been darkening steadily, but she had no fear. The time for diplomacy was past, and she was riding the crest of her anger and hurt.

"You ride roughshod over others, Henry, but do you ever turn and look over your shoulder to see all your bleeding victims rising behind you with revenge in their hearts?"

His voice congested with rage. "By Christ, madam, you go too far! Do not threaten me."

"I merely hold up a mirror and tell you to look in it and see yourself. You are the one who has gone too far, but who will hold a king to account? Who has the right to tell him no? An archbishop?"

John squealed, clamoring to be put down again, and staggered to his father. "Papa," he said, pulling himself up on Henry's legs. Henry ignored him, his eyes boring into Alienor. "Certainly not you," he said with a curl of his lip.

"Indeed, I thought not." She nodded at a notion confirmed. "Your son is clever to have learned that word for 'father' *in absentia*, although I am not sure he knows what it means. Perhaps none of your children do."

From being livid with fury, Henry's complexion was now bone-white. "I am warning you, madam, do not bait me," he said. "I have the power to crush you, as I would crush a wasp. It might sting me as it dies, but it will still be dead." He stepped over John and stormed from the room.

Alienor sat down on the bench and clutched her stomach, her emotion so strong it was painful. She had wounded him but in doing so had caused more damage to herself. She hated him but she hated him because she still cared. She needed to find a state of blessed indifference, and perhaps that would happen once she was back in Poitiers, once she was home.

# 34

ALIENOR CLOSED HER EYES IN BLISS AND ABSORBED THE WARM benediction of the sun on her face as she rode. Another month and that sun at midday would be as hot as pepper, but just now it was perfect. A warm breeze ruffled the trees, shaking loose the last late petals of cherry blossom and softly bumping the green nodules growing on trees that had set their fruit earlier in the season. The sky was the wonderful shade of blue she remembered from her childhood, and the scents of greenery and spring made her feel youthful and alive for the first time in many years.

Alienor and Henry had traveled to Poitiers shortly after Christmas. Henry had spent time putting down rebellious vassals in the north of the region and then returned to Brittany to deal with yet more upheaval. Their parting had been formal and gracious, their manner to each other tepid as they exchanged the kiss of peace. Sixteen years ago, straight from their marriage bed, he had left her in Poitiers and ridden off to deal with pressing issues elsewhere. Back then she had felt hollow and bereft at his leaving, so consumed by love and lust for the red-haired energetic youth that all she had wanted to do was bury her face in the shirt he had discarded at the bedside and dream of him. Now, she had barely been able to contain her relief at his going.

Opening her eyes, she glanced at the strong young hearth knight keeping pace beside her on the sun-drenched path, one hand on the reins, the other resting on his thigh. She had first encountered Patrick of Salisbury's nephew William when Thomas Becket had been preparing his menagerie for France, and a smiling, playful boy had given Harry a ride on one of the big bay wagon horses. Now she was coming to know William the man as a knight in the Earl of Salisbury's entourage and to appreciate his talents. He was courtly without being obsequious, intelligent, reliable, and astute. They shared a sense of humor. She loved his rich singing voice and that he appreciated music and song as much as she did. Beyond the skills of the court, he had already gained battle experience in skirmishes with the French in Normandy and had taken part in several tourneys where he was making a name for himself.

Although William's posture was relaxed, he was vigilant too, constantly looking around. There might be a truce after several uprisings of Alienor's unruly vassals, but the dust was still settling.

"Do you always wear your hauberk on everyday journeys?" Alienor asked. "Surely you must be stewing in all that mail?"

He turned in the saddle to study the members of her entourage, strung up on the path behind. A few of the sergeants wore padded tunics, but the knights' equipment was mostly borne on pack horses, with the destriers on leading reins. "I had some new links put in my hauberk yesterday, madam, and this seemed a good opportunity to test the fit and see if more adjustment was needed." He flexed his right arm.

She studied him with a sharper eye, noting a section on his shoulder where links of a different color had been patched in but were certainly not new. When she asked him about it, he made a face. "It happened soon after I was knighted, at the fight to hold Drincourt against the French. Some Flemish mercenaries cornered me and put the hook of a thatch pole through my mail to try to drag me off my horse. I managed to fight them off, but they tore open thirteen links from my hauberk and gashed my shoulder."

"You were fortunate to win free."

"Indeed, madam, although I did not think I was fortunate at the time," he said with a rueful shrug, "and I still have a scar."

Alienor marked that his battle experience was of close-up hard fighting, not just as part of a mob. Perhaps it might be worth stealing him from Patrick and giving him a place in her household. "What do you think of Aquitaine now you have been here a few months?" she asked. "How does it compare with England?"

"There is no comparison, madam, they are very different."

"That is a courtly reply," she said with a smile.

"But a true one. Aquitaine is steeped in sun, whereas in England it often rains. Aquitaine is a land of good wine and sweet red grapes. England is one of sheep and ale and blazing fires…"

"…as the wind whistles under the door," Alienor said.

He grinned. "I grant you that, but the grazing is good. The English have a reputation for being clods and drunkards, who then want to brawl except when they drink too much, and then all they can do is fall in the gutter. But they are tenacious. My mother's kin were landholders long before William the Bastard came to our shores. It is my homeland, but for the moment I would rather be in Aquitaine in April, and riding among present company."

"You will go far," Alienor said with a laugh. She tilted her head to one side. "Someone told me the other day that all English men have tails. Is that true?"

He glanced at her sidelong with a mischievous sparkle in his eyes. "No more than all men do, madam, and not that you would ever notice or be exposed to in polite company."

"I am pleased to hear it. You have set my mind at rest."

He bowed in the saddle and then gathered the reins. "We should pick up the pace, we are falling behind."

Alienor clicked her tongue to her mare. William excused him-self and rode ahead to join his uncle. She studied with appreciation his long, straight spine and the effortless way he controlled his horse. It entertained her to jest with him. He played the game with skill.

They stopped to water the horses at a wayside stream. Some of the party produced food from their saddle packs and started to eat. Alienor's seneschal Geoffrey de Rancon helped her dismount and presented her with a cup of wine, which she drank with gratitude, being parched from the dusty road.

Patrick of Salisbury joined them. The bony arch of his nose was sun-reddened, and sweat glistened in the creases of his throat. "We should keep the troop closer together, madam," he said. "Strung out on the road we are vulnerable."

"I will make sure to take closer order when we move off," she promised, adding, "Your nephew mentioned it too. He is a fine young man."

Patrick glanced at William, who was watering his horse in the stream and jesting with the younger knights in the troop: something to do with a mouse in someone's bed roll. "He plays the fool at times as they all do at his age, and he eats enough to feed an entire troop never mind one man, but yes, he shows promise. I…" Patrick turned at a sudden yell from a squire who had gone into the bushes to empty his bowels.

"Ambush!" the youth howled, charging back into their midst, his hose flapping around his thighs. "Ware arms!"

Amid a frantic scramble to mount horses and draw weapons, Patrick bundled Alienor back onto her mare. "Go with the queen!" he roared to Geoffrey de Rancon. "Take her to safety!" He whacked his hand down on the mare's rump and then turned, snarling orders at his men as soldiers rode out of the trees, armed for battle. Her heart in her mouth, Alienor spurred her mare. If she was caught, God alone knew the price they would exact. They might take her for ransom but were just as likely to kill her or cause her to have an "accident." Behind her the clash and clamor of violent battle tore the air, and she knew that the screams of the dying and wounded were mostly from her escort who were all unarmed—except for the young William Marshal in his repaired hauberk, and what chance did he stand?

"Holy Mary!" Her mare stumbled on a rut in the path and she was thrown forward and almost unseated. She loved to gallop—it was pure exhilaration to feel the speed of a strong horse beneath her—but she was terrified that they were hurtling too fast and would take a fatal fall, yet if they slowed they would be caught and slaughtered. When she tried to look back to see if they were being pursued, her wimple flapped in her eyes like a sail and blinded her. Henry's sister Emma galloped at her side. Fortunately, she was an accomplished rider.

De Rancon drew level. "Slow down!" he bellowed. "Madam, slow down. We will founder the horses, and we have many miles to cover before we are safe!"

Wild-eyed, Alienor drew in the reins and eased the blowing mare to a trot. The horse was trembling, and so was she. De Rancon's face was anxious and grim. The two other knights who had ridden with her were breathing hard and looking worried. One wore armor; the other was clad in his ordinary tunic but took the opportunity to pull a leather jerkin out of his saddle pack and struggle into it.

"We must double back to Poitiers. That is safest," de Rancon said, fingering the hilt of his sword. "But by a different road, not this one."

Behind them they heard the thunder of hooves and saw a cloud of dust rising from the road. Alienor gripped the reins and swallowed.

"They're ours," Geoffrey said. "Praise God, they're ours."

There were four of them, battered and bruised, one man pouring blood and missing the ends of his fingers down to the first knuckle on his right hand, but no one mortally wounded.

"The earl!" one of them gasped, spitting out blood and pieces of broken tooth. "They've murdered our lord—speared him through the spine like a fish in a pond before he could reach his warhorse and armor. It's a butchering ground!"

Alienor stifled an exclamation of shocked dismay. If Patrick had been slain, who was the commander of Angevin military strength in Aquitaine, then what did it bode for the rest of them? No attempt to capture, but to kill. Still, she was alive and free, even if in grave danger; the attack had partially failed, and her sons were safe behind defended walls.

"Who?" she said. "Do you know who?" She would have their heads. And their dismembered arms and legs. She would grind their bones to dust and cast them into the sea.

"Guy and Geoffrey de Lusignan," the knight with the mutilated hand said as his companion leaned across the saddle and bound the bloody stubs with the cloth in which he had been carrying his bread and cheese.

The de Lusignans were troublemakers, often descending from their fiefs in the north of Poitou to wreak havoc. Six brothers, all as bad as one another and with a wide network of affinities—magnets to whom the disaffected flocked. "There will be repercussions for this," she said, her voice harsh with the effort of controlling her fear and rage. "The de Lusignans will pay, I swear it."

❖❖❖

They rode into Poitiers with the hot afternoon sun on their backs, their lathered horses dripping sweat in the dust. Alienor held herself proudly, but she was devastated. No one had spoken for many miles. What was there to say when faced with the sudden severing of life midthread, no matter who you were? The utter treachery of spearing a man in the back? Alienor thought of the young knight William Marshal, of the conversation and jests they had been enjoying as they rode, and how she had intended to offer him permanent employment under her banner. An image of him lying dead and bloody in the dust beside his uncle flashed across her mind, making her nauseous.

News of their return had been carried throughout the palace, and it was plain to all that there had been a calamity. Ela, Countess of Salisbury, was one of the first to arrive as Alienor entered with her escort. Ela was too experienced a military wife to ask in front of everyone what had happened, but her spine was rigid with tension. The knight with the severed fingers was taken, staggering and dizzy with blood loss, to be treated by a physician. Alienor went immediately to her chamber, issuing orders for the captain of the garrison and the remaining senior knights to attend her there, and then she turned to Ela and told her what had happened.

"Dead?" Ela said blankly. "Patrick is dead?" Her expression registered disbelief. "That cannot be."

"I am sorry," said Alienor. "If I could pull back today like unpicking stitches and weave them anew, then I would."

Ela took a deep breath and pressed her hand to her heart. "And Patrick's nephew, William? Is he lost too?"

"That I do not know, my lady." Alienor braced herself against emotion. Tears could come later. For now, she had to cope. There were letters to write, aid to seek, men to rally. "I pray not."

Ela laced her hands together, white-knuckled, and nodded. The news had plainly hit her hard, but the blow had yet to connect at a deeper level. "I must go and pray," she said, "and I must send a message to my son in England. You will excuse me."

Alienor took Ela's hand and squeezed it. "Yes, of course. I will join you when I have dealt with what must be done."

Ela departed with her maids, walking as if she was in the act of turning to stone. Alienor washed her face and changed her travel-soiled gown. Her hands shook as she drank a cup of wine. Nowhere was safe, and Henry for all his energy and prowess could not deliver her that safety. He would come stay for long enough to rectify the worst of the problem and then leave without proper resolution, and it would all begin again.

She was adept at doing battle diplomatically, but the sword and the warhorse were also required to stamp authority on Aquitaine, and no woman could take such a road. Even the inimitable Empress Matilda had had to delegate authority to her half brother Robert, Earl of Gloucester, because men would follow his lead and balk at following hers. When Richard was old enough he could take on the role of warlord, but that time was not yet ripe. She had to endure; she had to deal with these things as best she could.

"Go and admit the men," she said to her chamberlain in a firm voice, revealing none of her doubts. "I will speak with them now." And they would know her anger and see her grief, but they would never see her fear.

❖❖❖

A detail of soldiers rode to the ambush site and returned with the bodies of the slain in a covered cart which they brought to the church of Saint-Hilaire.

Alienor steeled herself to look at the bodies as they were placed side by side on yards of gray burel cloth in a screened-off part of the nave. Lying on his back, the vicious spear wound that had ended Patrick of Salisbury's life could not be seen, but his shirt was saturated in the blood that had poured from his mouth. Someone had tried to close his eyes, and had wiped his face, but his lids were still half open, and his parted lips showed red-stained teeth.

Ela had insisted on coming to see her husband's body, saying it was her duty and she owed it to him, as his wife, but the sight was grim. She gazed at him, her face bleached of color. "When he rode out this morning I was angry with him," she said. "He'd let his gazehound pup into the chamber and it had chewed my embroidered shoes. He told me not to be a foolish woman complaining over trifles, and I called him an inconsiderate boor..." Her throat worked.

Alienor touched her arm.

"He always gave of his best," Ela said. "He was an honorable man. He made me proud. I am proud now. He died doing his duty. I wish I had told him..." She bit her lip. "A pair of chewed shoes is indeed nothing but a woman's folly." A shudder ran through her body. "Let him be buried in Poitiers," she said, composing herself. "The road home is too far in this fine weather, and he loved this church."

"It shall be done as you wish," Alienor said.

"Thank you." Ela wiped her forefinger under her eyes. "At least he will receive Christian burial and a tomb where his kin may mourn, which was never granted to my first husband, God rest his soul."

Alienor admired Ela's pragmatism. The countess's first husband, Isabel's father, had died in an ambush too, cut to death by the Turks and left to rot on the desolate heights of Mount Cadmos. "Indeed, I will make sure he has a fitting memorial."

Alienor cast her eyes over the other corpses with a deep welling of grief and rage that this should have happened. Reaching the end of the line, however, a fragile spark of hope kindled. "The earl's nephew is not among the slain," she said. "Where is William Marshal?"

A knight from the retrieval detail answered her. "His horse was there, dead, but there was no sign of him. I would say taken for ransom, madam."

The spark of hope became a small flame. William was one of the few wearing a hauberk, and that would have set him apart immediately as a man of rank. Patrick in his old riding tunic must have been viewed as a no one—just another servant to be cut down.

"If he has indeed been taken for ransom, then I will pay the price since he was taken in service protecting me," she said to Ela.

"That is kind of you, madam." Ela's voice was thin and preoccupied.

Two women arrived supporting each other, one elderly and toothless, the other in her middle years. Clinging together, they paced the line of corpses, their eyes intent. The younger one uttered a sudden spine-tingling wail and fell on her knees beside one of the bodies. She tried to lift him and clutch him to her, and when she could not because he was stiff in death, she spread herself across his bloodstained body and howled. Her companion gave a low moan as if she too had received a mortal wound. "My son," she said, her voice cracking. "My boy, what have they done to you?" She knelt painfully beside the younger one and began to keen.

Alienor made herself witness the raw and terrible grief of wife and mother. Where there should have been tranquillity and reverent praise to God, there were cries of grief and despair over the bodies of the slaughtered. She had lost children as babies, and she often thought of the lives they might have had, but to lose a son or a husband or a father in the full summer of his life was a bitter curse indeed.

Ela had not fallen on Patrick as the two peasant women had done upon their beloved man, but she gave quiet orders that she desired to wash his body and care for him herself before he was placed on his bier in front of the altar. Control had settled over her like a stone mantle. "I shall not wed again," she said, dry-eyed. "Ever."

# 35

## POITIERS, SUMMER 1168

*I*N THE WAKE OF THE ATTACK, THE DE LUSIGNAN BROTHERS took to their heels and lived a nomadic existence, traveling from one castle to the next, never spending more than one night in any place so that they could not be pinned down and brought to justice. Henry left in abeyance the truce he had been organizing with the French and his continuing difficulties in Brittany and rode south at speed.

Arriving in Poitiers, mired from the road, he went directly to the church of Saint-Hilaire and stood before Patrick of Salisbury's grave, his fists clenched and his mouth a straight, thin line.

"He was one of my most able commanders," he said to Alienor. "His loss is a sore blow, God rest his soul, and God rot his murderers in hell."

"Amen to that," Alienor murmured. She saw the exhaustion in his face, the lines of care that had not been there before, and was almost sorry for him.

"I cannot stay in person to deal with the matter," he said with impatience. "I do not have the time. Brittany is in turmoil, and I do not trust Louis to keep this truce. I can spare no more than a few days to sort out this mess."

It was all in danger of getting away from him, but she could tell he would rather face all the demons of hell than admit to it. He was still determined to exert complete control. "Then a few days will have to do."

He scowled and bit at a ragged thumbnail. "I thought sending you into the duchy would quell their rebellious tendencies. I did not expect to have to come here and deal with matters again so soon."

She raised her brows. "I hope you are not blaming me."

"No," he said tersely, "but your subjects are quarrelsome and difficult to rule."

His tone of voice suggested that he thought her no different to them. "It did not prevent you from marrying me," she said. "Indeed, you were eager for the match as I recall."

"Perhaps I was too young to know what I was getting into."

"Perhaps I should have thought better of it before it was too late."

They glared at each other. Then Henry turned without a word and left the church. Alienor sighed, lit a candle, and knelt to pray.

❖❖❖

"I am going to appoint William de Tancarville governor in Patrick's place," Henry announced. "He is experienced in border warfare and will hold the Lusignans to the point." He lifted his goblet and drank. Washed and changed, he was pacing his chamber at the top of the Maubergeonne Tower and making plans.

Alienor's lips tightened, but she inclined her head. De Tancarville was another who believed the world revolved around his demands; nevertheless, he was courtly and courteous, a patron of young knights with chivalric notions.

"I need to find someone to take his place in Normandy, but that's less of a problem than dealing with your barons."

Alienor absorbed the jibe without comment. Her barons had always been willful and disinclined to accept a strong rule, be it from man or woman, a fact Henry had known when he married her. "Patrick's nephew, William Marshal," she said. "He survived the ambush and the Lusignans are demanding a ransom of thirty marks for his return. I told the Countess of Salisbury I would pay the sum."

The corner of Henry's mouth rose in a mocking half smile. "Another of your projects?"

She smoothed her sleeve. "I believe him worth cultivating. Both his loyalty and fighting abilities are proven."

"You could do worse," he said, "although it remains to be seen if thirty marks is a bargain or not. His father was staunch but inclined to go his own way about it, and his older brother serves me well enough." Henry refreshed his cup and after a moment changed the subject. "This truce I am negotiating with the French," he said. "One of the terms we have agreed is a betrothal between Richard and Louis's daughter Alais."

Alienor's stomach lurched downward. She stared at him in horror. "Is one son not enough for you?" she demanded. "How could you? I will not agree to this, ever!"

Henry heaved an exaggerated sigh. "We discussed all this before when Harry was betrothed. The match will secure our borders and bring peace. We won't have to worry about French hostility anymore or whom Louis might select to marry the girl. The daughters you bore him are wed into the Blois family, and we need to counteract that. It will be good for the boys. Two brothers married to two sisters—it will keep our own family ties strong."

The notion of having Louis's daughter as a future duchess of Aquitaine sickened Alienor. Even in her Poitevan heartland he was dictating to her. Richard would never wed Alais. So steely was her resolve in that moment that it immediately settled her down. "As you wish," she said and had the satisfaction of seeing Henry look taken aback. Clearly he had been prepared for a fight. His eyes narrowed in suspicion and when she returned his look blandly, he pointed his finger at her. "I warn you not to cross me," he said. "I will be watching."

❖ ❖ ❖

Richard's deep blue gaze widened with shock and then filled with anger and disgust. "Betrothed to Alais of France? The younger sister of my brother's wife? She's a nothing. I won't do it. I don't want to be betrothed to anyone."

Alienor had summoned Richard to her chamber to give him the news. He stood in front of her, his chin jutting with mutiny. He was vibrant and beautiful, and her heart ached. "Your father deems it necessary for peace with France. I cannot go against his decision to make this betrothal, but you are too young to wed."

"So was my brother, but it still happened to him," Richard spat.

"It will not happen to you," Alienor said fiercely. "I promise that on the bones of our ancestors. You may have to suffer a betrothal, but it will not lead to a wedding, I swear on my soul."

Richard fell silent while he digested her words. Then he said, "When I am duke of Aquitaine, I shall do as I please and wed whom I choose." He sent her a forceful look. "No one shall stop me."

Alienor's heart brimmed with love, pride, and sadness at his ferocious intensity. Marriage was always a matter of choice—a political one. Begetting this man-child was one of the rare blessings of her match with Henry, and she would not allow Richard's father to tarnish that brightness. "Indeed," she said. "You will always be a player, never one of the pieces."

❖❖❖

The August sun beat down upon Poitiers, drawing the blue from the sky until it was a burning white. House timbers were almost too hot to touch, and the dazzle on harness fittings was blinding to those inadvertently caught out. Lizards basked, soaking up the heat. Dogs sprawled in the shade under carts, and people retreated to the depths of their dwellings to await the lessening of the sun's intensity.

Within the ducal palace, protected by the insulation of thick stone walls, Alienor was holding court, Richard at her side, a golden coronet binding his red-gold hair.

Negotiations were still continuing with the French, as was sporadic warfare, and Henry was in Normandy dealing with the situation. William de Tancarville had been working to control the Poitevan rebels and had seen off the threat posed by the Lusignan faction—for the time being at least. Alienor was not optimistic that their ambitious, warlike tendencies would remain quelled for long, but all was relatively quiet for the moment.

The next petitioner summoned to the dais by the ushers was

Patrick of Salisbury's recently ransomed nephew, William Marshal, who had returned to Poitiers two days ago, his captors having been paid the requisite thirty marks.

Alienor had sent the young man new clothes from her livery cupboards, and he was dressed in a fresh shirt of soft linen, a rust-red tunic, and close-fitting blue chausses. He walked up the hall, the slight check in his step a sign that he was still recovering from the leg injury he had received during the skirmish that had killed his uncle. He knelt without difficulty, however, and bowed his head. She noted with approval that he had taken care with his appearance beyond the clothes. His neatly trimmed brown hair, his clean-shaven jaw, and an astringent aroma of herbs suggested time spent in a bath and the services of a barber. Closer up, she noted the dark shadows under his eyes, and he was thinner than before his ordeal, but he still possessed that vital, resilient spark.

"Come, sit by me." With a sweep of her sleeve, she indicated a stool at her left-hand side, lower than her chair but still a place of privilege. "Now we have you returned to us, we must consider your future."

"Madam." He did as she bade him, managing to fold himself into the position with grace despite the length of his limbs.

"I know you have nothing to your name," she said gently.

She saw the flicker of trepidation swiftly concealed and knew its reason. A knight who had nothing could easily become nothing. And more than trepidation, she recognized his pain at having to admit he was beholden for his freedom. "Madam, that is true, saving my honor."

Alienor acknowledged his reply with a smile. "Well, your honor is worth the highest ransom in itself, and I intend to help you make your way in the world. You will need equipment if you are to serve and protect me as courageously as you served your valiant uncle."

William said nothing, but his jaw was taut.

"I now stand in his place and take on the responsibility of seeing to your welfare and equipping you. You have become mine."

"Madam, it is a great honor and privilege you set before me—one I can never repay."

"The debt is mine," she replied. "And you can repay it best by serving me well. I had your spare destrier cared for during your absence, and I gift you with a replacement stallion for the one you lost, as well as a palfrey and a pack horse. They are waiting for you in my stable."

Sudden tears swam in his eyes, and he swallowed. "Forgive me, madam. I am overwhelmed by your kindness. I never thought to be offered such things."

"I would be foolish not to bestow them on you and bind you to my service," she said with a shake of her head and a smile. "It is not all kindness, William." His genuine response moved her and reinforced her opinion of him. The court was full of dissembling and sycophancy and the power play of young men striving to climb fortune's wheel by stepping on their companions. William had an easy way—he instinctively knew the right thing to say at the right time—but his tears and the ragged edge to his voice were proof to her of greater depth.

"You must be measured for your new hauberk," she said, "and order what you desire from my armorers in the way of weapons and accoutrements. See my chancellor and he will issue you the necessary writs." She reached down to the side of her chair and produced a leather pouch, fat with coins. "This is for your immediate expenses. From this moment forth you are a waged knight of my household." Having given him the purse, she waited until he had composed himself, and then she took his hands between hers and gave him the kiss of peace on his smooth, shaven cheek. Rosemary, she thought. And pine. "We will talk later."

He bowed from her presence, and she watched him leave with warmth in her heart and a smile on her lips. For the outlay of a modest sum of money and some pieces of good equipment, she had just attached to her entourage a young man of high caliber and talent, and she was well satisfied with her bargain.

She turned to Richard. "Mark the men you believe will be useful to you," she said. "Treat them well and they will repay you a hundredfold."

He gave her an innocent look. "Like Papa treated Thomas Becket?"

"You reap what you sow," she replied. "I think you understand."

"Yes, Mama. Only give power to men you trust, and always make sure you have more than they do."

Alienor smiled. "Just so," she said.

# 36

## POITIERS, JANUARY 1169

WRAPPED IN A SABLE-LINED CLOAK, ALIENOR LOOKED OUT from her window in the Maubergeonne Tower on a bitter winter's morning with frost silvering the roofs and covering the ground like gritty loaf sugar. In the gray dawn William Marshal was blowing on his hands as he supervised the assembly of a pack train of pack horses and servants. He wore his own heavy winter cloak—a gift from her at Christmas—and a fur-edged cap pulled well down over his ears.

Alienor had witnessed a change in him since his return from captivity. The arrogance of young knighthood had developed into something more mature and serious, although he still had that heart-melting smile and that gleam in his eyes. She was giving him great responsibility by trusting him to take Richard to his father at Montmirail where a conference was to be held with the French, aimed at securing future peace and stability for all.

She watched him go to his new destrier, stroke its face, and blow his breath in its nostrils. Beausire was a powerful dark bay, by far the best in her stable. Many knights above William in seniority did not own a warhorse of this quality. He had cost Alienor more than William's ransom, but she had wanted him to have the best.

The stallion nosed William, seeking a titbit, and he produced a piece of bread on the flat of his hand. Observing the pride on the young knight's face as he took a moment with his horse, Alienor smiled with the pleasure of knowing they were both hers. As if sensing her scrutiny, William raised his head and glanced toward her window. He patted the stallion's neck, spoke briefly to his squire, and set off toward the tower.

Alienor withdrew from the embrasure and went to sit before the fire at her tapestry frame. The pair of dozing gazehounds raised their heads and thumped their tails on the floor. Not wanting to encourage them to climb in her lap, she ignored them. Moments later, her chamberlain ushered William into her presence.

"Madam," William said and knelt, immediately becoming the dogs' victim as they greeted him with enthusiastic licks and wags. Laughing at his plight, Alienor bade him rise and join her on the bench. He fondled the dogs, speaking their names and rubbing their ears while they pushed at him and swiped him with their tongues, demanding affection.

"Is everything ready?" she asked.

"Yes, madam, all is prepared." He smiled ruefully. "I have a new appreciation of my father's skills after organizing all this."

"I did not know him well, but enough to recognize him as a resourceful man."

"Indeed he was, madam—he had to be."

Alienor had heard the story of how William had nearly been hanged as a child when taken hostage for his father's pledge of faith to King Stephen. John FitzGilbert had broken that faith because of his more binding promise of allegiance to Henry and the Angevin cause, and only King Stephen's soft heart had kept William from the gallows. William must know a great deal about the cost of loyalty, and she suspected it had given him a deeper strength on which to draw. "I am entrusting you with the care of my son," she said. "To protect him on the road and to deliver him whole to his father."

"With my life, madam, I swear."

"I know you mean that with more than words." She removed a ring from her middle finger and put it in his hand together with a pouch of silver for expenses on the journey. "I want you to report back to me on what you see and hear at Montmirail. I am not asking you to be my spy, but I want you to observe and garner impressions—and I wish to know how my sons comport themselves."

A look of keen understanding crossed his face. "I shall be glad to serve you, madam."

"I leave it to your discretion."

William knelt to her again and left the room, his step smooth and confident.

Alienor resumed her seat before the fire and gazed into the red heat. She had spent Christmas in Poitiers while Henry had celebrated the feast at Argentan. Another Christmas apart, further widening the gap between them, and she had been perfectly content to let it be so. Presiding over her own court, she had enjoyed the company and the merriment, the games, the songs, the camaraderie of a gathering where the Normans, Angevins, and English were the outsiders.

She had not missed Henry, and the only minor cloud in her sky was that although she was queen of England, duchess of Normandy, countess of Anjou, all those titles had an empty ring when Henry had marginalized her in Aquitaine. She was not invited to this conference at Montmirail, but her sons were. Harry was to do homage to Louis for Normandy and France, and Geoffrey would do the same to his father for Brittany. Richard would kneel to Louis for Aquitaine and be betrothed to his daughter Alais. Alienor's gorge rose whenever she thought of that particular term of the treaty; she remained determined it would never come to marriage.

Richard arrived to bid her farewell, his eyes bright with anticipation. He was dressed for the journey in a heavy cloak lined with squirrel fur and a hat of blue wool, the brow band embroidered with golden lions and eagles. A tooled belt with a fine new dagger girded his waist.

"Comport yourself as a prince of Aquitaine, and the son of a king," she said. "I want to hear well of you when you return to Poitiers."

"Yes, Mama," Richard said with short patience. "I know my part."

Embracing him, she felt his recoil. He thought she was making a fuss, and he was too manly now for that.

Her pride tinged with the sadness of watching her chick prepare to leave the nest, she came to the courtyard to see him off and give him into William Marshal's care. The latter had donned his hauberk and surcoat under his cloak and had buckled on his sword, ready for business. In public now, Richard knelt to Alienor and she took his hands between hers and gave him the kiss of peace in the manner of a lord to a vassal.

She watched him ride out with his entourage, the knights glittering in their hauberks as if encased in frost, the banners fluttering red and gold, and the line of attendants and soldiers clouded in a vapor of misty breath. When the road was finally empty, Alienor returned to her fire and her younger children, Alie, Joanna, and John. But she did not intend to be idle or to mope. Even in the dead of winter she had plans afoot for spring.

❖❖❖

A month later the weather was still cold, but with a scent in the air suggestive of winter's end and of life stirring in seed and root, in den and barnyard. Alienor had been poring over plans for a new great hall in the palace complex, a space fine and beautiful to reflect the power and grace of the duchess of Aquitaine. And large enough to encompass the dealings of the court, and provide room for banquets and gatherings. She especially wanted it to outshine the great hall at Westminster. The masons were due to arrive next week, and she was eager for work to begin.

She studied her youngest son, who sat on a fleece rug near her feet, making marks on a slate with a piece of mason's chalk as he chattered to himself. For a two-year-old he had an extensive vocabulary. What inheritance Henry would provide for this last son when the lands had already been parceled out to the older siblings she did not know—unless it be a bishop's miter or somewhere far-flung such as Ireland or Jerusalem.

He glanced up, saw her watching, and immediately covered his work from her view. A secretive child was John, his ways so different from the open boldness of his older brothers.

Her chamberlain arrived and stooped to murmur that the party from Argentan had returned, bringing Harry with them. Her heart kicked into a faster rhythm, and apprehension mingled with pleasure as she bade her sons be brought to her chamber.

They arrived, tired from their ride but still full of themselves. Alienor received a shock when she set eyes on Harry, because he was taller than she was and by a full head. A line of light bronze hair fuzzed his top lip. His skin wore an oily bloom and a few blemishes, but his eyes were every shade of blue from sky to sea, and he had become handsome in the way a grown male was handsome. She could clearly see Henry in him, but oh, she could see herself too, and his smile was beautiful.

"Mama." He knelt to her. His voice had changed too, no longer a boy's.

"Who is this man who calls me mother?" she asked with a breathless laugh, on the verge of tears.

Harry's complexion reddened. "A future king, Mama," he said with pride. "Papa says that after my next year day he is going to have me anointed and declared king at his side."

Behind him, Richard slouched as if bored, but his face was taut with irritation. Richard was big and strong for his age, but Harry's growth spurt had given him the advantage, and the added promise of kingship was not sitting well with Richard's notions of dominance. Geoffrey merely looked speculative.

"So then my father will be the 'old' king and I will be the 'new' one,'" Harry said with a slight smirk.

"Do not let him hear you say that," Alienor said but had to stop herself from smiling.

"Oh, but I did, and he laughed," Harry said with a grin. "And then he had to prove he was still the strongest by beating me at arm wrestling. Of course I let him win."

Alienor shook her head. That was typical. Men and their constant attempts to dominate one another and everyone else. If Henry had laughed, it would have been more like a snarl.

She wanted to smooth the scowl from Richard's face, but the resentment in him was too strong for such a gesture to be of any use. Better to let the brothers relax with food, wine, and comfort, and then tend to their self-esteem.

❖❖❖

Later, that evening, when her young men had retired, Alienor sent for William Marshal and bade him make his report. He had exchanged his mail for a warm tunic of rust-red wool and, with his gilded belt and gold rings on his fingers, was every inch the courtier.

Alienor gestured him to sit with her at the fireside. "I have heard all about Argentan from my sons and advisers," she said, "but now I will have your impressions."

"Madam." William's dark gaze met hers. "Your sons comported themselves as princes and were a credit to you. I heard many comments upon their nobility and fine looks."

"I would expect that." Her acknowledgment was tinged with impatience. "Even were it not true, men would still spout such compliments within hearing."

"Indeed, madam. The lords of Blois were not overjoyed to witness the betrothal of my lord Richard to the Princess Alais, but there was nothing they could do to prevent it. Both kings were very satisfied with the situation."

As they would be, she thought with contempt. "And Alais?"

"She is a pretty child," William said, "and so quiet her presence was barely remarked upon. Her conduct was modest and appropriate."

A mouse then, and malleable, but not what she wanted for Richard.

"The homage-taking went smoothly also."

"What are you not telling me?" She studied his face. "I asked you for honesty, yet I feel you are withholding things from me."

William shook his head. "I have left nothing out, madam. There is little enough to tell. Your sons comported themselves well in public and you would have been proud of them."

"And out of public?"

He gave a rueful shrug. "I used to fight with my brothers all the time when we were boys, but we were—and still are—united for the good of our family. You expect spirited horses to pull on the reins. Whatever quarrels there were, were of the usual kind and not worth reporting."

She pursed her lips. "My sons told me that the king's reconciliation with the archbishop of Canterbury was not a success?"

"No, madam." William looked pensive. "Everyone thought that the quarrel would be resolved at last. The archbishop had sworn to make his peace with the king, but when it came to taking the oath, he balked and said he would serve the king in everything 'saving the honor of God.'"

Alienor clucked her tongue, irritated at the folly of men who refused to compromise.

"The archbishop left Argentan with King Louis but without his approval or favor. Everyone's patience is at an end."

"It should never have come to this," she said. Becket was a millstone around their necks. She supposed he thought he would be needed when it came to crowning Harry and was expecting to win in the end. Little did he understand his opposition.

"Was Rosamund de Clifford with the king?"

A flush crept up William's throat.

"It is not something I would ask my sons, but I will know both the official business and the gossip of the court."

"Yes, madam, the lady was there," William replied with obvious discomfort. "I did not see her—she was kept in seclusion—but she had a tent near the king's."

So, the great affair was still continuing, and his mistress had been present at this prestigious gathering while she, queen of England, duchess of Normandy, and countess of Anjou, mother of the sons swearing allegiance, was left in the cold. What kind of example did that set? What did it say of a man that he left his queen at home and brought his whore?

After William had gone, Alienor sat by the fire and quietly took herself to task. What did matter in all this was that she was duchess of Aquitaine in her own right, not Henry's. What did matter was that her sons would rule over a glittering empire, and they were her flesh and blood as much if not more than Henry's. And when she thought like that, he could not touch her whatever he did.

❖❖❖

Henry came south to Poitou and once more turned his attention to dealing with insurgents. With brutal determination he brought the counts of Angoulême and La Marche to heel and continued to pursue other pockets of rebellion.

One warm spring morning in April, Alienor watched William Marshal teaching her sons and the youths of the household how to spar on horseback using swords and clubs. William had a way with the youngsters, and they were all enjoying themselves and learning at the same time. He was what they aspired to be; they all wanted to achieve his level of prowess and skill, to make something difficult look as easy and casual as he did. A simple flick of the wrist, a particular twist on the rein. Richard in particular was very driven but trying too hard and making mistakes.

Henry's deputy, William de Tancarville, joined her to watch. He was in Poitiers for a couple of days, replenishing supplies while waiting for Henry to return from his latest expedition to the hinterland.

"You cannot take the boy out of the man," he said with a chuckle as they watched William fighting off three at once and laughing.

"I think that is part of his success," she said. "But there is more to him than that." She gave him an interrogative look. "You trained him, did you not?"

He folded his arms. "Yes, and it wasn't always easy. Like all young lads, he had to be licked into shape. He'd had an excellent grounding from his father, but he needed honing and maturity." De Tancarville grinned. "My men used to tell me that any man who took him on as a hearth knight was a fool because William would eat him out of house and home to no good return. I lost count of the times we had to kick him out of bed or haul him away from the kitchen door." He watched William teaching the youths how to make a particular sword blow on a difficult turn. "It wasn't that he was lazy, more that he picked things up so quickly that he easily grew bored. In truth I never had a squire who learned as fast as he did and knew how to deal the blows after a single demonstration. He was often picked on because of his skill, but it never soured his good nature. I told those who said he would come to nothing that one day they would eat their words, and I was right."

"But even so, you did not keep him as a hearth knight after his training?"

De Tancarville shook his head. "Even I can only keep so many young knights in my entourage, and he had a sponsor in Patrick, God rest his soul. I knew William would make his way in the world."

"Perhaps he is destined for greater things yet," she said and turned at a shout from the gate. Henry was back. Her stomach churned with conflicting emotions: anticipation, trepidation, defensiveness, and anger. What she desired to feel was indifference, but the more she tried, the more elusive it became, rather like her sons' efforts to manage the moves William Marshal was demonstrating with such ease.

❖ ❖ ❖

Tired and dusty, Henry eased himself into the warm bath that Alienor had organized in his chamber. A narrow board was spread across the middle of the tub on which servants had set out platters of bread and chicken. He looked well, for he was lean and tough from days spent in the saddle, and his freckled skin wore a pale golden glow. Once she would have shared the tub with him and they would have enjoyed an intimate meal of laughter and conversation, followed by delicious lovemaking. Such closeness was now a thing of the past, like a song which she remembered the tune of but when she tried to sing it she couldn't. However, she brought him soft white soap of Castile, scented with oil of roses, and a fresh jug of hot water.

"Now you have quelled the worst of the rebellion," she said, "I think I should go on progress and show my face to the people so that they see me as well as your iron fist. I shall bring Richard with me and give him a prominent place at my side so that they may know my heir. He is ready, I think."

Henry gestured assent. "As you wish. Just don't get ambushed again."

Alienor bristled at his tone, which managed to suggest that it was her fault it had happened the first time. "Surely not if you have mopped up the rebels," she said sweetly. "Besides, I will have William Marshal for protection."

"Ah, the dashing young knight." Henry took a chicken leg and bit into the roasted golden skin. "I was impressed by him at Montmirail," he said around a mouthful of meat. "You made a good bargain when you ransomed him."

She raised an eyebrow. "Mostly I am a good judge of men." A pity that judgment had deserted her when she married Henry.

He grunted, leaving her to interpret the sound as she would, and when he had finished eating, left the bath and stood impatiently while the servants dressed him in a soft shirt and loose robe. He picked up the copy of *La Chanson de Roland* that lay on the chest. "Warlike reading," he said.

"Richard's studying it. He was very keen to know that Roland's sword and the Oliphant horn are relics of Aquitaine." She looked wry. "He also has a burning desire to go and fight Saracens like both his great-grandsires did."

Henry turned a few pages before putting the book down. "Well, that is a noble undertaking, but one he may yet grow out of." He went to pour himself a cup of wine. "Becket is still being obdurate," he said after a moment. "I had more letters yesterday. He is holding out because he thinks I cannot crown Harry without him, but no law of God says I must have the coronation performed by the archbishop of Canterbury."

"But you still need a papal dispensation. You do not want anyone to declare Harry's coronation invalid."

Henry gave an impatient shrug. "I have a second archbishop in that of York. Pont L'Évêque will be willing even if Becket isn't. And I have my dispensation—Pope Alexander granted it to me years ago in return for my favor."

Alienor did not think that that pope had intended the dispensation to be used in such circumstances, but still, as a document in the hand, it was valuable leverage. "What about Marguerite? Is she to be crowned too?"

Henry stroked his chin. "That remains to be seen. Louis is desperate for his daughter to be made a queen, but he will want the archbishop of Canterbury to perform the ceremony to make it binding. So he will put pressure on Thomas to reconcile with me too."

"You think Thomas will capitulate?"

Henry exhaled with irritation. "God knows. Behind my back he excommunicates my bishops and threatens an interdict. He says he will obey me in all things saving his oath to the Church. Well and good. I say in that case I am willing to have him back in all things saving the kiss of peace."

Alienor knew that no kiss of peace meant Henry would not guarantee Becket's safety in England, and that he would still shun him. It was like watching two stags run against each other and lock horns, both seeking the advantage and neither able to gain one.

He began his customary pacing. "I have been thinking about the children," he said as he turned, "the younger ones."

Alienor was immediately suspicious. Henry's policies concerning their offspring were usually destined to give him power and take it from her. "Indeed?"

"Since there has been so much unrest, and since they both require an education, I am sending them to Fontevraud for a while. John might have a career in the Church depending on what happens, and it will suit his needs whether he does or not." A nostalgic look softened the usual sharpness in his eyes. "I often stayed there as a child when my parents were otherwise occupied. You would not have to make arrangements during your progress, and be constantly worried for them."

Alienor eyed him. It might also mean he did not want her influencing them too much. Nevertheless, she could see the advantages and she too loved Fontevraud. "I think it a good notion," she said after a pause. "I shall write to the abbess."

"Good." He wandered around the chamber touching this and that while silence lengthened between them. What was there to say? They had no reason to sleep together because there were no children to beget. All business they needed to discuss had been dealt with.

Eventually, Henry left the room and went to join his cronies. Alienor watched the laundress gather up his travel-stained linens and take them away to be washed. A lingering aroma of acrid male sweat permeated the atmosphere, a smell that at one time had made her almost queasy with desire. Now with a different queasiness she desperately needed to be out of the room. Having ordered her women to burn incense to purify the air, she took her cloak and went for a walk, Marchisa accompanying her.

Passing through the hall, she saw that her three eldest sons had joined their father and his entourage and were reveling in the hard masculine company, puffing out their chests and pretending to be men. Henry's arm was across Harry's shoulder, but he was talking to all of them. He glanced briefly at Alienor but his attention was for his sons, and she might have been no more than a cat crossing his path. He would take them all, she thought bitterly. Pretending she had not noticed, she entered the tower on the other side and climbed to the battlements where she could gaze out over all of Poitiers, shining in the spring sun. The sight gave her sustenance and calmed her turmoil. Henry would be gone on the morrow.

She was still recovering her breath from the climb when Hamelin joined her. He had been among the men downstairs but had obviously seen and followed her.

"Your new hall has grown apace since last I was here," he said, nodding at the timber scaffolding caging the building works.

"We have made a good start," she agreed, "especially now the fine weather is here. I cannot wait to hold a great summer banquet and hear the troubadours sing their lais."

"Indeed, that would be an experience to savor," he said. "I intend building a new keep on my Yorkshire estates when I return to England."

"And will you hold banquets with troubadours?" she teased.

Smiling, he leaned against the stonework. "Not in the way of Poitiers, but fitting, I hope."

Alienor was gently amused. Hamelin had a preference for plain food, albeit of fine quality. Give him a perfectly baked loaf, a hunk of cheese from cows grazed on lush pastures, and a decent wine, and he was supremely content. No spices or food in decorated disguise for him. Banquets were a symbol of status, endured rather than hosted for personal pleasure. "I trust Isabel is well?"

He rubbed the back of his neck. "That is why I followed you," he said, "to speak on her behalf. She is with child again, and was very sick when she crossed from England. She is resting at Colombiers. It is peaceful there, and it would cheer her greatly to see you."

"Of course I shall visit, and as soon as I am able. She is dear to me both as a sister and a friend." The sickness of early pregnancy could be vile. Hamelin was often overprotective of his wife, who looked fragile but in reality was as strong as an ox. She gave him a mock frown. "We have barely spoken since you married her and took her away."

He grinned. "I will not apologize to you for that."

"I would not expect you to." Impulsively she kissed his cheek. "I am pleased for you both. Such closeness in a match is rare indeed."

"I know my good fortune and thank God for it."

The air between them filled with the tension of unspoken words, bridled because neither wanted to be compromised.

Alienor turned once more to the glittering view spread below the walls of her tower. "Indeed," she said. "Count your blessings."

❖ ❖ ❖

Henry departed the next day with a baggage train of laden pack ponies. The knights rode side by side, row upon row in glittering harness, followed by sergeants in leather jackets and quilted tunics. Richard, Harry, and Geoffrey joined the troop and rode with the army for a few miles, escorted by William Marshal. As the dust settled behind the last horse, Alienor breathed a sigh of relief but felt bereft too, because it seemed she was always the one left standing in the dust.

# 37

## Colombiers, Anjou, Summer 1169

$\mathcal{I}$T WAS A GLORIOUS SUMMER DAY STEEPED IN SUNSHINE. FURRY bees burrowed among the roses and lavender, collecting bulging trousers of golden pollen. Isabel sat with Alienor in the castle's pleasance while the children played around them. Isabel's eldest daughter and namesake, Belle, had just turned four years old, a beautiful little girl, her hair dark like Isabel's but rippled with amber lights. She and Alie were deeply absorbed in a game with their dolls.

Under the eye of their nurses, Belle's younger brother Will and his cousin John were building a tower from wooden blocks. Isabel's new baby, another girl, christened Adela for her grandmother, slept in her cradle in the shade of a fig tree, watched over by a nurse. She had arrived a fortnight early, and Alienor had not been present for the birth but had ridden into Colombiers to find her new niece already thriving in the world.

"I am sorry Hamelin will not see her for a while yet," Isabel said, "and he will be sorry too, because he dotes on the children. I have never seen such a fond father."

Alienor raised her eyebrows. "Doting on small children is not usually a masculine trait, especially when those children are daughters."

"They are his haven from his duties. He comes to us to be cleansed and to find himself again."

"Like washing your hands after a day spent grubbing in mire," Alienor said neutrally.

Isabel bit her lip. "I did not mean it like that. There are fewer burdens on him. He can sit the children on his knee and watch me sew and fall asleep if he wants to. At court he has to be on his guard all the time. He is the king's brother, and men are always seeking things from him. He shields the king too, and that takes its toll."

"Henry won't notice or thank him," Alienor said. "Henry takes it all as his due."

"Hamelin renders it as his duty, because that is his purpose. He does not begrudge that, but every man needs a haven, somewhere he can retreat and find peace."

"Henry would rather hunt his horses into the ground and ride other women than come home to his family," Alienor said and then looked away. "He may do as he chooses; it no longer matters to me."

Isabel shook her head. "I do not believe that is true, because if it did not, you would not look so grim."

"You are foolish," Alienor snapped.

"Am I? It seems to me that it matters a great deal."

Alienor was horrified to feel tears prickle her eyes. "It only matters where it applies to issues of land and inheritance," she said brusquely.

"But surely too in what is due to you as yourself? I speak as your friend—and as your sister-by-marriage."

Alienor dropped her gaze. Isabel was indeed a true friend, who would not seek favors of her and exploit their bond, but she did not trust her to keep quiet with Hamelin. While she and Henry had numerous secrets and angry grudges boiling between them, Isabel and Hamelin had none. Isabel shared everything with him and, sooner or later, whatever she said would get back to Henry, because Hamelin's first loyalty was to his brother.

"I know you do, and I thank you for your care," she said. "Henry is what he is, and nothing will change him. I thought when we first married that he could be molded. He was a very young man and I did not know him, but I realize what a vain hope it was. And when you realize your hopes are in vain, of course you care—but it also means it does not matter, because you will never have what you want."

"Oh, Alienor."

"I warned you not to pity me," she said, her voice developing a ragged edge. "I have my own path to tread, and I have my children."

"But you are taking them to Fontevraud?"

"Only John and Joanna, and only for a little while. They will be safe there while I go on progress with Richard and then to Normandy. Of course I shall visit them, but this is a practical solution. And Alie will stay with me too."

Isabel could not imagine doing that with any of her children, but she and Alienor had different responsibilities and attitudes. At least John and Joanna would have each other.

"I need to move freely without constant worry and heartache," Alienor said. "John's future may lie with the Church, and this will be a good time to discover if he has a vocation. And Joanna...well, a mother should not become too attached to her daughters. Parting with Matilda was a great grief to me, and it will be the same when Alie goes to her marriage." Her voice caught. "Negotiations are already afoot with Castile, and it will not be long."

"You are putting on a brave face," Isabel said. "I could not do that."

Alienor made no reply. Isabel would have to if the right dynastic marriage came along and Hamelin chose to send their girls away. "They say that a woman's daughters are hers for life, and perhaps that is true for some, when they can live close to one another and visit often, but a queen must send hers into the world, and it is the sons who sustain her and become her glory." She glanced at Richard, who was playing with some other youths, watched over by William Marshal. They were engrossed in a game in which they had to try to touch their opponent while avoiding being touched themselves, and Richard was like lightning. So quick, so physically intuitive.

Servants arrived with a tray of small, crumbly pastries and wine that had been cooling in the castle well. The baby woke and began to fret. Isabel lifted her from the cradle, opened her gown, and put her to suckle.

"Don't you have a wet nurse?" Alienor was astonished.

Isabel shook her head. "I would rather feed them myself. I know what goes into them is of me, and it nurtures them. Why would I have milk in my breasts and not use it for the purpose intended?"

"What does Hamelin say?"

"He thinks it good that a child should suckle the milk of its mother's nobility."

"But it means you are at the beck and call of a nursing child all hours of the day, and a woman who is giving suck is not supposed to lie with a man."

Isabel blushed but held her ground. "That is the lore, but you are not telling me everyone obeys it? Besides, there are other ways, and Hamelin is in the field with Henry. By the time he returns, Adela will be weaning onto goat's milk."

Alienor marveled at Isabel. She had never suckled any of hers, not even Richard; there had always been a wet nurse waiting on hand to take the child so that Alienor would be ready to conceive again the moment she had been churched. Watching the baby nuzzling Isabel's milk-heavy breast, seeing the tenderness in Isabel's expression as the child began to nurse, Alienor felt a pang of regret.

Isabel changed the subject. "You certainly got a bargain when you paid the ransom and bought the service of that young knight."

Alienor glanced around. The game had turned to wrestling. William was adroitly avoiding Richard's assault and teaching him how to twist out of a particular hold. "He is a valued part of the household," she said. "I sometimes receive the impression he is marking his time. He could perform his duties with one hand tied behind his back. When I give him permission to attend a tourney he never returns empty-handed." She smiled at Isabel. "Strange to think your mother is his aunt by marriage."

"He could have been in my and Hamelin's entourage," Isabel said with a mischievous twinkle.

Alienor wagged her finger. "He is mine," she warned, laughing. "No matter how much you bid, you are not having him back."

"That valuable?"

"Let us say a sound investment that will accumulate with time."

Isabel deftly transferred the baby to her other breast. "Have you heard any more about Richard going to France?"

Alienor bristled. "Henry may have made that covenant with Louis, but I will not have the heir to Aquitaine raised at the French court, whatever he says!"

"I did not think so," Isabel replied. "But knowing Henry, I wondered what choice you have."

Alienor firmed her lips and watched the children at play. Isabel's little daughter was trying to interest John and her brother in playing a ball game. John grasped the ball of soft leather strips and, with a shout, threw it in the flower bed. "Henry may believe I must do his will, but Richard stays here," she said with quiet conviction. "I know this as I know my heart beats in my body. You would have to wrench it from my chest before I would allow such a thing to happen."

## 38

CAEN, FEBRUARY 1170

ON A COLD DAY ON THE CUSP OF SPRING, BLEAK BUT WITH glimmers of a brighter light behind the clouds, Henry prepared to return to England. He hadn't set foot there for four years, but preparations to crown Harry were afoot, and there were pressing matters of government with which to deal. Forty ships stood ready to transport the court to England, although Harry would not follow his father until the summer.

Alienor had ridden north to Caen at Henry's summons. He had intimated in his letter to her that he needed her help, and her curiosity was piqued because for him to admit that, he must be in a tight corner.

When Alienor arrived with her entourage, the great donjon at Caen Castle was bustling with retainers about the business of packing for the move and as usual gave the impression of chaos, although there was an underlying semblance of organization if one looked more closely. Richard gazed around, sniffing the air like a hound in a strange but interesting place.

Alienor prepared to dismount, and William Marshal was immediately at her stirrup. She paid him little heed for her attention was all on the two youths advancing across the bailey. Harry had grown again and walked with an assured confidence that was almost a swagger. He was nearly fifteen years old, a similar age to his father when the latter had crossed to England on his first impromptu battle campaign.

At his side, his bastard half brother Jeoffrey wore a quilted tunic, a dagger slung low at his left hip. He had already cultivated a beard, albeit sparse and downy.

Both young men knelt to her. She gestured them to rise and embraced Harry. Jeoffrey lowered his gaze and took a step back.

"Well," she said. "My young king-in-waiting."

Harry puffed out his chest. "Not for much longer, Mama."

"Indeed not."

Harry embraced Richard, who had dismounted in his own time. "Papa's bought me a new horse—a stallion," Harry said, his countenance bright with pleasure and a little smug. "Do you want to see him?"

Richard's expression was torn between enthusiasm and envy. Not wanting to appear impressed or eager, he shrugged. "If you want."

Alienor watched her sons and their bastard half brother head off in the direction of the stables.

"Go with them," she said to William Marshal. "Keep an eye."

"Madam." William bowed and departed.

Alienor followed an usher to the chamber prepared for her. Braziers had been lit but had yet to take the chill from the day, and the wind direction was creating a cold draft on the tower stairs. Her bed and some of her baggage had arrived yesterday but had yet to be arranged, and although the room was ready for use in a basic form, it was not particularly welcoming. She huddled into the warmth of her cloak and went to gaze out of the window. Charcoal-colored clouds scudded across a paler gray sky, populated by a few wind-tossed seagulls. From a distance she saw Henry advancing on her, immediately recognizable by his short cloak and his brisk stride. A woman crossed his path and he paused to speak to her. Her gown was the color of speedwells and her hair was covered by a full wimple of white linen. Alienor's eyesight was not as sharp as it had been and she could not be sure, but she thought he touched her face. The woman moved on with a swift glance over her shoulder at the tower. She clambered into a waiting litter and was borne out of the castle gates. Alienor narrowed her eyes.

Turning from the window, she instructed her women to fasten the shutters and light more candles.

Moments later Henry breezed into the chamber and with a swift command bade everyone rise from their obeisance. "I am glad you are here," he said to Alienor without preamble. "We have been looking out for you these past two days." He came to her, gave her a perfunctory kiss on the cheek, and moved away.

"We made the best pace we could." She wondered why, if he had been looking out for her for the past two days, he had not removed his mistress from the vicinity before now. If he was glad to see her, it was for political and not personal reasons. "I did not want to ride the horses to exhaustion."

Servants arrived with small pastries and a flagon of spiced wine. Alienor took her cup and went to stand before a brazier to absorb the heat. She had become accustomed to sunshine and warmer climes in Poitiers. This February morning in Normandy made her bones ache. "When do you sail?"

"Early next week if the wind holds. I shall leave Harry in your care, and also his wife." His gaze lit on a box of books, and he stooped to investigate the titles.

"Is she here?" Alienor tried to keep the distaste from her voice.

"Not yet, but she will be arriving soon. I want you to care for her among your women while she and Harry grow accustomed to each other."

"Have you decided what to do about crowning her with Harry?"

Henry picked up a book and turned a couple of pages. "I have a mind to crown Harry without Marguerite. She is but twelve years old. It will be more appropriate to make her queen when she is older and ready to assume all the duties entailed."

"Louis will not be pleased."

He let out an impatient breath. "I can deal with Louis, but he does not have to know yet. Better to leave the choice open and prepare for a double coronation even if there won't be one." He waved a dismissive hand. "Let the girl have some new gowns out of it. It is not as if she is never going to be queen."

Alienor nodded with satisfaction. She was content with such a state of affairs because it meant she remained sole queen of England and could bring better influence to bear on her daughter-in-law. "I take it Thomas Becket will not be performing the ceremony?"

Henry looked at her as if she had given him vinegar to drink. "I have no need of him when I have a dispensation to have Harry crowned by whomsoever I choose."

"I heard he has excommunicated the bishops designated to crown Harry and that he intends putting England under interdict."

"Hah! What he intends and what happens are two different things." Henry closed the book and, picking up his wine, came to stand at the brazier. "That is why I have need of your diplomacy and skill."

"Indeed?" Alienor's smile was acerbic. "That is a novelty. Your usual view is that I am an interfering woman who should keep to her sewing and innocuous pleasant chat with envoys and bishops."

Henry scowled at first, but then his gaze warmed with reluctant humor. "That is true, if I am being honest."

"Are you?" She gave him a hard look. The harsh winter weather had roughened his cheeks and his eyes were bloodshot from standing too close to smoky fires and spending too many nights straining to work in dim candlelight. There was barely a glimpse in him of the limber, smooth-skinned youth she had married. But then she too had aged and lost her optimism.

"It is your duty to support me and our heirs."

She sipped her wine and watched the smoke twirl up from the coals. Had his mother still been alive, he would have used the empress to govern Normandy; he had summoned Alienor from Poitiers because he had no other choice. He was right about the duty she owed, but his decisions were all about his schemes and plans and not paths she would have chosen. "What do you want me to do?"

"Becket will try to prevent Harry's coronation. He wants to force me to let him keep that blasted 'saving God's dignity' oath, which I will never do. He will attempt to serve notice of interdict the instant my feet touch English soil. I want you to prevent any cleric with orders from Becket from crossing the sea. Until that notice makes landfall, no clergy in England are bound to obey it. If I can stop him and the pope from interfering, our son will be anointed king, and their quiver will be short of arrows indeed."

"They will claim it is not legal in the eyes of God," Alienor warned.

"It will be no more than squawking of old women," Henry said contemptuously.

Alienor inclined her head. "As you wish. I will have the ports watched and have my knights detain anyone who might prove a threat."

"The bishop of Worcester in particular, so my informants tell me." He raised a cautionary forefinger. "Treat anyone you capture with diplomacy, and do not tell them I have ordered their detention."

Alienor curled her lip. He was placing her in the role of queen as intermediary and peacekeeper but making her his scapegoat into the bargain. "So you draw me here to do your underhand work and to take the blame."

"You are here to share the work of ensuring that our son is crowned," he snapped.

"I shall do it," she said regally. "Not for you, but for Harry and his future."

"Good, then it is settled."

"And Richard shall be made the count of Poitou in my name the moment he reaches his fifteenth year day."

He gave a dismissive wave. "Of course."

Alienor was not yet finished. "Concerning Richard, since we are speaking of the future of our sons: I want him to stay with me and finish his education in Poitou. I will not have him being sent to court in Paris at this stage."

"By all means. There is plenty of time for that; Louis can wait awhile."

Alienor was not fooled. He was only agreeing because it suited him for now.

He rose to leave and picked up the book he had put down. "I'll borrow this. I've been wanting to read it."

After he had gone on a flurry of cold air, Alienor ate a small tart from the platter and mulled over what had been said. Despite her irritation with him, she was buoyed up by the challenge of the task he had set, and it brought a smile to her lips.

❖❖❖

On the training ground used by the knights, and watched by his parents, Harry was trying out the horse that his father had given him to mark his fifteenth year day. The stallion was a chaser, a bright golden chestnut with a metallic sheen to its coat and a white marking in the shape of a lightning zigzag on its rump. Harry had named it Flambur, meaning "glittering," and the horse lived up to his name, as did his harness, the leather stamped with gold and decorated with pendants that jingled with each high-stepping movement.

William Marshal was tutoring Harry in horsemanship among a small group of other youths, and Harry, aware of his audience, was showing off. Grinning, he urged Flambur into a fast canter and tried to execute a tight turn, but he had not allowed himself sufficient room for maneuver. The stallion slipped to his haunches and twisted. Harry lost his seat in the saddle and was unceremoniously dumped in the dirt. Other than being winded, he was unhurt, save his pride, and he struggled to his feet, brushing soil from his fine clothes while Flambur bucked and cantered around the field, shying from everyone who tried to catch him, reins and stirrups flapping.

William Marshal reined his horse around and trotted up to Harry. "Quickly, sire." He reached down and with his strength and Harry's leverage pulled the youth astride his mount's rump. Flawlessly executing the same tight turn that Harry had just failed to accomplish, he cantered after the loose chestnut and, riding up alongside him, grabbed the bridle while shouting to Harry to leap over into the empty saddle.

His face taut with determination, no grin now, Harry scrambled and jumped. The maneuver, albeit clumsy, still achieved the desired result, while William gripped Flambur's bridle until the lad was secure and could control the horse himself. They reached the end of the training ground, and Harry drew rein and trotted back, flushed and exhilarated, while William praised him and slapped his back.

"And that," said Alienor to Henry, "is a fall coming before pride." Her heart warmed toward William, who had turned the moment around for Harry, and at the same time demonstrated a rescue technique for battle and tourney situations.

"The young Marshal is good with the squires," Henry remarked.

"They look up to him. He is a skilled teacher," she said. "Harry might not sit still to listen to a tutor, but he takes notice of William because he absorbs the lesson without it being a chore."

Henry rubbed his jaw. "When Harry is crowned, he will need a larger household. Appointing Marshal to a position in his retinue is worth considering, I think."

Alienor nodded, although she was ambivalent. She had been thinking of making him tutor in arms to Richard. However, she knew William was ambitious, and since he had saved her life, she owed him the opportunity to better his lot. "He is worth bearing in mind," she agreed.

"Good." Henry gave a firm nod, turning a suggestion into a reality there and then.

❖❖❖

Alienor looked around the chamber vacated by Henry when he sailed to England. Harry was taking it for his, and his servants were transferring his accoutrements. The room had just been swept and there was a smell of settling dust and a slight aroma of smoke and incense from braziers. Harry's bed and mattresses of stuffed down and straw had been moved in together with sheets and blankets, chests, and a hawk perch.

The fleet had sailed for England in blustery but decent weather with good visibility, but during the night a storm had brewed up and battered the harbor with howling winds and lashing rain. This morning the sea was frisky and the wind had returned to its usual bustle, but everyone in Caen was on tenterhooks awaiting news of the king's safe arrival in England. Alienor had given thanks to God at morning Mass that Harry had not sailed with his father.

Still, the storm clouds had a silver lining. She had received news that Becket, on his way to Caen to talk to Henry and serve the coronation ban on his bishops, had learned of the sailing and turned back because of the atrocious weather. Not that it would stop him from making another attempt. She would have to remain vigilant.

An item on the window seat caught her eye: a bone needle case, exquisitely carved out of walrus ivory. What it was doing in Henry's chamber was a mystery. He sometimes mended bits of harness himself, but this was a delicate woman's item. Alienor removed the small stopper, attached by a plait of silk, and tipped several silver needles into her hand. Their eyes and thickness were of varying sizes for working on different fabrics. A length of narrow red ribbon was tucked down the side of the case and, when drawn out, proved to be embroidered with tiny golden lions. It was skilled and beautiful work. One needle was threaded with gold wire mingled with strands of fine honey-brown hair. There was no need to ask whose possession this was or who had been here. Alienor's throat constricted. Once she might have sewn something like this for Henry herself... Not anymore. Taking the ribbon to the brazier as if holding a dead snake, she cast it into the coals and watched it shrivel and burn. And then she threw the needle case after it.

As the silk twist crumbled into ash, her chamberlain arrived to tell her that Henry had landed safely at Southampton.

Alienor said nothing, because at the moment she was wishing him and his paramour at the bottom of the sea.

"The fleet was scattered by the storm though and one ship lost with the king's physician on board and Gilbert de Suleny."

"That is indeed sad news." She rallied herself. Even if Henry had been on the ship that sank, there would have been others drowned too whom she cared about, or who had no part in her anger toward him. "I will have prayers of thanks said and alms given for the souls of the dead."

Harry arrived, red-cheeked from a vigorous ride out on his horse, his energy very similar to his sire's as he prowled into the room.

"Your father has arrived safely but had a rough voyage," she said neutrally. "One ship was lost though, with Ralph de Bellamont aboard and Gilbert de Suleny."

Harry manufactured a look of concern. "I am sorry for that, and I am glad I wasn't with them," he replied. "Papa always seems to attract storms."

"Yes, he does," she agreed, "usually of his own making, although Becket would see it as being brought upon him by God's wrath."

"Becket would see anything not to his liking as being brought about by God's wrath," Harry said with a grimace. "I am pleased I did not have to stay in his household."

"It was valuable time you spent there," she said. "Not just with the archbishop but all the learned men around him."

Henry gave an indifferent murmur. Alienor considered this bright son of hers, handsome, intelligent, and so easily bored. He found it difficult to learn by sitting still, unlike Geoffrey who excelled, or Richard, who could focus like a spear point when his interest was caught. Harry had Henry's restlessness but not his depth. He was like a butterfly, and that concerned Alienor. He needed to acquire knowledge and wisdom in order to rule, but sitting with a tutor was plainly not the best way.

"I have been thinking about your household when you are anointed," she said. "Your father suggested Richard Barre for your chancellor."

Harry scowled at that. "He's my father's man and an old fusspot."

"He's also widely experienced," Alienor reproved. "You need that as part of your administrative backbone. Besides, he is in Rome at the moment, so he won't be immediately joining you. Walter can stay as your chaplain and I thought to promote that young clerk Wigan to your chancery. Also, what about William Marshal as your marshal and tutor in arms?"

Harry's brow cleared as he decided not to sulk. "I would have chosen them myself," he said. He sat down on a cushioned bench before the brazier, spread his arms, and crossed his legs. "I want Adam Yqueboeuf, Philippe de Colombiers, and Baldwin de Béthune too."

"As you wish." Not all were to Alienor's taste, especially the sycophantic Yqueboeuf, but a young man had to have his friends as well as the checks and balances set there by his parents.

Harry's gaze fell upon the burning needle case and his nose wrinkled at the smell of scorched bone.

"I found it on the embrasure sill," Alienor said, "with a red ribbon inside embroidered with lions. I will not have evidence of your father's concubine tainting the places where I have to walk."

Harry avoided her gaze. "I do not blame you, Mama."

"You have been in her company? You know her?" She was repelled to think that Rosamund de Clifford was acquainted with her sons.

He shrugged assent. "She does not argue with him," he said. "She is not interested in political doings, and he can talk to her of ordinary things."

Alienor curled her lip. "He can talk to me of ordinary things if he so chooses."

"But you are fierce like an eagle, Mama. You might fly away with his goods in your talons or dig out his eyes. Rosamund is like a kitten. If she scratched him it would be an accident, and he could destroy her with one squeeze of his fist—but he doesn't want to do that. He wants to play with her and put a belled collar around her neck."

Alienor wanted to retch. "I see."

Harry stirred his toe on the rush matting of the chamber floor. "He needs both of you, Mama."

She made an aggravated sound. It was all about the desires of men, even with her sons. "I am not so sure that I need him," she said. "And what he fears of me, I know well of him."

❖❖❖

A fortnight later Harry's bride Marguerite arrived in Caen together with her younger sister, Alais. Alienor had not set eyes on Marguerite since her farce of a wedding to Harry ten years ago. The dumpy toddler had become a robust child, heavyset and solid, quite unlike her slim, silver-haired father. She lacked his height, and her features were doughy and landscaped with adolescent blemishes. However, her brunette hair was wavy and lustrous, and her eyes soft brown and rather beautiful. Her sister Alais was fair like their father, a small, gray-eyed mouse. Alienor had been prepared to dislike these girls, yet something turned within her. For better or worse Marguerite was her daughter-in-law, and even if she was not about to be crowned, it would still happen at some point. Soon too she would be old enough to bear children. Whatever her antipathy, Alienor had to bring her into her circle of influence.

Harry was not impressed by the French princesses. Although polite to them, he showed little interest. He viewed being wed to Marguerite as a necessary duty. She did not care to beautify herself, regarding it as frippery, and her opinions were set and stolid. To Harry's bright, quick nature, she was as stimulating as a bowl of cold pottage.

Alienor set about the task of preparing Marguerite for her new life. She had arrived with a baggage of sober gowns and none of the trappings of high royalty. Alienor employed a seamstress to fashion new robes for her. Marguerite's warm coloring suited reds, golds, and greens, but when clad in her new finery, she resembled a plow horse in the harness of a high-stepping palfrey.

Nevertheless, Marguerite had her attributes. She was dogged and steady. While not a good rider when it came to anything faster than a trot, she could hack for miles without complaint. She had stamina and endurance, and a way of seeing things through to their conclusion. Such qualities would be of great use to Harry, who needed that kind of grounding—although first, of course, he had to notice his wife.

Alienor sent them out together with the hawks, and that proved successful because Marguerite relished the pursuit and Harry was able to show off his white gyrfalcon and his considerable skill in handling the bird. Marguerite admired his prowess, and the day's sport was passed in mutual enjoyment. At the table later,

Marguerite was more animated than usual, and her sparkle made Harry pay her more attention than was his wont.

Alienor watched them with a judicious and political eye. She had never wanted their marriage, but since it was a fact, it would be for the best if the couple could find fulfillment in their roles and their formal partnership. At some point she had to tell Marguerite she was not crossing the sea with Harry to be made queen at his side…but not quite yet.

❖❖❖

Alienor was in her chamber reading correspondence from Poitou when William Marshal requested an audience and she bade her chamberlain admit him.

William entered the room and came to kneel at her feet. He had arrived straight from patrol and was still wearing his mail and sword belt, although he had left his weapon at the door. "Madam," he said without preamble, "we were watching the roads as you instructed, and intercepted the bishop of Worcester and his servants. You said you desired to speak with any English clergy we might meet, so I courteously invited him to accompany us."

Alienor smiled with satisfaction. "You have done well, William. Bring him to me, but treat him as a valued guest, and have us provided with refreshment. I want you to stay and keep your ears open—but remove your mail first. I do not want to intimidate the good bishop."

"Madam," William replied with a gleam of understanding. He returned shortly, wearing his court tunic and escorting with deference Roger, Bishop of Worcester. The latter was Henry's cousin, older by fifteen years, a handsome, well-spoken man with dark hair graying at the temples and a closely cropped beard of badger-striped white. He had long been a friend of Thomas Becket, who had raised him to his bishopric seven years ago. Since Henry was his kin and well known to him, he had a foot in both camps.

Alienor liked Roger of Worcester, even if he was bearing letters of excommunication from Becket that would destroy Harry's coronation should they reach England. He was devout but not inflexible. Whereas some bishops she knew, Gilbert Foliot the foremost, would have entered the room in a roaring temper at being detained, Roger knew how to play the game and came forward as if he was indeed an honored guest.

Alienor greeted him by kissing his ring and he acknowledged her with a bow and a smile.

"It is a pleasure to see you again," she said. "It has been too long."

"And I have missed your company too, madam, and that of the king," he answered graciously.

Servants arrived with a rock-crystal flagon of the best Gascon wine and dishes of fried pastries, small cheese tarts, roasted chicken, and fresh salmon cooked with ginger and currants. They arranged the repast on a trestle table covered with a white linen cloth and set it with platters of fine silver gilt and expensive glass cups. "Come," Alienor said. "Will you dine? I have need of your advice and I am sure you are keen to refresh yourself."

He studied the dishes being laid out and the delicate curls of steam rising from the crisp chicken skin. "You are kind, madam. Traveling always does sharpen the appetite, and it is a while since I and my companions ate."

"Their needs will be seen to also, and we shall provide you with sleeping accommodation."

"Madam, there is no need to go to such trouble on our account." He was in a bind but plainly that did not prevent him from fighting with diplomacy.

"Oh, it is no trouble at all, my lord. Indeed, I must impose on you to stay a little while because we have much to talk about."

She watched him look around the room. Her musicians had arranged themselves in the window splay and were tuning their instruments. Her chamberlain was lighting more candles. William stayed in the background, his presence a subtle statement: a reminder to the bishop that he was a guest, but not free to leave.

"I am at your disposal, madam," he said graciously and seated himself at the cushioned bench between wall and table.

Once they had washed their hands and Roger had blessed the food, Alienor said, "You are traveling to England, I assume?"

The musicians started to play a soft, harmonious duet on harp and citole. She accepted the thick slice of chicken breast he expertly carved and laid upon her platter.

"Madam, you are right," he said. "I was on my way to England, on a matter of urgent business concerning the king."

"I am sorry to say the seas have been very rough for the time of year, and crossings have been difficult." She reached to her cup and took a dainty sip of wine.

"Indeed, I heard that the king's fleet suffered a bad storm on their recent crossing, but the weather is fairer now."

"Perhaps, but still too variable to take chances."

"If you will permit me to leave, I will be very glad to be on my way."

Alienor smiled. "Of course, my lord bishop, but I am afraid it will still not be possible until the tide turns—whenever that may be. You will be housed with every comfort and sent on your way as soon as possible."

He grimaced with wry acknowledgment of his situation.

"Should you have letters for the king, I shall be glad to see that he receives them by a swift messenger. If you gave them to me, you could be on your way by tomorrow morning."

"Madam, I appreciate your offer, but any correspondence I have was entrusted to me, and it is incumbent on me to deliver it in person."

"I understand," Alienor replied. "I but thought to save you a wasted journey."

"That is thoughtful of you, madam," the bishop said, not concealing the irony in his voice. "No journey is ever wasted, but I appreciate why mine will be delayed." He wiped his lips on his napkin. "You do know that your son's coronation will have its legality questioned if it is not performed by the archbishop of Canterbury?"

"The king has a dispensation from the pope," she replied

smoothly. "As I understand, the archbishop of Canterbury's role is only tradition and not an unassailable right. But I take your point. I am sure in the future the situation will be clarified by additional ceremonies and, God willing, the participation of Canterbury, but for now it remains as you see it."

"The king of France will not be satisfied with such an arrangement for his daughter."

"We shall deal with that when the time comes. It behooves the king of France to help resolve this matter if he wishes to see his daughter crowned by the archbishop of Canterbury, does it not?"

Roger of Worcester said no more on the matter, and the meal continued with less pointed conversation. Indeed, after their initial exchange, he seemed to have resigned himself and even appeared to relax and take pleasure in the music, which surprised Alienor because she thought he would have been more concerned.

When he retired to his prepared chamber for the night, she told William to put a guard outside his door.

"You think he will try to escape, madam?"

"I do not know, but he seems to have accepted his detention with less complaint than I expected."

"Perhaps his heart is not in it?"

She shook her head. "Far from it—I think he is very concerned. He is a close friend of the archbishop's. He is also a consummate player, and I need to make sure this is not a ruse on his part."

"Perhaps there are duplicate sets of letters. The archbishop must know that a lookout will be kept."

"That is my thought too," Alienor said, "so we must continue to be vigilant. But even if letters do arrive, I suspect they will not be heeded."

William bowed and made to leave, but she caught his arm and gestured him to sit. "Before you go, I want to speak to you on another matter."

"Madam." His expression was attentive and pleasant, but Alienor could tell that he was shielding his doubts and uncertainties.

"I have been thinking about your situation," she said as he

folded his long body onto the bench. "It seems to me that I have been keeping the equivalent of an expensive fast horse in my stables for pulling the plow and carrying goods to market. I know you chaff at the constraints."

"Madam, I…"

"No." She raised her hand to silence him. "You are not being used to your full potential, and that is a waste of your talent and my largesse."

He looked at her with a spark in his eyes—surprise and anticipation, she thought. "Madam, I am content to serve you…"

"No, you are not," she contradicted. "You are willing and loyal, which are different matters. You need more than I can give you. Before the king sailed for England, we discussed the men who would form the nucleus of Harry's household. Harry likes you and you have a talent for educating the squires and young lads in the warrior skills. You are proven in battle, in diplomacy, and in loyal service to my household. I am appointing you, with the king's agreement, to the post of Harry's marshal and his tutor in chivalry when he sails to England to be crowned."

William's complexion grew ruddy. Rising from the bench, he fell to his knees before her. "Madam, you honor me."

"Yes, I do." Smiling, she extended her hand so that he could kiss her ring. "This is to your great advantage. Use it well."

"Does my young lord know?"

"He asked for you when we were discussing who should form his household." Dark amusement entered her voice. "He does not want you training Richard and giving him an edge. I thought about giving you that position but decided it was better for you to serve Harry. You are English by birth; you know their ways and will be of great use to him in that capacity. I also expect you to keep him steady and to the mark—and to report to me on how he fares. Use Wigan as your messenger. He's to be employed as Harry's chancery, and I know he keeps tourney tallies for you."

"Madam."

"I trust you to look after Harry, as does the king. Thus far you have not failed us. Loyalty and good service will take you far, William, but you could go further still. You have it in you to be more than a hearth knight, but it is up to you what you make of the opportunity."

He inhaled deeply, taking in her words, and she saw that he understood very well indeed. She gave him a wide, warm smile like a jewel. Even though she had set him free to leave her, she still had his support for life.

❖❖❖

The bishop of Worcester spent the night without incident, attended Mass in the morning, and then met to converse with his fellow clergy. He continued to treat his house arrest with equanimity. On meeting Marguerite and Harry, he was reserved but courteous, and seemingly unbothered by his situation. Although he showed no inclination to abscond, Alienor continued to have him closely watched and wrote to Henry telling him that the bishop of Worcester was her guest.

A week later another visitor arrived in Caen in the form of Mary de Boulogne, Isabel's sister-in-law, whom Henry had forced out of her convent and into marriage with Matthew of Alsace. Mary had borne her unwanted husband a second daughter in January, and after ten years of marriage had finally obtained her annulment and was seeking to return to the religious life.

The woman who was ushered into Alienor's chamber was like a winter sparrow, thin and small. Her cheeks were hollow, her dark eyes troubled, yet there was a determined set to her jaw, and she had a straight, upright bearing. Her narrow frame was clad in a robe of plain dark wool bagging over a leather belt. A white wimple arranged in severe folds covered her hair and outlined her jaw.

"I wish to cross to England to deal with my affairs and make my peace," she told Alienor. "As one royal woman to another I request safe passage. I have endured ten years in the world." She set her jaw. "My marriage was begun in rape. Never did I consent; it was unlawful from the start. Now, praise God, the Church has finally found its conscience and granted me an annulment. I shall be glad to retire from the world."

"I understand your need, my lady," Alienor said. She was deeply sympathetic toward Mary and guilty because she should have protested more at the time—although Henry had been set on his policy and she doubted it would have changed things. "You are welcome to lodge here for as long as you wish."

"Thank you." Mary folded her hands in her lap, gripping them together until they were a single white knot.

Later, the women dined with the bishop of Worcester. Mary was quiet and dignified, and Alienor could see in her the powerful Mother Abbess she had been before Henry had ripped that life from her. Mary did not ask why the bishop was lodging here, even though she must have known the reason. She was quiet and introspective, although she and the bishop spoke briefly upon theological matters.

The next day Mary departed with her small retinue, bidding Alienor a formal farewell in the courtyard before mounting her white mule. In her dark dress and plain woolen cloak, her lips pursed. The impression Alienor received was that Mary dwelled in a world from which all the colors of joy had been sucked out. All that remained was a gray and steely resolution, and, in a way, Alienor knew how she felt.

# 39

## CAEN, JUNE 1170

*T*HE FINAL PREPARATIONS WERE IN HAND FOR HARRY TO GO TO England. The weather had turned fair and fine; the wind was in the right direction, and the crossing of the Narrow Sea was set fair.

Seamstresses and tailors had been working day and night to complete the coronation robes. Marguerite, still unaware that she would not be accompanying her young husband, was flushed with anticipation almost to the point of giddiness. Although clothes usually meant little to her, she was excited about her cloth-of-gold coronation gown, ermine cloak, and gem-embroidered shoes, and twirled around the chamber after the most recent fitting, her eyes shining as she chattered about being anointed queen in Westminster Abbey.

Alienor thought Marguerite looked as if the clothes were wearing her, but even if it was impossible to make a silk purse out of a sow's ear, the magnificence was the message. Alienor felt a glimmer of satisfaction that Marguerite even in her finest moment would never look as glorious as she had done on her own coronation day with Harry curled in her womb. Even now, Marguerite would be insignificant beside Harry's splendor—if and when she was crowned.

Marguerite eventually changed into her everyday garments. The women were folding the coronation robes into a cedarwood chest when William Marshal arrived to speak to Alienor. The young knight had taken on a new gravitas since being promoted to his position in Harry's retinue. He had been dealing with loading the ships and the logistics involved with the journey, and the heat of the summer sun had flushed his face and put tawny streaks in his deep brown hair. Some of Alienor's ladies sent coy glances his way, of which he was obviously aware but did not acknowledge beyond a slight bow in their direction.

"Is all going well?" Alienor asked.

"Yes, madam." He bowed to Marguerite too and she smiled at him. Like everyone else, she relaxed under William's charm.

"While I was at the dockside, an English ship arrived with a messenger aboard." He turned to indicate the man standing outside the doorway.

Alienor bade him come forward and took the packet. He knelt and handed it to her. Reading the contents, she pursed her lips. "You may go," she said, "but return by compline for the reply."

As he made his obeisance and departed, she turned to William. "I know now why Roger of Worcester was so amiable about being lodged here," she said. "The letters of excommunication have reached England."

His gaze filled with chagrin. "I am sorry, madam. I have been vigilant, but obviously not vigilant enough."

"It is not your fault. The archbishop sent the letters with the lady of Boulogne." She gave a short laugh. "All the time she was here, paying an obligatory visit and requesting permission to go to England, she was sitting on those excommunication documents!"

William winced, but appreciation glinted in his eyes. "What will happen now?"

"Nothing. The king will still go forward with the coronation because he is set on it. Doubtless he will burn the letters and claim they never arrived, but it will have given the Countess of Blois satisfaction to serve the notice, and Becket will have scored a moral victory by winning through the blockade. There was other news in the letter too." She looked over her shoulder, but Marguerite was playing with her small terrier dog out of earshot. "The king deems it unwise to crown Marguerite. She is not to sail to England with Harry but will stay here with me for now."

William raised his brows. "Does my young lord know?"

"No," Alienor said. "He does not need to be told until the morrow. I trust your discretion."

"Indeed you have it, madam, but I am sorry for the princess."

"This is but a momentary delay. She will still be crowned."

"Yes, madam." His expression neutral, William bowed and took his leave.

❖❖❖

Next morning at dawn, Harry embarked for England, the sunrise marking a path across the sea as it crested the horizon in a flash of gold. Many of the entourage had not retired until late because of the light summer evening, and heavy-eyed squires and knights curled up on deck and went back to sleep the moment they were on board.

Alienor embraced Harry, who had just stifled a yawn. His breath smelled of sour wine and the cardamom pods he had been chewing to sweeten his mouth. "God speed you," she said. "When I see you again, you will be an anointed king." The last two words gave her a frisson of pleasure. "Be mindful of that, and live up to your part."

"Of course, Mama." His tone was dismissive. She could feel his impatience to be away and pursuing masculine things. He had been thoroughly equable when told that Marguerite was not to accompany him; indeed, even a little pleased, because it meant his coronation was an opportunity for him to shine on his own, and he would not have to share any accolades. Alienor only wished she was accompanying him to see his moment of triumph, but there would be other occasions.

"Go with my blessing," she said, kissed him again, and watched him board the ship that would take him to his destiny.

❖❖❖

Marguerite dragged her coronation dress out of its chest, hurled it on the floor, and stamped on the yards of gold silk. "You knew!"

She sobbed. "You knew! You betrayed me! What use is this gown now?" She kicked the dress. Her small white dog took the opportunity to dart in and attack the cloth, tearing at it with his sharp little teeth and snarling.

Alienor eyed her daughter-in-law with surprise and speculation. She would not have thought stoical Marguerite the kind to throw a tantrum. "It is for the best," she said. "It is because of the dispute with the archbishop of Canterbury. The king has a dispensation to have Harry anointed by a bishop of his choice, but that dispensation does not include you. It would not be binding, and your father would never permit that. Your coronation has to be above reproach. It will happen later on once everything is settled."

"But it was planned for now!" Marguerite said tearfully. "I do not trust you. I shall never trust you again. I shall write to my father and he will come with an army and soldiers and he will deal with all of you! You will all pay!"

"That is enough!" Alienor said, her anger rising. "Matters of state are involved of which you know nothing. If your parents by marriage and your husband see fit to delay the coronation then so be it. Your loyalty is to us. I thought better of you than to behave like a thwarted child."

Marguerite's shoulders heaved. She jutted her jaw and stared at Alienor without apology like a pugnacious little dog.

"We shall talk in a while when you have calmed down and are able to have a sensible discussion about this," Alienor said and left the room.

Returning an hour later, Alienor found Marguerite in a state of quieter but simmering resentment. The dress had been picked up and draped over a clothing pole, although bits of straw and a snag from the dog's teeth were evidence of the abuse it had received. Marguerite held the dog in her lap and stroked it repetitively.

Alienor sat beside her on the bench. "If you are to be queen of England you must behave as befits that role," she said.

"Yes, madam," Marguerite replied, still stroking her dog. Her voice was dull and flat. Alienor remembered being a similar age and having Louis's mother, this child's grandmother, telling her what to do for the good of the country so as not to disrupt matters of policy. How powerless and angry she had felt. And she had been a deal more knowing than Marguerite. She understood what the girl beside her was feeling but could also now empathize with her former mother-in-law.

"I still want to write to my father," Marguerite said defiantly.

Alienor restrained her irritation. "Do as you will, but this is only a delay. You shall be crowned queen, I promise."

Marguerite cuddled the dog, and it licked her face.

"I could have done nothing to prevent this even had I wanted to. You have a deal to learn about the position and power of a queen—what is possible and what is not. Your loyalty to your husband is commendable and it must see you through now."

Marguerite's set expression remained, but she nodded stiffly. "Yes, madam."

"Good." Alienor took the girl's hand in hers, even though it was not her natural inclination to do so. The flesh was clammy and soft. "I know this is hard for you, but you are young; you will have your time."

❖ ❖ ❖

A fortnight later, following Harry's coronation, Henry returned to Normandy, landing at Barfleur and from there heading to Vendôme to speak with Louis, who had already mustered an army and was preparing to invade Henry's territories over the insult offered to his daughter. He demanded to know why she had not been crowned with Harry and insisted that the situation with Becket be tackled once and for all. Isabel had arrived from England with the royal contingent and she joined Alienor at Fontevraud with John and Joanna before moving on to Poitiers.

Alienor milked Isabel for the details of Harry's coronation, eager to know everything.

"Harry was magnificent. You would have been so proud of him," Isabel said as she and Alienor sat by the hearth drinking wine. "He looked every inch a king, so tall and handsome. He was made to wear a crown. Not only did he know his part, he became it. The crowds adored him. I have never heard such a roar of acclaim before."

Alienor smiled with pride and a certain satisfied pleasure. That accolade would have pleased Henry and yet lodged like a splinter in his heart, because the tribute was for his son, not him.

Isabel said ruefully, "I remember him as a baby in the cradle, so tiny. It was so strange to see him almost a man."

"Time passes too swiftly," Alienor said, remembering the grip of his infant hand around her smallest finger.

"I am truly sorry you could not be there to see his anointing, but I know you had other duties."

Alienor made a face. "Indeed, for what use, other than to be Henry's scapegoat. Did you see Mary de Boulogne?"

"Yes, she visited me and we prayed together. She was worried that I had been coerced into my own marriage, but I told her I was happy with Hamelin and I hoped she would be able to live in peace now that she could return to life in a convent." Isabel contemplated her cup. "She is very bitter about what happened: she will not forgive, and she will not forget."

Alienor shrugged. "Would you in her position? I know I would not. I wish her peace and I will pray for her."

Isabel touched the cross around her neck. "I do so every time I kneel in church. I so wish that the king and the archbishop could be reconciled."

Alienor raised a skeptical eyebrow. "Hell will freeze over first, I tell you that now."

"Hamelin says Henry has come to a boulder in the road with no way around. He no longer knows what to do to reach the archbishop. But they were such allies when he was chancellor."

"Well, it's either blame the man or blame God," Alienor said grimly. "I agree with Hamelin. I do not know how they will resolve this because neither man will back down. It has gone beyond the peacemakers. It will only end when one of them dies, and that includes the pope."

Isabel gasped and looked shocked, but Alienor was unrepentant. "It is the truth," she said. "I do not know Thomas well, but I know my husband. At least in Poitiers, I am well out of the argument."

❖❖❖

Alienor returned by gradual stages to Poitou accompanied by Isabel. The women spent a fortnight at the ducal hunting lodge at Talmont and rode out most days with the hawks. Alienor chose a new gyrfalcon from the mews and named her Blaunchet. Watching her climb into the blue and carve the air with her wings, and strike her prey with ruthless accuracy, Alienor's heart filled with joy and she remembered that she too had been born to soar.

Soon she would go to Poitiers, but now was a time for replenishment in the company of her friend while allowing Richard time off the leash before he settled into the duties of learning to rule a duchy.

Even so, amid the leisure, messengers rode constantly back and forth on the business of government. One morning in early September, Alienor sat in the garden at Talmont enjoying the perfume of the late summer roses, the most recent correspondence in her hand. She turned to Marguerite, who was sitting on a turf seat next to her, and forced a smile. "The king has agreed that when Archbishop Becket returns to England, another coronation ceremony will be held at Westminster, and you will be anointed queen."

Marguerite's eyes brightened. "Does the letter say when that will be?"

"Before the Christmas feast," Alienor replied.

Marguerite's entire posture became more erect. She lifted her head and looked imperiously around, as if she was already balancing the weight of a crown.

Isabel, who was sitting on Marguerite's other side, touched the girl's hand. "That is wonderful news. At last we have a concord."

Alienor looked down at the letter. "Henry has also given the archbishop leave to reprimand those bishops who performed Harry's coronation." That too was a powerful concession from

Henry; it also served to shift the blame from his shoulders. Nothing would be his fault.

Isabel's smile faded and her expression became serious but not dismayed. "At least honor will be satisfied."

Alienor made a noncommittal sound. What Henry had not done was give Becket the kiss of peace, which meant he had not forgiven him and was not prepared to put the past aside. What Henry was saying was that Thomas was free to come to England but that he would not grant him a safe conduct or guarantee his safety once there. On his own head be it. While she was deliberating what to say, her chamberlain arrived accompanied by a messenger, and their grave faces made her heart leap with anxiety.

"What is it?" Her thoughts flew to her children. "What has happened?"

The servant knelt and presented her with a packet bearing Hamelin's seal. "Madam, the king has been taken grievously ill at Domfront of a fever, and he is in peril of his life."

Swiftly she broke the seal and read what Hamelin had written. He said she must come as swiftly as she could. Henry had made his will, dividing up his lands between his sons, and if she wanted to see him alive, she had better come now.

"Dear God," Isabel whispered, signing her breast.

"I must go to him." Alienor rose to her feet, her mind already on the journey. "Let prayers be said in every church in the land and offerings made that he might recover." She often thought she would be better off without Henry, but not yet. Their sons were still very young for rule, and predators would be waiting for their moment: hyenas circling a dying lion. Only let the youths come into their full majority, able to lead men, and then God could do what he wished with him.

❖❖❖

Alienor rode into Domfront a week after receiving the news and found Henry weak and febrile but recovering, closely watched by his physicians. The wound in his thigh caused several years ago by a horse kick had become infected and brought him down with a debilitating fever before finally erupting and subsiding into a leaking sore that was being dressed daily with herbs and unguents.

Alienor entered his chamber and found him propped up in bed, gaunt and hollow-eyed. Removing her cloak, she sat on a stool at his side. "I came as soon as I received the summons," she said. "I am relieved to find you still alive."

He gave her a heavy, bloodshot look. Beneath his eyes, the skin was pale indigo with exhaustion. "You have always been a good liar," he said hoarsely.

"I am not lying." She took the cup of wine a servant presented to her. "It would be inconvenient if you were to die now. Our sons are not old enough to take the reins, and I do not wish to be put in the same position as your mother and have to fight for every last piece of ground. I prayed for you night and day as we rode." She offered him her cup and he took it and drank. It shocked her to see how his wrist shook with the effort, and the emotion that ran through her shocked her too. It was like dropping a precious crystal goblet and then receiving cuts as you picked up the shards. Just when you thought there were no shards left to hurt you, you would discover another needle-thin spike and you would bleed.

"If you are going to die, at least leave it until Harry has attained his majority," she said.

He grunted with sour humor. "I am touched that you raced to my bedside in such haste. I will comfort myself with your concern for my well-being and not be cynical enough to think you came in order to exert political control in event of my death."

"Think what you will, but I am here—as I was the last time you were sick unto death. Back then you thanked me, but I have received enough at your hand not to expect that now. I came because I am worried for you."

His expression grew peevish. "I do not need your pity or concern."

"You may not think you need it, Henry, but you do. This is a warning sign…"

Hectic color flushed his cheeks and his eyes flashed with temper. "Not you too—do not you dare! I am sick of churchmen telling me I should make my peace with my perfidious archbishop and whispering that this is my entire fault and I should kiss the treacherous whoreson. Hell will freeze over first, I swear to you!" He paused to suck breath into his lungs, panting as if he had run uphill in his armor.

Alienor continued as if he had not interrupted her. "…a warning sign that you need to ease your burdens. Accept that others are capable of carrying them and let them go. If you do not, they will kill you." She took the cup from his trembling fingers. "You need peace and you do not have it. Look at where you have been brought. Unless you change, you will die."

"Since when have you grown so wise?"

"I am not wise, merely sad and experienced." She rose from the stool. "I will leave you to sleep and to think upon what I have said."

Henry turned his head away. "Go back to Poitiers," he said. "I do not need you here."

"You do," she said, "but you do not know it. You never have."

She left the room and had to stop outside for a moment, her hand to her mouth. She was shocked at how sick and frail he was. Last time it had happened, he had been a young man, well able to fight it off, but now he was a similar age to his own father when he had died, and she had seen the fear in his eyes. They both knew he was still fighting and that he might not survive.

Hamelin was waiting for her and kissed her cheek. "Sister," he said. His eyes were bruised hollows revealing his exhaustion, and his usually neat appearance was unkempt.

"I did not expect him to look like that," she said. "Like a starved child, or an old man." She shuddered.

"We all thought he was going to die," Hamelin said somberly. "And the fact that in his lucid moments he was sincere about his will…" He broke off for a moment and rubbed his palms over his face. "He needs time to recuperate," he said. "We all do."

"He will have to delegate," Alienor said firmly.

Hamelin massaged his temples. "That is going to be difficult."

"It has to be done. He is not fit to make decisions as he is."

"I do not deny you are right," Hamelin said. "I just do not know how it will be accomplished. There have already been wild rumors flying around that he has died." His eyes filled with pain. "He is my brother, and I do not want it to become a truth."

Alienor looked away. She did not know what she wanted anymore, but Henry was so sick and vulnerable that, almost against her will, she was forced to feel pity and compassion for him. "Such rumors are dangerous. They will lead to unrest," she said. "We must tell everyone he is alive and recovering. It must be made very clear indeed."

Hamelin nodded. "I agree. I have already sent out messengers with that news, and I have left the sickroom door open when he is awake, so that people can see for themselves, but he will not be capable of taking up his duties for a while yet."

"Then for now he has no choice but to delegate."

❖❖❖

For the next few weeks, Alienor tended Henry as he slowly recovered. There were setbacks where his fever rose again or his stamina gave out and he would spend most of the day asleep, but slowly he clawed his way back to a semblance of health.

For Alienor it became not so much a period of truce between them while he got better but a loop of time cut out of their lives, like a meander in a river. For a short while, they could set the past and future aside and exist in the moment. She sat at his bedside as she had done the last time he had been dangerously ill. She kept him entertained, cared for his welfare, and assisted with the deal-ings of the court. Fortunately there was a lull in matters requiring serious political attention. Henry had patched up a ragged peace with Thomas Becket, who had sent his good wishes and prayers for Henry's recovery, to which Henry had raised a cynical eyebrow.

She sat with Henry in the window embrasure where they had earlier played a desultory game of chess. Although dressed, he was wrapped in his cloak and was occasionally sipping from a cup of hot sugared wine.

"Becket says he will join me in Rouen in November for the

crossing to England." Henry glanced at the letter he had just been reading. "Then we can arrange to have Harry and Marguerite crowned together."

"Will you give him the kiss of peace?" Alienor inquired, toying with one of the chess pieces.

"Not unless I must."

"And if it comes to that?"

He shrugged. "We shall see." An obdurate look entered his eyes and Alienor did not press the issue.

They moved on to discuss the matter of their second daughter's marriage. Before Henry's illness a union had been mooted between Alie and the fifteen-year-old Alfonso of Castile. "It is a good match," Henry said. "It will give us security on that border, and Alie will be a queen."

Alienor inclined her head. She was amenable to the match because the bridegroom was a similar age to Alie, not thirty years older as in the case of Matilda's husband. They would have time to grow up together, and at a southern court. It still brought its own set of difficulties and there was the heartache of parting from another daughter to distant lands. What price an empire spread far and wide?

"The betrothal should take place before winter," Henry said. "Let them come to Poitiers or Bordeaux."

For a short while there was silence between them, but not noticeable because court musicians were playing softly in the background. Several times Henry inhaled as if about to start a conversation, and then changed his mind. Alienor was content to wait and to think upon practical matters pertaining to the betrothal. When it should be, how much work there was to do in preparation.

Eventually, Henry set down his cup. "My father was my age when he died. I know I could now be lying in my tomb. Who knows when God will take us?"

"Indeed." She eyed him with interest, wondering what this was about.

He chewed his lip and then said abruptly, "I have been thinking about going on a pilgrimage for the good of my soul before I return to my duties."

Alienor blinked in surprise. Henry was only devout when he had to be and in pragmatic ways. "I suppose it might aid your recuperation," she said.

"It will also show how devout I am—that even while I argue with my archbishop, I have a suitable respect for God. Louis takes all the acclaim for piety. It seems to me I should have something with which to reciprocate."

She ought to have known. Here was the practicality in his religion. Killing two birds with a single stone. "Have you somewhere in mind?" she asked.

Henry folded his arms. "I thought perhaps Compostela."

"No, not there!" Alienor shook her head. "My father took that road and did not return, and Louis has already been there anyway." She took a sip from his cup and felt the hot sweetness warm her throat.

"Then where do you suggest?"

Alienor pursed her lips and considered. "Perhaps the shrine of Our Lady at Rocamadour in the Limousin? It is holy to Saint Martial, who has the power to cure fistulas—so it is said."

For a time Henry said nothing. He continued to drink his wine and absently rubbed his thigh. She could see he was tiring again and needed to sleep. "Your courtiers can bring you messages, and it is not that far from Poitiers or Bordeaux," she said, softly persuasive. She gestured gracefully with her wrist, allowing her silk sleeve to whisper and send out an earthy, musky perfume. "You could meet informally with friends and vassals on the road if you wished."

Henry narrowed his eyes but not in rejection. "I will think on it," he said.

Alienor dipped her head and did not press the issue. He would have to believe it was his own idea. But she resolved to begin preparations.

❖❖❖

Henry, Alienor, and their entourage set out for the shrine of Our Lady at Rocamadour, journeying by slow stages. They spent the heat of the day resting in castles or monasteries in the shade and rode in the cool early mornings and during the hour before sunset and on through soft blue twilight. Nothing arduous, everything measured.

Henry traveled in simple garments. A fresh linen shirt each day, loose upon his body, a plain tunic, and a pilgrim's straw hat. The fact that he was riding a fine dappled palfrey and accompanied by a large entourage marked him as a person of importance, but he eschewed the trappings of kingship. "Harry has borrowed all my gold and jewels anyway for that progress of his," he told Alienor when the subject cropped up as they rode. "He wanted to make a full impression on the English as a shining king."

Alienor laughed. She had mellowed toward Henry over the last few days; for the moment, they were still lost in the meander of the river. "And you think he will give them back?" Following his coronation, their eldest son had gone on a progress around England, a sort of pilgrimage of his own, intended to acquaint him with his future subjects.

Henry chuckled but then grimaced. "The boy does have a taste for fine things, I admit, and money trickles through his fingers faster than spring meltwater."

"Ah, but you indulge him in that vice."

"He is the son of the wealthiest king in Christendom," Henry replied, "and a future king himself. He has much to learn about government and kingship. He does the feting part very well indeed, even if he does need to curb his tongue on occasion. I have let him start with parades and furbelows because that is a simple task and he is suited to it, but I shall ease him into the rest and give him responsibility when he is ready."

Alienor made a wry face, knowing that the "ready" would be later rather than sooner because Henry would not want to let go. He might say he was willing, but his hands would have to be pried off the reins. "Did you not lead an army to England when you were his age?"

"Hah, I was younger than him!"

"Of course you were," Alienor said sweetly.

Henry shot her an irritated look. "I had to battle every step of the way for my kingdom. My parents fought for that right and I knew from an early age it was my duty to continue where they left off. Every fiber of my being was focused on achieving my goal." He gazed into the distance. "I was fourteen when I crossed the Narrow Sea to bolster my mother's failing cause. She thought me a hindrance, but that wasn't true. I rallied the barons to my support. They saw me and they saw hope." He struck his chest. "Without my intervention then, I would not be king now."

"She told me the story," Alienor said. "How you had no money to pay your ragged band of mercenaries and when she refused to help you in order to teach you a lesson, you went to Stephen and asked him to pay you to leave the country."

Henry grinned. "Yes, and Stephen did. It was typically generous of him, the fool, even if he wanted me out of the way. But by then I had infiltrated his barons and shown them what a good prospect I was for the future." His smile faded. "I do not want the same for my sons. I want them to inherit what is theirs in right and dignity without wasting all that time. When I was Harry's age, I was constantly beset, sometimes not knowing where I was going to find the next meal or afford nails to shoe my horse, let alone pay my men. I lived hand to mouth and on the run. I don't want that for my sons. I want them to rule in splendor when their time comes."

"Assuredly they will."

He gave Alienor an opaque look. "I suppose you heard that at Harry's coronation, I undertook to serve him at table because it was his coronation day and I was proud of him. I said it was not often that a king served another king, and Harry replied against all grace that it was not uncommon for the son of a count to serve that of a king."

"Yes, I heard. Isabel told me," Alienor replied. "That was a little too clever, I thought."

"Yes, indeed, and I was angry," Henry said. "But do you know what? Part of me was satisfied and even pleased to have bred this creature of privilege—a privilege that was never mine because I was too busy carving out my inheritance in bloody handholds on naked rock. He shines, Alienor, and everyone sees that he shines."

Her heart swelled with pride in which there was a piercing shard of affection for the man at her side. Another piece of the broken crystal.

"Of course he will have to be ruled and shown the right way, but let him have his moment in the sun that I never had at his age. He has the time that I did not."

"Indeed," Alienor said, "but you must let him become a man, which means giving him responsibility and allowing him to make his own decisions—and mistakes."

"I know that," he said testily. "I am not a fool. I plan very carefully for the future of my heirs."

Which meant involving them as little as possible, she thought. A child should never dictate to its parent, but sometimes Henry's rule was too rigid.

The road turned and a distant gorge came into view, and, clinging to the rugged cliffside of creamy-gray rock, the shrine of Our Lady of Rocamadour.

A different kind of silence fell like a gauze veil over the heat haze. Henry exhaled softly through parted lips and murmured an involuntary word of astonishment. Alienor gazed at the buildings, amazed and awed at the way they seemed to hang suspended between heaven and earth, like an eagle's aerie but for humankind.

According to legend, Saint Amadour had been tutor to the Christ child before coming to Gaul. His mummified body had been discovered here eight years ago. A Madonna statue, carved from ebony wood, had been found beside the corpse and was said to perform healing miracles, especially for those afflicted with fistulas and old wounds that would not heal. Here too thrust into a crevice in the rock and held there by a loop of iron chain, was the sword Durendal, which had belonged to the great and tragic hero Roland, defender of the pass at Roncesvalles against the Saracen horde.

"The hair has risen on the nape of my neck," Henry said and he shivered. As if compelled, he dismounted and knelt in the dust of the road to pray, and everyone scrambled to follow suit. The stones were rough under Alienor's knees as she clasped her hands. Henry appeared to be genuinely moved by the sight of the shrine, and she looked at him with speculation for a moment before she bowed her head. She dared not hope a change was in the air, but she could pray.

The pilgrim party continued on its way as the sun dwindled westward and the dying light splashed the rock with tints of ruby and fire. By the time they arrived at the pilgrim hostel at the foot of the rock, it was late dusk and the stones were almost purple.

❖❖❖

Visiting the shrine involved climbing more than two hundred stairs—on the knees with prayers on each step. Henry and Alienor began the ordeal early next morning after confession and Mass and continued until noon, without food or drink, by which time they were sore and exhausted, Henry especially. His lips were compressed to a thin line, and Alienor could see the strain of effort in his jaw. However, the deed was a powerful symbol of humility and his will carried him through. Hamelin followed immediately behind Henry, ready to catch him if he swayed or fainted, but there was no need. Alienor heard Isabel muttering prayers as they climbed each step, entreating forgiveness for her sins, although Alienor could not imagine Isabel having any to confess.

Henry prostrated himself before the shrine of the Black Madonna. Alienor suspected it might be by way of taking a respite, but it looked like piety to the priests, and she joined him, kissing the cold, stone flags under her lips. The scent of incense pervaded the space and made her light-headed. The relief at having climbed so far and achieved her goal became a sense of achievement and, as she looked at the wise, all-knowing half smile on the ebony visage of the Madonna of Rocamadour, she was infused with a deep feeling of spiritual tranquillity and oneness.

Later, she stood beside Henry and gazed out over the valley misted with cloud below, and it was indeed like hanging between heaven and earth. In the blue above, an eagle soared and Alienor watched its outspread wings, a deep feeling of exultation coursing through her, straight as a lance, and with her spiritual eyes open, she knew it was a portent. Henry watched the eagle too. Then, after a moment, he turned and left, tugging Hamelin away with him to go and study the sword in the rock, withdrawing into practical things.

Isabel joined Alienor and the women stood side by side, gazing across the vastness of the clouded gorge.

"Henry seems ready to rejoin the world," Isabel said. A tress of hair had escaped her wimple and the cloud had frosted it hoar-gray.

"Indeed. He will not want to linger here now. It will all be back to the business of ruling and controlling." The eagle had vanished and the mist unfurled gray tendrils across the sky. "I thought we might have more time."

"More time for what?"

Alienor gave a poignant sigh. "My first husband could not tear himself away from pilgrimages. We spent a full year in Jerusalem after everyone else had returned to France while he traipsed around shrines, and Abbé Suger's pleas that he come home grew ever more desperate. But Henry has never been one for such seeking. Things are only of value if they are practical. He would rather study a sword than open himself to God's vastness. For a while, I thought that the severity of his illness had given him a different perspective—perhaps it did for a while—but now he is better, and he sees this visit as a matter accomplished, his dues rendered. He will return to the world—and to his old ways, I have no doubt."

# 40

## Bures-le-Roi, Normandy, Christmas 1170

ALIENOR CUPPED HER HANDS AROUND A GOBLET OF SPICED wine and shivered. Rain spattered against the shutters and the wind that whistled through the gaps was icy but not quite cold enough to turn the rain to snow. The roof of the log shelter was leaky and had soaked the wood. Fires belched acrid smoke and gave out meager heat. Everyone wore their heaviest winter garments and stood around in shivering huddles, muttering about the weather.

Harry and his entourage might have alleviated the gloom, but they were keeping court at Westminster. John and Joanna had arrived from Fontevraud to spend the Christmas season with their parents, and that at least brought some cheer to the occasion, although there was a gap at Alienor's side where Alie would usually have kept her company. This year, Alie would be celebrating the Christmas feast with the Castilian court in Burgos, and the mountain passes would all be closed with snow.

Henry, fully recovered, was restless. He had intended going to England at the same time as his troublesome archbishop, but that had been impossible because on his return from Rocamadour he had had to deal with problems on the French border where King Louis had been fomenting trouble. The dispute was still rumbling on, but a truce had been agreed over the winter. Henry had chosen to spend Christmas at Bures and cross to England in the New Year. Becket was already at Canterbury.

Alienor watched four-year-old John play with some bone discs strung on a wooden frame. He was clacking them across, counting to himself and then counting them back, adding and subtracting, making patterns. Alienor was amused, imagining him like a little clerk at an exchequer board. In typical fashion he was secretive about his play and not keen to share. He preferred to sit in a corner, his back to the wall, and observe people, and the looks he gave them were intense, calculating, and not at all childlike.

Alienor called him over to eat a slice of sugared pear from the box at her side and listen to the tale that Master Matthew the story-teller was preparing to recite. John set his lips and for a moment looked mutinous, but then he carefully hid his toy under a cushion and came to her. Alienor lifted him onto the bench beside her and smoothed his hair in a tender gesture. Joanna pressed against her other side and cradled her soft cloth doll, a look of anticipation brightening her face as she waited for Master Matthew to begin.

Master Matthew hailed from the Welsh borders and recounted his tales—of which he had a vast repertoire—to the accompani-ment of a small boxwood harp from which he plucked notes like clear jewels. He had sparkling brown eyes and a thin, expressive face that could change on the instant to suit his tale, one moment full of mirth as he narrated the story of a talking donkey, but turning to menace as he told another about a fearsome monster that came from the moors and tore people limb from limb before devouring them until finally a hero was found to slay the creature. Joanna cuddled up to Alienor with delicious fear. John was fasci-nated and alert but not afraid. He thought it might be interesting to capture and chain such a creature and bend it to his will to use it as a deterrent against others.

When Matthew had finished, Richard came forward, lute in hand, and sang a hymn to the Virgin Mary and the Christ child. His voice was at that deep, bell-toned stage that meant it would soon break, and Alienor's eyes filled with tears. Caught in the fleeting moment between boy and man, Richard's beauty was heart-stopping.

As the last note thrummed and resonated, her chamberlain tiptoed over to her to murmur in her ear that the bishops of York, London, and Salisbury had arrived and were requesting an audience.

Alienor praised Richard and gave him a gold bezant for his song, which pleased him mightily. "Admit them at once," she said. "It is too foul a day for them to be waiting without a fire. I assume the king has been summoned?"

"Yes, madam."

Alienor sent John and Joanna off with their nurses but allowed Richard to stay. She had a feeling of foreboding because for the three bishops to have risked a crossing in such difficult weather spoke of necessity. It must have something to do with Thomas Becket, and that was ominous.

The bishops arrived, saturated from their rough sea voyage followed by their ride in wild weather. Their draggled state reminded Alienor of a clutch of soggy poultry, huddled and muttering. She rose to greet them and ushered them to the hearth, commanding servants to bring towels and hot wine.

Henry strode into the room on a new flurry of cold air from the stairwell and stared at the dripping men in astonishment. "What is this?" he demanded.

Robert of Pont L'Évêque, Archbishop of York, ceased mopping his face with a towel and bowed. In the heat from the fire, his cloak had begun to steam. "There are grave tidings from England, sire, and that is why we have been forced to come to you in person."

"What sort of tidings?" Henry snapped. "Don't beat around the bush."

The archbishop's chins wobbled with indignation. "The archbishop of Canterbury has declared us excommunicated. He read out the sentence during his sermon at Canterbury, and to the entire congregation. He has also been putting it about that your eldest son has been falsely crowned and should be deposed. He claims he has authority from the pope to excommunicate whomsoever he pleases—excluding you and the queen."

"His knights are riding around the country raising sedition," Gilbert Foliot interjected. His voice was gravelly with a heavy cold. "They have been urging folk to rise up and see justice done."

Alienor stifled an exclamation of shock. Becket was stubborn and bitter, but she would not have thought him capable of treason.

A muscle bunched in Henry's cheek. "Then by God's eyes, am I next?" he demanded. "Where does this man stop? Or perhaps he doesn't?"

The archbishop of York handed the by now saturated towel to one of Alienor's servants. "We have come to bring you this news all as one, but it is not for us to tell you what to do now. You must take counsel and decide how to deal with the situation. We must go and petition the pope to overturn the sentence. For now, we are excommunicates, and Christian men must shun us or risk excommunication themselves."

Gilbert Foliot said forcefully, "Sire, while Thomas lives, you will have neither peace nor quiet nor see good days. He is set on a path of contention where the only rule that matters is his own."

Robert de Beaumont, the new young earl of Leicester who was attending on Henry, spoke out with conviction. "The archbishop of Canterbury has shown he is a dangerous man, sire. He ought to be made an outlaw for this and cast out himself."

"Indeed, he should be hanged on a gibbet," said Ingelram de Bohun, who was related to the bishop of Salisbury and plainly appalled at the sorry state of his elderly kinsman. Looking around, he received vigorous nods of approbation. "No priest should be allowed to cause insurrection like this. It is treason."

Alienor's breathing quickened. If Becket was truly raising riot in England and threatening to depose her son, he had to be stopped.

Henry's chest inflated and fury blazed in his eyes. "What miserable drones and traitors have I nourished at my court who now let their lord be treated with such shameful contempt by a...a lowborn clerk! A man I have raised from the dust, who has eaten my bread and grown rich on my largesse. Now he draws up his heels to kick me in the teeth!"

The mood was becoming ugly. Alienor could see men turning dark looks on the three disheveled bishops. It would only take one step more to turn them into scapegoats. The tension was such that any churchman was fair game and Henry, in his current mood, would not help them.

"Come, my lords," she said, raising her voice above the muttering. "I will find you a chamber where you may recover from your journey and your ordeal. I will have food put outside your door. In the meantime, as you have said, the king will discuss matters with his advisers."

❖ ❖ ❖

Alienor came to Henry's private chamber, walking calmly past the squires and attendants who stood outside, looking concerned and uncertain. No one prevented her, but she saw the exchanged glances.

Outside, the rain still spattered against the shutters and the candles guttered in an icy draft. Two had blown out and the smell of singed wick caught at the back of her nose. Henry was pacing the room like a demon: chest heaving, eyes glittering. She saw the overturned chair and the torn bedcover. A red starburst of wine dripped down one wall, and on the floor beneath it, a dented silver-gilt cup lay on its side.

"Throwing things around in a temper will not improve matters," she said.

"If you have come to lecture me, then get out," Henry snarled.

Alienor picked up the fallen cup and poured wine into it, pretending to be calm, although she was alert to the violence in him. "I have long since given up lecturing you. I might as well talk to the wall—and receive the same treatment you have just meted to that cup. This concerns me as much as it does you. I have paid little heed to the archbishop's ranting before now, but when he threatens our son and says he will depose him, and when he excommunicates the bishops who crowned him, then it is an insult too far." She gave the cup to Henry and bit her tongue on the admonition not to throw it at the wall this time.

"He will not rant for much longer," Henry growled. "I am sending de Mandeville and de Humez to England with their knights to seize him and put him under house arrest. I shall set the thing in motion at first light, and Thomas will reap what he sows."

Alienor gave a cautious nod of approval. Thomas Becket had overstepped the line and had to be contained, but it was a risk because it escalated matters. It was disappointing too. She had thought Henry and Becket had been coming closer to a truce.

"I gave him the world," Henry said bitterly. "I raised him from his petty merchant background and he spits in my face, and I do not understand why."

"He wants what you cannot give him, and you want what he will not give you. But…I sincerely think he has gone mad if what we have just heard is true."

"Oh, it's true," Henry sneered. "He would do anything to keep a grip on his rights as archbishop of Canterbury, even down to deposing our son—even down to deposing me!" He drank back the wine and slammed the goblet on the table this time. "I cannot make the man see reason. I need the pope to revoke that sentence of excommunication and then return him to exile. If that does not happen, I shall confine him so closely that he will never see the sun again. I will not have him and his minions riding around causing sedition." He waved his bunched fist. "You see what he does to my lawful bishops?"

"For that I do not care, but I care what he might do to Harry."

"You don't care what he does to me?"

"No, I do not. You have made your own bed of nails in which to lie, but I do care about the insult to kingship and to our line. The quicker this is dealt with the better."

They looked at each other, linked in common purpose, but in a bond still rough with the friction of hostility. "On the first ship to England on the next tide," he said.

There was no reason for her to stay, and he did not encourage her. She left him to his business and ignored the servants who knelt in obeisance as she collected her maid and swept past.

Halfway back to her own chamber, she stopped, suddenly aware of hooded figures in the darkness, the clink of sword fittings and rustle of cloth, men talking in low voices. In the smoky torchlight she recognized Reginald FitzUrse and William de Tracy, both of whom had been sworn in service to Becket when he was chancellor. Were they deserting Henry? Plotting treason? They had recently been vociferous in their oaths of support, but that meant nothing. Things were often not what they seemed.

She advanced to block their path and for a moment there was panic as they reached for their hilts, then dropped to their knees, realizing whom they faced. The fear in their expressions mirrored her own.

"What are you about, messires?" she demanded.

FitzUrse licked his lips. "We are on a mission for the king, madam. I cannot tell you what it is."

Her heart pounded in her chest. An icy draft blew along the ground and fluttered the hem of her cloak. She was cold already, and his reply made her colder still. She considered her options. She could raise the household and make a public outcry. She could march back to Henry and demand to know what was happening, or she could be blind.

"Go," she said with a brusque gesture. "We have not seen you." She threw Marchisa a warning look.

The knights rose, bowed, and melted stealthily into the night. Jaw chattering, Alienor almost ran back to her chamber, where she ordered Marchisa to bolt the door. By mutual assent, neither woman spoke of what they had seen.

❖❖❖

In the dreary January weather the court moved to Auvergne. It was always dank, never cold enough for snow but sufficient for icy rain. The days were dark and the light was gone almost before it was born. Most of the shutters remained closed and candles were devoured at a phenomenal rate.

Alienor had not told Henry about encountering his knights on her way from his chamber. Indeed, she had tried to banish the incident from her mind. Clandestine activities abounded at court and, on this occasion, it was safest not to know about them.

Alienor and Isabel sat in a window embrasure with their sewing. It was late morning, and the shutters were open to let in the weak, pale gray light. Isabel was with child again and feeling queasy. She was pondering whether to return to England or go to Hamelin's estates in the Touraine.

"I am sick enough as it is without chancing the sea," she said, screwing up her face. "I think I shall go to Colombiers until late spring. It depends where Hamelin is. I like to be near him." Alienor said nothing. She had had enough of Henry and her own intention was to make her way to Poitiers and continue Richard's education in statecraft.

"He likes to see me and the children," Isabel continued. "I sometimes wish we were an ordinary couple, just a merchant and his wife, living day to day with no great cares."

"Even if you were a merchant's wife you would have cares," Alienor said, "and they would seem no less worrisome to you."

"Indeed," Isabel conceded, "but the fate of countries would not..." She ceased speaking. The women turned their heads toward sounds of turbulent commotion in the antechamber. Alienor rose to her feet as a servant burst into the room and hastened to kneel at her feet, almost cowering. "Madam, terrible news. The archbishop of Canterbury has been slain in his own cathedral on the altar steps."

Isabel gasped and put her hand to her mouth. Alienor stared at the messenger in shock. "Slain? By whom?"

"By four knights of the king's household, madam." The young man proceeded to name the men Alienor had encountered slipping through the darkness. That night in Bures-le-Roi she had stumbled upon men intent on assassination.

"They broke into the cathedral where the archbishop was hearing Mass and they cut him down." The man swiped the back of his hand across his mouth and nose. "They slashed open his head and pulled out his brains on the edge of a sword and smeared them all over the altar step."

Isabel cried out as the words brought the image to life, and she doubled over, retching.

Alienor's jaw was so tight with tension that it ached. Dear God, how were they going to deal with this? Where was the way out? "Care for the countess," she commanded her women and, dismissing the messenger with a sharp flick of her hand, went to find Henry.

There was no sign of him in the hall where knots of courtiers stood around discussing what had happened, their shock and agitation palpable. She made her way to his chamber at a rapid walk and found the door barred and a guard set outside. "I will see the king," she said and stared the man down. "Do not tell me he refuses to admit anyone. I am the queen and this is a matter of the utmost importance."

The guard hesitated, and then cleared his throat and opened the door for her.

Henry stood by the hearth shivering and clutching a letter, which obviously contained the news of Becket's murder.

He spun around as Alienor entered and closed the door firmly behind her. "I suppose you have come to gloat and tell me it would always come to this," he said harshly.

"What would be the point in that?" she replied. "Done is done and now we must face the consequences." She lowered her voice. "I saw those men at Bures, the night they were setting out to do this deed. Tell me one thing: Did you send them, Henry?"

His eyes glittered. "Would you believe me if I said I hadn't?"

"Did you?" She increased the pressure but not the volume of her voice. "Tell me the truth and I will believe you."

"No, I did not." He clutched his hair. "Yes, I was sending men to arrest Becket, but not those four, and not with that intent. They took it upon themselves to do what they did. I…" His face twitched. Swiftly taking his arm, she made him sit down on the hearth bench.

"When I heard the news, my first thought was, 'Good, he is dead. Now I can hear my own thoughts without him trampling on them; now I can have peace.' I'm still glad that the thing he became as archbishop is no more, even if I feel regret for the man who was my chancellor." A shudder ran through him.

He would find it difficult to mourn. She had never seen him grieve properly over anything. It was as though all such feeling was disposed of in a deep, internal well, and the more emotion that poured in, the deeper down he dug, and one day the top would cave in on him and he would drown alone in darkness. He had used the word "regret," but it came from the surface. She knew that underneath lay all the things with which he could not cope. "There will be repercussions," she said.

Henry pulled his cloak around his body. "The deed is done. I cannot bring him back from the dead. The pope may do as he wishes. Without his vacillating and indecision, none of this would have happened. He should have taken Thomas's resignation when he tendered it."

"But he didn't, and the blame for this will land at your door. Men will say your words were the catalyst. They will accuse you of ordering those knights to go and murder the archbishop. Those who intend rebellion will have a cause on which to hang their swords."

Henry bared his teeth. "Then they will be dealt with. I refuse to take the blame for this." He jerked to his feet and took several agitated steps across the room.

"Whether you do or not, you will be charged with complicity in the act. The murderers will be excommunicated and you will face the same."

"The pope would not dare." Henry turned and flashed her a look bright with rage and underlying fear.

"Who knows what the pope will do. I advise you to conciliate. To murder an archbishop, no matter how contentious, on his own cathedral steps is a heinous act, and one you must condemn if you are to survive."

"I have already drafted a letter to the pope."

"What did you say?"

"That Thomas brought it upon himself by preaching sedition and that he was cut down by men of whom he had made enemies. That I did not incite anyone to murder." He gave her a bleak and bitter look. "He is going to haunt me more now that he is dead than he ever did alive, isn't he?"

"Yes, he is," Alienor said, "because now he has become a martyr." Henry should have walked away from making Becket archbishop, but that was only to go around in circles of hindsight. What was done could not be undone, only dealt with.

"It will take at least six weeks for my messengers to reach the pope, so that gives us time to prepare." He returned to the bench, put his head in his hands, and groaned.

Alienor set her hand lightly on his shoulder. "He insulted your kingship and our family dynasty. Even if his death is a shocking thing, it is an outrage that he treated you as he did."

He said nothing.

"Is there anything you want me to do?"

He raised his head. "Yes, leave me alone. Go back to Poitiers. It is better if you are not here. And send everyone away. I don't want to talk to anyone."

She went to the door, thinking that she would be glad to return to Aquitaine and immerse herself in its affairs. Let Henry deal as he would and continue to dig his well.

Hamelin was waiting outside, shifting from foot to foot. "He will not see you," she said, "not for the moment at least. Let him be."

Hamelin looked dazed. "I cannot believe this terrible evil has been committed," he said. "I disagreed with Becket many a time. I called him a traitor once and would again to his face, but to murder an anointed archbishop in the house of God and mutilate the body is a mortal sin. If a leader of the Church is murdered, then how much closer do people come to murdering a king?" He swallowed hard. "I can understand it happening in the hot blood of the moment, but not setting out and with time to think." He looked somber. "The fear of God is upon us all. Even without excommunication, there will be terrible repercussions. What if Henry is excommunicated?"

"That will not happen. The pope is contrary, but he is not a fool." Or at least she hoped he wasn't.

Hamelin looked sick. "This will turn him into a martyr."

"And that makes him more dangerous dead than he ever was alive. Henry will never be free of him. I am returning to Poitiers. You should look to Isabel. The news made her unwell."

"I shall send her to the Touraine until this is over," he said. "England is not safe."

"She can travel with me as far as she needs to go."

"Thank you." Hamelin palmed his face. "I have to stay with Henry. He is still my brother and my first loyalty."

"Then God send you his grace, for you will need it." She stood on tiptoe and kissed Hamelin's cheek and thought it ironic that she could kiss her brother-in-law with affection but not her husband.

# 41

## POITIERS, OCTOBER 1171

ALIENOR GAZED AROUND HER NEW GREAT HALL. IT WAS STILL open to the sky, but the walls were almost complete—and it was going to be magnificent. A fine haze of stone dust filled the air and the clink of the mason's chisels was a pleasant sound in the crisp morning.

Richard stood at her side, flushed from training with his tutors. His practice sword was still in his hand and battle light gleamed in his eyes. Since last Christmas he had grown faster than spring wheat and towered over her. He reminded her of her uncle Raymond, Prince of Antioch, who had been killed in battle in the Holy Land. He had that same leonine grace and watchful gaze that absorbed and assessed everything within his vision, that same astute political judgment. Occasionally too he resembled Henry's father, Geoffrey le Bel, from whom he had inherited his burnished hair. He was beautiful, the best of her sons and the one in whom she had invested the most because she knew he could do anything. Next midsummer he would receive the regalia of the counts of Poitiers and take another step on his road to power.

Richard spun the sword end over end and then tossed it high in the air and caught it neatly by the hilt before grinning at the way she tensed.

"A letter came from your father while you were at your training," Alienor said and refrained from commenting on his tricks, knowing it would only make him dare more. Besides, she had never told Richard to be careful. She had always encouraged him to venture, to climb, because only by so doing could he develop absolute confidence in himself. However, he had to learn the art of politics and diplomacy too. "He has arrived safely in Ireland and the sea crossing was brisk but not too rough."

"It is a long way to go for somewhere to hide." Richard flipped the sword in the air and caught it again.

"Your father would not call it hiding. He would call it expanding his influence and preventing others from forming kingdoms on his flank. It is better to take the homage of Richard de Clare and prepare the ground for your brother than have Ireland fall into anarchy. It can be his for the sake of a show of force, and then he can let others hold it until John comes of age." De Clare had gone to Ireland at the request of the high king of Leinster, who had hired his sword and offered him land in exchange for defeating his enemies.

"Little John Sans Terre." Richard's tone was one of patronizing amusement. "Why doesn't Papa let him enter the priesthood? It would be useful to have a bishop in the family."

"That path is already marked out for your half brother."

Richard snorted. "Does Jeoffrey know that?" He looked sidelong at his mother. "I suppose John is the spare child," he said. "Should one of us not flourish, he still has one not in holy orders to take our place, but it is going to be difficult wooing the fathers of heiresses when it comes to making John a tempting prospect. Ireland is the back of beyond and filled with bog-dwelling savages and of no relevance to France or Germany or Spain. It's hardly the first choice for a man to place his daughter."

"There is time for change," Alienor said. "John is still very young."

Richard examined the hilt and gave it a polish on his sleeve. "While Papa is in Ireland, he can avoid the difficulties caused by Becket's death too."

"That had not escaped my attention." Alienor firmed her lips. There had been much to-ing and fro-ing between England and the papal court. Henry had engaged the best lawyers to help him talk his way out of the situation. Canterbury Cathedral had reopened its doors but no services had been held there as yet, and the tomb area had been sealed off but was due to reopen—fortuitously enough—on the anniversary of Becket's death. Alienor had heard rumors of the growing popularity of "Thomas the Martyr" and knew Henry would not be able to silence the voices. In dying, the archbishop had produced a many-headed monster. Henry had not helped himself by refusing to punish the knights involved, saying they must make their own penance with God.

"Thomas will be waiting for him when he returns," she said grimly, "and larger than the life he no longer has."

❖❖❖

On a hot June morning eight months later, in the abbey church of Saint-Hilaire, Richard became duke of Aquitaine. Although the sun beat down outside, the interior of the church was still relatively cool and spiked with the scent of frankincense that rose from the gray-gold lumps in braziers and censers.

Richard was not fifteen until early September but already knew full well how to project magnificence and authority. Alienor was almost bursting with pride. This more than recompensed for missing her eldest son's coronation and Geoffrey's investiture as duke of Brittany. Richard would be the greatest of the dukes of Aquitaine, the pinnacle of his ancestor. Now Richard was entitled to rule, Henry would rapidly become redundant and she would govern at her son's side and advise him as matriarch of the dynasty.

Seated upon the bishop's throne on a raised dais, Richard was invested with his right and title by the archbishop of Bordeaux, assisted by the bishop of Poitiers. The coronet of the dukes of Aquitaine, bejeweled with pearls and sapphires, adorned his brow, and the lance and the banner of his ancestral line were placed in his firm young grip. The light in the window arch sparkled on sharp steel and rippling silk as the hymn "O princeps egregie" was chanted by the ecclesiastical choir.

After the consecration, Richard and Alienor processed from the cathedral into the hot summer light to be feted by the crowd. All of Poitiers had turned out to see the newly invested young duke emerge from the basilica. They were cheered amid a shower of blooms and petals and, in return, sent silver coins spinning amid the crowds, and small loaves of bread, marked with the sign of the cross.

Alienor, resplendent in cloth of gold, gestured to one of her knights, and he led forward a striking palfrey for Richard to ride. The stallion's coat was a gleaming cream-gold, its mane and tail fire-chestnut. A tasseled red saddlecloth hung almost to the ground, and the breast band was adorned with a double row of gold bells. Richard's eyes widened with tears of pride and wonder. Taking the stallion's bridle, he patted its satin neck, ran his hands over the shoulders, withers, and rump to feel the trembling strength and then set his foot in the engraved stirrup and swung into the decorated saddle.

The sight of him, the sheer, imperious joy and splendor, took Alienor's breath. Richard's smile was as wide as the sun as he turned his new horse on a tight rein and raised his right hand, clutching the banner of the dukes of Aquitaine. As the silk rippled and flowed around him, the roar from the crowd and the tossed flowers caused the horse to prink and sidle, but Richard mastered him with confident ease, and Alienor allowed the tears to spill freely down her cheeks as she watched her son grasp his destiny.

❖❖❖

Six months later, on a bitter winter day with snow blowing in the wind and the heat of June a distant memory, Alienor and Richard arrived at Chinon. Richard, secure in his title, wore a cloak of rippled blue-and-cream squirrel fur, the ring of Saint Valerie gleaming on the middle finger of his right hand. He rode his cream-chestnut palfrey, Jalnice, and the golden bells jingled on the red leather breast band with each movement of the stallion's muscular shoulders.

Alienor shivered as the towering fortress walls of Chinon mantled them in its shadow. She had wanted to spend Christmas in Poitiers, but it was a political necessity to come here. This would be the first time she had seen Henry in two years, and she was not looking forward to the encounter.

Approaching the castle, Alienor became aware of another entourage preparing to enter a dwelling house and, with an unpleasant jolt, recognized Rosamund de Clifford. Her cloak was also lined with squirrel fur, and her gown was an expensive Madonna blue. Framed by a soft veil, her pale complexion was flawless and virginal.

Richard made a sound of disgust when he saw her. "I cannot believe he has brought her here to Chinon," he said.

Alienor made an indifferent gesture, although the sight of all that false innocence sickened her. "Why not? He brings her everywhere else. I no longer care what he does," she said. "Only let us govern in Aquitaine without his interference."

Richard raised one eyebrow. "I doubt that, Mama. He will still try to find ways of keeping it in his hand."

Alienor grimaced. "Your grandmother the empress advised him to keep his barons hungry—to starve them like hawks in order to make them sharper."

"Peck out his eyes more like," Richard said.

They rode past Rosamund, who swept them a deep curtsy and lowered her head, but not before Alienor had glimpsed the resentment and challenge in her eyes. She had grown bolder since their last encounter, but then she was no longer a girl, rather a woman in her full beauty—although that in itself was no guarantee of keeping Henry's affection. He liked his women innocent and malleable.

Richard turned his head away. "My father's whore," he said, loud enough to be heard.

Alienor said nothing and gazed straight ahead as if Rosamund did not exist.

"She wants to be queen," Richard said. "I have heard her inveigling my father."

"That will never happen," she replied with world-weary amusement. "He will not risk his grip on Aquitaine for a concubine, no matter her charms. She may be of noble blood, but not rich enough to put her on the right side of the blanket." She looked at Richard and saw his flushed complexion. If he had had experience of women, he was discreet and kept it from her. The way he spoke about Rosamund, she suspected that any dealings he had with whores would not be amicable.

Riding into the courtyard, they came upon Henry, freshly returned from the hunt and talking to a groom who was about to lead away his mired and sweaty mount. Alienor gazed between her golden son on his golden horse and the man with gray in his red beard standing beside a trembling chaser that had been ridden too far and too hard. Henry turned from the horse and focused on them, wrapping his hands around his belt.

Richard dismounted in a flowing movement, threw back his sleek fur cloak, and helped Alienor down from her mare. "Madam my mother," he acknowledged with a bow. Only then did he turn and bend the knee to his father. "Sire," he said, his sea-blue eyes full of pride and challenge.

Looking amused but wary, Henry advanced and stooped to kiss him. "My son, the count of Poitiers and duke of Aquitaine," he said. "And almost a man."

Richard tightened his lips. Alienor noted with approval that he had learned to hold his tongue. That particular discipline had been difficult for him to master.

"He already does a man's work," she said to Henry, "and that makes him a man in my eyes. If he had not been ready, I would not have named him my heir."

Henry gave her a narrow look. "Madam my wife," he said, "it is good to see you."

Alienor did not believe that for a moment. "And you," she said. Their kiss was a dry, cold meeting of lips. "You have been hunting, I see?"

"A man should always be active. It aids digestion and helps him to think."

Alienor raised her brows. His physique had broadened and grown solid as he approached middle age, although he was still clearly vigorous. There was no sign of a paunch, and yet his years rode him as hard as he rode his mounts.

"I hope both are in good order," she said. "I am pleased I do not need to race a horse into a sweat to exercise my own wits."

Henry curled his lip. "Absence has not softened the sharpness of your tongue."

"Nor made the heart grow fonder," she retorted. "I notice you have not been pining for my company if a certain house in the town is any indication. Does she help you to think too?"

"Rosamund helps me with many things," Henry said stonily, "and her tongue is not a blade."

"Oh, I am sure she has other weapons at her disposal."

Ignoring the remark, Henry changed the subject by admiring Richard's palfrey. "It was a gift from me at his investiture as duke of Aquitaine," Alienor said.

Henry examined the horse, grunting approval as he ran his hands over its firm, muscular body. "You have always liked these since you were a little boy," he said. "The tawny horses."

"They are gold," Richard said, emphasizing the word. "Men will always mark where I am, because they will see my golden horse and know."

Henry gave Richard an inquiring look. "What will they know?"

Richard jutted his jaw. "That here is leadership. That here is a man they can follow through thick and thin. That here is a man who will take the reins and use them to forge his destiny."

Alienor smiled.

Henry raised his brows, creating three horizontal pleats across his forehead. "You look every inch the prince," he said. "I grant you that. But power does not come from fine clothes and horses and courtly flourishes. Standing here as I am with burrs in my tunic and mud on my boots, I have more power in my little finger than you have in your entire being. Power comes from within, and you still have much to learn, boy, even if you think you know all."

❖ ❖ ❖

"You did not have to be so harsh on Richard," Alienor said to Henry later as they sat before the fire in his chamber. She noticed that he kept rubbing his leg, but when he saw her looking, he pretended everything was all right.

Across the room, a group of courtiers were playing games of dice and chess, Richard among them, marked out by his height and his bright hair.

"He is far too sure of himself," Henry said. "He still answers to me."

"Yes, he does, because you are his father and because he is one of your heirs, but he is maturing swiftly. He is a duke and count in his own right and I shall give him more duties when we return to Poitiers. He will not answer to you for Aquitaine because Aquitaine is not your vassal and never has been."

Henry rubbed his chin. "I see. And that is why you are no longer acknowledging me in your charters? Did you think I would not notice how you have changed the salutations on your documents to exclude me?"

"Why should I not change the wording? It is my prerogative. Richard is old enough to undertake military duties and some government, and that leaves you free to deal with other arenas."

Henry's expression grew hard. "Our lands must be ruled with an overall policy to be effective, especially where France is concerned. I do not want to find that one part has been working for its own gain or strengthening itself and making alliances at the expense of others. Suppose Richard took it into his head to attack Toulouse? Or to go raiding where he should not? My sons are too young and inexperienced. They still need my hands on the reins."

The hands of a man who did not want to relinquish one iota of control. "Is a woman's touch not good enough? Richard is my project, and he has excelled himself. Do you think I would go pushing my own son into war? I will guide him through each stage until he is ready. He still has much to learn, but you should give him a little loose rein. Think of yourself at fifteen, your pride and how sure you were."

Henry gave her a jaundiced look. "Yes," he said, "and that's why I say he needs keeping on a tight rein. Besides, what I was at fifteen does not apply to my sons."

The discussion was going around in a circle. Henry would do nothing that lessened his control on any situation. Changing the subject, she asked him about Ireland.

"The matter is settled for now," he said. "I have been acknowledged king and allegiance has been sworn. When John is grown he can rule there if he is not fitted for the Church."

Alienor inclined her head. She had no argument with that notion. "He should be arriving with Joanna and their nurses by tomorrow," she said and glanced up as Hamelin joined them. "Is Isabel coming to court for the Christmas season?"

"Indeed she is. I expect her any day."

"And the children?"

"Belle and William both. Adela and Mahelt will stay in Touraine—they are too young and traveling with them would make the journey twice as long." He looked wry. "Isabel will be reluctant to leave them, but it will not be for long." He cleared his throat. "I take it you have heard the news from England? The latest about Canterbury?"

"What news is that?" She glanced at Henry, who shrugged and opened his hands but looked wary.

Hamelin dug in his pouch and handed Alienor a small lead ampulla with a string threaded through it. "One of my men was given this the other day."

The object was shaped like a horseshoe and inside the upward curve was a small container etched with a figure on a bier attended by two priests. The legend in Latin around the outside read: "Thomas is the best doctor of the worthy sick." She gave the trinket to Henry with a grimace of distaste.

"They are diluting his blood and brains in water and selling the stuff to pilgrims, declaring it is a cure for the sick," Hamelin said. "There have been claims about miracles for a while, but the cult is growing. They started selling the water earlier this year in wax-lined boxes, but now it's been refined to these ampullae."

"Thomas was ever good at schemes to make money," Henry sneered. "The Church will sit on its overflowing coffers and bleat piety until Judgment Day."

"He has also made himself a martyr in the eyes of the people and the cult will only grow. Your son has already attached himself to it by visiting the shrine."

"What do you mean?" Alienor asked sharply.

"Harry visited the shrine earlier this year," Hamelin said. He looked at Henry. "And in so doing, he has increased his standing and thrown the blame back onto you."

Alienor saw Henry stiffen. Hamelin was frowning. There were undercurrents here, things she needed to know that were not going to be said.

"You make too much of the matter," Henry snapped. "I have admitted that my words may have set those knights on the path to murder Becket, but it was of their own volition and unwitting by me. I have done penance and been absolved."

"To the letter of the law, yes," Hamelin replied doggedly, "but is that enough?"

"Of course it is!" Henry's eyes glittered with impatience. "I will go no further."

"But they have gone further with these ampullae and miracles. If you want stability and honor and rule, you have to be greater than that. People see what you have said and done, and it measures up lacking against Becket. You swore at Auvergne to go on crusade and to give money to Jerusalem. You have sworn to restore the Church's property and do right by Becket's relatives, but have you set any of this in motion? If you do not make a great show of remorse or humility, people will turn from you and look in the direction of your sons to make things right."

"Of course I intend it!" Henry's face reddened, and his chest inflated with anger. Alienor had never seen Hamelin confront Henry like this; plainly he was deeply concerned, perhaps even afraid.

"You are not going to ride off to Jerusalem even if that is what you have said you will do. You would be far more organized by now if that was the case. I do not believe anyone else expects you to do it either, but you must demonstrate your remorse over the archbishop's death. Unless you show your contrition, these little ampullae of the 'Water of Canterbury' will bring you down, and the rest of us with you."

"You talk like a fool, Hamelin," Henry scoffed. "You're becoming an old man."

"Hah, I want to live to become an old man!" Hamelin retorted and stalked off.

Henry shook his head and glowered at Alienor. "Do not look at me like that."

"Perhaps Hamelin is right about the penances and showing that you mean it," she said. "Can you afford to ignore his advice when he is so loyal to you?"

Henry said nothing, but his jaw clamped like a vice.

"What did he mean about people looking in the direction of your heir?"

"Nothing. It's just Harry trying to flex his wings before he has the feathers to fly. He wants me to give him lands to rule for himself and won't accept it when I say he is not ready. I know full well that Louis has rubbed a sore spot on his pride and is now grinding salt in it just to cause trouble. He keeps telling Harry it is beneath the dignity of a king not to have land and power."

"But why should he not flex his wings?" Alienor asked. "He will soon attain his eighteenth year day. Your father was only your age when he willingly ceded you Normandy, and you were only seventeen."

He drummed his fingers on the table in irritation. "You do not need to tell me my own history."

"Do I not? You cannot give your son money and distractions and expect him to be satisfied. He is beyond monkeys named Robert now; he needs to be independent."

"He is holding his own Christmas court at Bonneville with Marguerite, and she has been anointed queen by the archbishop of Rouen," Henry said. "I have been more than indulgent."

"Yes, you allow him to play at being king, to hold feasts and entertainments, and then you complain about how much it costs you. You must give him proper responsibility. If you cannot loosen your grip, what room in your life does anyone else have?"

"Plenty when they show they can be trusted."

"Ah, trust," she said. "And who can trust a king who does not keep his word?" She rose, knowing that like Hamelin she had to escape. "You must give him something to occupy him and soothe his dignity. Not just as a sop to a youth, but as an exercise in power. You have raised him up, but now you must give substance to his crown, otherwise you will make him a laughingstock."

"I shall do as I see fit."

"Of course you will, and then watch it all tumble down because you have no foundations." She left the room in exasperation and climbed to the battlements because she did not want to bring her anger and irritation into her own chamber.

The guards on the walls bowed to her and made way. Gazing out into the star-salted night, the moon a luminous white disc, she observed a female figure crossing the ward, escorted by a soldier bearing a torch. Rosamund, she thought with scorn. Poor, deluded, silly girl. Why would anyone want to be Henry's queen? What kind of power was that? He would use her as he used everyone and discard her when he had had enough.

Hearing voices further along the battlements, an interweaving of masculine cajolery and soft feminine giggles, she frowned. The only people who should be up here were the soldiers on duty and those who had authority. It was not a trysting place for lust-struck squires and their conquests. The voices came closer, shushing and whispering, and Alienor stood tall to confront the approaching lovers. By the gray light of the moon they were an odd sight, for they were bundled into a single cloak, hence the hilarity as they strove to match footsteps and bumped against each other.

Their meander stopped short as they came up against Alienor. The girl gave a frightened scream and the youth stifled an expletive.

"Do you not kneel before your queen?" Alienor demanded icily, her annoyance exacerbated by what she had just seen in the courtyard.

With a desperate flurry the pair struggled to their knees, the girl falling over and the youth yanking her up.

"Madam, forgive me, I did not realize…"

She recognized the voice now, and with it came recognition of the features too. Jeoffrey, Henry's bastard, and perhaps about the business of begetting another one.

"What are you doing here?"

He made a gesture of appeasement. "I was showing Sara the battlements under moonlight. I didn't think…"

"Indeed, you did not," Alienor said. "This is no place for trysting. Do not think to persuade the guards to look the other way just because your father is the king and you think it gives you privilege. It doesn't. Get up."

He lunged to his feet and extricated his partner from inside his cloak. Alienor vaguely recognized the trembling girl as belonging to the dairy. "Go," she said to her. "And thank God on your knees that I am not going to order you whipped."

The girl ducked her head and beat a hasty retreat, disappearing into the darkness of a turret entrance.

Alienor looked at Jeoffrey. Henry had appointed him arch-deacon of Lincoln in September with an eye to confirming him to the bishopric at a later date, but the young man, although enjoying the fiscal benefits of the post, showed no intention of taking vows. If anything, since his appointment, he had turned the other way and could be found constantly training in the military arts, swaggering about and making trysts with silly girls who should know better. "I wonder what your grandmother would say if she could see you." She moved to the wall and looked out over the starlit landscape. "What sort of man do you want to be, Jeoffrey?"

He adjusted his cloak, pulling it straight. "I want to serve my father," he replied after a short but prickly silence. "I want to do my best for him as he has done for me."

"And this is it? Your best?"

"It was a moment of fun," he said sulkily.

"Indeed, but you have responsibilities and a position to uphold. And clandestine fumbling with dairy maids is not part of that position if you desire to be honored." That was how he had been begotten—a result of his father's tumbles with a common woman. She did not say so; he was intelligent enough to make the connection. "You have a life of privilege, granted to very few. Will you use it, or abuse it? Think on what I have said."

When he had gone, she closed her eyes and breathed deeply of the cold starlit air. She had asked him what sort of man he wanted to be, and she feared that the answer he had avoided giving her was that he wanted to be just like his father.

❖❖❖

Despite the various frictions, the Christmas sojourn at Chinon had its pleasures and entertainments. Alienor went hunting with her gyrfalcon and her sleek white gazehounds. There was the exhilaration of the chase in the bright, brisk cold and, as always, the sensation of a fast horse under her saddle and the wind flurrying against her mantle made her laugh aloud with exultation. Each day, when they returned in red winter sunsets with the trees stark and black behind them, there was feasting and merriment and tale-telling in the hall. She played chess with Jeoffrey. Occasionally he defeated her, but most of the time she still won.

John and Joanna arrived from Fontevraud and Henry was delighted to see his youngest son, now turned six years old, so nimble and intelligent and eager to please him. Joanna was a delightful, pretty little girl, and Henry derived great pleasure from having her sit in his lap where she fed him preserved fruits from a bowl, seeing how fast he could devour them. Observing him with his youngest offspring, Alienor remembered when he had been like that with the others—until the girls approached marriageable age, and the boys became old enough to potentially challenge him.

Henry took John up on his fast courser and cantered him around the yard before setting off to hunt, and John was exhilarated until he was put down and left behind with his nurse. Alienor noticed how hungrily John watched his father. He would emulate his walk and dog Henry's heels everywhere he went. Richard treated his youngest sibling, nine years his junior, with amused indifference, occasionally verging on scorn. He would cuff him and bowl him over, the way he did when playing with his father's half-grown pet gazehound. He called him "John Sans Terre" and laughed when John became angry—until the day that John stole Richard's sword and hid it under a pile of dung in the stable yard.

The ensuing fracas was cataclysmic. John denied all knowledge despite having been seen lurking in the area by a groom, but it didn't save him from being held upside down and shaken by Richard, who had then thrown him into the dung heap and threatened to slit his windpipe with the sword. By the time a passing knight intervened and came to John's rescue, he was a shaken wreck, tears and mucus streaming down his face, and he had pissed himself. But he wasn't sorry. Forced to own up and apologize, he spoke the words by rote, but his eyes flashed fire and retribution. Richard, taken to task by Henry for excess violence against a child and his own brother, was not sorry either and stormed off to clean his sword, muttering that he would kill John if he came near his weapons ever again.

There was constant turbulence. The heavy tension was like waiting for snow to fall as the sky darkened. The silence from Bonneville, where Harry was holding his own Christmas court. The late evenings when Alienor knew that Rosamund was slipping through the postern to Henry's chamber. All under their noses and all unsaid while their Irish harpist plucked sweet notes that trembled in the air as he sang songs of betrayal and deception. Alienor's white gyrfalcon preened on her perch, and men rested their cups on their bellies, listened to the musician, and cast one another sidelong glances.

The Narrow Sea was an expanse of hurtling gray waves with spindrift blowing off their tops before they crashed into the shoreline in explosions of silver spray. In other halls in England, men talked at fires, warming their hands and sharpening their blades, ready for next year's campaign season. At Canterbury the common folk crowded to the tomb of Thomas Becket and, in the scarlet glow from the shrine lamps, heard tales of miracles as they made offerings in exchange for vials of the "Water of Canterbury" and called for their king-slain martyr to be made a saint.

❖❖❖

"I wish Henry would give Harry and Marguerite their own lands," Alienor said to Isabel as they sat together in Alienor's chamber. Outside, the ground was covered with a light dusting of snow, but it wasn't enough to interfere with the court's preparations to move on to Fréteval. The sounds of bustle carried up through the narrow window arch. "He will be eighteen next month, and he needs a focus." She watched John and his cousin Will constructing a castle from wooden blocks. Despite the usual childhood squabbles, the boys had formed a firm friendship, which pleased her, because John was generally aloof with other children and they tended to avoid him.

"It doesn't seem a moment since Harry was a little boy playing with his toy knights and castles," Isabel commented with a fond look at their sons.

"And that is the problem," Alienor said, her tone heartfelt. "That is how Henry would see our son even now that he is on the cusp of manhood. He gives him playthings—money and gifts—but not responsibility and then complains when the money is gone and he is asked for more. What does he expect? If he does give him tasks, they are no more than sealing charters and witnessing covenants. There is no meat to the matter. Harry needs more than that for his own sake and the country's, but Henry does not wish to see it. It is not the same for Richard because I give him leeway and he can perform a man's duties in my dominions, and when Geoffrey comes of age Brittany will be his. But what is there for Harry to govern? Henry would have to give him Normandy, England, or Anjou, and he will never do that."

"I do not know what to say."

"Because there is nothing to say," Alienor replied. "The solution is for Henry to change, and that will happen when the seas run dry." She looked at the children playing around their feet. "You have but one son; that is precarious, but at least you will not face squabbles over inheritance."

"Indeed," Isabel agreed and put her hand on her belly. "I do not think there will be more than these four. My fluxes are scant these days and Hamelin is absent much of the time with Henry."

"You miss him, don't you?"

"I do," Isabel said softly. "Things are so difficult because of what has happened. I do not want Hamelin—or me—to change so much that we no longer recognize each other. I still want to take his hand, and have him take mine."

"It is too late for me and Henry," Alienor said bleakly. "I shall be relieved to return to Poitiers."

"I am sorry."

"I took someone's hand once." Alienor gazed into the distance. "But I lost him a long time ago." Isabel started to ask a question and then changed her mind, and Alienor was glad, for she would not have answered it, no matter how firm their friendship. Some things were best left unspoken.

❖❖❖

Alienor was sorting out a box of tangled embroidery silks when Henry came to her chamber. He had taken John out riding, and the latter was dancing at his side, his small face still alight from the pleasure of the experience. A small pang went through Alienor, another shard. Henry was so good with small children—while they were easy to control, and when he could be bothered.

"To what do I owe the pleasure of this visit?" she inquired. Normally Henry would have given John to his nurse and not come anywhere near her chamber.

"Pleasure?" Henry smiled and ruffled John's hair. "I think we are past that stage, but I wanted to keep you informed since we will be parting company soon."

"Well, that makes a change from keeping me in ignorance." She raised her head from the knotted silks. Henry had picked up one of John's toys—a cone on a string attached to a ball, and was busily popping the ball in and out of the socket. "But that is obviously not your intention today."

He chose to ignore her sarcasm. "I was talking earlier with

emissaries of the Count of Maurienne. You'll meet them at dinner. Count Humbert has a daughter, and is interested in matching her with John if terms can be arranged to our mutual satisfaction."

"Maurienne." Alienor pursed her lips. "That would mean lands in Piedmont and Savoy?"

"Yes, and the opportunity to become count of Savoy."

Alienor glanced at John, who was listening with interest. "What of Ireland?"

"There is still that possibility, but the Maurienne lands are strategic for controlling the mountain routes through the Alps."

She heard the eagerness in his voice. Once again he was building worlds, expanding his territories and horizons, and in spite of herself she felt an echo in her bones. "And in exchange?" she asked. "What does Humbert of Maurienne want to trade for such a treasure?"

Henry cupped the ball. "That is to be discussed. I have invited him to Claremont in two months' time to see what can be arranged. I shall want all my heirs there since we did not have a full gathering this Christmas."

"Will I still be king of Ireland?" John demanded.

Henry chuckled. "We shall see, my little hawk," he said. "We shall see."

A gleam entered John's eyes. "Richard won't be able to call me John Sans Terre anymore."

"No, he won't." Henry handed him the toy in dismissal and ruffled his hair. "And certainly not when I am by."

"I will be interested to see just what you are going to give Humbert of Maurienne in exchange for his daughter," Alienor said when John had gone.

Henry tugged on his earlobe. "I am thinking about it. Enough to make him commit but as little as I can get away with."

When Henry had made his will during his last serious illness, there had been nothing for John. She failed to see what there could be unless Henry raided his coffers and offered coin and treasure in lieu, and she knew how reluctant he would be to do that.

# 42

## Fréteval, Anjou, January 1173

*M*AMA!" HARRY STOOPED SO THAT ALIENOR COULD EMBRACE him. His smile was warm, his hair shone like gold, and his eyes were as clear as a calm northern sea. Since last she saw him he had become a man, gaining another finger joint in height and broadening out.

"It is so good to see you!" Alienor was laughing and crying at the same time. "It has been too long! You've grown so much!" She turned to embrace Marguerite. "And you look well too, Daughter."

"Yes, madam, I am." Marguerite responded with a curtsy and a dutiful kiss. She was as plump as a pink silk cushion, her forehead and chin spotty with adolescent blemishes. Yet her brown eyes shone and the smile on her lips made all the difference. Alienor noted the possessive look she sent toward Harry and the one he returned to her. It wasn't adoring, but there was a knowing air of complicity that excluded Alienor and reminded her of her first marriage where she and Louis had done the same before Louis's mother—who was this girl's grandmother. Marguerite was now a queen in her own right, although not anointed at Westminster, and not by Becket. Alienor imagined a small, almost hidden crown on her head, as opposed to the great diadem she envisaged on Harry's.

Richard came forward and the brothers embraced. Richard was taller than Harry but slighter of build, still being only fifteen. "Well," said Richard with a mocking smile. "Here he is, the king-in-waiting!"

"Not for much longer," Harry retorted.

"Has Papa been promising you things again?" One side of Richard's mouth curled upward. "Don't believe a word. You should listen to Mama instead."

Alienor was exasperated by her sons. Already the needling had begun, and bore a sharper edge now that Richard was duke of Aquitaine and Harry still had nothing beyond an income that ran through his hands like water.

"Come," she said. "Enough of that. There is plenty of time for other talk when we reach Montferrand."

Harry turned to greet John, who had not returned to Fontevraud because of the betrothal negotiations. "Little brother." He tousled John's hair. "So Papa has found you an inheritance and a bride, hmmm? I wonder how long you'll be waiting." Going to one of his baggage chests, he produced a horse's breast band of green leather with silver bells tinkling on it. "I brought this for your horse so that everyone in Montferrand will know a true prince is coming."

A rare smile lit up John's face as he took the breast band, and he looked at Harry with an expression that was almost hero worship.

"That was kind," Alienor said.

Harry shrugged. "Papa made me responsible for him in his will. One day he will be a man, and perhaps a useful ally." His expression said he was willing to be magnanimous because John was a child and he did not consider him a rival. There was no such gift for Richard.

Henry arrived then and greeted his heir with loud and superficial bonhomie, hugging him to his chest and slapping his back. There was a hearty kiss too for Marguerite and a comment about how buxom and well she looked, hinting that he hoped she was fecund.

Alienor observed Henry's jovial performance and was not fooled. The smile was on his lips, but his eyes were steely, and his movements were dominant and forceful. She knew already that Montferrand would be a family gathering where Henry told everyone what they were going to do, and they would obey him or face the consequences.

Later, while they were all seated at table, Henry casually mentioned to Alienor that there was a meeting planned for after Montferrand at Limoges, which would be attended by various magnates and royalty and was an opportunity for diplomatic talks. "I hope to build a lasting peace and make firm alliances on our southern borders," he said.

"Very laudable," Alienor replied and wondered if Henry was trying to box her in too by making arrangements surrounding Aquitaine. "Whom may we expect to see other than Humbert of Maurienne?"

Henry rinsed his mouth with wine and swallowed. "Alfonso of Aragon and his advisers." He gave her a calculating look. "He wants me to mediate in a dispute with Raymond of Toulouse."

Alienor went very still. "So Raymond of Toulouse will be present?"

Henry shrugged. "Whatever your opinion of him, he is part of the process and needs to be present." He toyed with the gems studded around the base of the goblet. "We can turn this to our advantage. If I can successfully negotiate John's marriage, it will weaken Raymond's position in that he will have potentially hostile neighbors on both sides. To save himself, he will have to pay homage for Toulouse."

Alienor swallowed revulsion. "Then do not bring him near me, except he be on his knees. You know my feelings about Toulouse."

"You have made them abundantly clear," he said stiffly. "I thought you would be delighted to have Count Raymond pay homage to Aquitaine."

"I am," she said, "but that does not mean I shall enjoy sharing his company, and I have no doubt he will wriggle out of the business if he can."

Henry pushed the cup to one side. "Nonetheless, he will do it," he said. "And we shall have peace." He gave her a warning look.

Rather than being delighted at the news, Alienor was deflated and wary. There was something about Henry—a thin, tensile undercurrent that gave her cause for more than the usual suspicion.

❖❖❖

Alienor was hungry and impatient. The discussion between Henry and Humbert of Maurienne concerning the proposed marriage between his small daughter and John had begun after morning Mass, several hours ago. Her sons, including the prospective bridegroom, were with their father at the negotiations, but the women had been left to their embroidery and conversation in another chamber. A formal feast was to be held later, followed by informal discussion where Alienor's duty would be to smile, play the gracious hostess, and smooth out any remaining rough edges.

Her first impression of Count Humbert of Maurienne had been of a quiet, genial man, but his eyes were heavy-lidded, and it was not sleepiness that lurked behind them, but a shrewd and calculating brain every bit as sharp as Henry's. He would drive a hard bargain for the lands that came with his infant child.

Raised voices sounded outside the chamber door and Harry burst into the room, his face scarlet with fury and his fists clenched. Hamelin followed on his heels, remonstrating with him.

Alarmed, Alienor pushed aside her sewing frame and went to them. "What is this? What's wrong?"

Harry's eyes glittered with tears of rage and humiliation. "My father," he choked. "He has taken the castles of my inheritance at Chinon, Loudun, and Mirebeau and offered them to Humbert of Maurienne as John's contribution to the marriage bargain! He refuses to let me rule anything, and now he eats into what I am due, and barters it away in a marriage settlement for my little brother!"

Marguerite rose from her chair and hastened to his side.

"How much more is he going to take from me?" Harry demanded raggedly. "I'm not a child. I'm a crowned king in my own right without an inch of ground to my name. I might as well wear the ears of an ass on my head and ride a mare!"

"There is a time and a place to discuss this and in the right manner," Hamelin said, his face ruddy with anger. "You should not have left the council chamber as you did. You have undermined your position already, you young fool."

"Hah, I couldn't undermine it any more than it has already been!" Harry spat. "Was I supposed to sit there and swallow it while my father gave away my patrimony?"

"Younger sons always receive those castles by tradition," Hamelin replied, "but that is not the point. The point is you raging out of there like a child having a tantrum. Now Count Humbert may want to rethink his position. You should have had the control to sit still and discuss matters like a man, not an undisciplined boy. Is it any wonder your father has doubts about giving you responsibility? You have just enforced his opinion of you that you are not fit to rule."

"I know full well why you take my father's part," Harry sneered. "Those castles would be in your administration until John came of age. You have a vested interest, Uncle, so don't pretend you're impartial. My father always sends you out like his dog to bark at those who displease him."

Hamelin's chest heaved. "If you were mine—" he said in a congested voice.

"My lord, enough, I pray." Alienor hastened to stand between them. Isabel was on her feet too. "Harry, peace. Your uncle is right. You do yourself no good by raging like this."

Harry glared at her. "Did you know he was going to do this, Mama? Did you?"

"No, and if I did, I would have advised him against it, but your father never heeds any voice but his own. He is quite capable of talking himself into riding off a precipice. It does not mean you should do so too."

"I won't let him do this to me," Harry said with bitter pain. "He has given me nothing, and now he takes away even from what he promised me. What am I to think of the value he sets on me? My father-by-marriage loves me better than he does."

Alienor shuddered. "Do not confuse love with political machinations. It well suits Louis to encourage strife between us."

"But he's right, isn't he? And my own father has just proven that." Taking Marguerite by the hand, he left the room, his stride so rapid that Marguerite stumbled. Hamelin made to follow, but Alienor held him back.

"Let him be," she said. "You will make things worse than they are if you pursue him." She turned to one of the squires on duty. "Find me William Marshal."

Hamelin ground his teeth. "He cannot be allowed to behave in that manner before our allies."

"Why not?" she said scornfully. "His father does, and I suppose he has learned by example. If Henry has done what Harry says, then he has reason to be upset."

Hamelin stood his ground. "Indeed, but it was not the time or place… What if he leaves? What will that do to the negotiations?"

"He won't. Where would he go?"

The squire returned with William Marshal in tow. The knight was clad in the padded tunic he wore under his mail shirt. He had been tending to the latter garment, picking over it for flaws, and his hands were black with grease and ferrous residue. "Madam," he said and knelt.

"Your lord has received some upsetting news," she said. "Find him and make sure he does nothing rash. He will listen to you. Calm him down and prevent him from leaving should he take it into his head to do so. Be about the business in haste."

William gave her a shrewd look. "As you wish, madam." He rose, bowed, and hurried from the room.

Alienor turned to Hamelin, who was slightly less red in the face by now. "I pray you return to the king," she said, "and see if you can repair the damage. I will also do what I can."

Hamelin gave a brusque nod. "I am uncertain of success," he said, "but if anything is to be salvaged, some kind of peace must be made."

"Indeed." Alienor's mouth twisted. "After all, is it not said that a queen's most important role is that of peacemaker and that the meek shall inherit the earth?"

❖❖❖

Typically, Henry did not want to talk about his decision. "It is made and that is final," he told Alienor when she tackled him in his chamber. "And I was right to make it. Until my son learns to govern himself, I am not about to let him govern others—and I will brook no interference from you, madam, on that score."

"But you must have known that giving those castles in surety for John would incense Harry. Surely you could have promised something else? You are throwing him into the arms of the French by doing this."

Henry made an exasperated sound and threw up his hands.

"What would you have done if you had been in his position at eighteen? I watched you strip your own brother of those castles. Henry, you must bend, or else the tree will break. You have enough trouble in your life to deal with already."

"How can I give him lands while he is incompetent to govern them? He says he will only learn by doing so, but I cannot trust him, and I know Louis has gotten his claws into him. I never thought I would fear betrayal from my own son when I saw him lying in his cradle."

"You are only reaping what you have sown," she said with weary contempt.

"And what you have encouraged to grow," he accused.

"When have I seen him of late to do so?" she demanded incredulously. "You took him away from me when he was still a little boy."

"You bore him, madam. For all that I own him my son, he has your taint within his very bones."

Alienor gasped. "Is that how you see it? You who have betrayed me again and again? With my lands, with other women, with all the promises you have made to me through the years and broken without a second thought? Look in your mirror, sire, before you throw stones at me, and do not blame me if what you see does not suit you."

"I will not stand for this," Henry snarled. "I will curb that boy—indeed, 'boy' is what he is."

"And you will not allow him to be a man, because that threatens your own manhood!"

The argument had gone around in a circle. Precious little peacemaking, but she was too angry to be interested in peace now. She looked at Henry's clenched fists and wondered if he would strike her, but he drew a deep breath and turned to pace the room like a caged lion.

"When I was his age I had no choice but to fight for my inheritance. If I had not, I would not have had one. He has no need. He will inherit my kingdom in the fullness of time. There is no cause for any of this fighting." He paused and wagged a warning forefinger at her. "You will follow me on this. You will do as I tell you."

"Are you threatening me, my lord?"

"What is left when talking sense to you is like pissing against the wind? I expect his obedience, and yours. You both owe your allegiance to me."

Alienor raised her head. "Is there anything else, sire, or do I have your leave to retire?"

"You may go," he said. "But think well on what I have said. Cooperate, or face the consequences."

❖❖❖

Harry was waiting in her chamber when she returned and almost sprang on her as she walked through the door.

"Oh, in God's name, pour us both some wine and sit down," she snapped. She sat down before the hearth and rubbed her aching temples.

"I won't let him have those castles, Mama, I won't."

"It is not settled yet for certain," she replied. "Things change and you must take a long view of the game."

He gave a puff of frustration and handed her the wine.

"You did your cause no good by storming out like that."

"What else was I supposed to do?" His voice rose with indignation. "Accept it meekly?"

"You could have conducted yourself in a more mature manner in front of other men. You diminished yourself in their eyes by behaving as you did."

"So you take his side?"

Alienor restrained the urge to strike him for being so imperceptive. "No," she said. "I do not, but you play straight into his hands by acting as you do. Do not give up. You will have your lands and your esteem."

"When?" Harry said bitterly. "When he is dead? When I challenge him for it at sword point?"

"That is treason!" Alarmed, she put her hand on his wrist. "You must not say such things! That is what I mean about taking responsibility."

He stiffened under her touch, but not with rejection. Rather he appeared as if assimilating a new angle. "Yes, Mama," he said after a moment. "Thank you for your advice." He leaned over to kiss her cheek. "I will not apologize to him though."

"I do not expect you to, only behave in a dignified way at the oath-taking, and mind what you say. Your time will come."

He gave her another of those looks. "Yes," he said, and his tone was so expressionless that it held a wealth of meaning. "Yes, it will."

❖❖❖

The ride to Limoges for the main conference was a mixed affair, rather like the weather, which was raw and cold but with flags of blue between the clouds and moments of weak sunshine that almost hinted at warmth on her skin. Raymond of Toulouse had joined them but stayed back off the pace, having little to do with anyone, and Alienor was glad, but even the awareness of his presence made her feel like a cat that had had its fur ruffled the wrong way. The sooner he swore his oath and departed, the better.

Harry had been quiet and subdued, but Alienor was positive he had little intention of obeying his father. Earlier she had seen him strike one of his clerks and dismiss a scribe, both of whom were in Henry's pay and spied for him. She was also aware of Henry keeping a close watch on Harry's knights. The air was full of dangerous tension, and her nape was prickling the way it always did before a thunderstorm.

On reaching Limoges, the baggage was unpacked and the participants changed from their traveling clothes into formal garments for taking the oaths of homage.

Alienor donned a gown fashioned from cloth of gold patterned with eagles, their wings outspread. She wore a ring on the middle finger of her left hand set with a large topaz, which she called her phoenix egg because of its fiery golden color. A gold net encased her hair, and she wore a silk veil secured by a gem-set coronet.

Richard arrived, ready to accompany her to the great hall. He wore crimson and gold and his cloak was lined with the chevron furs of blue squirrels. A coronet decked his hair too, and the ducal ring of Saint Valerie shone on his right hand.

"Well," Alienor said, "this is an auspicious day, is it not?" Alight with pride, she arranged the drape of his cloak.

Richard smiled and said with relish, "It is going to stick in Raymond of Toulouse's craw to bow to us."

Alienor grimaced. "Indeed, and it ought to be a sweet taste, but I am wary. It seems to me he has been backed into a corner. He has no choice. And when people have no choice, their oaths and allegiance are given with resentment and reneged upon at the first opportunity. Yes, I badly want to see it stick in his craw, but what will he do afterward? Choke it up perhaps."

Richard drew himself up. "He will do nothing, Mama, because I will not let him." His tone was proud, and slightly affronted. "He will be my vassal too, and I will keep him to his word."

She took his arm and squeezed it, and felt the new strength of muscle under her hand. "I know you will," she said, "but I still do not trust him."

"Harry says that if Papa does not give him lands, he will seize them for his own because it is his right."

Alienor felt a jolt of alarm because such words were an escalation of intent. Harry often postured and threatened to do things, but he seldom followed them through because it was too much trouble. However, he might well be testing out his ideas on Richard and looking for support. "And who does he think will aid him, apart from those impecunious knights of his?"

Richard shrugged. "His father-by-marriage, I suppose, and anyone else Papa has ridden over in the past."

"Did Harry ask you?"

Richard fiddled with the jeweled hilt of his dagger. "Not in so many words, but he is truly considering it, Mama. He is not strong enough to take on Papa by himself."

It had gone further than she thought. It would not be a wise idea to tell Henry. She needed more information before she could decide what to do for the best. Louis would definitely finance anything that split up Henry's domains and caused divisions, but at the same time his daughters were united with her sons and Harry's proximity to the French Crown was inevitable.

"That is a very dangerous game," she said. "Your father will come to hear the rumors, and he will deal ruthlessly with anything he regards as betrayal. You should not speak so where you can be overheard."

Richard glanced around at Alienor's women, but none were within earshot. "I do not, Mama, but Harry is less discreet; he does not care who knows. He hinted to me that he's been quietly seeking support and finding it. He says there is huge unrest in England since the death of the archbishop."

Alienor's alarm increased. "Just how far has this gone?"

"I do not know, Mama. You must talk to Harry."

She saw the doubt in his eyes lurking behind the veneer of manly confidence. This was new territory for him, and he was still in need of guidance. "I am glad you have spoken to me," she said. "You have done the right thing. I will speak with Harry after the ceremony. Leave it with me."

Together, Alienor and Richard descended from her chamber to the public space of the great hall where everyone was assembling to witness Raymond of Toulouse kneel in homage to Richard and Alienor and concede that he was Aquitaine's vassal. Henry was already seated on the dais, watchful and alert, his gaze moving from person to person, marking and assessing. For once rings adorned his fingers and he wore a dalmatic of purple silk which set off the ermine lining to his cloak. Harry sat beside him, upright and still, mirroring his father's pose, but his usual smile had been replaced by set lips and an inscrutable expression.

As Richard mounted the dais and received a kiss from Henry, Hamelin stepped forward, blocked Alienor's path to the steps, and drew her to one side. If Harry's face was inscrutable, then Hamelin's revealed deep discomfort and unease but dogged determination. Alienor gazed at him in surprise and alarm.

"Madam, the king requests that you remain here for the moment," Hamelin said stiffly.

"What is the meaning of this?" Alienor tried to shake him off, but he tightened his grip.

"Madam, forgive me. The king will explain all in a short while, but for now he wishes you to remain here." He drew her to stand beside Marguerite and her sister Alais: observers, not participants. The path to the dais had been blocked by Henry's household knights.

Raymond of Toulouse came forward from a group on the opposite side of the room from where Alienor stood. Even though he was on his way to bow the knee and pay homage to his enemies, he walked with a defiant swagger. At the foot of the dais he paused, took a deep breath as if about to plunge into deep water, and then mounted the steps. Kneeling before Henry, he put his hands between his and swore him allegiance, acknowledging him duke of Aquitaine and overlord of Toulouse. Alienor's breath stopped at the top of her chest in utter shock. Henry had no right to accept that oath. Indeed, it could be construed that because Raymond of Toulouse was swearing fealty to the king of England, Aquitaine was England's satellite. She would die before she let that happen.

Rooted to the spot, she watched Raymond place his hands between Henry's and Henry give him the kiss of peace. And then Raymond turned to her sons, first kneeling to perform homage to Harry for Toulouse, acknowledging him Henry's heir. Harry glanced at his father and swiftly at Richard but accepted the homage, a flush spreading across his face. Finally Raymond turned to Richard, who hesitated for a long moment before finally completing his part of the ceremony, his expression rigid with strain.

Rage surged through Alienor so strongly that for a moment she could not see. This was the vilest betrayal of all: that Henry should snatch away from her the kernel of her authority, of who she was, and use Raymond of Toulouse as his instrument.

"You serve the devil," she hissed at Hamelin. "Let go of me, you traitor. I will not be restrained by the likes of you." She wrenched herself out of his grasp and flung from the hall with its tableau of treachery. Storming into her chamber, she ordered the startled servants to pack the baggage for an immediate return to Poitiers. She swept several gowns off a clothing pole and threw them on her bed for her women to fold and then dug her fingernails into her palms, seeking control.

Isabel arrived, flushed and tearful with distress. "Alienor, I am sorry. I swear I did not know!"

"If you did, would you have told me?" Alienor glared at her with furious contempt. "I think not, because your loyalty is not first of all to me, is it, but to your perfidious henchman husband! Get out before I say something to destroy any bridges remaining between us."

Isabel bit her lip. "I am sorry. I truly am. I do not blame you for sending me away."

Alienor refused to look at her. There was a pressure in her stomach and saliva in her mouth. "Just go," she said.

Isabel hesitated and then made a deep curtsy. "I shall pray for all of you, and do what I can, however little that might be," she said and, with a sob, fled the room.

Alienor ran to the latrine shaft built into the thickness of the wall and hung over it, retching bile. When a worried Marchisa inquired if she was well, she waved her away and choked that she wished to be left alone.

Eventually, the spasms subsided and she collected the shattered pieces of herself and strove to put them together. She knew Henry would not come to her and explain. Why should he? He had already revealed the kind of store he set by her. Returning to the chamber, she rinsed her mouth with wine and returned to the matter of packing. Once back in Poitiers and away from Henry's poisonous presence, she would consider how best to proceed.

Richard arrived as she was putting her topaz ring in a wax-lined jewel casket. He was panting from his run up the stairs, the gold sunbursts on his tunic flashing with each hard breath.

"How could he do this to us?" he demanded, his voice almost breaking back to boyhood with the pressure of his anger. "He must have known what Raymond was going to do."

"Of course he knew," Alienor spat. "It is your father's ploy to make Aquitaine a vassal of England and Normandy and at the same time save face for Toulouse. Doubtless he thinks he has been clever, but that oath will not stand. You are duke of Aquitaine independent of anyone but me, and since I accepted no oath, it is invalid." She drew a deep breath. "Should you not be at this triumphal feast of your father's?"

Richard grimaced. "I said I had to visit the latrine. Harry is furious too. He says the oath-taking was a sop that's not going to salve his pride or compensate for those castles just because he took precedence over me. He says it's all Papa's trickery again. He's going to defy him because if Papa won't listen to him, then what else can he do? What is there to lose?" As he spoke, Richard controlled his voice, and it dropped to its deeper resonance.

A taut silence fell between them, then Alienor said, quietly bitter, "Your father is a consummate player. Harry must take consultation and advice, and be committed beyond the superficial to any undertaking. There is a great deal left to lose."

"And to win," Richard said hawkishly.

"Rebellion goes far deeper than a complaint about not enough land or responsibility. Rebellion risks all," she warned. A part of her felt a sensation of reaching out, of excitement and yearning. It was like inhaling freedom, but she knew the danger and was afraid for her sons and herself. She touched his arm. "Let us talk once we are back in Poitiers. For now there is nothing we can do."

❖❖❖

"Your brother tells me you are considering folly," Alienor said to Harry when he came to her chamber, having absconded the feast.

Harry shot an angry look at Richard. "I do not know what you mean."

"You know exactly what I mean," Alienor said curtly. "I am your mother and I know what goes forth. If you are intending what you intend, then you must be very sure, and you must plan carefully. You cannot treat this as a sudden enthusiasm or a child's outburst where all will be forgotten tomorrow. Either you mean this with all your heart as a man, or you must step back."

Harry set his jaw. "I mean it, Mama. I've been thinking about it all day. I am going to return to the French court. There are many in England, both common folk and barons, who desire to cast off his yoke. He has made enemies everywhere. All we are to him are pawns on his chessboard, and he thinks he can move us about wherever he wants."

"And what would you do?" she asked. "How exactly do you intend to become a player instead of one of his pieces?"

"I am a king," Harry said proudly. "I shall make him acknowledge me. There are many who will join my banner when I summon them." He gave her a wounded look. "I have not spent all my time reveling and pouring my allowance down the drain."

"Aquitaine is mine," Richard broke in swiftly. "I will not let you or Papa take it from me."

Harry turned to him. "It is not my fault that Raymond of Toulouse swore to me first rather than you. It wasn't my doing, as well you know."

"Perhaps, but even so I will never kneel to you for Aquitaine."

Harry brushed the words aside with an impatient wave of his hand. That issue was not his current focus. "As you will. Come with me to France if you desire, and kneel to Louis as your overlord."

Alienor was frustrated by their quibbling, and afraid too. "Do not be in such haste," she said, rubbing her aching temples. Everything was unraveling, and she did not know which way to turn because there was betrayal of one sort or another in every direction and no sanctuary anywhere.

"I tell you, Mama, I am not staying. I am going to Paris because I cannot call anywhere in my father's domains home. He dishonors me at every turn. I am constantly being told to act like a man. Well, now I am, and the rest of you may do as you see fit, but my mind is made up." He departed the room with head down like a charging bull in a manner totally reminiscent of his father.

Alienor's headache had become an intense sawing pain, and she could not think. "We shall talk about this tomorrow," she said to Richard. "Tonight I am too exhausted, too sad—and too angry."

❖ ❖ ❖

Hamelin sipped his wine. It was always magnificent in the south, and this one was exceptional. Even so, tonight it cloyed his palate and he did not want to be in this room. The feast to celebrate the homage ceremony had been a mockery. Humbert of Maurienne had been royally feted and superficially all had seemed well, but excuses had had to be made for Alienor's absence. Harry and Richard had been present because they were forced but had left early. Hamelin suspected they had gone to keep company with their mother. Geoffrey had remained at the feast, watchful as usual, keeping his thoughts to himself and observing the proceedings with a keen eye. John, seated at the high table on an embroidered cushion, had behaved with aplomb. Now, he was leaning sleepily against Henry, being very quiet and good, obviously loving the treat of being allowed to stay up with the men.

"I should go," Hamelin said to Henry, who seemed unconcerned by all the undercurrents and was paring his fingernails with a small antler-handled knife. "If we are to start out at dawn, I need to sleep—I cannot keep your hours."

Henry looked amused. That he was sitting down and acting as a leaning post for John was only because his damaged leg was paining him. "I cannot keep my hours either," he said wryly. He gave Hamelin a searching look. "You have said little this evening, Brother."

Two frown lines appeared between Hamelin's brows. "I have been turning things over in my mind and thinking that there are going to be some storms to ride out."

"There are always storms to ride out," Henry replied with weary cynicism and looked up as an usher approached him.

"Sire, the Count of Toulouse requests to speak to you urgently."

Henry raised his brows. "So urgently that it cannot wait until tomorrow?"

"He seemed to think so, sire."

Henry flicked his hand. "Bid him enter then," he said and looked down to tousle John's hair. "Time for your bed, my little bridegroom. Geoffrey, you too. Time you left."

Geoffrey narrowed his eyes but rose to his feet.

"I want to stay with you," John protested, stretching. "It's not fair."

Henry smiled sourly. "Life never is, even for those who make the decisions. We shall be riding early tomorrow morning and for a long time. Here." He gave him the knife he had been using, sheathed now in lion-stamped leather. "You can have this. I trust you to be grown-up enough to care for it well."

John's eyes lit up and he thanked his father, but his feet still dragged as he was handed into the custody of his older brother and taken from the room.

"Was it wise giving him a knife?" Hamelin inquired. "God knows what—or who—he will stick it in."

Henry chuckled. "Let him be," he said. "He pleases me well—more than his older brothers."

Raymond of Toulouse was admitted to the chamber and knelt to Henry, although again with a slight hesitation that showed his reluctance. His cloak was fastened askew and his clothes were rumpled as if he had donned them in haste. The expression on his thin features was wary and satisfied at the same time.

"I thought you would have retired by now, my lord," Henry said with neutral courtesy.

"I had, sire," Raymond replied, "but I have news you need to hear."

❖❖❖

Isabel lay in bed waiting for Hamelin. He had been gone for what seemed forever, and the lamps were almost out of oil. She had been putting tiny decorative stitches on the neck of an undershirt she was making for him, but now her eyes were strained and sore. She knew she would be unable to sleep until he returned. She had her chaplain read to her for a while, and she prayed, because there seemed a lot that needed praying for. Everything felt dark and ominous, even though the world was turning toward spring. And although spring brought new life, it also heralded the campaigning season, and there was trouble afoot. She hated Hamelin going to war. She feared for him each time he kissed her farewell, but she knew better than to cling and weep. She was afraid for Hamelin and afraid for Alienor. She was like a grain caught between two millstones, for she loved both, yet to support one was to be disloyal to the other.

At last, in the small hours, Hamelin returned to their chamber and made his way to the bed by the light of the cresset lamp. Sitting down, he removed his shoes, then leaned forward and put his face in his cupped hands and groaned. Isabel sat up and crawled across the coverlet to him. "Hamelin, what is it?" She set her arms around his shoulders.

He lifted his head. "I do not know if I can tell you. Christ, I feel so tired and sick—heartsick."

Alarmed but outwardly calm, Isabel left the bed and rekindled two lamps. She stirred the fire to life and brought him a cup of wine. Hamelin drank, put the cup down, and lay on the bed, propping himself against the bolsters. "I do not know what to say or do anymore," he said bleakly. "We have reached a precipice and the only thing to do now is jump."

Isabel strove to steady her voice. "What has happened?"

He grimaced. "Raymond of Toulouse came to see Henry and told him he had overheard Alienor, Harry, and Richard plotting treason against Henry."

Isabel stared at him in shock. "No! I do not believe that!"

"It is true," Hamelin said grimly. "They have every cause, and it is within them to do so, especially after today."

"And how fortuitous of Raymond to overhear it, and report back! How can you be certain he is not just causing mischief?"

"Because he had been paying one of Alienor's servants to report to him—her water bearer. Harry is preparing to ride to Paris and foment rebellion from there, and Alienor is supporting him."

"Dear God!" She put her hand to her mouth. What had Alienor done? There was no going back from this. "He could still have misconstrued what was said. Perhaps he is making mountains from grains of sand. Nothing would suit Raymond of Toulouse better than to set father against son, and if he could harm Alienor into the bargain, so much the better."

Hamelin shrugged. "And no smoke without fire, they say. Henry has to take this threat seriously."

Isabel shook her head. "This would never have happened if Henry had not ignored her right as duchess of Aquitaine and accepted Raymond's homage himself. By doing that he was saying he has bound Aquitaine to England. There are many things for which Alienor will not forgive Henry, but that one will be written on her heart at her deathbed."

"He had to do it." Hamelin's tone was defensive. "Raymond of Toulouse could not have been brought to swear any other way. He would never kneel to a woman—to Alienor."

"But the pressure was on him, not on Henry," Isabel pointed out. "Raymond would have had to swear eventually or be brought down. Henry had as much interest in what came about today as Raymond did."

Hamelin said nothing, his mouth set in a tired, stubborn line, revealing that he knew very well what she was saying but would argue no further.

"What will happen now?" she asked.

He sighed. "Henry is going to take Harry on a hunting trip and keep him at his side for a while."

Under house arrest then. "And Alienor?"

"He will keep a close watch on her, but there is little she can do on her own from Poitiers." He pulled off his shirt and left the bed to go to the basin and wash. Isabel looked at him in the grainy lamplight. In the years since their marriage his frame had thickened, but he remained strong and muscular. His hair was threaded with silver but curled at the nape in a way that still made her ache with tenderness. She loved him dearly, but she was not happy because she knew he would follow his royal brother to the ends of the earth, whether he agreed with him or not, and do his bidding as he had done at the oath-taking ceremony.

"I have heard certain rumors too," she said quietly.

He turned around from his ablutions, squinting through water-blurred eyes. "What about?"

"About Henry considering annulling his marriage to Alienor on the grounds of consanguinity."

"That is a ridiculous notion." He buried his face in a towel, a ploy that Isabel noted with foreboding.

"Not to a woman who has been lied to and pushed aside."

"And what do these rumors say?"

Isabel clasped her hands together. "Some say he is planning to put Alienor aside in order to wed Rosamund de Clifford, and some say the French princess Alais."

"That's preposterous!" Hamelin lowered the towel, and she saw genuine astonishment in his eyes.

"Is it? Alais is rising thirteen, of marriageable age. And he still keeps the de Clifford girl as close to him as his shirt and braies. There are times when I think nothing is beyond your brother."

Hamelin gave a vehement shake of his head. "He will not do that."

"But what does it say that people think him capable of it?"

He returned to bed and pulled up the covers. Isabel pressed against him, seeking the warm security of his body, not wanting to argue but still with a heavy conscience. "I want to go to Poitiers with Alienor," she said.

"Why would you want to do that?" He tensed as she had known he would. "No, you will go to Colombiers and wait for me there until we can return to England."

She stroked his cheek. "I know that is your plan, but if I accompany Alienor, perhaps I can smooth the situation. Queens are not the only ones who are mediators."

He grasped her hand. "If Alienor is caught up in rebellion, I cannot afford to be involved in it through you. Your heart is too tender, and I do not want to see it bruised or taken advantage of. We cannot have conflicted loyalties in this."

"That will not happen. If matters become too difficult, I shall leave for the Touraine." She ran her hand over his chest, feeling the wiry curl of his hair. "I know you are troubled, but Alienor is still my sister-by-marriage—yours too. Her sons and daughters are our nieces and nephews—cousins to our own children. John is close friends with our William. I will not disobey you, but I am asking you to give me a few weeks with Alienor to see what I can do. And then I can bring the children away with me if necessary."

She bit her tongue in the long silence that followed and made herself stay still. Eventually, Hamelin pulled her into his arms. "Very well, go, but I trust you, and if you break that trust, know that it can never be mended."

"I won't fail you. I swear on my soul." She kissed him on the mouth, and he tightened his embrace, claiming her for his own, even while his words agreed to let her go.

❖❖❖

Shortly after dawn, Alienor rose and prepared to face the day. She had slept badly, and her dreams had been vivid, disturbing, but impossible to grasp, so she could not recall their content, only their unsettling effect, which left her feeling as if the walls were closing around her, pushed inward by unseen enemies on all sides. Yesterday's headache still thumped at the back of her eyes, and she sipped a bitter tisane of willow bark to combat the pain. Marchisa was combing her hair, ready to plait it. It was still sleek and strong but more silver than gold these days, and she was contemplating abandoning the dyes and letting it become a natural waterfall.

As Marchisa added a lotion perfumed with nutmeg to the final strokes of the comb, Henry arrived together with servants bearing bread, cheese, and jugs of wine.

Alienor eyed him in surprise as the attendants assembled a small trestle table, spreading a white cloth and arranging the food on it. "I thought you would be gone by now," she said. Her anger had frozen overnight and she was numb.

"I am sorry to disappoint you, madam, but the pack horses are not ready, and I have to wait on the rising of slugabeds. I thought we might break our fast together while I wait."

Alienor dismissed her women and swiftly wove her hair into a plait herself. "Why should I want to break bread with you ever again after yesterday's oath-taking?"

Henry waved his hand and sat down at the trestle. "You should pay no heed to that. It was the easiest way of getting Raymond of Toulouse to kneel in homage to me. He would never have knelt to you, so I represented you to make it easier. You are still duchess of Aquitaine. Richard is still duke." He reached for a piece of bread and looked at her in that way she hated because, while ostensibly focusing on her, he had in fact detached himself and spoken as if she did not matter.

"So you would rather Raymond of Toulouse was assuaged and pandered to than Richard and I be acknowledged overlords in a public ceremony?" The numbness began to thaw and tingle with pain. "You had no right to do that, Henry. Aquitaine does not belong to you. It is only yours by marriage. It is mine and Richard's by right of birth and blood."

Henry chewed and swallowed. "Raymond of Toulouse was ready to make peace and I had to seize the opportunity. I need everything settled before I go to fight in Outremer."

"Ah yes, Outremer." Alienor picked up her own goblet, the drape of her sleeve shimmering in the light from the high window. "I wondered how long it would be before we came to that. If you ever set foot there, it will be more of a miracle than those purportedly being performed at the tomb of Saint Thomas. I can see straight through you. Even the money you give to the cause in Jerusalem remains yours. You are just stockpiling it elsewhere in case of emergencies."

A red flush crept up his throat and mottled his face. "You have a vicious tongue."

"Any tongue is vicious that does not wag in support of your desires," Alienor said flatly. "You shall not annex Aquitaine to England, whatever subterfuge you employ. Far from settling things down, do you think my vassals will be overjoyed to see their hereditary rulers set aside as if of no consequence while Toulouse kneels to the king of England?"

"I dealt as I saw fit," he snapped. "Nothing will change." He rose to his feet and paced to the window, goblet in hand.

The door opened and Harry walked in. "Mama, I..." He stopped and looked warily from one parent to the other.

"Ah," Henry said with false bonhomie. "The prodigal son. Come break your fast with us." He gestured to the table.

Harry eyed him warily. "I'm not hungry," he said but went to pour himself wine. His eyes were pouched and bleary from the previous night's excess.

"Even so, you should eat something before we set out."

Harry blinked at him. "Before we set out? I am staying here in Aquitaine. None of my baggage or Marguerite's is packed."

Henry's smile was narrow and intense. "No matter. I was not thinking of your entire household, just you and a few retainers. There have been too many misunderstandings between us of late. I thought it would be good for us to go hunting together. Marguerite can stay here with your mother."

Harry flushed and shot a glance at Alienor, who sent him one back with an infinitesimal shake of her head before she dropped her gaze. "I am not ready to leave."

"Then I will wait for you." Henry finished his wine and dusted crumbs from his tunic but did not leave the room, making it plain that he intended to take Harry with him here and now. "I've given orders to have your horse saddled," he said, "and your baggage packed." He spoke in a jocular tone and came to put his arm across Harry's shoulder. "We can pick up supplies as we head into Anjou. Come, if you are not going to eat, let us leave your mother to make herself presentable for a public farewell."

He ushered Harry to the door and, as he opened it, he looked over his shoulder and gave Alienor a glittering look that said, *Checkmate*.

Alienor pushed aside her platter, her bread barely touched. Henry obviously knew something was afoot; he had spies everywhere who would carry tales. She thought back over what had been said the previous evening and gnawed her lip. Enough for suspicion, certainly; enough for Henry to want to bind his eldest son to his side. Perhaps he would talk Harry around. Perhaps he would offer him more baubles and allowances to fund his lavish lifestyle without addressing Harry's true discontent. It would not be the first time.

She summoned her women so they could resume her toilet and she chose to wear the same finery as yesterday, including her jeweled hairnet and coronet, to show everyone that she was still the proud duchess of Aquitaine.

The courtyard was packed with people mounting their horses, making their farewells, and adjusting their traveling baggage. She watched Harry mount his palfrey with a set jaw and a hard expression in his eyes. He smiled though for the crowd, a fierce smile, bold as a troubadour, and tossed a profligate shower of coins into a group of watching children, as if to say that this largesse was nothing, and there was plenty more where that came from: all from his father's coffers.

Richard watched the performance with arms folded and a cynical twist to his lips. Envy glinted in his eyes too. For two pins Alienor knew he too would be on a horse and away with the men, even though he would vehemently deny such desires. He was attracted by his father's mantle of power and at the same time scornful; he knew he could wield that power so much more honorably and effectively.

From the corner of her eye, Alienor noticed William Marshal preparing to mount his palfrey and she went to him. William immediately removed his foot from the stirrup and bowed. "Madam."

"I do not know what is going to happen in the future, but as you value your oath, keep my son safe," she said, touching his mailed sleeve. "I am laying this task on you."

"Madam, I swore to serve you all my days, and I swore to serve my young lord when he became king. I shall not veer from my word but do all in my power to protect him."

"Then God protect you and keep you strong because Harry will need you."

"I shall not fail you, madam." William kissed her sapphire ring. She took it off her finger and gave it to him. "There is sufficient worth in this to buy a spare horse or other requirements," she said. "It is for the unforeseen. Keep it close, and tell no one you have it."

"Madam." William threaded it around his neck on the same thong as his cross and tucked it down inside his shirt.

Alienor left him and went to embrace Harry. "Be careful," she said, her voice strong with warning. "Do nothing rash. I shall be thinking of you and holding you in my prayers."

Harry gave her a broad smile. "Do not worry for me, Mama," he said blithely. "Indeed, this hunting party of Papa's may turn out to be a fine suggestion after all."

Alienor arched her brows and wondered just what he was hiding under that smile. All or nothing? He was becoming as difficult to read as his father.

Henry rode up on his white palfrey and reined it back hard. Its nostrils flared, showing their red lining, and bloody foam dripped from the bit. She had never seen him ride a beast that was at peace with him. "Have you finished with the fond farewells?" he demanded.

She swept him an ironic curtsy because she had no fond farewells for him. "Indeed, sire, I have."

"Good. I shall send word from Chinon."

She watched them ride out and tightened her jaw. At her side Richard said quietly, "What now, Mama?"

"Now," she said, "we play a waiting game."

Returning to her chamber, she felt sick but elated. At least with Henry gone, she could breathe again, and she had much to do. Summoning her scribe, she dictated letters to her vassals to try to reverse the damage done by Raymond of Toulouse's oath to Henry. Richard expended his energy by riding out on patrol with his knights as a demonstration of his ability to command and to prove that Aquitaine was in firm hands both administratively and militarily.

Isabel remained with Alienor, keeping her company but staying in the background. She showed Joanna and Belle how to work a certain floral embroidery stitch, and then she set up her braid loom so that Joanna could make a collar for her pet squirrel. Alienor watched her and frowned.

"You did not have to stay," she said, taking a moment away from dictating her letter. "Indeed, it might have been better if you had left."

Isabel gave her a look of measured calm. "I discussed it with Hamelin last night. I said you might need company, and someone other than nursemaids to watch over John and Joanna. I can take them back to Fontevraud when I do leave if you wish, but our sons are good friends and I thought they would enjoy each other's company for a little longer."

"What else did you and Hamelin discuss?" Alienor said. "Did he leave you to spy on me?" She heard the bitterness in her voice but did not draw back; it was like relieving the pressure on a sup-purating wound.

"Of course not!" Isabel's hazel-brown eyes widened in distress. "Henry surely has better spies than me if he wants to observe what you are doing."

"What else am I supposed to think after yesterday? If you had any sense in you, you would have left with Hamelin."

"I care for you," Isabel said. "And I thought I might be of use. If I had gone with Hamelin, it would only have been as far as the Touraine, and then I would have been left to myself. Indeed, Hamelin wanted me to leave, but he let me have my way in this."

"You should have listened to him," Alienor said. "I know Henry has me watched—and you will be under suspicion and watched too."

Isabel smoothed her hands over her knees. "He thinks you are plotting to overthrow him and have your sons rule in his stead. Raymond of Toulouse came to him late last night and told him that you were. Hamelin was there and heard it all."

Alienor was not surprised, but the words still took her aback. Expecting a blow was not the same as being struck. "That is exactly what I would expect of a snake—nay, a worm like Raymond of Toulouse." She curled her lip. "He would connive at anything to save himself and drive a wedge into our household, although he hardly needs to do so with Henry as he is. That explains why Henry wanted to take Harry with him. They might go hunting together, but Henry will watch his every move." She shook her head at Isabel. "I know you want everything to be right, but I cannot make it so. If Henry tries to take Aquitaine from me using underhand methods, I shall fight him with every means at my disposal until the last breath in my body. He will have to kill me to stop me."

"Oh, Alienor!" Isabel held out a hand toward her in distress, her eyes liquid.

"Save your compassion," Alienor snapped with a flash of temper. "Henry's perfidy I can deal with, but not your doe-eyed looks of pity." She narrowed her eyes. "It's about more than that, isn't it? You are going to tell me about the rumors of an annulment." She gave a bitter smile. "You are not the only one who knows things. The gossip has been so rife on that score I would be deaf not to have heard it." She rose and went to the window embrasure. "I wanted to come to Aquitaine, but it suited Henry too—putting me here out of the way as he saw it. If he can attach my lands to England by ties of allegiance and vassalage, then that gives him more control and diminishes my power. He can use

Richard as a puppet count and retire me to a nunnery—or so he thinks."

Isabel said quietly, "You will have heard rumors about a new marriage too then."

Alienor grimaced. "Yes, I know about that, but Rosamund de Clifford is not of sufficient birth to be a queen, no matter her aspirations."

"And Alais?"

"Oh, you have heard that one too? Hah, what a match that would be. He would become his own son's brother-in-law and make his second son a cuckold." She looked over her shoulder at Isabel. "Knowing his weakness for young women I would not put it beyond him, but for now, that is one for the mischief makers—and there are plenty of those. He has enough to contend with dealing with the aftermath of the murder of Becket without further incensing the Church's sensibilities." She gave Isabel a tight smile, like a wounded soldier ignoring the blood. "Certainly I shall retire to a nunnery—when my bones are so frail that they can no longer bear my weight, when every tooth has fallen from my skull. By that time, either by mercy or retribution, I shall no longer care."

❖❖❖

Three weeks later, at home in Poitiers, Alienor was preparing for bed when William Marshal was ushered into her chamber. It was raining hard and he was soaked to the skin. "I am sorry to be dripping on your floor, madam, but the weather is foul and I have ridden hard," he said with chagrin, his teeth chattering.

One of her women brought a towel while another took his sodden cloak. Alienor sent a squire for bread and wine and made William sit before the hearth where a maid was stirring the embers to life. She saw him glance at her hair, which was combed down and loose ready for bed, and her lips twitched. "You may well look," she said. "It is given to few men to see a queen with her hair unbound."

"Madam, it is a memory I will treasure for the rest of my life," he said gallantly.

She waved her hand in a gesture that both accepted and dismissed the flattery. "What news of my son?"

William wiped his face with the towel. "He is safe in Paris, madam."

Alienor raised her brows, not certain that she would call being in Paris "safe." It certainly meant matters had escalated. "And how did that come about?"

"The king and my young lord went hunting and continued to discuss their differences without resolution. My lord realized there was no further point in talking to the king, so we left Chinon secretly at night and rode for the French border. When the king found out he gave chase, but he was too late." William's brow furrowed. "My lord asked me to knight him while we were on the road. I said it should be done by a man of greater standing, the king of France perhaps, but my lord did not wish that. He desired to be knighted so that he would be worthy to lead men…and since his father had not done so at Limoges he felt the lack…" He sent her an apologetic look. "Madam, I did as he bade me and I knighted him on the road because he would have it at whatever cost."

Alienor thought it a trifling matter when compared to the rest. "That is not to his detriment or yours," she said. "Go on…"

"We reached Paris and King Louis welcomed us. He was greatly disturbed to learn that the Count of Toulouse had paid liege homage to King Henry."

Alienor gave a cynical nod. That particular move would stick in Louis's craw just as much as hers, if for other reasons. He had done everything in his power to bring Toulouse into his own domain. To see it veering now toward England would infuriate him.

"He promised to support my lord, and they have set about courting allies, of which there are many." William gave her an uneasy look. "King Henry sent the archbishop of Rouen to Paris to demand that Louis return my lord to his custody." William paused as food and wine arrived. Alienor waited until the servant had set them down and moved away.

"Go on," she said.

"The archbishop came before Louis in full court and said, 'The king of England asks you to return his son.' And Louis replied that he did not know what the archbishop was saying because the king of England was sitting right beside him."

The comment was to the point and cutting. There was satisfaction to Alienor in hearing what had been said but no pleasure. "It is in Louis's interests to foment a quarrel between father and son," she said. "His support may be strong for now, but it cannot be relied on as a rock, as I have good cause to know. What else?" She poured wine into a cup for William and waited for him to take a few swallows. The firelight gleamed on his strong throat and the raindrops still trembled in his hair.

"Matthew and Philip of Flanders have rallied to my lord's side. So have the king of Scotland and the earls of Leicester and Norfolk. England is poised to rebel and Normandy too. My lord is of no mind to conciliate."

"I am sorry it has come to this." Alienor rubbed her arms, and even standing close to the fire felt the cold invading her body. "Now I must choose between my obligation to my husband as his queen, and my love and loyalty to the heirs born of our union." And since her sons were her future, and since Henry had slighted her, that choice was obvious. "I trust you," she said to William. "I trust your utter loyalty to me and to my boys."

"Madam, I swore my oath to you and to my young lord," William said stoutly. "I am troubled by the divisions, but I hold to my word." He left the bench and fell to his knees. "I swear it again to you. I shall protect my lord with my life and serve unto death."

Alienor took his hands between hers, still cold from the rain, and gave him the kiss of peace. "Let us hope it does not come to that," she said, "but I accept your service, and you shall be rewarded for it, I promise."

William resumed his seat. "Madam, there is more. My lord wishes the lords Richard and Geoffrey to join him in France.

That is the reason he has sent me to Poitiers—to bring them to safety—and yourself if that is your wish."

Alienor dug her fingernails into her palms. So, Harry wanted to be head of the family and Louis wanted all the young fledglings to roost with him—although not, she suspected, herself. It would come as a nasty surprise if she did turn up with her sons. The scenario of Richard and Geoffrey going to France was one she had wrestled with, feeling as if she was trapped in a box with the lid coming down.

"They are not yet men," she said, "even if they believe they are. They are susceptible to the manipulations of others. Harry might think he is taking control by rebelling against his father, but Henry has the devil's luck, and I know what a fierce fighter and organizer he is. Harry and Louis don't have those skills. Richard will come to them in time, but he is only fifteen years old, and Geoffrey even younger."

William cleared his throat. "If they stay here the king will come for them," he said.

And there was no telling what Henry would do then. He had already revealed his intention of marginalizing her and seizing Aquitaine. In that case why should she support him? Better that Aquitaine go to France. "Find a bed for the night," she said. "And be ready to leave at dawn with my sons."

He rose to his feet and bowed. "And you, madam?" His gaze was troubled. "What will you do?"

She shook her head. "I shall not leave unless I must, but I want my boys kept safe." She bit her lip. "This is going too far and too fast, William. God protect us all from the storm."

❖ ❖ ❖

It was still raining at dawn, but no more than a light mizzle and the air was mild. Watching the grooms loading the packhorses, Alienor was bereft but also relieved that her sons would soon be out of Henry's reach.

Richard joined her, his cloak covered by a cape of waxed linen to keep him dry. "Take care," she said, embracing him hard. "Know that you are in my prayers every day."

"And you in mine, Mama."

"Look after Geoffrey." They were still so young. Fifteen and fourteen. That was no age to be caught up in this squabble. They were learning difficult and bitter lessons that were not beneficial, even while they were gaining experience of the world. Richard thought it all a great adventure, his face aglow and his eyes fierce.

Geoffrey, true to his nature, was enigmatic and self-contained. It was often difficult to know what he was thinking, whereas with Richard she could almost feel his every thought and movement as part of her own. If Eve was Adam's rib, then she felt as if Richard had been formed from one of hers. She hugged Geoffrey to her heart and he gripped her lightly in return, giving little beyond convention and courtesy, and his dark gray eyes were inscrutable.

Watching them ride away into the misty rain under the watchful supervision of William Marshal, her heart was full of pain. Had she done the right thing? She no longer knew. Geoffrey did not look around, but Richard turned gracefully in the saddle to salute her, and then they were gone, swallowed up by their journey, and she was alone.

# 43

## Poitiers, Summer 1173

ALIENOR SAT ON HER FAVORITE SEAT IN THE PALACE GARDEN, surrounded by a trellis of red Palermo roses, a gift many years ago from the king of Sicily. This place was a somnolent haven from the upheaval, discord, and strife beyond the sun-drenched walls, but she knew that the moment she opened the letter sitting in her lap she would bring that turmoil into her sanctuary.

The summer had been one of sporadic warfare and uprising against Henry. In England, the earls of Norfolk, Leicester, Derby, and Chester had rebelled against him. King William of Scotland had marched south and the counts of Boulogne and Flanders had invaded the country.

In Poitiers, Alienor held court in her magnificent new great hall and sifted the news of the skirmishes and engagements, the gossip and the rumors. She stood accused of inciting the fires of revolt: her sons were not old enough to foment a rebellion on their own, so obviously she must be manipulating them and the treachery was all hers. Such righteous and biased opinions from Henry's supporters had given her much cause for caustic mirth.

The letter bore the seal of Rotrou, Archbishop of Rouen, one of Henry's particular friends, but a man for whom she had always had deep respect.

"Are you going to open it?" Isabel asked, snipping off a thread from the embroidery on which she was working.

Alienor grimaced. "In truth I am tempted to burn it," she said but steeled herself and broke the seal. Having unfolded the parchment, she read aloud what the archbishop had written.

> *To Alienor, Queen of England, from Rotrou, Archbishop of Rouen, and his Suffragans. Greetings in the search for peace.*

She grimaced at that.

> *Marriage is a firm and indissoluble union. This is public knowledge and no Christian can take the liberty to ignore it. What God has joined let us not put asunder. The woman is at fault who leaves her husband and fails to keep the trust of this social bond. A woman who is not under the headship of the husband violates the law of Scripture: "The head of the woman is the man." She is created from him, she is united to him, and she is subject to his power.*
>
> *We deplore publicly and regretfully that you have left your husband and what is worse, you have opened the way for the lord king's, and your own, children to rise up against the father. We know that unless you return to your husband, you will be the cause of widespread disaster. Your actions will result in ruin for everyone in the kingdom. Therefore, Illustrious Queen, return to your husband and our king. In your reconciliation, peace will be restored from distress, and in your return, joy may return to all. Against all women and out of childish counsel, you provoke disaster for the lord king. Before this matter reaches a bad end, you should return. We are certain that he will show you every possible kindness and the surest guarantee of safety.*
>
> *I beg you, advise your sons to be obedient and respectful to their father. He has suffered many anxieties, offenses, and grievances. Either you will return to your husband, or we must call upon canon law and use ecclesiastical censures against you. We say this reluctantly, but unless you come back to your senses, with sorrow and tears, we will do so.*

By the time she had finished reading, Alienor was shaking with fury, fear, and revulsion.

Isabel was pale and wide-eyed. "Holy Mary!" She reached across to touch her hand. "This is terrible. Is there no way around this?"

"Oh yes," Alienor said grimly. "Henry's way. I am being made a scapegoat here and fitted for shackles."

A second letter had accompanied the first, this one bearing Henry's seal and including a gift of prayer beads fashioned from amber and rock crystal. Alienor was tempted to take the jewels and hurl them in the nearest midden but restrained herself. They were valuable, and she could sell them or use them as a bribe. Henry greeted her as "his dear wife," and she had to swallow bile.

*I rely on you to be faithful to me and do all you can to bring our sons to heel so that they may be taught the error of their ways. I do not doubt your sincerity in this matter, and yet, if you prove insincere, I shall treat you likewise.*

And then a standard salute of farewell. How had it come to this? How had she let herself be brought to this?

"Harry will listen to me every bit as much as his father does, which is not at all," she said. "I am the one being ground to forcemeat between the two of them when it is all of their doing, not mine. They blame me for their faults."

"But if you went to Henry and threw yourself at his feet, you would save yourself," Isabel said. "What then could Harry, Richard, and Geoffrey do except return to the family fold? If you continue to defy Henry, it is akin to jumping off a cliff."

Alienor set her jaw. "So you counsel me to return to him?"

"What is the alternative?"

Alienor looked away to where the summer light flickered through the leaves of a cherry tree, the same one she had played around as a little girl. The same one where the archbishop of Bordeaux had told her that her father was dead and that, aged thirteen, she had become duchess of Aquitaine.

"The alternative is to defy him," she said. "If I go to him, it will make no difference. He will treat me the same as he has always done, and I shall still be blamed." She touched Isabel's arm. "You should leave for your own good. Go to Touraine. It is not safe for you here. Take John and Joanna to Fontevraud for me, and Marguerite—she cannot stay here. Everyone must go."

"Alienor, do not do this," Isabel pleaded. "Henry is an anointed king and your husband."

"Harry is an anointed king too, and my son," Alienor retorted. "Henry lost the right to my loyalty when he ignored my authority in Aquitaine. He has pushed me to the edge, which is why I find it so easy to step over it now. It is all very well for you to speak of obedience to your husband, but you see it through the glow of your match to Hamelin, who can do no wrong in your eyes. Do not say he is your husband and it is your duty to obey him; that much is evident." She spoke these last words with a curl of her lip and bitterness surged, followed by remorse when she saw the hurt in Isabel's eyes. "For your sake and mine, you must go."

Isabel set her sewing aside and embraced Alienor, giving her a tender hug, and that made Alienor feel guiltier still.

"Tomorrow then," Isabel said. "I will not part from you in upset and anger. You are my sister-by-marriage and you are my friend, whatever comes of this."

Alienor's throat tightened. "Say nothing more, you foolish woman," she said, squeezing Isabel in return. "You will make me weep, and I cannot afford to do that. I need all my strength and I refuse to drown it in tears. My path is set and nothing you say or do will change it…" Swallowing, she gently pushed Isabel away. "We shall not speak of it. Indeed, we shall celebrate instead."

A leaving feast was hastily organized, held later in the day than the usual dinner hour to give the cooks time to prepare the dishes of sugared pastries, the stews and roasts, and fruits marinated in honey. Alienor had the tables set out in the garden and horn lanterns hung from the trees. Cresset lamps pooled the tables with gold, and candles flamed on every stone plinth and surface until the garden was a twinkling arena of fallen stars in the gathering dusk.

The songs and music of Aquitaine flowed from lute and pipe and the emotive, pure voices of court minstrels and troubadours. Songs of desire and longing, of springtime and bursting hawthorn buds. Of love requited and love spurned. There were scurrilous tales too, which filled the space with laughter as people ate their food and drank the potent wines of Bordeaux from cups of Tyrian glass. There was dancing, and the children, wild with excitement, ran about shrieking and playing games of tag and hide-and-seek. Poignant, bittersweet moments filled for Alienor with memories of her childhood with her sister Petronella and her small brother Aigret. Once they had been the little ones chasing one another around the columns while the adults feasted, listened to music under the stars, and talked business and pleasure. She felt the validation of tonight within those recollections and was achingly sad, knowing that in the morning it would all be gone, perhaps never to return save in memories.

❖❖❖

"Be good for your aunt Isabel," Alienor told John and Joanna as she adjusted their traveling cloaks and kissed them both. "I know you have made this journey before with your cousins but it is still a long way."

Both children nodded, although John huffed with impatience, considering himself a big boy beyond need of coddling. Joanna was already looking over her shoulder at her cousins who stood waiting. Alienor felt a pang that her children were so eager to be off. Yet they were fond of their cousins and loved their aunt Isabel and that was all to the good—for them. She would not think on her own sorrow. Her sons were at the court of her former husband; their wives and their future wives were best dwelling within the safety of Fontevraud for now. She embraced the young women and exhorted them to look after one another and was moved to see tears welling in Marguerite's eyes.

"Come now," she said briskly. "You are a queen. You must set an example to the others and be their strength. They will look to you for guidance."

Marguerite sniffed and surreptitiously wiped her eyes on her sleeve. "Yes, madam," she said in a tight voice but raised her head and straightened her shoulders, and in that moment Alienor warmed toward her daughter-in-law.

Isabel took custody of John and Joanna, shepherding them with open arms, her cloak like the wings of a mother hen. Waiting in the courtyard, Isabel's traveling wain was painted with the blue-and-gold de Warenne checkers, and the covered top had segments rolled back to allow light and air to those within while still affording a degree of seclusion. In went the children and the young queen. In went the small pet dogs, while the larger gaze-hounds were left to trot at the sides of the cart.

A strong contingent of de Warenne household knights stood ready to escort their countess and her wain north into Anjou and they too were decked out in the de Warenne blue and gold.

Alienor gave Isabel an emerald ring that Isabel had long admired. In return, Isabel presented Alienor with a soft woolen blanket in shades of lavender and misty green fashioned from cloth woven on her own Yorkshire lands.

"I wrap myself in this when I am cold and I cannot sleep, and it always comforts me," she said. "I want you to feel the same and think of me when you use it."

Alienor swallowed. It was a humble piece of cloth, but what it stood for was priceless. "Assuredly I shall," she said with tears in her eyes.

"May God keep you," Isabel said, "and may I see you soon in happier circumstances."

"And you, my sister."

Alienor stood in the courtyard until the traveling cart and its escort had rumbled from sight, and then she folded the blanket around her shoulders, crossing her arms over her heart, and returned to her hall. With everyone gone, the vast space was one of lost footsteps where only hers scuffed on the flagstones with no one to hear.

❖ ❖ ❖

The season's wheel rolled through summer to autumn in Poitou, but the colder days were slow to make their impression and the leaves stayed green on the trees long into September before slowly yielding to crisp, dry gold.

Messengers arrived with news and rode out again with bulging satchels. Verneuil had burned to the ground. Alienor learned that Henry had sold one of his gold crowns and was hiring Brabançon mercenaries in huge numbers to exert his will and quash rebellion wherever it rose. As a result of his speed and expenditure, he had secured his rule in Maine and Anjou as far as the Poitevan border. England was in a state of flux, but the rebels had failed to prevail. Indeed, Henry's bastard son Jeoffrey, far from embracing his role as archdeacon of Lincoln and turning to the clergy, was proving to be a competent general and had secured victories over the English insurgents. Negotiations at Gisors for a peaceful solution had broken down because Harry, Richard, and Geoffrey refused to yield to their father's demands. The young Earl of Leicester had gone so far as to threaten violence to Henry, matters had become so heated.

Alienor read the latest letter in her chamber by the open window. The October air was mild and balmy, giving the lie to the calamitous news at which she was staring. The rebel earls of Leicester and Norfolk had fought a battle and suffered a major defeat at Fornham Saint Genevieve, near Saint Edmund's shrine. The Earl of Leicester had been seized together with his wife, who had been with him at the battle and captured wearing a hauberk. She had cast her gold rings into the swollen River Witham rather than let her captors loot them from her fingers.

Alienor's heart sank. Ever since the failure of the talks at Gisors, she had been considering quitting Poitiers to join her sons in France. They had urged her to do so because Henry was at Chinon and poised to strike down into Aquitaine with his Brabançons. She could not depend on the loyalty of her own barons. Some would stand firm, but others would seize the opportunity to tear free of their feudal oath and increase their territories at her expense.

Alienor bit her lip. She could go to Henry and try to put out the fires on the burning bridges between them, but the notion of facing him as a supplicant filled her with revulsion. She could ride to Paris and try to persuade her sons to make peace with their father, but if they would not conciliate at Gisors, she doubted she would succeed. Or she could ride to Paris, make an alliance with Louis, and fight Henry to the bitter end. Three choices, all with their own poisonous barbs. Where was peace? Where were grace and tranquillity? Whatever decision she made, she was damned.

Undecided, but knowing she could not remain in Poitiers, she summoned her household and gave the order to pack the baggage for a journey north.

"Where are we bound, madam?" asked Saldebreuil de Sanzay. His hair, once as black as polished jet, was badger-streaked, and his lively dark eyes were surrounded by seams of hard experience.

Alienor frowned. "I have not decided yet. I will know when I come to the crossroads." But she wondered if she would. Since none of her options were palatable, she might just stay at the intersection, suspended between choices.

Saldebreuil raised his brows. "And you are taking a full baggage train?"

"I shall go as I choose, and it will not be as a pauper," she said regally.

"Indeed not, madam. Even clad in naught but the clothes you stand in, you would never be that," he replied with a gallant bow. "But I should know how to prepare."

She tapped her forefinger against her lips while she considered. It was impractical to take everything. She would pack the portable items she could not bear to leave for Henry's mercenaries should he seize Poitiers. Her father's chair, a wall hanging stitched by her mother, the contents of the treasury, the painted glass in the ladies' chamber at the top of the Maubergeonne Tower. She would send the items to Fontevraud for safekeeping and Henry would not touch them there.

He had already stripped her of so many precious things and trampled them underfoot. Her standing as duchess of Aquitaine, her place as a rightful consort and powerful queen. All given to men raised from the dust and in some cases the gutter. She knew he had it in him to be rid of her, and as she pondered Saldebreuil's question, she realized that in truth she had no choice but to side with her sons.

"The full baggage to Fontevraud," she said. "For which you will need carts. I shall ride with pack horses only."

❖ ❖ ❖

Alienor walked around the environs of the palace, bidding farewell to the fabric of her life. As a girl of thirteen she had left Poitiers for Paris, but on that day she had been the future queen of France and royal consort, not a refugee in search of succor and sanctuary. Her heart was dull with pain; she had traveled so far for so very little.

Here was the Maubergeonne Tower where her grandmother had dwelled as her grandsire's mistress. The room was bare, the window glass carefully removed with its lead tracery wrapped in cloth and packed in one of the panniers. The wind whistled through gaps in the apertures, now covered by waxed linen. If she listened hard enough she could hear the echo of voices and laughter. At the side of her vision, she could see her grandmother reclining on her bed draped in a loose scarlet robe, her lips stained by the juice of the sweet dark cherries she was eating as she listened to the beguilement of troubadours. Alienor was aware of her childhood self, playing hide-and-seek with Petronella, discovering the nooks and crannies, the special, secret places of the Maubergeonne. And years later Petronella sneaking away from the hall to be with her French lover in this very chamber. The echoes of anger and betrayal, lust and bloodshed were powerful here; this was more a place of shadows than light. Alienor shivered on the threshold as she turned for one last look and wondered if she would ever return.

Her escort waited in the courtyard, the palfreys and pack animals harnessed and ready, panniers packed and saddles uncovered.

Alienor stroked the nose of her dappled mare, taking comfort from the palfrey's hay-scented breath and soft muzzle. With a brisk nod she accepted Saldebreuil's boost into the saddle. Once settled, her crimson gown arranged, she drew on a pale leather hawking glove and had her falconer hand Blaunchet to her. The gyrfalcon flapped twice and then settled on her wrist, talons gripping the glove. Inspired by the bird's fierce look and her firm weight, Alienor raised her head and looked toward the gate with regal pride. She nodded the command and Saldebreuil saluted, swung into his saddle, and led the troop away from the palace, banners rippling against a deep blue sky sown with flying leaves of autumn gold. Alienor departed Poitiers in full and magnificent array, a triumphal parade, never a retreat.

❖❖❖

That first day, they covered twenty miles to Châtelleraut where they spent the night. Alienor woke at dawn to the sound of the wind hurling rain against the shutters. Reminded of autumn days in England, she rose and dressed for the next leg of the journey. The weather suited the moment. Yesterday had been one of defiance as she left Poitiers, the proud duchess of Aquitaine with her banners flying and her white gyrfalcon on her wrist. This morning that fire had died and she was faced with the cooling embers and ashes of reality.

Going to the hawk perch near the window, she set Blaunchet on her wrist and fed her small gobbets of rabbit meat. Stroking the falcon's gleaming breast feathers, looking through the distorted window glass at the driving rain, she wished she could soar high and free.

"Madam, I doubt we shall make thirty miles today unless the downpour eases," Saldebreuil said gloomily as they broke their fast on hot wheat frumenty mixed with dried fruit and spices.

"We shall just have to do our best and push on from that," Alienor replied. "We endured much worse when traveling to Jerusalem, you and I."

Saldebreuil gave her a wry look. "We were twenty-five years younger then."

"Well then, we have experience under our belts, and the conditions are better because we know the terrain. We are not yet in our dotage." She eyed him with amused irritation. Her constable hated the rain as much as a cat, and it always put him out of humor.

"Madam, you will never be in your dotage, but I am not so sure about myself," Saldebreuil answered. "But I shall do my best to keep up."

A drenched messenger arrived with the news that scouts from Henry's army had been sighted reconnoitering to the north and that Brabançon raiding parties from Chinon had fired at least two villages.

"Then we must be swiftly away and on the alert," she said. After another glance at the foul weather, she discarded yesterday's riding gown for male attire of thick hose and stout boots under a full cloak and a hood of waxed leather. Hardly the dress of a queen, but they needed to make good progress, rain or no rain.

In the courtyard, Alienor mounted her mare and prepared to ride. Blaunchet was confined to a draped cage on one of the packhorses. Today the mood was one of brisk business, devoid of festivity.

The party traveled as swiftly as the muddy roads allowed, scouts trotting ahead to check the route. The wind dropped and the rain eased to a steady drizzle. Saldebreuil hunched over his saddle, head down like a molting owl. Alienor retreated into herself and continued to ponder what she was going to do. If her sons did defeat their father, what would happen to him? They could hardly imprison Henry; to do that to an anointed king, their own father, was untenable. Send him to Outremer? Henry's own grandsire had been of Henry's years when he began a new life as king of Jerusalem. But she could not see Henry accepting that as an alternative, even if he had sworn to go there. That was for show, not reality. If they made a peace treaty, whatever concessions were hammered out would not hold, because Henry never kept his word—or only for as long as he needed to, and he would immediately seek to grab the upper hand again. He would not stop until he was dead, and that in turn made her feel dead.

The autumn afternoon darkened and the rain continued to fall, eventually penetrating cloaks and working its way through tunics and linens to set a damp chill in the flesh until Alienor was shivering.

Through the rainy gloom she saw sudden movement ahead on the road: the glitter of ring mail and a flash of color on a shield. Saldebreuil shouted a warning and her men scrabbled for their weapons. Suddenly Alienor found it difficult to breathe. She turned her mare to spur her back the way they had come, but her bridle was caught by her knight Guillaume Maingot.

"I think it best if you stay, madam," he said, the rain dripping off the nasal bar of his helm. "You could become lost in the woods, or your horse might throw you."

His eyes were expressionless and steely and she felt a cold blade of shock slice down her spine. "You traitor!" she spat. She tried to wrench her mare away and the horse reared, forelegs flailing. Maingot held on hard as the knights who had been blocking the road advanced and encircled. Another of her coterie, Porteclie de Mauzé, closed in on her other side, ensuring she was trapped.

Ambushed, outnumbered, unable to flee, Alienor's troop had no choice but to surrender. Maingot led Alienor's mare forward to the commander of the knights who had ambushed them. Dull gray light shone on helms and rivet mail. Alienor swallowed bile. A further handful of her trusted household guard had joined the other troop, and she realized how badly she had been duped and betrayed. They had just been waiting their moment.

"Madam, I am Thierry de Loudon," her captor announced with a courtly but perfunctory bow. "I have come to escort you to shelter and safety forthwith by order of the king."

However she responded, Alienor realized she would be like a cat spitting at a pack of dogs. They could tear her to pieces at their whim. "And where would that be?" she demanded, retreating into regal hauteur.

"We are taking you to Chinon, madam. The king awaits you there."

She felt as if she had been pierced by a shard of frozen crystal. "What was it worth?" she asked Guillaume Maingot scathingly. "What did he promise you to betray me? Lands? Power? How much did you sell your honor for, my lord? Thirty pieces of silver?"

He gave her a hard look in which there was neither guilt nor shame but perhaps a glint of defiance. "It is not about honor, madam, it is about survival. What use am I to future generations if I squander myself like those men in your entourage who will be taken and tortured or thrown out of their patrimony? Better to be rewarded and put in a strong position. If others would rather die, then that is their choice."

"I hope you rot in hell for this," she hissed.

"I must take that chance, but it may be that God intended me to bring you here and I am doing his will."

Alienor pressed her lips together and looked straight ahead, saying nothing, because he might be right and she did not want to think along that path.

It was full dark when they rode into Chinon and still raining. Alienor was pulled down from her horse and taken within. She stood dripping, shaking with cold and suppressed emotion in the hall where she had been accustomed to give peremptory commands from the high dais. Her captors hemmed her around and she glared at them with contempt. Where did they think she was going to run? She knew they were going to imprison her, but whether in the oubliette or the tower remained to be seen.

She had been in this situation before, as her former husband's captive when she had desired to remain in Antioch with her uncle and to end the marriage. Louis's henchmen had abducted her by force. Her treatment then led her to be terrified now, but she kept her head up and her spine rigid, showing her captors no sign of fear. Even so, she was weak with relief when they brought her to a chamber high up near the battlements.

The room was icy and bare of furnishings but, as she entered, servants arrived with a straw-stuffed mattress, a blanket, a piss bucket, a jug of wine, and a small loaf. The darkness was illuminated by a shallow cresset lamp, only three of its dozen depressions lit with oil. There was neither a hearth nor a brazier in the room to provide heat, and the smell of damp was pervasive.

"Madam, you will rest here until the king is ready to see you."

It was pointless to say they had no right to keep her here; no one was going to listen. "Then at least grant me water to wash," she said, "and dry clothes from my baggage. Or does the king desire me to be brought before him sick with the ague that will surely consume me if you leave me here like this?"

"I shall see what can be done, madam," de Loudon said with distant courtesy and, with his companions, left the room, locking the door behind him in a deliberate jingle of keys. Alienor shivered and rubbed her arms, but that only pressed her damp garments against her flesh. Although no one had manhandled or insulted her, she had not seen a single glance of compassion or support among her captors, and their expressions, when not neutral, were filled with hostility. She was truly surrounded by her enemies.

She had spent so much time here with her children. This fortress had sheltered her as a home and been a place of refuge, but now these walls entombed her and were perhaps her last sight on earth. From home to prison cell to death chamber in one fell swoop.

Facing the shuttered window, she fell to her knees, put her hands together, and prayed in the weak ray of light slanting through a gap where the slats had warped apart. She prayed to the Virgin and Saint Martial for herself, for her sons and for their deliverance. She prayed too for the strength and fortitude to bear what was to come.

She was still on her knees in the almost darkness shivering with cold and shock many hours later when a servant accompanied by two hefty guards brought her a bowl of broth and replenished the oil and wicks in the cresset lamp. She was given items from her baggage—a clean chemise and gown, a comb, and a wimple. There were no jewels, no unguents and perfumes: none of the items Alienor had always taken for granted.

"Am I not to have a maid?" she demanded.

No one spoke, and their action was her reply before they went out, once more locking her in solitude.

Alienor had often thought that her life was a prison, but with freedom gone and no one to answer her smallest command, she realized how much worse it might yet be. She told herself she was still a duchess and a queen. No matter what Henry did to her, he could not take that away.

She rose from her stiff, aching knees and drank the broth, cupping her hands around the bowl for warmth and comfort. She changed into the dry chemise and gown, wrapped the blanket around her from the bedding, and returned to her prayers, entreating God's mercy, for she knew Henry had none in him.

❖❖❖

In the morning a different servant brought her more bread and wine and cold water in which to wash her hands and face. She was not hungry, but she forced down the food and performed her ablutions. There was no one to comb her hair smooth and straight, and she had to do the best she could before plaiting it and concealing it under her wimple.

She heard the tramp of hard footsteps on the stairs, the scuff of shoes outside her door, the turning of the key, and the door opened upon Thierry de Loudon and two guards. They were not wearing mail shirts now, but all had swords at their hips and grim faces. "Madam, you must come with us," said Thierry. "The king awaits you."

She faced them with her head up, but her heart was pounding. Without a word she stepped from the room. One soldier went ahead of her down the winding stairs, dark save for the weak illumination of a single squint light. Aware of the men following her down, Alienor's shoulder blades prickled.

They crossed the courtyard where a long gallows had been erected. Four corpses swung, hands tied behind their backs, necks tilted obscenely to their shoulders. Men of her escort, including the young lad who tended her mare, their only sin being loyalty to her service and lack of value in ransom. Her stomach lurched with nausea. Now she truly knew where she stood.

On entering the great hall, her vision blurred and she staggered. The soldiers grabbed her to hold her up, and although she tried to shake them off, they held her fast and marched her toward the dais at the far end where Henry waited, sitting on what was to all intents a throne of judgment with statues of gilded leopards either side. He wore his coronation robe of embroidered crimson wool and clutched a gilded staff of office in his right fist. His hair, once as red as a squirrel pelt, was the color of dusty tow and thinning. She saw the weariness in him, the bitter, querulous anger—and the power. She had steeled herself to be unafraid, but, seeing him now, the fear still came, and the need to be as far away from him as she could.

Henry beckoned the guards to bring her to the foot of the dais and forced her to her knees before him.

In the long silence that followed, Alienor stared at the steps, her mind and body numb. *Only let this moment be over.*

When he spoke, his voice was harsh as if his throat was filled with gravel. "Do you kneel before me now, madam? You have been brought here to answer for your betrayal and treachery. Your perfidy in turning my sons against me." He drew a breath, but it was swift and left Alienor no place to speak. "You have thwarted me at every turn and despised the rule of law." He clenched his fist on the chair finial. "You deserted your own husband, and now you desert your duchy to fraternize with my enemies and drive my sons deeper into rebellion. You should have stood by me and defended our lands against all comers. In defying me you have lost the right to govern those lands ever again. You have disgraced the honor of your own sons." His fist came down and his voice grew raw and cracked.

"You are a termagant and a liar. You have concealed things from me and gone behind my back. You have used information like a knife to cut me open and then turn the blade in the wound when you should have been my helpmate. You should have been my honor, and you have become my dishonor."

He paused again to pull air into his lungs. Alienor's own chest was hollow. She could not breathe because he was dragging the life from her with each statement, and from the surrounding silence she knew that all were listening with a mingling of relish and shock. She withdrew into herself, folding herself around her soul to protect its flame. Not Aquitaine, God have mercy, not Aquitaine.

"All that I can salvage from this is to thank God that he has given me the chance to run you down like a common criminal and give you the dues you so dearly warrant." His tone crawled with revulsion and he gestured to the guards. "Take her away. I no longer want to look on her and what she has become."

Once again Alienor felt the hard grip of the soldiers' hands on her arms as they jerked her to her feet. As she rose, she looked Henry in the face and saw the implacable eyes of an enemy. The eyes of the man who had sent Thomas Becket to his death. The eyes of the man who would hold on to everything in those knotted fists until death melted his strength.

Henry compressed his lips and, still holding her with his gaze, raised his hand and commanded his musicians to play.

Alienor was escorted from the hall to the sound of harp, tambour, and lute, the latter beloved of her southern lands. He had done it intentionally to intimidate her and show her that she did not matter, that the life of the court would continue unchanged.

Pushed into her prison chamber, she was again left with her slop bucket and a single candle. There were no attendants, nothing to pass the time save her thoughts, and those were unbearable. She lay down on the thin straw pallet and stared at the chamber ceiling. Her eyes were dry; the wounds inflicted by Henry's words had gone too deep for tears. She pressed her hand to her stomach where there was a vile pain, as if everything had been ripped out of her, creating a hollow cavern surrounded by a brittle shell.

Later in the day a surly attendant brought her a bowl of thin onion gruel, half a loaf of stale bread, and a jug of sour wine that was almost vinegar. When she protested that it was undrinkable, he gave her a blank look and backed from the room.

She was considering whether to drink the wine or pour it in the slop bucket when the door opened again and Henry walked in. He gazed around the chamber and sniffed the damp stone air in a disparaging way. A scribe had followed him in, bearing a lectern and his writing effects.

"You will write to our sons," Henry said without preamble. "You will tell them of my displeasure at their continued defiance, and you will order them to yield immediately."

Alienor's hands were shaking, and she folded them at her waist so he would not see how cold she was, how distraught and afraid. "You think they will listen?" She almost laughed from suppressed hysteria. "They are becoming men. If you don't listen to me, Henry, why should they? You think I planned all this? That I betrayed you?" The laugh escaped, and with it all the words that had been burning inside her for days, months, and years. "You purblind fool. You betrayed yourself when you sent me down to Poitiers and then tried to make me and Richard vassals of the English Crown. When you treated me and your sons as pawns on your chessboard—the same way you treat everyone. I tell you this for a certainty—you will die alone, unmourned and uncomforted. Your archbishop will be lauded and you will be vilified!"

Henry clenched his fists. "Dictate the letters and be done, you virago."

Alienor gave him a look of utter loathing. She felt sick with tension and fear, but there was a dark, miserable triumph in answering back to him. "You need light and heat for your scribe to see to write and to hold the pen," she replied. "Although perhaps letters like this should be composed in the cold and the dark."

Henry sent for more candles and a brazier because obviously she was right, but he bit out the commands with suppressed fury. Once the scribe was ready, Henry turned to her. "You inveigled our sons into this; now you will put a stop to it."

"I did not inveigle them," she said wearily. "You pushed them to rebel by your own deeds, and now your birds are coming home to roost. You think them too young? How old were you when you took up the fight for your inheritance? You were younger than Richard, much younger than your heir. I did not turn Harry against you, and it is not my influence that keeps them in Paris. Do you seriously think I would collude with Louis?"

"I no longer know what you would do," he snapped, "but you will dictate those letters, and you will put your seal to them, and you had best pray that they heed them, because I have you in my custody and at my mercy."

She curled her lip. "You think that threat means anything to me?"

"I would hope it means something to them."

"Then you hope in vain, sire, if you believe it will bring them to heel, but since you desire these letters, you may have them. I care not."

She dictated to the scribe, warning Richard, Harry, and Geoffrey of their father's anger and saying that it was incumbent upon her to demand they return and face him. She was honor bound in her role as mother and queen to be a peacemaker. She hoped that her sons were sharp enough to take her meaning.

The ink dried, the letter was folded, and Henry produced the seal he had taken from her confiscated strongbox and pressed it into the melted wax.

Henry sent the scribe away to make another copy of the letter from the rough draft on his wax tablet. As the door closed behind him, anxiety tightened Alienor's throat. Henry approached her with slow deliberation intended to intimidate, until he stood over her, close enough to steal her breath. Reaching out, he ran his hand down her arm.

"There was a time when you were very desirable to me, my lady," he said hoarsely. "When I would as soon bed you as look at you and when my blood burned at the very sight of you. I would imagine your sleeves trailing over my body, and I would grow hard at the very thought. It is such a shame that those days are gone."

Alienor swallowed. Her back was to the wall and there was nowhere to run.

"Yet, make no mistake: I will have my way when I want it, and you will render to me the marriage debt because that is the law between husband and wife." He rubbed his hand at her waist, then down her leg and between her thighs, pressing hard to hurt, and then he dragged her to the pallet and pulled up her skirts.

Alienor chose not to fight him. She could have raked his face with her nails, she could have tried to bite him, but he would only take more pleasure in bending her to his will. Instead, she gave him indifference and lay passive, gazing at the rafters as he pressed her into the mattress. It was painful because she was dry, no love or lust to moisten the channel, and he was vigorous and violent. The episode was conducted in grim silence except for his grunts of exertion, and the stifled sounds she made in her throat. And then she felt him jerk and flood her with his release.

"There," he said, panting, his hips still bucking. "You are still good for one thing, even though you can no longer conceive a child. But then I look at the sons you have given me and turned against me, and I think it a blessing." He withdrew from her with such force that she almost felt dragged inside out. "We will talk again," he said as he left the bed and adjusted his garments, "but for now I shall leave you to ponder the error of your ways." He thrust his face close to hers and seized her jaw. "Be thankful I have not beaten you witless or thrown you in a dungeon, but I tell you this much: you will never see Aquitaine again as long as I live. You betrayed me, and for that I shall never forgive you."

After he had gone, Alienor lay on the bed for a long time, taking shallow breaths because she knew if she drew deeper ones they would become sobs. The place between her legs was on fire and she felt defiled by his seed, where once she had been exalted. He had committed this act, this rape, to show he was the conqueror, the all-powerful, virile king, and that she was subject to his will.

She vowed that if he attempted to take her again, she would have a weapon ready, even if only a hair pin to pierce his throat.

One of them would not survive. She hoped her sons would understand the underlying message in the letters and not yield to their father, yet, if they did not, what did it say about the value they set upon her person? However she looked at the situation, the future was bleak. She closed her mind. If she thought about the situation too hard, she might end up like Petronella, driven mad by the lies and perfidy of men.

# 44

## FALAISE, JULY 1174

ONE DAY BLENDED INTO THE NEXT FOR ALIENOR. FROM Chinon, Henry transferred her to Falaise and once again incarcerated her near the top of the keep, her only access to the outside world via the clergy who came to pray with her, although the chaplains were always of Henry's choosing. She was not permitted to speak to anyone who might tell her what was happening beyond the walls. If she asked questions, she received either bland replies or no reply at all. The guards were changed every couple of days, making it impossible for her to form a rapport with any of them, and she thought she would indeed go mad—she was not meant for the hermitage.

She had been permitted needlework to pass the time, but it was penance sewing of chemises and shifts for the leprous poor, not embroidery, and all she had to work upon was plain gray linen and matching thread. It was worse than dwelling in a nunnery, for even nuns had recourse to a cloister, and all she had were four bare walls and a narrow window that showed her nothing but a thin sliver of sky.

Henry had not visited her again, and she thanked God for that mercy, but she was constantly worried that he would. She had nightmares where the door burst open and he stood on the threshold, ready to batter her to a pulp. She had other dreams where her sons defeated their father and came to set her free, but as the days passed and the seasons turned, they faded and became as dull as the linen over which she toiled in the pale light from her window. Day in, day out, pecking at the stitches, creating garments for people whose lives she would never know. Her hands grew rough for lack of unguents, and the clothes she wore were the same as the kind she was stitching. Her world was a gray chamber, stitching gray linen and looking to a future where she faded into the walls and became nothing.

Lacking a scribe and the wherewithal to send messages, she wrote letters in her mind to her children as she worked, some of them filled with grief and outpourings of love, some dark pools filled with anger at the events that had led her to this. And then she was disgusted with herself for such thoughts.

Worse than all the fighting and arguments was being deprived of company and conversation, of being forgotten and consigned to this sackcloth existence. This chamber might as well be an oubliette.

She had taken to pacing up and down between stints of needlework to keep up her strength, but the act reminded her of Henry's pacing and filled her with hate as she walked from wall to wall to wall, muttering to herself.

One morning, hearing footsteps outside and the murmur of voices, Alienor rose to her feet and faced the door, needle at the ready. When it opened, she could only stare at Isabel, who had her arm around Joanna and John, one on each side. Tears scalded her eyes and overflowed. Joanna ran to her with a cry of "Mama!" and flung her arms around Alienor's waist, pressing her face into the hollow beneath her heart. John, more reserved, joined his sister but waited for Alienor to put out her arm and draw him in. She felt their hair under her hands, their soft skin, their supple bodies. *Dear God, dear God.* "Oh, I have missed you!" Her voice cracked. "So much!"

"Papa said you had to be taught a lesson," John said, giving her a narrow look. "He said he was going to put you so far up a tower you would never come down for what you had done, and that's what happens to traitors!"

Isabel made a sound in her throat and started forward, hand outstretched.

His words struck Alienor like a blow. So Henry would set her youngest children against her too and use them to wield the club. "You must not believe everything your father tells you," she said, unable to keep the anger out of her voice. "It is not always the truth. Whatever happens, I love you, and that love is without boundaries." She forced a smile through her tears, and touched each of their noses to emphasize what she was saying.

"But it is true, you are in a tower." John looked around, taking everything in, the bare, crude simplicity.

"But not forever," she said. "And I am not a traitor... Go and sit by the hearth while I greet your aunt."

The children did so, hand in hand, solemn as small adults. Alienor turned to Isabel and embraced her, although it was more as if she were drowning and clutching the side of a small boat amid the waves. "He has consigned me to a living death," Alienor wept in grief against Isabel's neck. "He might as well have put out my eyes, because he has left me blind. You are the first visitor I have had beyond a priest."

Isabel returned her clasp. "I would have come to see you long before now, but Henry would not allow it. Nothing anyone could do or say will ease his bitterness. He is a changed man."

"Henry has not changed." Alienor wiped her eyes on her cuff and straightened up. "If he appears changed to you it is only because the cloak has been stripped away and you are seeing him as he really is." She went to the children and embraced them again, unable to believe they were here in the room with her. She was overjoyed and she was grief-stricken. She wanted to be there to see them go forward into the world, but because of Henry, because of this dispute, it was denied to all of them. She had given all to her older sons and had nothing for these younger ones; her store was bare. The knowledge of what it meant for them and for her was a bitter draft indeed.

Thawing a little, John opened his mouth to show her where he had recently lost his front baby teeth.

Alienor gave a tearful laugh. "Ah, you are almost a man," she said and wanted to weep in earnest as he preened and puffed out his small chest. A man with all that entailed, especially in respect of his treatment of women under his father's tutelage.

She had nothing for them because all she possessed were the stark necessities, but Isabel had come armed with a merels board and counters so that the children could play while she and Alienor talked.

Alienor eyed the board and laughed harshly. "I made one of those at Chinon. I drew it in the ashes from the hearth one day after I was allowed a fire, and I played myself, right hand against left, using lumps of charcoal for counters. I pretended Henry was my opponent and I always won. In my room I always won, if nowhere else. Will you leave this behind when you go? There is a certain irony to planning strategies in cold ash, but this would be so much more elegant." Hearing the brittle note in her voice, she pressed her lips together.

"Alienor, don't," Isabel pleaded.

She drew a deep breath and steadied herself. "So," she said. "How did you manage to win your way through all these doors to visit me? What bribes did you use?"

"I didn't." Isabel gave a shrug. "I kept asking Hamelin to speak to Henry and he eventually agreed for my sake, even though the king was reluctant. Hamelin told him he should consider the wider implications and that it might be to his advantage. Henry eventually agreed to grant me permission to come and bring John and Joanna." Isabel's complexion flushed. "He also told Hamelin that no woman was trustworthy and he should have me watched because all women were scheming whores."

"That sounds like Henry. What did Hamelin say?"

Isabel looked away. "That not *all* women were thus marked."

A servant entered bearing a flagon, two goblets, buttermilk for the children, and some small pastries crusted with honey and nuts. Alienor's mouth watered. Her nourishment had been a penance of bread, pottage, and sour wine, with the occasional piece of chewy salt beef or stockfish. These sweet delicacies that she had taken for granted before were like treasure to her now.

"He would not give in just to humor Hamelin," she said after she had devoured one of the flaky, sticky pastries, which made her feel a little sick. "There has to be another reason." She gave Isabel a sharp look. "Is he receiving a drubbing from my sons and needs me to mediate? Is that it?"

Isabel looked flustered. "I was only permitted to see you on the condition I did not speak of the outside world."

"Oh, in God's name, I'm a prisoner!" Alienor spat. "Locked up with my own company for weeks on end. My clothes are checked for messages; I see no one but the guards. I don't even know what month of the year it is anymore! The sky in that window does not tell me, and neither does the priest. Why are you here if you cannot speak? Shall we just talk about sewing and hair dye and the best way to get stains out of garments?"

Isabel reddened. John glanced up from the merels board at the sound of his mother's raised voice, and Joanna bit her bottom lip.

"I promised, and it was to Hamelin," Isabel said. "He trusts me, and I will not break that faith." Eyes liquid, she removed her cloak and poured wine for both of them. "I suppose it is not breaking that trust to tell you there have been skirmishes and truces and that the situation is similar to what it was when you were taken. Your sons are still fighting. So is the king." She handed Alienor a cup. "And it's July."

Alienor sipped the wine, which was strong and rich, the kind she used to drink before she was a prisoner. The wine of power and command, now no longer hers except by the whim of a man she loathed and the kindness of her sister-by-marriage. "Just tell me that my sons are well."

Isabel gave a cautious nod. "Yes, they are, all of them…and you are right, I am here for a reason other than just a social visit."

Alienor set her cup down. "I knew it," she said. "Henry would not be persuaded to do anything that did not serve his purpose. Tell me and let us have it out in the open."

Isabel clasped her hands. "Henry is going to England and taking you with him. He asked me to arrange for your things to be brought to the ship, and that I accompany you and the children."

"England?" Alienor raised her brows.

"The whole court is going, including Marguerite, Alais, and Constance of Brittany—and the earl and countess of Leicester."

Alienor gave a short laugh. "A veritable prison ship of hostages. What happens to us when we arrive there?"

"I have not been told. You are to have new attendants though. Emma is to wed Davydd ap Owain, Prince of North Wales, by the king's order."

Alienor stared at Isabel in dull shock. Henry could do anything he wanted and no one could stop him. Her heart went out to Emma, who had been raised by nuns and had then dwelled in her household as a gentle companion. She was still of childbearing age, but only just. "That is so cruel and unnecessary," she said.

"The king has disbanded your household," Isabel plowed on, her voice unsteady. "Marchisa is to go with Emma to attend her, and you are to be assigned to the care of Robert Maudit, who will be responsible for all your expenses."

Alienor's heart dropped like a stone. England was farther away again from Poitiers, and there would be an island of separation between her and her sons. It would be easier for Henry. He could complete the process he had begun and shut her away out of sight and out of mind until she had neither sight nor mind remaining. But she would surely have the company of attendants once settled, even if they were Henry's creatures, and they were a project she could work upon.

"I asked to be given the task of telling you this," Isabel said. "There has been enough cruelty done already. I will understand if you loathe me for it, but I had to do something to bring some decency and compassion into this terrible state of affairs." Her chin wobbled.

"Of course I do not loathe you, you goose!" Alienor said with exasperation. "You are as dear to me as a flesh-and-blood sister, not just by marriage. It may be too late for decency and compassion, but I love you for trying…and do not dare weep!"

"I'm not." Isabel sniffed and cuffed her eyes.

Alienor set her jaw. "I will not let him win. He may shut me up in the darkest oubliette, but he will not break my will."

❖❖❖

The journey from Falaise to Barfleur took four days at the sedate pace of the covered wain in which Alienor was secluded. She was able to see the rolling Norman countryside out of the back, decked in summer greenery, and feel the warm breeze touch her face. Observing fields and trees in full growth was a bittersweet shock after so many dark months with bare stone walls for company. She had become so accustomed to living within herself that the brightness of the world was almost painful to her dulled senses. Conversation was awkward because what was there to say? The political situation was out of bounds on pain of renewed isolation. All she knew was that her sons were still fighting their father, but from the supplies in their train and the well-equipped number of soldiers, Henry did not seem to be under any kind of strain, and such talk of their escort that she happened to overhear was bullish and cheerful.

Arriving in Barfleur on the fourth day was another shock to Alienor's battered senses, for the port was heaving with people like a fishing net straining at the seams. The rumble of cartwheels, the hard thud of horse hooves, the harsh voices of Brabançon and Flemish mercenaries, the pungent fishy miasma of a seaport town in hot weather assaulted her in a great wash of stench and sound. Henry was obviously shipping an army over to England, and men who fought for pay were more trustworthy than the vassals upon whom he dared not turn his back lest they stuck a sword in him.

"Make way, make way!" roared Robert Maudit's herald, his complexion the same hue as the boiled lobsters being served in the hostelries. "In the name of King Henry, make way!"

Not *Make way for the queen!* Alienor noted. Once that cry would have resounded, confirming her authority, but no longer, and the omission, more than her prison walls, more than all her endurance of solitude, made her realize how powerless she was and how low Henry had brought her.

The wain rattled to a halt in the castle bailey, and as Alienor was descending from it, Henry rode in on a lathered stallion, bloody foam spattering the bit. He was shouting over his shoulder, issuing brisk orders to his adjutants concerning matters of embarkation. New lines creased his brow, and deep seams were carved between nose and mouth corner. He saw her as he was dismounting and gave her a look filled with venom. She stared through him as if he did not exist, raised her chin, and refused to show him deference, even though beside her Isabel curtsied and bowed her head.

Henry abruptly turned on his heel and stamped away, bellowing more orders.

"It would be easier if you did not antagonize him," Isabel said softly.

"I shall not yield to him again in this life, whatever it costs," Alienor replied grimly. "Besides, it would make no difference to his treatment of me whether I curtsied or not."

"Madam, let me escort you to your chamber," said Robert Maudit.

Alienor gave him a contemptuous look. "Do I have a choice?"

"Madam, all the ladies of the household are waiting there until embarkation," he replied smoothly. He had served the empress as a steward, hence to outsiders it might look as if he was performing that service now, but to all intents and purposes he was her jailer.

"All the ladies?" That was interesting. "And are we free to come and go as we please?"

"That would be unwise with so many soldiers in the town. It is for your own safety, madam."

"And the Countess de Warenne?" Alienor inquired.

"That is a matter for her husband," Maudit said.

"I will accompany you," Isabel said swiftly. "The earl is busy elsewhere, and it will be simpler and safer to stay with you than to go to lodgings."

"As you wish, madam." Maudit summoned armed attendants

to escort the women to a chamber on an upper floor of the keep. Entering the room, Alienor found it already occupied by Marguerite; her sister Alais; Humbert of Maurienne's little girl Adeliza; Constance, heiress of Brittany; and Emma, Henry's sister. A full complement of royal hostages.

"Dear Holy Mary," Alienor said, thinking they were like a flock of hens, cooped up and waiting to be necked.

Emma rushed to her and hugged her tightly. "Thank God. We did not know what had happened to you! I thought I would never see you again!"

Alienor returned Emma's fierce embrace and laughed through threatening tears. She would not cry, because if she did, she would never stop. "I'm alive for now; that is all that can be said."

"I am to be wed…"

"Yes, I know, my love, I know."

Emma straightened and put on a brave face. "I never thought to be, nor to a Welshman, but I have no choice, and there must be worse fates in the world."

"Yes," Alienor said bleakly, "there must."

"Harry and Richard will come for us," Marguerite said stoutly as she too came to curtsy and then to kiss Alienor. "My father will put a stop to this."

"He has not done so yet," Alienor said. "England is a fortress moated by sea. Who will be interested in women of France, or Brittany, or Aquitaine?" Her political mind was stirring and stretching. "What I want to know is why all those mercenaries are being amassed to go with us."

"The Scots are threatening Carlisle and Alnwick," Emma said. "And Nottingham is in the hands of the rebels. Philip of Flanders has promised to send aid and has already embarked mercenaries of his own."

"Why do we have to go?" Marguerite asked with a small flounce. "He took us from Fontevraud almost by force as it is."

"Because he dare not leave any of us in Normandy lest an attempt be made to rescue us in his absence," Alienor replied.

"We are hostages, and he is keeping us confined and close. He won't leave us one side of the Narrow Sea and himself the other, especially when he is threatened."

❖❖❖

The weather changed overnight. Clouds rolled in, first white but churning to dirty gray, and the hostage party left their lodging for a sea of surging green waves, white-veined and crested with spray. The crossing was going to be brisk and possibly stormy. Both John and Joanna were wide-eyed and tense; they had been infants the last time they had made this journey, too young to be daunted. Alienor eyed the sea with misgiving. She did not want to set foot on the galley because it was another step away from herself.

She looked at Isabel, who had joined her as the crew secured the gangplank. "Twenty years ago I sailed from here with Henry to be crowned queen of England," she said and stared out to sea, feeling a tug in her heart like the surge of the waves. "Harry was curled in my womb and Will's hand was clasped in mine. Now, my womb has ceased to quicken, my best years are past, and I return as a prisoner and hostage. Harry is squandering himself in rebellion against a father who refuses to validate him with any kind of power, and my firstborn son is naught but bones and dust in a tomb." She turned to look at Isabel. "That is what it comes down to—bones and dust. Is what lies between worth it?"

"It is what you make of it," Isabel replied staunchly and touched her arm. "It is for God to judge, not us. All we can do is our best; let others choose as they may."

"I am not sure this is my best," Alienor said, swallowing. "Or if it is, then it is a poor effort, is it not?"

"You do yourself a disservice."

Alienor grimaced. "Indeed, and that disservice happened long ago when I wrote a letter of proposal to Henry FitzEmpress and agreed that he should become my husband."

The wind strengthened as they boarded the ship, and by the time the gangplank was pulled in, the crests on the incoming tide tossed like the manes of wild horses. At least with the children on board with her, as well as Hamelin and Isabel, Alienor knew Henry would not try to stage an accidental drowning on the crossing, although the wild weather might accomplish that anyway. She watched the golden lions rippling on the red silk banner at the prow of his galley further along the moorings, and the swirl of his cloak as he prowled the deck. He had neither been to see her nor so much as looked at her since that stare across the courtyard, and she was both relieved and wary. She noticed the figure of a woman on board with him—blue cloak, white wimple—and felt weary indifference.

As the tide turned, the English fleet weighed anchor and cast off from their moorings. The ships cleared the harbor and entered the open sea where the swells grew bigger and stronger, heaving against the side of the ship, exploding spray over the top strake. The saturated crew toiled to adjust halyards and stays while the steersman fought to hold her steady and keep her course true. Squalls whipped across the surface of the sea like running wolves, savaging the fleet and moving on. Lightning veined the charcoal-colored sky with dazzling striations that left an imprint on the eyelids. The sea threshed beneath the ships, driving them forward at a hard pace, straining the sail, and the passengers huddled miserably in the deck shelter. Little Adeliza of Maurienne had never been on a ship before, and between bouts of retching, she whimpered and shivered. Isabel tucked a blanket around her and held her tightly, rocking and soothing her. John, who was enjoying the drama, gave his future bride a disgusted look.

Feeling as if she were about to be suffocated, Alienor left the shelter and stood on deck, breathing deep gulps of the salty air and letting the wind batter against her.

Robert Maudit, who was also on deck, shouting to the steersman, saw her and, holding on to the halyards, made his way in her direction, his face taut with anxiety and anger. Before he could reach her, however, Hamelin too emerged from the deck shelter and waved him away.

"Madam, it is not safe out on deck," he shouted. "You could be washed overboard. You must go back inside!"

"Would it be any worse than my fate when I reach England?" She faced Hamelin. "Let me have this moment. I have always thought your nature less cruel than your brother's."

A powerful wave crashed against the ship, and she was flung into him and deluged in a shower of icy spray. He gripped her hard and she felt his solid, muscular body and strong arms, and it was strange because it was so much like being held by Henry, but very different too.

The ship steadied and Alienor pushed away from him to stand on her own.

"Now will you go inside the deck shelter?" he asked.

"In a moment," she said and took his hand. "Promise me you will be good to Isabel, and do your best for John and Joanna."

He raised his brows. "Those are already given. You do not have to bind me with oaths."

"Yes I do." She gave him a long, measuring look. "It is all I have within my power to do. And I will say this too. For all your loyalty to Henry, Hamelin, beware. Do not let him destroy you. Henry is a storm few survive."

"I am adept at weathering him by now," Hamelin replied evenly. "The main difficulty is negotiating all the treacherous rocks offshore."

"Promise me."

"I do so swear," he said and removed his hand from hers, "but not for your sake."

"I would not ask that. I know where your loyalties lie, my lord."

Alienor returned to the deck shelter. Hamelin was conservative, but always scrupulously fair to his own way of thinking. She supposed it was a small mercy.

Isabel's chaplain was leading prayers, and the atmosphere had become less fraught. People were still retching, but their bellies were empty. Alienor knelt, closed her eyes, and bowed her head to murmur words over the string of prayer beads clasped in her hand.

Shortly after noon, the wind veered and lessened in intensity, and the fleet was able to race for the English shore like galloping horses controlled on a tight rein. Sails were tattered rags, the crews were exhausted, and the passengers buffeted and draggled, but they were alive. An hour before sunset the clouds broke up and evening light burnished the sea, illuminating the port of Southampton in hues of gold and bronze as the storm-battered fleet limped into harbor. Amid the cheers and embraces of her fellow passengers, Alienor viewed their landfall with resignation. She had seen Henry's flagship ahead on their starboard side. It had been too much to hope that her prayers had been answered and that it had foundered in the storm.

# 45

## Southampton, July 1174

FOLLOWING THE PREVIOUS DAY'S WILDNESS, THE SEA HAD
calmed to a benign humor and licked the bruised and weed-
strung shoreline almost tenderly under a sky of broken cloud.

At Southampton's timber keep, there was no respite beyond a
single night for the storm-tossed English court as Henry prepared
with his usual demonic energy to move inland. Even before dawn,
the cargo from the ships was being unloaded onto the carts and
pack horses procured in the town.

Alienor, draggled and still in the same salt-stained garments
from the crossing, was escorted under guard to Henry's chamber.
The room was bare save for a bench before the hearth, everything
else having been loaded into the baggage wagons. He stood before
the empty fireplace, tapping his fingers against his belt, his expression impatient and his mouth a hard, thin line. How had she ever
derived pleasure from his kiss?

"So," she said, holding herself tall and straight despite the state
of her garments. "Have you brought me here so you can claim the
marriage debt again?"

He shot her an irritated look. "In truth I do not want to see
you at all, but I am conscious of my duty, even if you are not
conscious of yours."

Alienor raised her eyebrows and said nothing.

"I am sending you to Sarum, and there you will remain in

Robert Maudit's custody for as long as I deem necessary. You are to have no contact with our sons and daughters except by my express permission."

"How you must fear me," she said with a mocking smile, although inside she was devastated. "You have done everything to take my power from me. You cannot live with it, can you? You fear your sons too, and rightly so."

He shot her a glance in which there was hatred. "You turned them against me with your conniving, but they will come back to the fold in the end. They cannot stand against me."

The same old arguments and the same old blame and delusions. "The fold? They are not sheep. They are lions, and they are younger than you. Cage them as you will, their time will come."

"Yours is over, madam, I am certain of that."

"And you always deal in certainties, Henry. You are so certain that everyone will betray you that you have made it a self-fulfilling prophecy. Send me to rot then, but I promise I will haunt you all of your days. Banish me from sight, but I shall remain a thorn inside you."

"Your threats are as empty and as powerless as you are," he retorted. "Whatever happens, it will be of my design, not yours. Yes, you will trouble me, but no more than a louse bite does, and I hold you between my fingernails. Think on that. I could crack you at any time. And do not think your sons will side with you. They are becoming men, as you are always telling me, and once I have resolved our differences, they will cleave to me because I hold the power, not you." He showed her his clenched fist to emphasize his point. "Yes, even your beloved Richard. I shall send him into Poitiers and let him rule with me overseeing from afar—unlike you perching on his shoulder. Your time is finished, madam. Whatever you threaten is no more than the hissing of a cat."

He adjusted his cloak. "You will retire to Sarum to rest and confer with God. Those who inquire after you shall be told that you are unwell, that you need a long rest and solitude. Those who remember your sister will know what I mean." His gaze lit upon the pearl ring she was wearing, given to her by the empress not long after Harry's birth. "I will take this for safekeeping," he said. "I doubt my mother would want you to have it now, and as far as I am concerned, you have lost the right to wear it." Grabbing her hand, he worked the ring from her finger, and when Alienor struggled and tried to pull back, he gripped the harder until she let out an involuntary sob. Panting, eyes bright with triumph, he cupped the jewel in his fist and left the chamber. Alienor squeezed her eyes tightly shut, a terrible sense of desolation and despair sweeping through her. But still she did not weep.

Two of Henry's hearth knights entered the room to escort her down to the courtyard, and she went with them, feeling numb. Three baggage trains awaited, one Henry's, the others prepared for the women, although Henry himself intended riding ahead and his white palfrey stood saddled and ready. Without looking at her, Henry set his foot in the stirrup, swung astride, and heeled the horse to a canter. A host of knights and sergeants followed him, including Hamelin, although Isabel remained behind with the other women and the children.

Alienor was bundled into a traveling wain separate from the others, and Isabel turned to Robert Maudit with narrowed eyes. "I shall travel with the queen," she said. "And so will the lady Joanna and the lord John."

"The king—"

"—is my brother-by-marriage and has other business on his mind. I shall speak to him as soon as I may, but in the meantime, I leave it to your compassion and good judgment, my lord."

Maudit frowned but after a moment acceded to Isabel's wishes. She ushered the children into the wain and then clambered in herself and settled next to Alienor amid the cushions. "It is not seemly," she said, smoothing her gown. "How dare they do this?"

Alienor shook her head. "Henry can do anything he chooses, and always to suit himself," she said. She looked at the paler band of skin on her finger where the empress's ring had left its mark and memory.

The cart trundled away from Southampton, leaving the sea behind, and they entered open countryside fragrant with all the rain-released scents of summer and sunlight sparkling in the puddles. A fine day to be out riding with the hawks. Not one to be traveling into confinement under heavy guard.

"Where is Henry bound?"

"Hamelin said to Canterbury," Isabel replied. "To pray at Archbishop Thomas's tomb and to atone for whatever part his words played in his murder."

"Atone?" Alienor gave a mocking laugh. "Is that what he says?"

Isabel looked troubled. "Perhaps he is truly penitent."

"About having to perform the atonement, certainly," Alienor replied, curling her lip. "But if he is going to kneel at Becket's tomb, it is not from remorse. Fear of the consequences if he does not. He would never have knelt at his feet in life and begged forgiveness. He considers him a greater nuisance now that he is dead. No," she said cynically, "Henry will pray at Becket's tomb and make the greatest show of remorse and piety anyone has ever seen, but just because he knows the only way to maintain control is to create a spectacle that will upstage Becket and become the talk of Christendom. It will settle the country down, and in the places it does not, then his Brabançons will wreak havoc."

Isabel stared at her with shock.

"Do not look at me like that," Alienor said wearily. "I have every reason to say these things. You always see the best in people, and that helps you to live your life, but I cannot turn a blind eye to what is really under my nose. I trust you as much as I trust anyone, but whatever you do for me, and no matter how much you desire to help me, Hamelin and your children matter to you more, and Hamelin is Henry's brother. You will come to the edge with me, but you will not leap—and I do not blame you…"

Isabel bit her lip. "I do always see the best in people," she admitted after a moment. "I cannot do otherwise." Her eyes were liquid with tears. "I will help you all I can. I might not leap, but I will hold a rope down to you, I promise, and I shall never let go."

❖❖❖

They reached Sarum toward the end of day, their wain creaking up the hill to the white-painted castle standing on the hill. Sarum in winter with bitter winds driving across the Downs, and sleet hammering on every shutter, was a wild, desolate place, gray, cold and dark as despair. Even today in fine weather a hard breeze was blowing over the ancient raised mound and snapping the banners on the tower walls. For how long, she wondered, would Henry incarcerate her here? Until she died of cold and neglect? Until she became a faded voice swirling in the wind?

Alienor stepped from the wain and looked at the sky. Storm clouds were massing again, and yet there was a silver brightness behind them and swords of radiance shafting out to dazzle the palace buildings and the cathedral enclave beyond.

The darkest prisons were those of the mind. She could either fall into a well of black despair or hold on to the light and keep hope alive. If she could find freedom within herself, then Henry would be unable to touch her, and even in losing everything, she would still have won.

Her greatest challenge was about to begin.

# Author's Note

*The Winter Crown* is the second novel in my trilogy about Alienor of Aquitaine, one of the most famous and iconic queens of the Middle Ages. As I said in my author's note to the first in the sequence, *The Summer Queen*, what we think we know is not always the whole story and dependent on what filters are applied.

Two comments I frequently come across with reference to Alienor are that she was one of the most powerful women of the Middle Ages and that she was ahead of her time. Those statements say a lot about how we have chosen to portray her image with reference to our own culture, and I don't entirely agree with them, although I would say that she had a strong constitution and an indomitable will. My take is that Alienor was a woman of her time, striving to deal with controlling husbands who knew their place in society and that a woman's place, by natural law, was subordinate to theirs, especially in the case of Henry II, who preferred not to share power with anyone.

In the earlier years of the marriage, Henry did entrust Alienor with the regency of England while he was about his continental concerns but, at the same time, seeded her household with men of his choosing, including her steward and chancellor. Rather than having a free hand, Alienor was expected to work closely with regnal deputies such as Henry's powerful justiciar, Richard de Lucy. As Henry's reign progressed, men like de Lucy were to take over the main role and the queen's position and influence became further diminished. If anything, Alienor had less say than her predecessors and her mother-in-law the Empress Matilda, whose hand can be seen governing Normandy throughout the 1150s and early 1160s and whose advice Henry frequently sought.

I strongly suspect that Henry was ambivalent about having a wealthy, cultured wife who was as mentally sharp as he was and had nine years' more experience in the world. The dynamic with his mother was different; whatever happened, he could trust her and know she was always on his side. I believe he never felt quite the same about Alienor.

For the first fourteen years of her marriage to Henry, Alienor seems to have been either pregnant or recovering from pregnancy and childbirth. Between 1155 and 1158, she bore four children in rapid succession. Henry Junior (Harry) was born in February 1155, Matilda in the summer of 1156, Richard in September 1157, and Geoffrey in September 1158. Some historians suggest that she suffered a miscarriage either between Geoffrey and little Alienor's birth in 1161, or between 1162 and Joanna's birth in 1165. Whether she did or not, the constant pregnancies were a physical strain on her body. One of the major roles of a queen was to bear the heirs, preferably male, and Alienor would have viewed that aspect as an important part of her duty and one only she could do. To be fecund as a medieval queen consort was to succeed.

It was a medieval belief that pregnant women lost their ability to think rationally while in a gravid state. There was also the fear that their wombs were liable to go wandering around their bodies (the origin of the word hysteria). It was viewed as a serious medical complaint for which one of the remedies was to burn an eagle feather under the afflicted woman's nose, the stench of which was supposed to send the womb hastening back to its proper position.

Henry did not confine himself to sharing Alienor's bed. Before he married Alienor he already had one bastard son in Jeoffrey FitzRoy. The boy was rumored to be the son of a common whore named Hikenai, but my belief is that such a name is the product of the rumor mill and jaundiced clergy. Hikenai may be a pun on the term for a riding horse. In both *The Summer Queen* and *The Winter Crown* I have named the Hikenai character Aelburgh.

We have no detailed record of Jeoffrey's early life, so I felt that it was not beyond the realms of probability that he spent some of that time with his grandmother in Normandy, but I admit that it's speculation that fits the plot. Some of his childhood may have been spent in Wiltshire because he was mocked later in life for speaking French with the accent of Marlborough.

Henry had at least four (and possibly six) bastard children with different mothers, but other than Jeoffrey, they are not within the scope of *The Winter Crown*. Henry is not known to have had any children with his long-term paramour Rosamund de Clifford. It would seem from what is known of his several mistresses that Henry preferred very young women—in their midteens rather than more mature. I would guess this was because they were unwritten pages and easy to manipulate—unlike his wife.

Researching the characters of Isabel de Warenne and her husbands was interesting. Isabel's first spouse, William, was something of a tragic character: the youngest son of King Stephen and a potential heir to the throne. William and Isabel were married when they were both very young; he was still a boy. He gave up his right to the throne during the peace settlement of 1153, but there must always have been an uneasy relationship between him and Henry II, who was his second cousin. William died during the retreat from Toulouse. Isabel, now a young and desirable widow, was then earmarked as a potential husband for Henry's youngest brother, also named William (at times I wondered rather desperately who wasn't named William in the twelfth century!).

Unfortunately for William FitzEmpress, Thomas Becket was determined to teach Henry II a lesson following the latter's disgraceful deed of forcing Mary de Boulogne from a nunnery and into marriage with Matthew of Alsace. The legend goes that the young man was so distraught, he went home to his mother in Normandy, pined away, and died. I suspect a strong dose of political and artistic license here. For a start no Angevin ever pined away! The likelihood is that William died of a wasting disease or other natural causes, but the anti-Becket faction found it expedient to put the blame on the recalcitrant archbishop. Indeed, one of his murderers, Richard Brito, is reputed to have said that he delivered his blow on Becket's body for his former lord whose household knight Brito had been. I suspect that Brito had been promised land from the de Warenne estates and was unhappy to find himself with nothing.

Henry still had his way by marrying his illegitimate half brother Hamelin, Vicomte of Touraine, to Isabel, thus securing her vast estates to the Angevin line. I have imagined the relationship between Hamelin and Isabel to be a good one, partly to mitigate the vitriol in Henry and Alienor's marriage as it degenerated, and partly because they do seem to have made excellent partners during their forty-year marriage. Isabel bore Hamelin three daughters and a son, and between them the couple would go on to build the great keep at Conisbrough, having all the creature comforts that an earl and his lady might desire, as well as being a formidable fortress and statement of power.

On her marriage to Hamelin, Isabel de Warenne became Alienor's sister-in-law. I strongly suspect that they enjoyed a warm friendship down the years and that their children and families were close. Some of the reasons for those strong suspicions, I am saving for the third novel in the trilogy, *The Autumn Throne*, but suffice to say I have good grounds for believing that Isabel de Warenne and Alienor of Aquitaine were closely acquainted. As a side note, it also made me smile to discover that Isabel de Warenne was William Marshal's stepcousin, her mother having married William's uncle Patrick. Needless to say, I am highly delighted to bring William Marshal himself into the narrative. It has been wonderful to visit with him again and to know there's more of him to come!

My focus in *The Winter Crown* is upon Alienor and her life and times from her viewpoint and concerns. I was aware that I could not write a novel about the reign of Henry II and not deal with the issue of Henry's poisoned relationship with Thomas Becket.

However, while it remained an important element in the story, I deliberately chose not to set it center stage except in the moments when interactions with Becket became pertinent to Alienor. It is her story, after all.

It has often been said that Alienor was responsible for setting her sons against their father. It's argued that they were too young and immature to have rebelled as they did. It is also said that she turned against Henry because she found out that he was playing around with Rosamund de Clifford. I believe both arguments are flawed. I do believe that Alienor was disillusioned and angry at Henry's behavior toward her in several arenas, including that of controlling her duchy and hogging power to himself. With Rosamund, I think it was just the same old thing, with perhaps an extra nuance of concern because Rosamund was more to Henry than a one-night stand, but hardly grounds for a full-blown rebellion to someone as pragmatic as Alienor.

Quite simply Henry II was a dominant, controlling alpha male—which made for both good and bad medieval kingship. He liked to micromanage and was reluctant to relinquish power once he had it in his grasp. There was to be no delegation to his sons or his wife. Having failed to take Toulouse, which had been a project dear to Alienor's heart ever since she had been queen of France, Henry eventually brought the lands into his own sphere by political maneuvering. He secured a marriage alliance for his youngest son John, which meant that Toulouse was surrounded by pro-Angevin interests. To survive, Raymond of Toulouse deemed it prudent to swear homage to Henry. Crucially he did not make the oath to Alienor, who, as duchess of Aquitaine, should have been the recipient. By swearing to Henry, he gave him precedence, and perhaps this was the final straw.

When Alienor's sons rebelled against their father, she had a stark choice to make between her husband—who had belittled her and let her down time after time, year after year, but to whom she was beholden as a wife and partner—and her sons, who were the future and who might look to her for matriarchal guidance, especially her beloved Richard. (Incidentally, that letter from Rotrou, Archbishop of Rouen, is reproduced verbatim.) I believe that the young king was ripe for rebellion without any goading from his mother. Henry II was perfectly capable of alienating his sons on his own. Indeed, the young king spent more time with his father than he did with Alienor in the years leading up to the rebellion. While writing *The Winter Crown*, I came to think that while Henry II was a great king in many ways, he has been allowed to get away with far too much for far too long!

To cover less sweeping brush strokes in the novel, I thought readers might find the following incidental details interesting too.

I have called Henry's heir Harry to differentiate him from his father. Harry is an early anglicized version of Henry. I have differentiated between Henry II's legitimate and illegitimate sons by calling them Geoffrey and Jeoffrey. One of the nightmares for an author of historical fiction is the medieval propensity for giving everyone the same name!

Readers of *The Greatest Knight*, my novel about William Marshal's life, might notice that Marguerite's position in the narrative has changed slightly, but this is because the course of research never stands still. King Louis made a stipulation that Alienor was not to have the raising of his daughter and it seems likely that, until she was twelve or thirteen, she was actually raised away from the Angevin court and not in Alienor's household.

I have to explain why I have named the monkey Robert in chapter 12. In the Middle Ages it was a given that all animals and birds had a name relating to their kind. All cats, for example, were either Gylbert or Tybald (hence Tibbles); all sparrows were Philip. All redbreasts were Robin, and wrens were Jenny. And all monkeys were Robert.

Still on the subject of animals, I have given Henry a menagerie at Woodstock. Certainly his grandfather Henry I had one there, with camels and a porcupine as mentioned. King John kept at least one lion. So I considered it feasible, if not remarked upon in history, that some exotic animals were in residence during Henry II's reign.

Visitors to the United Kingdom can visit the ruins of Old Sarum in Wiltshire where Henry II imprisoned Alienor following the rebellion of 1173. There is not a great deal to see now, but English Heritage's information plaques give the visitor some idea. What it still does have is atmosphere by the ton. A papal document of 1217 said of the cathedral site adjacent to the palace: *The continual gusts of wind make such a noise that those celebrating the divine offices can hardly hear each other speak.* On a warm summer's day, Old Sarum is glorious, with the green scent of the Downs blowing across the ancient slope. For the twelfth-century traveler it was situated less than a day's ride from the great medieval city of Winchester and the port of Southampton, but in the bleak and desolate days of midwinter it must have seemed like the end of the world to a prisoner incarcerated there—a winter crown rising out of the remote landscape.

Alienor's story continues in *The Autumn Throne.*

# Select Bibliography

Below are just a few of the books and sources I found useful while researching *The Winter Crown*. I can particularly recommend John Guy's biography of Thomas Becket. For any readers interested in viewing my full research library, it can be found here: http://elizabethchadwickreference.blogspot.co.uk.

Aurell, Martin. *The Plantagenet Empire 1154–1224.* Translated from the French by David Crouch. Pearson Longman, 2007.

Bull, Marcus, and Catherine Léglu, eds. *The World of Eleanor of Aquitaine: Literature and Society in Southern France between the Eleventh and Thirteenth Centuries.* Woodbridge, Suffolk: Boydell Press, 2005.

Chibnall, Marjorie. *The Empress Matilda: Queen Consort, Queen Mother and Lady of the English.* Oxford: Blackwell, 1999.

Farrer, William, and Charles Travis Clay, eds. *Early Yorkshire Charters, Volume 8: The Honour of Warenne.* New York: Cambridge University Press, 2013.

Flori, Jean. *Eleanor of Aquitaine: Queen and Rebel.* Edinburgh: Edinburgh University Press, 2004.

Gillingham, John. *The Angevin Empire.* 2nd ed. London: Arnold, 2001.

Guy, John. *Thomas Becket: Warrior, Priest, Rebel, Victim; A 900-Year-Old Story Retold.* New York: Viking Penguin, 2012.

King, Alison. Akashic Records Consultant.

Norgate, Kate. *England under the Angevin Kings V2 (1887)*. Whitefish, MT: Kessinger, 2010.

Salzman, L. F. *Henry II*. London: Constable, 1917. On-demand print accessed from Amazon.co.uk.

Strickland, Matthew. "On the Instruction of a Price: The Upbringing of Henry, the Young King." In *Henry II: New Interpretations*. Edited by Christopher Harper-Bill and Nicholas Vincent. Woodbridge, Suffolk: Boydell Press, 2007.

Turner, Ralph V. *Eleanor of Aquitaine*. New Haven, CT: Yale University Press, 2009.

Warren, W. L. *Henry II*. London: Eyre Methuen, 1973.

Wheeler, Bonnie, and John Carmi Parsons, eds. *Eleanor of Aquitaine: Lord and Lady*. New York: Palgrave Macmillan, 2003

# Acknowledgments

I would like to say a big thank-you as always to my publishing team at Sourcebooks. My lovely editor Shana Drehs and production editor Heather Hall. My thanks to these ladies for help and teamwork during the editing stages, and to everyone else at Sourcebooks who work so hard to deliver books into the hands of readers.

I have been with my agent Carole Blake since the beginning of my publishing career, and I want to thank her and everyone at Blake Friedmann for providing a stable platform, fighting in my corner, keeping me solvent with publishing deals—and for all the fun and friendship!

Thank you to my readers for all the pleasure and friendship too. I so enjoy talking to you all on my Facebook group. You're lovely, and you so enrich the writing life.

On the domestic front, I must give an accolade to my husband, who continues to be a stalwart and, other than the fact that he seldom sits still, is nothing at all like Henry II! And to my dear friend Alison King, whose remarkable talent has helped me in countless ways to write this novel.